UNHOLY GHOSTS

To Alexandre Quintanilha

And for those whose lives have been ended, threatened or dimmed by the viral eclipse over sexuality, particularly Harold, António and Miguel

With thanks to Alex, Ruth G. Zimler, Dorothy Bryant and David Fernbach

This project was supported in part by a grant from the U.S. National Endowment for the Arts

Richard Zimler

Unholy Ghosts

THE GAY MEN'S PRESS

First published 1996 by GMP Publishers Ltd,
P O Box 247, Swaffham, Norfolk PE37 8PA, England

World Copyright © 1996 Richard Zimler

A CIP catalogue record for this book is available
from the British Library

ISBN 0 85449 233 X

Distributed in Europe by Central Books,
99 Wallis Rd, London E9 5LN

Distributed in North America by InBook/LPC Group,
1436 West Randolph Street, Chicago, IL 60607

Distributed in Australia by Bulldog Books,
P O Box 300, Beaconsfield, NSW 2014

Printed and bound in the EU by The Cromwell Press,
Melksham, Wilts, England

Part I

1

Dear Carlos,

In the seventh century, Bishop Ferreolus of Grenoble excommunicated a loaf of bread, which promptly turned black and hard as coal.

What had the bread done to deserve such a fate?

The legend of Ferreolus offers us no answer. But since any loaf of bread in any century can't do much more than be itself, its crime must have resided in its very nature — its *breadness.*

It is not necessary to *do* anything to be damned in this world. That is what our good Bishop was teaching the Christians of Grenoble. A man, like a loaf of bread, can be punished — even sentenced to death — because of his nature.

Or he can be compelled to hide his love for the rest of his life as if he were an untouchable leper.

I'm talking about you, Carlos.

Forgive me if this seems exaggerated. I've been guzzling ouzo on and off all day. And I'm remembering the shocked face of a guy whom I stabbed a few hours ago. I didn't run after him. After a while, I only cared that he bloodied up the fluffy blue throw rug where we wipe our feet just inside the door.

No, you don't know him.

I don't think he'll go to the police because he's like you. I could be wrong though.

You were sure you'd never hear from me again, weren't you? I guess that I've been squirreling away words. I realize, of course, that you won't want to read any of them unless I give you something in return. So here it is... Remember how you were always wondering what intimate secrets I was sharing with my brother? Now's your chance to find out; I'm enclosing the letter which I wrote to him nearly a year ago, just after my last visit to New York; the same letter you and I fought so bitterly over because I refused to let you see it. You'll be happy to hear that you're mentioned briefly, in the very first paragraph. So grant me a small favor and read on. Here it is...

Monsaraz, Portugal

Dear Harold,

I've just had a strange and lovely encounter that's left me feeling really happy for the first time in months — since Carlos starting slipping from me, I think. It all started this morning at about ten a.m. when I met an old man at the main entrance to Monsaraz. You'll find this town on the map I gave you, about three inches to the right of Lisbon, just by the Spanish border. I'd gotten up shortly after cockcrow and left Carlos snoozing away in bed to go for a stroll through the surrounding farmlands. I was just getting back to the town when I met him. He was one of those aged peasants who inspire Italian novels: tiny, barrel-chested, with giant, sun-coarsened hands. He had dirt under his fingernails, stubble on his round cheeks, closely-cropped gray hair bristling behind his ears. His dark, Sunday-best jacket and woolen pants were dusted with dry soil. He wore no necktie, yet his white shirt was buttoned to the collar. He carried an old-fashioned gray felt hat with a thick black band, walked with slow, awkward, side-to-side movements as if uncomfortable with the freedom of unfettered shoulders.

He looked like he was made for a turn-of-the-century photograph of the Portuguese hinterlands.

And his eyes! They were clear green, beautiful, deeply set into his tan skin, more youthful and alive than the rest of him. Eyes like a saint should have. He looked about seventy, but peasants grow old early under the weight of the medieval plows they still use here in Portugal. He might have even been as young as fifty-five or so.

As I passed through the stone archway guarding the main street of the town, he waved to me with his hat. He was sitting on a low wall fronting a house in whose garden blood-colored roses were blooming. I said hello in my heavily accented Portuguese. When he stood, I noticed that his pants were way too tight. It seemed really sweet that he was unembarrassed. It seemed to say something about village life, you see. That people were accepted here with all their eccentricities. Maybe that's all an illusion; maybe it's even more difficult to be different and vulnerable in a nowhere-land like this. Anyway, his own sudden toothless smile seemed well-wishing and generous. With hands of presentation, he gestured down the main street of the town and said something I didn't quite get. His voice was hoarse, came to me like wind across stone. "*Donde é?* Where are you from?" he asked when he saw that I didn't understand what he was saying.

"*Os Estados Unidos, Nova Iorque,*" I replied.

"Ah, Ronald Reagan," he said, with a knowing nod. He pronounced our ex-President's first name as "Roonal."

"Exactly," I replied.

"*Minha aldeia,* my village," the peasant said, sweeping his hand in an arc. His eyes closed for a moment as if forced by a difficult memory, but then he nodded and smiled at me.

We began to walk together, slowly, me towering over him. We went down the main street of Monsaraz in silence, without even looking at each other, until he stopped to offer his hand to a small crimson and amber butterfly that was flexing its wings atop a weed that dared to sprout out of a crack in the cobblestones. He knelt slowly, and the descent of his hand was gentle. When it came to a rest against the butterfly's chosen leaf, the insect closed its wings and stepped its black, spiky feet onto this new pedestal. It was like the little creature sensed how kind-spirited he was. Or like they knew each other, were friends.

The peasant lifted his visitor up to me. "*Uma borboleta,*" he whispered with a certain gravity, as if he now carried the mini-ature form of the town sorcerer. He slowly extended the butterfly toward me. When his hand was nearly touching mine, however, it flew off. We followed the fluttering together until it disappeared into the sky. He laughed, lowered his hand, shrugged.

It was really a great moment. Me and him there together, standing in the silence beyond a butterfly's departure. But that was just the beginning.

Sorry. Now I realize I've gotten ahead of myself because of my excitement. Let me tell you what Monsaraz looks like so you can see me and the peasant there together.

Imagine a village of white stone, an eccentric ivory crown on a pillow of moss — the highest hill for many miles around.

Can you see it?

Or imagine a village in a fresco of Giotto's, one of those hilltop towns in your beloved Umbria. Now paint all the walls of the houses white. (Yes, I think that's a better image for you.)

From afar, coming back after my dawn walk, I had imagined kids playing soccer in the streets, old women chatting at window-sills. But once I was inside the rim of the ivory crown, walking with the peasant, I could see that the town was empty. I suppose everyone was already at church. Or still asleep. It was Sunday morning, after all, and the Portuguese sleep late on weekends. Not that the streets were entirely empty; stiff, tiny, bearded dogs often passed us looking over their shoulders. One fawn-colored mutt with threatening black eyes stopped to bark till my host calmed him down with his supplications. "*Não ladre...sshhh... faça favor...sshhh...tudo vai melhorar. Pois...pois, exato, vai brincar com os amigos.* Don't bark, please, sshhh, everything's going to be fine. That's it, go ahead and play with your friends."

As he spoke, I looked out beyond the crenelated battlements which circle the town. Hundreds of feet below lay green and gold fields rustling with olive and cork trees. Somewhere in the distance, underneath the violet haze at the horizon, ran the Spanish border. The sky was the deep blue of summers dreamed. A gentle wind from the east was carrying the scent of dew and olive oil.

The old peasant led me down the blinding white street lined with single-storey homes, all topped by roofs of tawny-colored tile. Explaining carefully, pointing with a thick, leathery finger, he talked of the woolen-goods cooperative, the church, the café, the bullring — all the landmarks built with so many years of labor. He led me to his home, right at the end of the street, just next to the entrance to the bullring. It had pink geraniums growing in front. To the side of the door, a wicker basket of red poppies hung from the wall. "*Entre... seja bemvindo*, Come, welcome," he said. When I hesitated to enter, he added, "*Faça favor*. Please."

I had to bend to pass under the granite lintel of the threshold. Inside, he hung his hat on the hook of a wooden rack made from an ox yoke and was kissed by a young woman in a dark apron. She was about thirty, I'd guess, with brooding eyes, her hair pulled back under a headscarf of black linen. I couldn't see her real well because it was dark and my eyes hadn't fully adjusted from the sunlight.

She offered me a smile of welcome. We were standing in a low-ceilinged hallway. It felt like we'd entered a miniature world, as if space had shrunk. The old peasant waved for me to follow him, then caressed open a side door and beckoned me into an even darker room. I hesitated, but the young woman nodded as if to say, "It's okay — go in, follow my father."

In the room, the body of a tiny old woman was lying atop a neatly made bed. A brown shawl of crocheted wool had been draped over her face and hair, and she had been dressed in black. Except for her feet. They were shriveled and tan. Feet like roots out of soil. Three white candles on a small wooden table cast glaring light and shadow across the old peasant, the walls, the woman, me. I felt as if I shouldn't be there. Then again, as if it were right. As if death, too, were part of my reason for visiting this town.

The peasant showed yearning in his face as he looked at the woman, the kind that comes, I suppose, from having shared joys and griefs for half a century. From this, I understood, of course, that she must have been his wife — and not his sister or another relative, I mean. I searched for Portuguese words of solace. But my host put a finger to his lips, nodded so I knew that I didn't

8

have to say anything. He stood at the side of the bed.

Now comes the part which floored me. The peasant linked his thumbs together and made a fluttering motion with his hands over her chest. The flutter seemed to free itself from confines, then rose slowly into the air until it was high above his head. He said to me: "*O corpo é só um casulo, e ao morrer, a alma volta para Deus como...* The body is just a cocoon, and upon death, the soul returns to God like a... " As he spoke, he edged his hands toward me, cupping them as if they carried a tiny gift. He whispered as if it were a sacred secret, "*...uma borboleta.*"

After that, he sat on the bed by his wife, his back hunched, praying. As I stared at him, it seemed as if the idea of a soul was something totally obvious and indisputable, like my being at that moment in a small town in Portugal. With certainty I was thinking: *we all have a butterfly inside us waiting to fly free.* (To you, as a practicing Christian, such a metaphysical notion may seem mundane, and the metaphor itself may seem clichéd, but as I've told you, I *never* entertain such ideas.)

As he prayed in silence, I began to doubt myself, began wondering why he had led me to his home and shown me his wife. I was angry. Had he seen something in my face which told him that I needed faith? What gave him the right to interfere with me, to make me see death, listen to his sermon about souls?

I wanted the distance of the tourist returned to me. But I was frozen there. Finally, after maybe two or three minutes of watching him pray, I felt as if his invitation was an intimate gift which I didn't deserve. It was like I had crossed an invisible threshold into a magical landscape, passed beyond a border I'd been searching for without knowing it. And that both you and he had led me there.

Does this make any sense to you?

You'll think me insane, perhaps, but I even began to wonder whether he really wasn't some sort of village saint. Looking at him — at the gray stubble on his cheeks, his great hands, his hunched back — goosepimples shivered on my skin. I felt as if the heat of my normal existence had been stolen from me.

His daughter took my arm suddenly and escorted me to the door. As I left the bedroom, the old peasant waved and smiled again. "*Uma borboleta,*" he repeated, pointing at my chest this time.

It was like a reminder. And like what I've been needing to hear for so long, since the onset of your Aids, maybe longer — what I've been afraid of hearing, as well. (Is it harder to give up *dis*belief than it is to give up belief? What do your Christian sages say about that?)

As I walked back to the inn, I felt as if I were about to burst into tears, that I was weighted with responsibility. It was like all the clocks in the world had just stopped and were waiting for me to pronounce an incantation so that they could begin counting time again. And yet, I also felt as if I were returning home. Like I was walking on Maplewood Road toward Mom and Dad's house. That I was about to find safety and protection.

Is that what faith is all about — the irrational certainty that one is safe and being watched over?

What do you think is this great responsibility such faith implies?

One other thing. I know you'll understand, because we share the same childlike attraction for things of color, but I swear to God that there was another crimson and amber butterfly sitting on the white stairs leading to the inn's front door. Right on the top step, flexing its wings. Maybe they're really common around here, so the coincidence is no big deal. Before it flew up and away, it seemed so beautiful against the white background — like a stained-glass figurine come to life — that I wished I could slip inside its little body.

That's it. I don't know what the lasting consequence of all this will be, but I knew that I had to write to you. About death and faith and Portuguese butterflies.

P.S. Why do the worst thoughts occur to me at my best moments? When I finished this letter just now, I made the mistake of looking into the mirror behind the desk I'm writing on. My own face, particularly the translucent depth in my eyes, provoked fear. Do I dare write to you about this? I hesitate, because I don't need any more terror in my life. But if I'm going to live up to the agreement we made that day in your room at Mt Sinai Hospital and discuss these important matters, then you've got to know all my feelings.

What I now know, of course, is that the metaphor of the *borboleta* is no good, is just like those so-called 'promising' drugs the doctors were stuffing you with. But there's a deeper fear. For even if the peasant is right, even if we all carry a soul like a butterfly at our center, his wife was an old woman. It was time for her soul to depart from its cocoon. But it wasn't for you! It was simply too much for Him to ask you to leave. A man of thirty-nine? My brother? You were only just starting your metamorphosis. Your wings were not fully formed yet. How could you be expected to fly to God?

"Cut the poetry and don't get melodramatic!" I hear you say.

"The butterfly is only a metaphor. My soul didn't lose its way."

You always had such certainty in your voice when you spoke of such things. And maybe it's true. I don't know. But there's a swollen ache in my stomach when I picture your gaunt face as it was in the hospital which is no metaphor. And when I look in the mirror now and see the reflection of you in my tired gray eyes, all the dread of the last two years returns. Dear God, how very alike we look when we're three thousand miles and an eternity apart! The same curly brown hair, the same long, straight nose. The same half-smile when we fight sadness, as if we've been straining all our lives against some inevitable fate of destruction.

I never told you, but when we were kids, I'd sometimes look across at you in the middle of the night when you were sleeping. Curled there, your head on your flannel Spiderman pillow, you didn't look like the enemy I fought with over toys and comic books and most everything else. No, you were reduced to what was essential: a little boy dreaming — my elder brother.

And I wished that you would let me love you as I now do.

Sometimes, I imagined I looked just like you as I lay my head back into my pillow. Two little boys we were, making the same journey together.

And that's the deepest terror. You see, I wonder how alike we will look in years to come, now that you are no longer here and I keep advancing toward age forty, fifty, sixty... I'm going to leave you behind, lose more of you with each advancing year until I may not even be able to hear you in my voice or see the way you sleep at night as my own head hits the pillow. Your soul will fly out of me, as well. The space it occupies will desiccate. Memory will reach into a dry hollow. And in the mirror only my own abandoned face will be reflected.

2

My dearest Carlos,

Now that you've finished reading my last letter to Harold, I can tell you that something unexpected and terrible has happened, and that's why I have to write to you. No, I can't say what it is just yet; people who are scared need strict rules to live by or they flounder, so I've decided to tell you everything in chronological order.

I also need to tell you things about myself. Pretty soon, you may be the only one left. Maybe you'll be the one to save us all, and you need to know everything.

You see, Carlos, one upon a time I was eleven years old and

bicycling with my brother through a neighborhood smelling of barbecues and shaded by oaks. We stopped at Gardener's Hill, read comic books, played catch with a Spalding rubber ball. We sat on the curb and talked about our teachers.

Then, seemingly the very next day, Harold was dead. And I was writing letters to him that would never be mailed.

Maybe there's more time between childhood and death than I'm implying, but that's the way it seems.

If it doesn't seem that way to you then you're still enjoying your youth. Good for you.

But I can't wait any longer for you to grow up.

I ask only that you listen. Even after our nearly two years together, I know that you don't really know me and don't have any sense of the barriers which exist between the living and the dead. How, then, will you be able to respond to the offer which I'm going to make at the very end of this letter? Without understanding the dangers you face, how will you find the courage to accept?

I realized that I was going to have to write to you on Monday, May 22nd, about two weeks ago now. It's right there in my journal. Do you remember António, my best student? He was already sick, had just entered the hospital, but I didn't know about it yet. And even if I had, I wouldn't have put two and two together right away. I was at home. My new home. On the Passeio das Virtudes. The previous November, I left the place we'd shared and moved in with a goodhearted beast named Fiama who has a third-floor apartment there. The night of the 22nd she discovered that she was infested with crabs. Her pubic hair was a forest full of eggs, so I shaved her down below and put on some bitter-smelling liquid which I'd bought at the corner pharmacy. On the way home from buying the stuff, Zero had called to me from the Pérola Negra. Remember Zero, the poet with the Vandyke beard, the one who lived for a time in Istanbul and who's always eating pistachio nuts? Anyway, when I explained to him what I was up to, he raised his eyebrows like a lecherous old man and tugged on the tip of his beard. He informed me in a scholarly voice that a woman really trusts a man when she lets him shave her private parts. That's what started me thinking I had to write to you. Fiama trusted me, you see. And I realized that despite what I said at the time, I never really trusted you. Not completely. I'm sorry. I want to make sure you understand; *I'm* apologizing. I made mistakes too. Many.

I wanted to write to you and tell you that.

As I worked Fiama over with my Wilkinson double-edged razor, she lay back like Cleopatra, her arms under her head, her elbows splayed out, the little bushes under her arms infusing the room with the smell of dirty sheets. A dark woman, Fiama is, with a tangle of thick black hair creeping down her neck and over large, doe-eyed breasts — the kind which novelists are always mis-describing as *firm*. You know what they feel like to Fiama? A silk bag filled with ripe raspberries. When she gives herself a breast exam she imagines that they're blessed with the most luscious berries from the north of Portugal. A poetic woman, don't you think? Her only drawback is that she's got a face that looks older and more intelligent the closer you get. As you know, Portuguese bachelors panic when confronted with a women with brains, and she rarely gets a date with a guy who's anything but a third-rate gangster. Hence the crabs. She'd be a great catch, though. In addition to everything else, she's got a husky singing voice that sounds as if she's got fur in her vocal chords. She'd certainly be worth you painting, dear boy, let alone getting in the sack, assuming you would dare try to get your paint brush up for a woman who could see right through you. As it happens, Zero hit the nail on the head; she feels comfortable with me because the only thing I want from her is an occasional back rub or bedtime story. So as I was lathering her up, she started telling me her ideas about the human condition. She believes that life is based on eyesight — the better one sees, the easier life is. I didn't mention to her that there are some very happy blind people in the world because she's not easy to interrupt when she's got a few Super Bock beers sloshing around with the regrets in her gut. Her theory is that since the optic nerve weakens as we age, our lives invariably get harder. To be fair, and just so I don't give the impression that she's a lunatic, I should add that eyesight isn't a simple thing to her. It also implies reasoning. For instance, she says that now she's thirty-nine she can no longer tell the age of teenagers; a high-school kid looks exactly like a college student to her. When she's sixty, she says, she won't be able to tell the difference between a runny-nosed schoolboy and a bank president. She also believes that there's nothing to be done about it. Fiama's philosophy in a nutshell: you're born, your vision gets progressively worse, and when you're nearly blind, you think you can see God. Then, of course, you die.

Is that the true story of my brother and his conversion to Christianity?

In general, you Portuguese share Fiama's unflagging optimism. It's why I've gotten on reasonably well here. And yet, everyone I meet in Porto invariably tells me they're Catholic.

Catholics without faith — it's an interesting concept.

As for me, I still try my best not to consider the future. Just like in the old days, when we were a team. I count my blessings like sheep before I go to sleep at night: clear blue eyes; agile fingers; a nearly full head of curly brown hair; a brain that can still sometimes distinguish dream from waking reality. And of course, good vision. Maybe it's not twenty-twenty any more, but I can still read the sheet music on my stand without glasses. And it certainly hasn't deteriorated so far that I'm seeing God. So perhaps Fiama's got it right; I can't say that my life has been all that hard. I've got a little money, a job, a mother who's still alive. Most importantly, I haven't been to a funeral in over a year, and only one dear friend of mine looks as if he's dying. And, I'm not sick.

Did you think that that was the reason I decided to write to you? Did you have your fingers crossed in hope?

Imagine, it's already the end of my fourth year in Porto. Without having to peer at friends tucked neatly into the creamy folds of velvet in their pine coffins, the months pass by without noticeable markers. It seems only a few days since August 17th of last year, when you took all your things from our apartment while I was teaching and left behind a letter which began: 'You could be cured, but you have to really want it.' Remember? At first, I didn't understand. I thought: *Cured of what, for God's sake?* Then I figured I didn't understand your Portuguese. I looked up the word *curado,* cured, in my Morais dictionary. I found out that — sure enough — olives and sick people are cured. *But why would a healthy American need to be?* I couldn't figure it out. Because I'd lived so long in cities where anyone with at least a sixth-grade education has the good sense to know that my blessed perversions can't be cured...

not by shock treatment;

not by praying to Yawheh, Allah, Brahma, the Great Spirit or even Sean Connery;

not by aversion therapy;

not by magic crystals or psychedelic mushrooms;

not by watching Oprah Winfrey interviewing unhappy queers from every state in the union every day for a decade;

not by chanting macho mandalas penned by Robert Bly in a testosterone-induced trance while sitting in the lotus position on a butte in the Sonora Desert;

not by mainlining prozac while eating can after can of Bumble Bee tuna fish;

and not even by watching videotapes of teenage Asian girls smoking cigarettes with their pussies in a Bangkok Eurotrash bar (as was once suggested to me by a French therapist I had the displeasure to meet on Fire Island).

Then I understood that you really believed what you were saying. I laughed out loud; I'd never realized before what a dinosaur I'd fallen for. Tell me, Carlos, do you have nightmares about an asteroid hitting the Earth again and wiping out your whole pea-brained family of behemoths?

I've been raped and dumped by better men than you, so it wasn't because I was so damn hurt that I didn't write or call these past nine months. No, I didn't try to get in touch with you because hundreds of thousands of people *really are looking for a cure for a far worse disease than craving a kiss from a man or a short vacation in the city of Sodom.* You see, I despised you more than you can ever know for using that word *cure* so damn loosely.

On behalf of all the dead and dying I have known, I say (with all the compassion for your predicament I can muster): fuck you.

Shall we return to better memories?

Remember how we would come back from the Pérola Negra at midnight, after our verbena tea, and you'd rip your jeans off and lie there on the bed with your legs up like a dog wanting its belly scratched? Or has that all been neatly labeled under 'Bad Mistake', locked away in a steel box and buried under the floor of your Lisbon studio?

Even today, when I say your name to myself, the first thing I think of is the time shortly after we started sleeping together when you stroked my eyebrows with your fingertips like you were petting the most fragile of furry caterpillars and said, "I'd like to become part of you." No one had ever said that to me before, and I didn't think at the time that it was just a line. Your fingertips caressed down my forehead and nose, over my chin, across my neck and collarbone... Your black eyes were grave, and I knew that you were studying a body — anyone's body — for the very first time in your life. After thirty-three years of avoiding the physical world, it must have been quite a discovery. Your paintings changed after that. You put away the resinous circles, dots and squiggles you were always peddling and dared to put figures onto your canvases.

You actually decided to try to communicate with other people for the first time. I was touched when you began to paint scenes from the life of a little boy named Carlos who...

was born to António and Graça Mourão in the municipal hospital of Evora on April 12th, 1961, at exactly 6:37 in the morning and was therefore called the Dawn Baby for his next year of life;

has always loved codfish and fava beans and any dessert made with eggs;

discovered Kandinsky and De Kooning when he was twelve and taking art classes for the first time;

was ridiculed by the other boys because he preferred reading about the lives of saints to soccer;

attached stakes to the dahlias in his backyard so their pom-pom flowers wouldn't fall over in the wind coming from the Spanish plateau;

studied for a year at the Slade School of Art in London, but got so terrified at living in a big city *where anything could happen* that he ran home to Portugal with his tail between his legs;

had his first sexual relation with a neighbor boy named Mauricio when he was sixteen, but didn't repeat the experience till he met an American music professor when he was thirty-three. Me, of course.

Those first tentative efforts of yours at figurative painting weren't very good, I suppose. Maria thought they were terrible, as I recall, and refused to put them up at her gallery. But that wasn't important; you were learning how to accept yourself and fall in love.

And being a good lover is more important than being a good painter.

If you don't believe me, it may be because you haven't yet watched enough people die; a headstone doesn't lie about the insignificance of even the most brilliant career!

Want to see how much more I remember about you?

The crusty calluses on the balls of your feet.

Your Reebok sneakers squeaking when we had to walk home from the June Tabor concert in the rain.

Teaching me to eat pizza with a steak knife and fork.

Two espressos at the Pérola Negra every morning. Verbena tea before sleep.

The sketches for paintings which you used to take to bed with you at night, that I'd find in the morning under your pillow. The sound they made when they accidentally crunched between us at night. (Do you know that I saved every last one I could find and kept them in an envelope in my dresser. They're here with me now, below my socks.)

Watching you paint, your shirt off, smudges on your cheeks and forehead.

Your devotion to other people's dogs, how you used to go up to them in the street and rub their ears and let them kiss you.

How you brought me meals in bed when I had the flu.

The postcard of a Arp sculpture which you sent to me when you went to Nice, and which you signed, 'Eternally touching you...'

The photograph I took of you with your hair slicked back in which you looked just like Tyrone Power.

The smell of tobacco on your peasant fingers.

Feeding you slices of Granny Smith apples when your hands were too covered with paint to touch food.

You waking up in the middle of the night and being frightened and gripping both my hands.

Carlos, do you see how much I've committed to memory? It's crazy, I suppose, but I'd like to know even more about you. I feel cheated that you always painted the borders around you with such thick brushstrokes.

Now, as I whisper your name again, we are lying together on that mile-long strand of golden beach near Tavira. We're naked, and our foreheads are beaded with sweat and our scrotums are as loose as they can get because it's 100 degrees and we've just explored each other's deepest shadows in the thatched cottage with blue doors which we've rented and we're now so ready for sleep we can barely keep our eyes open. In a lazy slow voice, you're reading poetry to me. I fall asleep, and my dreams leave me in a land of olive trees and dew. I awake and watch you sleeping, and I sprinkle warm sand on your arm and begin to cry because you're the most beautiful thing I've ever seen and I wish I'd given birth to you.

Do good memories attract their opposite?

Using against me my half-jesting description of myself as part of an endangered sub-species *(Homo frequently erectus)*, you said in your poisonous goodbye letter, 'Why didn't you just stay in America where you and your fellow perverts were meant to become extinct and leave the rest of us the hell alone?'

I've always associated that inspired question with the time you asked me if I missed anything about the States, as if that were impossible. I said, "Everything, even the New York subway and L.A. freeways." But I'll admit now that was a lie designed to make you feel guilty because you were already distancing yourself from me with excuses about *too much work* and *things I would never understand about Portugal since I was a middle-class foreigner with no understanding of anything that couldn't be bought or sold.*

The truth is that the only thing I really miss is basketball. Not watching it, but playing it. There are no public courts here. And other than schoolkids, people here only play basketball in private clubs. No one over the age of twenty-five does any exercise at all, of course, except for a generation of old men who've rediscovered health after forty years of smoking two packs a day of unfiltered cigarettes and who are now running marathons.

Undoubtedly you will buy a blue and white tracksuit twenty years from now and start joining them on their training sessions.

You don't know it but you're blessed here in Portugal because you have the Atlantic Ocean; it makes all the difference — cool breezes at night, beaches with fine warm sand. What about your beloved French Riviera, where you dreamed of becoming famous and giving interviews on the deck of your waterfront palace? Forget it. The Mediterranean is no ocean, not even a real sea. It's a stagnant pool, reeking with Europe's waste. With beaches of mud and pebbles. Dive underwater at Saint-Tropez and you surface with a case of clap from some sunburned German tourist from Wupperthal who took a leak in the water.

Why do I make these sad attempts to be funny?

Isn't the answer obvious? I'm afraid you'll stop reading if I don't offer you little treats made with eggs and sugar from time to time.

It seems absurd to admit it now, but when I came to Europe I was going to write the great Jewish travel book: Lisbon to Moscow and everything with Hebrew origins in between. I told you about it, but you probably don't remember because my life always bored you. Back in L.A., my head had been so filled with the project that I couldn't sleep for months until I got here. But, as I told dear Libby, my agent, before we parted ways, I soon discovered that traveling was finished. Because sex is finished. There was a time when you could hop from bed to bed all the way to Istanbul, gay or straight, Jew or Gentile. But that's over now. So what's the point? To see yet another baroque cathedral built atop a ruined synagogue? Another cemetery with headstones written in Hebrew? I just couldn't keep writing about culture or history anymore.

It's probably a sin to say so, but culture and history without sex are all but useless.

Now, every time I see a church or synagogue I get narcolepsy. As for Europe's castles and churches and villas, they're all haunted by snot-faced Nazis and Communists trying to figure out what to do with their pitiful little lives until they can overtake the Social Democrats. Now that sex is in its death throes, if you want to see the world, rent the video instead.

As for what's appearing before you on the page, this is just a game. Like basketball. I toss the words into my screen and hope for the best. Let me spell things out even more clearly, Carlos: it is for you and me both that I abase myself in prose. You want to put on a nun's habit and crawl into a corner of your studio and scribble heartbreaking graffiti about life's solitude on dirty canvases. But I've finally decided not to let you hide yourself so easily. Dare I tell you my plan? It's obvious enough. I'm hoping, with the mad hope of medieval alchemists, that I'll happen upon some magic sequence of words, a formula, which might just turn your leaden life to gold, or, at the very least, revive you. Maybe I'll happen upon some arcane prayer that could even turn you into the Golem of Lisbon. You'll be the one to save us all, even me, defend us from the microscopic Cossacks swooping down on our ghettos in San Francisco, L.A., New York, Rio, London... Even now in Lisbon and Porto. Because how are we to know who will be chosen to save us? Maybe it'll be a cowardly painter from Evora who, if the lights aren't too bright and you slick back his hair, looks a lot like a bisexual Hollywood heartthrob from the 1940s.

Don't you get it? I mean you, Carlos...you.

So today is June the 7th. I've made it this far, and it is indeed something of a miracle. For a long while now it has seemed as if it were pouring everywhere over America and Europe except in outposts like Portugal. Ever since António started feeling ill, it's even begun to drizzle here. So if I'm still tossing words into this computer, it's not that I really think it's going to help. It's just that my constitution is not as strong as it once was and I've got to stay inside when it's pouring. And there's really nothing else to do but watch television. Of course, Fiama does own a ancient Philips black-and-white set with golden knobs, but she keeps it on the dresser in her room. She falls asleep listening to the news and lies naked and curled into a ball under her yellow blanket. I try not to watch with her because I'd like to die still believing that there is a real world somewhere if only we could find it.

A year after Harold's death and there are still days when I wake in the morning and feel his cold sweat beaded on my forehead.

And when I sip my morning coffee, the purple lesions which disfigured his face knot in my chest.

Harold is my enemy. As is António.

Why mention him in the same breath with my dead brother? Let me get the ouzo from Fiama's pantry and I'll tell you.

That's better; the truth seems to slip easier through your fingers when you've got fennel and alcohol on your breath.

Pardon my saying so, but a life of camouflaging yourself has made you rather slow, dear Carlos, so here it is: because António is the one who has summoned the Angel of Death to my refuge. He's undone all my ostrich plans to bury my head under the sands of Portugal. So where do I go from here? Africa? It's gasping for its last breath. And even if they find a cure for its ailments, it'll be too expensive for those poor slobs to afford. South America? Too hot except for Argentina. And the Argentines are so proud of being white that it makes me want to look like an Aborigine and spit worms at them. So maybe I should go to Australia and dig for opals. Or head to New Zealand and learn to yodel upside down. But I don't want to go anywhere they speak English. I prefer living where I can't understand everything people say because I'm able to make believe that they're actually sensitive and intelligent creatures.

As you can see, Carlos, I crave reality but live in a fantasy world. It's a paradox, I know. But then, so is my life. And yours — to say the least, my little closet case.

3

António was supposed to have a lesson with me on Tuesday, the 23rd of May. He left a message on my machine that morning saying he was sick and would have to cancel.

His voice sounded okay. I called him back, but there was no answer. I wasn't worried.

On Wednesday, a secretary at the Conservatory hunted me down while I was giving a lesson. António's father had just called, she said. The boy was in the Santo António hospital with shingles.

"But you don't usually go to the hospital for that," I replied.

She shrugged. "Must be a real bad case."

I got his room number and went to see him at visiting time, four in the afternoon. I met his doctor, a short unkempt man with an unruly beard, in the nursing station before reaching his room. His name was Silva. He told me in a calming voice that António had the flu and shingles at the same time. He was in the hospital to guard against pneumonia. He wasn't in any immediate danger.

I was relieved.

Then he said that he'd ordered an HIV test and that it would take a week to get the results.

Imagine your heart crashing through your bowels and falling on the floor.

I awoke on a metal cot. A nurse with pale skin and rubbery hands was touching my face. She brought me water.

There was gauze on my forehead. I felt it.

"You hit it against the floor," she told me. "Don't touch it. It's been cleaned and disinfected."

I took a cab home without seeing António.

You don't know my friend Pedro, because you were afraid to meet any of the other teachers at my school lest they get the idea that you and I were lovers. But you must have heard me talk about him.

Five foot three inches tall.

Uruguayan.

Colorful sweaters and jeans. Leather sandals with bare feet when it's warm; sandals with white woolen socks when it's cold.

A hooked Aztec nose; nostrils flaring as he plays guitar.

Straight. I mean, *really straight*. Not like you, because he doesn't need to fake the explosion in his brain when his desire meets the anti-matter world of a woman's moist shadow.

Does my language bother you?

Good.

On Thursday afternoon, after classes, Pedro introduced me to a

Brazilian man named Ricardo. We met at the tea house at Porto's Museum of Modern Art. We ordered scones and Earl Grey tea. We sat outside in the sun, under that magnificent arbor of wisteria which you thought was too exuberant because you have the fear of display which all closet cases have. We laughed from our bellies like Americans on holiday and juggled witticisms as best we could. Ricardo has green almond-shaped eyes, a thin, wily face and long black hair pulled back into a tight ponytail.

His mother is Japanese and his father Brazilian.

He teaches history at a high school in the Vila Indiana district of São Paulo.

He likes to go to carnival wearing masks with long pointed noses.

He cannot sleep if even one mosquito is in his bedroom at night.

He likes the quiet of Portugal.

When I first laid eyes on him, he was seated at a table at the Museum tea house. He was clothed in a kind of silence and elegance which made me jealous. I admit that I would have liked to sleep with him. Probably because the gauze from my fainting spell was still taped to my forehead and I was feeling so damned anxious.

I stopped craving him the moment he opened his mouth; despite his Brazilian accent and ponytail, he talked with the gravity of a European intellectual. He said he was forty-one and that he was visiting Portugal for the first time. When I asked why he'd become a history professor, he said that his older brother had been killed by the security police of the Brazilian dictatorship back in 1969.

Ever since his brother's murder, Ricardo had been interested in what he remembered of him and why it was so important not to forget *anything, even his scent.*

That was the expression he used: *even his scent.*

I stopped sipping my tea. We stared at each other. Was it recognition of a kindred soul?

This preoccupation with memory had led Ricardo to investigate history. "Why is the Trojan War fixed in our minds?" he asked me. "Why Auschwitz? What have we forgotten and why?"

"I don't know," I said. "What's the reason?"

"I don't know either. I'm still looking for the answer. That's one of the reasons I'm here."

I began sipping my tea again. I squinted at him suspiciously, as if he were holding back.

"I really haven't any answer," he repeated.

"Any guesses?" Pedro asked.

The Brazilian ate his last bit of scone, reached behind his head and tugged on his ponytail. He looked straight at Pedro and said, "I think it has to do with our perception of time as something through which we are moving. I believe that we remember, because if we didn't remember we would no longer perceive time this way. We would perceive it as static. In other words," he said, annoyed at himself for being so obscure, "we make a deal with ourselves." He stared at me. "We say, 'I'll remember my brother or my parents or some terrible event.' And why? So that we can continue walking ahead into the future. If we didn't make that deal, we'd be stuck in a world where time has ceased its flow. And human beings can't live like that very long."

I was more interested in him than ever now because I could see he was as insane as I am. I asked, "So why Portugal? Doesn't Brazil have enough history for you?"

"I recently discovered that my father and his ancestors were Jews... Jews from Portugal who hid their beliefs for centuries."

Was this another coincidental connection between us? One of occult significance?

Hardly.

Pedro had brought us together for this very reason. Take it from me, South American political exiles are all hopeless matchmakers.

At the time, this confession from Ricardo irritated me because I was so sick of Jewish history. So I was rather rude. In fact, thinking of our dead brothers, I said, "With all that's happened, who could possibly care about what happened to our ancestors all those years ago?"

Pedro rested his arm on my hand, looked at me like a parent beseeching his child to be reasonable and said, "What do you know about the kabbalah? That's really what Ricardo is interested in."

I rolled my eyes. "It's worthless. You want a useful philosophy, read Madonna's books."

Pedro frowned at me because he's delicate and intelligent, and doesn't like it when I curse and say stupid things. So I asked him, "Did the riddles of the Zohar help the Jews escape the Inquisition? And the magic manuals of Joseph Ashkenazi — did they keep my great-aunts and uncles out of the death camps? Could an amulet of a secret name of God really help anybody dying of Aids?"

"Hope..." Ricardo answered. His voice was urgent. He gripped his teacup as if he planned on squeezing it in his fist. I leaned back and hoped he wouldn't hit me with porcelain shrapnel. He said, "A long time ago I needed some philosophy that would bind me to hope. I didn't have one. That's also why I'm here. It wasn't just my brother. The security police arrested me a little while after him and took me to a house near Iguape. They wanted me to tell them things about him. A little man with a mustache, a man so puny you would never even notice him if he passed you in the street, put electrodes on me, on different parts of my body — the most sensitive parts, I mean. And the pain was like nothing I could ever tell you. It's when I lost hope. I remember the moment it evaporated from me. It was like one moment I was pregnant and the next I'd given birth to a still-born baby. I was empty. And I haven't gotten my hope back, not even after all these years. I'd have preferred keeping it. I just don't know how to bring a still-born baby back from the dead."

I looked down for a while, and he leaned back in his chair. When I faced him again, I said, "Even if hope is an illusion?"

"Even so."

"Then tell me this..."

And that's when my fears about António spilled out of me: "I've got a student in the hospital. He's a beautiful kid. Just turned twenty-four years old. Born to play classical guitar. I can't teach him anything but a little bit about music and passion. But he's probably dying. Slept with a dope addict, one of the other students, and now he's on his way out. The results for HIV will be in in six days or so. But I'm afraid I know the answer already. I pray I'm wrong. But maybe he's got no more than five years. Should he have hope? Should we give him hope?"

"You've never been tortured," Ricardo said.

I've trained myself to go silent when I'm enraged. Pedro began to speak, but I held up my hand as if to halt traffic. It was my turn to lean forward. "No, I don't qualify for your club," I snapped.

"It's not a club," he replied. "What I was going to say is that if you'd been tortured, you'd realize that hope is a kind of magic."

"Fuck you!" I said, because I'm so sick of people who think that life has a magic core that my ears run with blood when I hear it.

"Or maybe it's self-hypnosis," Ricardo continued. "I don't know the psychology of the brain. But imagine if you could make your body into hope...forge an armor out of hope. That would be a goal worth attaining, don't you think? And maybe it wouldn't save you from a death camp or a Brazilian bastard giving you electric shocks, or even save your student... But maybe you'd die in peace."

When I jumped up from the table, my chair crashed backwards. But I spoke with the calm of knowing my argument inside out. "You've got me all wrong. I don't want to die in peace. I want to die angry. Get it? I want to flail my arms and scream and kick and maybe put a bullet into the Pope. And this is the point... I want António to die angry, too. He should. He's twenty-four years old. Get it?! Not forty like me and you. Twenty-four fucking years old!"

Pedro held his hands over his ears because I'd begun to shout. He told me once that he was this sensitive before he was tortured, but I find it hard to believe. He was trembling. So I sat back down and covered his hands with my own and looked into his black eyes. He's such a fragile little thing. "I'm sorry," I said.

We lowered our hands together. I brought his to my mouth and kissed them. Pedro is a good friend, and I know I can be terrible.

I turned to Ricardo. "I saw too much in New York to stay there without mainlining valium," I said. "So I escaped first to Los Angeles, then moved to Portugal when my brother got ill. It was Aids, and it took too long. He died about two-and-a-half years after I moved here. And now, after a year of the most blessed freedom, of not knowing any friend who's going to have to say goodbye forever to the world, the Angel of Death has found me here. If you'd have come two weeks ago, you'd have found me reasonably happy. Free. But now, through António, I've been found. It's over. I'm angry because I don't know the secret words which will make him well. Guitar playing, writing, even loving — it's all worthless. Years and years of learning about music and writing and hunting for the kiss of a perfect lover and I still don't know one word that can help a boy who has to say goodbye to a world he's barely seen."

We sat in silence because confessions make people who've been wounded very quiet. For the first time, I realized what a failure I'd been because of this rage of mine.

It had even prevented me from writing to you.

I knew in that moment that I would not only send you this letter, but even had a vague presentiment of the form it would take.

I said, "Look, it may sound funny after my explosion, but I just want to be gentle with people now. What's left? After torture and hospitals and brain diseases, what's left except to try to take the pain from other people? And I can't even do that well. As you can see." I took out a teller-machine receipt from my wallet and wrote down the name of an old Jewish poet I once met. He told me that he wanted to get a thousand people who'd been abused and tortured together on a mountaintop in Portugal and have them face Jerusalem and shout in unison the name of God together. He wasn't sure what would happen, but he knew it would change things forever. "This one is pretty weird," I told Ricardo, handing him the slip of paper. "He'll point you toward the moon and give you a kick. And he says there's a clandestine band of kabbalists living near Belmonte. They meet together, know secret names of God. He says they sit and face Jerusalem and pray for the Messiah to descend to earth again. If his band of maniacs accepts you, I suppose they'll teach you how to breathe and dance and eat and maybe even make love like a kabbalist."

They smiled at my silliness. The Brazilian thanked me, then poured me more tea. "I want to meet your student," he said.

"António?"

"Can I see him?" he asked.

"Why?"

"Memory. Years from now, I want to be able to remember you and him together."

My throat was suddenly so dry that I couldn't talk. I excused myself and went to the bathroom at the back of the tea house and stood in front of the mirror looking in vain for signs of my brother's face and washed my eyes with cold water until I had my voice back. At our table, I said to Ricardo, "You still want to go?"

He nodded.

"And you?" I asked Pedro.

He nodded, too.

It was four-thirty in the afternoon, so visiting hours had already started. I drove us to the Hospital of Saint Anthony. In the car, these tortured South Americans were so silent and reverent that it made me want to drive straight into a granite wall.

In the hospital, Ricardo, Pedro and I stood together at the foot of António's bed, and the Brazilian asked the boy a question which changed everything. Suddenly, I was no longer thinking about escaping to New Zealand or South America or Africa.

My feet were rooted in place to granite paving stones.

And there was a steady drumbeat in the hollow left by my brother's death. And it was telling me, *I must stay with António.*

Amazing how meeting an acquaintance can change the future.

Dear Carlos, forgive me for ending this part of the game in the middle; I don't want to talk about Ricardo's question and António's reply right now. I can't even describe the boy lying in his hospital bed. So just wait a little while and we'll discuss it when I've had some more ouzo and we're both a little calmer.

I've just realized that I've gotten a little ahead of myself. It must be that my head isn't working properly since I started scenting the microscopic boots of the invisible Cossacks under my bed. I've forgotten that you never wanted to hear anything about António because of that little ailment of yours called jealousy which ate at you despite the fact that you told me: *God forbid I were really gay — it's just that for me, a hole is a hole is a hole.*

Did you think you were being clever?

Despite your contempt for everything from the United States, you were very American in your selfishness, you know; every conversation had to be a solar system revolving around your artist's ego. You couldn't see past the tip of your little cock and very often not even that far.

Did you really expect me to believe your juvenile parody of Gertrude Stein? But I respected your wishes and never told you anything about António and precious little about my past. Surely nothing that might drive you away.

In doing so, did I made a mistake?

Maybe you really did want to know those things.

Maybe they would have frightened you but made you hold my hand that much tighter under the covers when you woke up from your nightmares.

4

In retrospect, it seems to me as if I were looking for António all my life. Not someone to fall madly in love with, like you; that was always too easy for me, but a man or boy whose accomplishments would help to fill the emptiness. I can hear you laughing at that. But so much the better; your condescension will keep you reading.

When I was a little weed of youthful enthusiasm, all it took for me to fall in love was someone I'd slept with putting his arm over my shoulder in a movie theater, or pecking me on the cheek before sleep, or writing me a two-line letter of remembrance on his office stationery. One of these simple gestures of affection plus our mingled sweat and semen on some 200-threads-per-inch sheets and I was ready to sign my heart over to the bastard like a Jewish Cyrano de Bergerac who'd never heard...

of holding himself back;

of a handshake refused;

of getting hurt in bed.

I was an effortless mark. My blue-eyed stare of trust must have looked to the men I met like the yearning of a doe-eyed Mary Pickford for her aviator husband lost in a windstorm. More than one man told me I was really looking for it; *it* being betrayal, bruises, bombastic lectures on the nature of things; *things* meaning man's cruelty to man. The very first was Vincent, the Mozart-loving, amyl-snorting graduate of Andover and Harvard, who purchased his phony English accent for $10.95 from a BBC factory outlet in his home town of Lexington, Massachusetts; who knew Jackie Kennedy *personally* and who had eaten breakfast once in Gray Gardens with a hundred Bouvier-family tomcats licking his tits; who, when he first met me, read me Masoch's *Venus in Furs* at four o'clock in the morning after he'd had me twice from behind and eaten up all the semen stored like camel-milk for months inside my eighteen-year-old balls. He didn't believe it, but I'd been a virgin. *Venus in Furs,* of course, was about his fantasies, about a man dressed in nothing but sable fur, with a whip in his hand, dominating his slave. I took the words of the *Venus* to heart: 'Love...forgives and suffers everything, because it must. It is not our judgment that leads us; it is neither the advantages nor the faults which we discover that make us abandon ourselves, or that repel us. It is a sweet, soft, enigmatic power that drives us on. We cease to think, to feel, to will; we let ourselves be carried away by it, and ask not whither.'

Being with Vincent, I learned to accept this long-suffering and whimpering version of love. I set myself up for an Upper East Side door to be slammed in my face when I became an embarrassment and a chore, but mostly when I was no longer any *fun.* Fun, you see, is the be all and end all for a certain kind of American, straight or gay, and if they're not having any then they'd just as soon spray you full of bullets. Next time you see sociologists speculating about why an American would shoot up a restaurant with a machine gun, remember that it was because he *simply wasn't having any fun.*

At least, Carlos, that is not one of your faults.

I can see Vincent reading to me before bed, a goose-down pillow from Bloomingdale's behind his head, his bifocals low on his nose, his tone poetic, his manner affected. He was a little schnauzer of a man, always stiff and nervous, with a David Mamet close-to-the-scalp haircut. But he had Sal Mineo eyes, strong, hairy hands and a fire-hydrant cock. After he'd closed his book for the night, he always used to pound me like a jackhammer, in and out for ten manic minutes, never more than that, because there was nothing more important to him than being both macho and what he called *efficient.* Like the old Australian joke, Vincent's idea of foreplay was to grunt, "Brace yourself!" No matter, we'd go to sleep tucked safely into each other like timeworn socks. In the morning, he'd take his hand from around my belly, get into divorce-lawyer drag and head out to Pierce and Holbrook to make life miserable for some poor divorcée who never expected to get cut to shreds by the hired gun in the Armani suit whom her husband had had the good sense and megabucks to hire. Vincent, who took me to Sign Of The Dove and ordered me venison and a $125 Bordeaux from 1957; who skewered himself down onto me while riding up on the elevator to the Rainbow Room and who didn't care who saw us kissing before *Two Gentlemen of Verona* at the Shakespeare Festival in Central Park.

Vincent who, when he was no longer having so much goddamn fun, asked me to give him a blowjob in the tearoom of the Carlisle Hotel at midnight when no one was there and who threw a Maria Callas fit and dumped hot Earl Grey tea into my lap when I wouldn't do it. Vincent, who stopped letting me up to see the view from his seventeenth-floor Sixth Avenue office, who started to make believe I wasn't in his bed when the phone rang, who made me bleed by sticking a petrified seahorse from his Aunt Deborah in Florida up my behind as a *harmless little joke,* who bumped into Gore Vidal at Rizzoli's, whom he knew from a party at Edward Albee's *comfy little cottage* in Montauk and introduced me as a *little hustler from NYU with a nice ass.* All of which provoked fantasies about suicide inside me for the last six months of our year-long slide into humiliation but none of which made me leave him because I was in love. And because I thought that love meant that you hand over your independence and your body with no questions asked and never even suspect that there's any fine print in the contract.

Then one morning he slipped into one of the dozen suits he'd bought at Barney's and tied his white-and-black paisley Hermès tie, and woke me up with his mother-of-pearl pen knife from an Israeli discount store to my throat and spat this greeting to me: "I've met someone else who isn't such a whore. Take your smelly sneakers and your dirty jeans and don't be here when I get back." You'll know how naive I was, dear Carlos, when you hear what I said: "But I love you." Are you laughing hysterically? You should be. What a simp I was! Imagine thinking that *love* was a proper response! Imagine being so stupid that I never once imagined he was peddling his BBC accent on someone else. Imagine even defining love as letting someone scar your behind with a dead seahorse? He did me a favor by kicking me out. God, when I think of what I put up with... But what you'll find even more amusing is that after Vincent came Pietro, the romantic, fifty-two-year-old, silver-haired, *molto elegante* Professor of Italian Literature at Hunter College who made eyes at me over the foam of his cappuccino at the Caffe Dante and who led me with his confident smile to his apartment on West 11th Street and who sang Neapolitan ballads to me standing nude on the Persian rug he'd picked up *for the price of a blowjob* in Isfahan and who promised to *build a life around our love, our...amore.* Pietro, who used to tie me face-down to his bed with satin handcuffs and who never ever hurt me but who got drunk one night on Fra Angelico and too many dizzying looks in the mirror at the newest wrinkles searing his face and proceeded to beat me black-and-blue with the 'A to Coccinella' volume of a five-volume Italian-English dictionary for the fun of it and scream at me that I was *too young and beautiful and needed to be destroyed!* From Pietro, I have a broken rib that still hurts when it rains and a place in my throat reserved for vengeance which drips saliva like battery acid onto my pillow when I cannot sleep at night. After Pietro came Moishe, the bisexual Israeli taxi driver; who begat Miller the James Dean lookalike; who begat thirteen-inch Steven; who finally begat dearest Mark the Philosophy Graduate Student at Columbia. Mark, who bought me flowers every day for a month and whom I really thought was my lover for life but who asked me to move out one day short of our six-month anniversary when he told me that an assistant professorship position had opened up at Carlton College in Minnesota and who said *I won't be taking you with me* like I was an old piece of luggage.

But that cured me. Afterwards, *satori!* Fucking had nothing to do with love for most people and love had nothing to do with truth for all the rest. That was that. I understood. I snorted men and boys after that, across America and Europe, because I realized that all I could rightly expect in this life was the brief high that comes from a grope and a lick and a little penetration. It was the only way I was going to be able to fill up the despair of not being able to let myself fall in love. But don't you dare feel sorry for me, Carlos. I was lucky, one of the luckiest damn cocksuckers on the planet Earth. Why? All this promiscuity came before 1980 and the invasion of the invisible Cossacks who smell like pneumonia and who leave lesions in your skin with their microscopic swords. By the time they first appeared, I'd pretty much exhausted myself and given up on ever finding someone to share my bed forever. I was having the safest sex possible, that is to say, no sex except that which my right hand could gift me with. People make do with what they have, and I started to say in a schoolmarm's voice, *it's friendship that's really important.*

That's where my luck gave out. Because no sooner did I give in to that once-convenient rationalization then my friends started having their heads chopped off by the invisible Cossacks. The first to go was Malcolm the Breyer's Mint-Chip Ice-Cream Addict and Surrealistic Poet from Toronto, who came to the Village in 1976 looking like an overweight Cary Grant and who ended up as a goat-ribbed victim of the Killing Fields, who left me in his will all his unpublished poetry, a 17th-century silver candlestick from England and his dog, a twelve-year-old female Border Collie named Nancy — after Nancy Drew — who no longer recognized her master, the blotched rag-doll to whom I fed apple sauce and blended broccoli for the last month of his life. It was Malcolm who warned me back in 1983, "It's going to get a lot worse before it gets better." Did the extra pain of being one of the first to go give him a vision that many of our friends would soon be ash? Everybody on our West Village basketball team went down by the end of 1988, and a dozen others who were our fans and cheerleaders were dead by the time I left for L.A. in 1990. Except for me, the starting five all perished long before the first half of the game had finished.

The uniforms for Bob Jenkins, Henry 'The Beast' Davenport, Izzy Epstein and Carlo Foggia are all hanging from a special rafter in the Madison Square Garden of my memory. Bob, who was the cleverest, most talented bitch I ever knew and who could do perfect imitations of Daffy Duck, Bullwinkle, Patty Duke, Kevin Costner, Cher and a hundred other cartoon characters, who had light black skin which looked gold at sunset, who wrote a gay cowboy musical which was never performed — entitled *Oklahomo* — and who was working at Columbia University on some form of linear algebra so advanced that only three people in the world could talk with him about it, who dreamed of licking the sweat from the toes of his one God, Julius Erving; Henry The Beast, who got me started writing travel articles by saying, *you travel, you're relatively clever and you notice things other people don't so why not?* who contacted friends at the *Dallas Morning News* and got my first articles published even though they were shit, who was going to drive cross-country before he got too sick so he could die in the desert of New Mexico and who had decided to leave his body to be picked by vultures because of some romantic notion that he'd end up looking like a polished ivory skeleton on a Georgia O'Keefe canvas; Izzy, who had been kicked out of Yeshiva College in 1982 for having the compassion to feed his personal covenant with God to a starving orthodox rabbi named Koppelman in the basement bathroom of the main library and who turned me on to the kabbalah and taught me the Hebrew alphabet by writing the letters on the back of my hands and who left me in his will an autographed copy of Cecil Roth's *A History of the Marranos* and a seventeenth-century Russian-Jewish talisman against the demonic monarchs Lilith and Asmodeus; and Carlo, our point guard, who would have preferred being even a semi-professional basketball player in the sticks of North Dakota to being a $100,000-a-year corporate lawyer, but who stood only five foot seven inches tall and who met me every Sunday morning at eight a.m. at the court on Sixth Avenue and 4th Street so we could get in an hour of hoops before the junior high-school kids came and took over the court, who dribbled like Isaiah Thomas and hit the wildest thirty-foot bank shots one after another and who gripped my hand on his deathbed and said, "If you learn how to drive to your left, you'll never lose another game of one-on-one to anybody."

Of course, I got up at six a.m. for the next two weeks and went down early to the court and learned to drive like Bernard King to my left, but Carlo still died.

And yet it was Henry whom I mourned more than all the others; his dream of turning to ivory in the New Mexico desert seemed so fine. And it ended so poorly; he was prevented by his parents and sisters from leaving the hospital and was simply buried just like everyone else, in some flowery cemetery in Croton-on-Hudson. By then, I'd stopped going to funerals, so I had a private service at home — just me, Nancy the Border Collie and an altar composed of two white candles and a Georgia O'Keefe poster of an animal skull lying in the Sonora Desert.

After Henry died, I lost my resilience and started praying to the God curled up inside those little yellow pills my mother turned me on to. He, the God of valium, took a good deal of the pain away and made me feel as if I were spending my life crossing warm sand dunes.

A therapist I met through Carlo suggested *a change of locale.* So I rented a Honda and drove to Los Angeles with Nancy the Border Collie when a job teaching music opened at a Montessori School where Henry The Beast's ex-lover, Phil, was principal. By then people were dropping like flies in L.A., however, so barely fourteen months later, when Nancy the Border Collie got cancer of the liver and had to be put to sleep, I headed all the way to Europe. It was May of 1991. Harold started getting real ill shortly afterward, and I discovered that He, the God of valium, was fickle and needed more and more prayer for me to get through the days.

Harold, who shared a bedroom with me for the first fifteen years of my life and who complained that I always kept a night-light on, who was always teasing me because I liked sports and because he was unhappy and uncomfortable in his own body.

Harold, who was so precocious that he used words like *ostentatious* when he was only seven and who scared adults because they thought his stare was too knowing and that he'd stepped right out of *Children of the Damned.*

Harold, who had knobby knees and was relegated to the dodgeball team on inter-school playdays and whom the other kids made fun of because he had elephant ears and was too skinny and who started working out much later in life but lost all his newfound muscles when the Cossacks attacked.

Harold, whose revenge against all of us was his caustic bitchiness, who studied Dante and psychology at Swathmore like someone was going to whip him if he didn't get A's, who spent months working on a volunteer basis with an autistic kid named Eric to get him to simply touch his own nose, who did his doctoral thesis on learning in congenitally deaf children, who found God and lost some of his bitchiness and who never trusted me until six months before he died when he finally realized I wasn't some dumb schmuck who had all the breaks and who was secretly hoping for his older brother to die.

Harold, who couldn't be in the same room with our parents without going off like a gay grenade, who told me *I'd be an orphan if it weren't for you* and made me swear that I wouldn't abandon him.

But I did. I moved to Portugal, and I only flew in to see him five times in the last two years of his life, three of them when he was so ill that he might die.

When Harold's miseries were finally over, my Portuguese doctor said I needed to get off valium or I was going to *accidentally walk into an oncoming bus*. Which might be okay, I thought, except that I would traumatize the poor bus driver for life.

Did you know that I was reaching to you across a warm fog of valium for half the time we spent together?

I apologize for that too, Carlos. Who knows how many of your criticisms I misinterpreted as attacks and how many times I hurt you meaning to simply defend myself?

So many more people whom I once knew have been carried down to the Underworld that the list would make you put down this paper, so I won't go on. But I remember them all. Why? In order to keep moving into the future, like Ricardo the Brazilian told me? Could that be it? Or is it so I can pass on some sacred knowledge which I haven't learned yet? Why is it so important?

Someone to teach... I didn't know it, but I think what I was really looking for when I came to Europe was a man or a boy with an open heart and mind, who wanted to learn. And yes, I admit it; I was probably looking for an open mouth and rear end, too, if that was the most direct route to his brain. And I wanted someone who could teach me, too, because I think I'd learned all the wrong things when I was young and needed to unlearn them. Not that I even today know what the right things are. I'm only just beginning to get an inkling of what my life and yours is about.

And what might that be?

Patience, Carlos, we've only just begun this correspondence.

So I began to instruct António in the ways of the guitar. António, who's got the crystalline hazel eyes of a cat and who leaves a line of whiskers below his nose because he fears slicing off a nostril.

Keys always jangling as he lopes down the street.

Tight jeans contouring thighs made muscular by soccer and gymnastics. His hands tucked into his front pockets.

Thick white socks that soak up his boy-sweat until they stink like garbage.

Curly, dirty blond hair.

Sitting at my feet and begging me to read anything in English to him *just for the sound of it.*

Biting his cuticles.

Teaching me Portuguese curse words like *piça, pito, cona, cabra* while rolling on the ground at my grotesque pronunciation.

Asking waiters about the vintage of the Coca-Colas which I order at dinner so that they'll smile and we can laugh together.

Hopping on and off curbs downtown.

A nest of brown hairs at the center of his chest which is the best place to tickle him and make him fight you and then kiss you as deep as he can.

Nipples rimmed with a circle of delicious blond hairs which I once trimmed and then placed in an envelope marked 'Antonio's Nipple Hair, October 22nd', and which I've kept under my pillow of late to remind me that there is someone alive who has learned something good from me and who needs my help.

Memorizing new pieces so fast that I wonder if he isn't an alien in human form.

Concerts he hopes to give in Carnegie Hall and the Paris Opera and even the Antas Stadium in Porto before a soccer match between the home-town team and its Lisbon rival.

António, who will be famous and honored and warmed by the kindness of strangers if...

When he entered the practice room for his audition with me, I knew none of this, of course. I had no idea that he would change my life. Although I knew right away that he was gay. He sniffed me out, too. We exchanged that needful vampire stare that is the natural handshake of our kind, and then he looked away toward safety. He had dirty blond hair, cut so close to his scalp that he looked like an army recruit ashamed of the soft halo it might give to his face.

Carlos, do you know Titian's 'Portrait of a Man in a Red Cap' in the Frick Collection in New York? Of course you do; unless you've tossed the book I gave you for your thirty-fourth birthday into the garbage. The man in the red cap looks just like my António. Run now to your shelves and take a look.

Jealous? You shouldn't be. He's got youth and grace. But you've got eternal sadness and frustration in your eyes, and it's much more seductive.

António's father, too, has a lookalike in the Frick Collection, you know. But as of yet, that beautiful bastard hasn't entered our story. If you want, take a look through the book and take a guess which portrait he resembles.

'The Polish Rider', perhaps? Wait a bit, and I'll tell you.

António, as I say, was wearing his ever-present jeans and ratty leather jacket when he came for his audition. There was no doubt in either of our minds that he was horny and willing, but I hadn't traveled nine time-zones from L.A. to Portugal to wind up with a fledgling surfer boy looking for an excuse to come out, who'd then run off at the first sight of a perfect wave curling over the shore. Besides, I'd always considered students off limits. So I didn't think we'd ever share the same pillow.

I was also still afraid of venturing forth into the sexual world after two years in L.A. of right-hand pogo sticking.

Nevertheless, I'm not going to lie to you; I desperately wanted to slip my tongue into his mouth and lick all the way to his brain.

He fixed me with the stare of a sweet but hard-edged boy wondering if he'll get serviced by an older man. In a language which approximated English, he said, "What do you want that I play, Professor?"

"Anything," I answered.

"I no understand."

"Play anything you like that's short and isn't too loud. And please, nothing Spanish. I just got here from Spain and if I hear another mock bullfight for guitar I'll throw up."

Sweat beaded on my prince's forehead. He took off his jacket, folded it and placed it on the ground by his chair. In those gestures, I saw years of his mother nagging him to clean up after himself.

He was wearing a neatly ironed white shirt. He leaned over to take his guitar from its case, then lifted it onto his lap. It looked like it was made of balsa wood and purchased at the Toys-R-Us across the river from Porto in Gaia. The action on it was terrible; the strings were a centimeter from the frets. It was going to sound like a ukelele. He took a deep breath, as if he were preparing to swim a 100-meter freestyle. He sat up very erect.

As his hands took their positions, he flashed a self-conscious smile intended as a disclaimer for what was to come and said, "Me nervous."

"Me Tarzan, you Jane," I replied.

"What?"

I smiled. "Everything's going to be okay. Just play."

"Me very nervous."

"Let's just see what happens. Don't panic, just go ahead."

He stared at me as if I were expected to say something which would take away all his anxiety. When I didn't, his eyes grew glassy. I leaned back in my chair and folded my arms. I looked away. Amazing that I didn't realize how important this audition was to him.

He wiped his nose with the back of his hand. I coughed.

Finally, he started to play the first Gavotte from Bach's Sixth

Cello Suite. It was excruciating; his right hand fingered the tinny strings of his Toys-R-Us ukulele as if he were plucking out feathers from a turkey's ass. I nodded for him to go on out of perverse curiosity and a need to ruin someone's day. But António, God bless him, actually settled down. Considering the quality of his instrument, he played with admirable technique. And, more importantly, he put notes together into recognizable phrases and never lost his tempo.

"Enough!" I suddenly shouted.

He looked up at me. I frowned at him. Tears welled in his eyes.

I watched the water caught in his lashes and thought of my brother saying goodbye to me. "Put that toy guitar down!" I ordered.

He placed it atop his jacket.

I was free to say what I wanted since he wouldn't understand the more complicated English words: "Now get up, you little beast!"

He sat there gaping.

"Up, you beast." I raised my hands like a lion tamer. "Stand up!"

He stood. He wiped his eyes and his nose. I walked to him, took his cold hands in mine and squeezed them. "You've always thought that these were just the mittens of a little boy from Portugal," I said. "But these are the magic wands of a sorcerer. Why? Because they can summon the music of Bach across two centuries. When they touch the strings of a guitar, we can hear the composer thinking in his study in Leipzig and writing down the notes as quick as bunnies humping one another in their lairs. Can you see him there with his feverish quill?"

"Me no understand," he said.

I undid a button on my shirt and put his hand against the brown fur over my heart. "You feel that, my prince? Can you feel my faulty metronome?"

He started to breathe long and heavy, like he might faint. He nodded as best he could.

Our faces were only a foot apart. I said, "When you can feel Bach's heart, you will be playing this piece correctly. You understand?"

Of course, what I was saying was crap. But it was my performance which counted.

He nodded again. Gay kids have no resistance for affection from even moderately attractive older men, so I gave him a bear hug. He stiffened, but then hugged me back and melted into my arms.

Never let it be said that I take advantage of a desperate little boy, however; before it could go any further, I pushed him away and held him at arm's length. "If you're going to study with me, you've got to know something — I'm an asshole." He didn't understand. "Me asshole," I said, pointing to myself.

"Asshole?"

I didn't yet know that *chato* would have been a good translation, but I knew the words for 'crazy whore' and figured that that would suffice for now. In point of fact, of course, it was more accurate. "Me *puta louca*," I explained.

He laughed, then gave a big sigh.

"Watch... " I said, and I pointed to his toy guitar. "This is shit, pure *merda!*" I stepped on top of the damn thing. Strings groaned and snapped, wood splintered. I crushed the life out of it. António gasped and gaped. I handed him my guitar. "This, on the contrary, my little prince, is not shit. This good guitar. Good guitar." I petted its neck as he held it, then took his hand and made him stroke the deep contour by its sound hole. "One must be gentle. Treat it like you were playing with yourself on a warm beach." I made a motion with my hand imitating masturbation. "Like you are abusing yourself. Your cock may be hard, but it's fragile all the same. Take it easy." I sat down. "Now start playing again. And try not to pick at turkey feathers with your right hand."

He launched into the Gavotte. After a while, I stopped him because I realized that the biggest problem we were going to have was his inability to listen to the notes as he played them; everything was too disconnected, too staccato.

"Sing it!" I ordered.

"Sing what?"

"The Gavotte...the melody."

"The melody?"

"Just do what I say."

He sang like a prissy Lisbon faggot afraid to wake his granny up from her siesta. I ordered him to shut his trap. I sang for him, angrily, from my belly, linking all the notes together as if I were trying to forge them into a chain around his wrists. When I came to the end of the first long phrase, I said, "Now you sing like that."

Like most of you pitiful Portuguese, the boy was embarrassed to actually express himself. He acted as if his voice were trapped like a nasty little raisin at the very top of his throat. It was going to take some time to get him to listen to the music he produced. Was it worth my trouble? As he stared at me, I began to finally see in the clarity of his pale green eyes how much he wanted to study; I'm a thick son-of-a-bitch when I'm angry and horny at the same time.

"Where did you study before?" I asked him.

"I teach myself," he answered.

"How long ago did you start?"

"There are two years. Before that also...also..." His English faded to frustrated silence.

"And how well do you read music?"

"I no read music."

"What are you telling me?"

"I no to read music," he said emphatically.

"Then how did you learn the Gavotte?"

"From the disks." He pointed to his ear. "I play what here enter."

"You hear all the notes you played?"

"Yes."

If that were true, then he had a one-in-a-million ear. I got that tingle in my backside I get when I meet someone really talented or handsome. "Are you fucking with my head?!" I demanded.

"I no understand."

"How old are you?"

"Twenty-one."

"Most students enter here when they're eighteen. How come you waited?"

"I work with my father. We no money."

"So tell me why you want to study music."

He shrugged. "I want... I like. I no know." He licked his lips nervously, and his frightened eyes followed me as I put my guitar back in its case. "May I study with you?" he chirped suddenly.

"The audition isn't over," I said. "I want you to come home with me."

"Home?"

"Yeah. To my apartment, *meu apartamento*."

"Now?"

"Don't worry. No fucking." I made a hoop with my left thumb and index finger and stuck my right middle finger through it. I spoke like Boris Badinov: "Teacher and student no screw. Just music." I pulled him to his feet and put my hand up against his chest to feel his heartbeat. I rubbed his pectoral muscles and slapped his belly. "I crazy whore. Not you. You prince...dirty blond prince. You do nothing you no want to do. I no be mean to you. But I no promises make because I big crazy whore. And you...you try never to hurt me on purpose. Okay?"

He didn't know what I was talking about, but he said, "Okay."

"What my guitar?" he asked.

"I've got an extra guitar at home. You'll use that for now. Now step on yours once more for good luck. Crush it good!"

"Now?" he asked. When I nodded, he jumped on top of it and grimaced comically, like he'd done something delightfully naughty he was hoping nobody would notice.

We took a taxi to my house. He sat stiffly next to me like I might bite. I complained about codfish and unreliable people and traffic jams. He nodded and kept his hands trapped between his legs. Once inside my apartment, I cleared a space for him on the couch by tossing Fiama's laundry onto her bed. Then I put on Edith Piaf records, one after another: 'L'Accordioniste', 'Milord', 'La Vie en Rose', 'Les Trois Cloches'... Piaf's not a great technical singer, of course, but she's got vibrato that kills entire orchestras and legato which strings the words of her songs into the most lovely rusted iron chains. António had to learn the meaning of vibrato and legato right away or we'd never get anywhere. He sat with his hands still locked between his legs without saying a word, however, like he was an anxious little boy freezing to death outside his parents' house. I didn't want to watch him and looked out the window. Finally, when we'd had enough examples, I knelt next to him and said: "I want you to sing any song you know, but sing it as if you were Piaf. You understand?" I demonstrated with the chorus of 'Just Like a Prayer', your favorite Madonna song, Carlos. Remember?

"Now you," I said.

"Same song?"

"Anything."

António took his hands from between his legs and braced them on his knees. His eyes closed. He sang the Portuguese national anthem. He had a lovely voice, a masculine voice buried deep in his gut, a voice far beyond his years.

"That was great," I said. I caressed his cheek, and his eyes opened wide. "Very good," I said. I was strangely excited and was thinking that maybe I was so happy only because I wanted to sniff his every crevice in bed and obviously had him seduced. I hadn't yet realized that something more was happening. I picked up my guitar and played the first eight melody notes to 'Les Trois Cloches' with overdone vibrato, then sang it the same way so he'd see the connection: *Village, au fond de la vallée...* I told him that vibrato is not just an embellishment but serves to keep the true pitch of a note. He nodded. "And no space between the notes," I emphasized with my index finger wagging. "No space, because space *mucho* bad. Now, you do it." I handed him my guitar.

António had heard 'Les Trois Cloches' only once, but could play all the melody notes in tempo without a single error.

Do you know how unusual that is, Carlos?

He has the best sense of pitch of anyone I've ever met. He's one in a million.

As he played, I showed him how to relax his left wrist and jiggle it to create the proper vibrato. I cajoled and yelled and pleaded. He took deep breaths to steady himself. After a half-hour, he was doing well.

While I fetched some wine from the kitchen to celebrate, he played 'Les Trois Cloches' and added harmonized bass notes. I thought: *Hee hee! He's a natural. He's got more talent than anyone I've ever met. And he's a fucking vampire, just like me!!!*

As I walked back in with the bottle and two champagne flutes, I said, "Now stand and sing the Gavotte again."

António placed his feet apart like he was bracing for a blow. I licked my lips.

The boy channeled the Gavotte up from his balls into his chest and through his mouth. He was so proud of himself and so abandoned to the melody and now had such a nice semi-hard erection down the leg of his pants that I loved him as much as I could just then and even felt tears of pride knotted in my throat. I closed my eyes. Behind the darkness of my eyelids, I was standing at a train station watching everyone at whose deathbed I'd sat depart across an impassable checkpoint. I was the lone survivor. *I'm alive,* I was thinking, *and I've met a boy with greatness in his fingers!* It was the contrast that made me both sad and happy; here I was, left behind but listening to the sweet voice of a Portuguese youth who hadn't seen anybody he loved die yet and who had his whole future ahead of him. When he finished, I told him he'd learned well, then gave him his wine. "To António, who will know greatness," I toasted.

He smiled shyly. We sipped our wine. We stood there eyeing each other like two acrobats before a performance. We were wondering if we could trust each other without a net below. I said, "If I don't take the leap I'm going to explode."

He stared at me and sipped his wine.

"We have to do it before you become my official student," I explained. "We won't be able to do it afterwards."

He kept staring.

"Take a sip of wine, but keep the liquid in your mouth," I told him.

He did as I asked. I walked up to him and placed my chest against his chest and put my hands on his ass. I kissed him and took the liquid from his mouth. He moaned as if he were hurt. His cock swelled against me. I pulled away from him. His eyes were open and frightened. "You're a muscular little beast," I said.

After that, we simply *devoured* each other. There's no other word that could express our sexual hunger. In the living room, he opened my corduroys and fell to his knees. He groaned like he was being beaten. He licked and mouthed and nipped at me as if he were a slave trained from the age of two for this one activity.

A natural, I thought to myself again.

I rubbed his hair and caressed his shoulders and fell over his back like a cape as I came.

Yes, Carlos, he did what you always felt was disgusting and swallowed my offering. Greedily, I should add.

I freed him from his clothes and saw he'd concealed a dark cucumber with a blooming purple flower in his pants. "Lovely," I said in admiration. "Where'd you get it?"

"She is too big?" he asked.

"She is just fine," I replied. "And neither rain nor sleet nor snow shall keep me from my appointed rounds."

I did the best I could with my mammalian, unhingeable jaw, gagged a few times, but didn't give up; I wanted him to free himself in my mouth because I knew it would be over quick and the second time I wanted him to take me from behind and wanted him to be able to hold out for a good long while. Turns out, the kid had more bitter seed than could be stored in any normal set of balls. He grimaced in pain as he shot himself out. I kissed his neck, nuzzled around his underarms, told him he was beautiful.

After a minute, he started to groan again and breathe deeply. The magic latex of a young man's soul was rising between my hands, and I was holding a divining rod searching for a long-lost spring.

It hurt the boy to get hard again so soon, but we were too excited to stop.

Maybe we were both figuring that for the grand prize of an American rear end with a master's degree from the Manhattan School of Music he had to endure just a little pain.

I slipped a condom over him. "Please fuck me," I said.

But my poor behind was so tight from maybe five years without being sodomized by anything other than a green banana once in a moment of mad desperation inspired by ouzo and an old James Bond movie that it was knotted like an old pair of shoelaces. I had to pry my opening apart with my own forefinger and thumb, then lubricate it with KY jelly a half-dozen times to get a third finger in. Then and only then could we get him a little ways inside me. He had to pull out right away, because it felt like a big fat spiny lizard was trying to crawl up my bowel and make a home in my stomach. I kept cursing as I pried myself bigger and bigger with my fingers because it was taking so long to loosen me up. António thought I was mad at him and began to go soft. "Not you!" I shouted. "Not you, my dirty blond prince. Me, the *puta louca* is angry at *himself!*"

But I should've had more confidence in myself; another ten minutes and we had his bloom, if not stem, safely inside me. He was squatting behind me, panting with panic and lust, and he didn't know what to do. I told him, "Now, push slowly forward. Not too fast or you'll have to clean up my bowels and a lot of blood. And then the police will come and ask a lot of inconvenient questions about how you killed the American without any weapon in sight."

I tugged on his buttocks so he'd know to move forward. Slowly, the spiny lizard started to make its way toward my gut. He was splitting me open, and the pain made me go limp, but now getting him inside me was a question of personal pride — like soldiers taking a hill that is of no value in itself but means everything for morale. Finally, the damn thing was all the way in — flower, stem, leaves and roots. I slid forward onto the bed and took him down on top of me. "Just stay still!" I ordered.

He was nervous that he'd hurt me, and I could feel him going limp.

"I'll kill you if you go soft on me!" I told him. "Start thrusting when you want."

After he took me from behind, I flipped over on my back and put my legs over his shoulders. It was like being cleaved in half, and each thrust of his powerful hips took me back into a past before HIV, when you could let yourself be swept out to sea on sex and give yourself to Neptune and not expect to get beached on a desert island where you were going to waste away toward death. *"Fuck me!"* I kept shouting at him. *"Fuck me my prince."*

And like the sweet kid he was, he obliged.

I sobbed afterward. Like I hadn't cried in years. António's face grew white with fear. I caressed his cheek. I kissed all his fingers and inhaled their delicious scent of tobacco and shit. "Don't worry, I told him. "I'd forgotten that sex was like this... Long ago and far away, when touching a man could help you heal all your wounds." I placed the boy's hands over my closed eyes. "You haven't hurt me," I assured him. "You've just pushed me a bit into the past."

5

It's all in my journal. On Friday, May 26th, I got a call first thing in the morning from a reporter at *O Publico* preparing an article on foreigners in Portugal. His 'point of departure', as he called it, was that Brazilians, Americans, Germans and Brits were both enriching and destroying Portuguese culture. I didn't bother asking for an explanation. "So what's this theory got to do with me?" I asked.

He wanted an interview. I told him *no*. He insisted; I was the only American. "You'll be representing your country," he said.

This idea struck me as perversely amusing, so I agreed. I was to meet him next Friday at the *O Publico* offices. That seemed far enough away that I could cancel if need be.

I was dreading the classes that I had that day because I'd hardly slept a wink, and right away I ran into the director of the Conservatory, Ramalho. As a little kid he must have looked like one of those orphans painted on velvet; he's got the longest eyelashes you've ever seen — like fern fronds. Except now he's paunchy and jowled. Looks like a frog in a dramatic opera.

He pulled me into the staff room. It was empty. He told me with a proud smile that he'd screwed a whore the night before in Lisbon six times. *Six times,* he said, his head bouncing up and down like a bobble-head doll. He meant, of course, for me to compliment him. I did, because I need the job, but I was thinking that if he can get it up six times in one night he must have either the tiniest cock in Iberia or little Portuguese orgasms that don't flip his body over and over but merely raise a hiccup in his chest. *Six times,* he repeated, holding up his fingers in case I didn't get it. Yes, I said. She was sore afterward, he said. Rubbed raw. But the sweet *cabra* — the bitch — loved it. He had the smile of a little boy needing praise. To escape his conversation, I told him a joke I'd once heard. The Norse god of thunder, Thor, is very horny up in Asgard; he spots a comely young wench in the fields outside Copenhagen, falls upon her and keeps his immortal member in her for three days, back and forth, back and forth until he comes in an explosion. When he's done, he raises his sacred hammer over his head and exclaims, "I am Thor, god of thunder," at which the poor woman replies, "You're *thor,* I'm so *thor* I'm not going to be able to walk for two weeks!"

Ramalho laughed, but he didn't get it. While we were both wondering what to say, Rosa, the violin teacher with the speech defect and smelly breath, entered.

Ramalho cornered her and began the exact same conversation!

I suddenly interrupted him and said, "If I left school a week or two early, would anyone have a stroke?"

"What about the last classes?" he asked, irritated. "And finals, for God sake?!"

"I'm not saying I'll definitely go early. But my father's ill," I lied, "and I may have to fly back to the States at a moment's notice. I'd get someone to cover for me."

My real reasons for wanting to leave had nothing to do with this, of course, but rather with a crazy plan for me and António which had begun to coalesce in my brain.

Ramalho shook his head as if it weren't what his mother would find proper, but if it had to be...

You know, Carlos, there are only three things which really interest me now, and the first is recording what life was like before sex disappeared completely from the planet. Because one day, our survivors will not know. Sex will become so perilous that it will be declared morally unacceptable under any circumstances. Sperm and egg will meet only in test tubes. The little fertilized nothing will then be transplanted into the belly of a beast, say the womb of a pig, and Mrs Pig will carry our little Johnny or Betsy to term.

I realize I'm not in any position to record all aspects of sex. No one is. But I'd at least like for our descendants a thousand years from now to know that we...

loved to dive headfirst into any number of bodily orifices;

slobbered, gobbled, sweated and spurted with perfect strangers in the most perfectly strange places;

played with ourselves in churches and synagogues, schoolrooms and staff meetings;

and still could never quite get enough.

I realize that I'm not alone. Others are trying to scrawl the same message. One of our works will survive perhaps, be dug up on the shore of some dead sea by a wizened old Armenian and hidden in a cave until such time as it is safe for this information to be revealed.

My second and even more important goal is to do everything necessary to help my dear António.

At this point in the story I'd avoided him in the hospital for two days. Cowardly behavior, I know. But I was trying to summon strength from the hollow cavern of a body I'd lugged all the way from sunny California. What I had yet to learn is that if you imagine you're filled once again with all you were, strength can generate itself spontaneously — at least for a time.

Is this an example of the magic of hope which Ricardo the Brazilian told me about?

The third goal is to drag you, dear boy, out of your Lisbon cave, kicking and screaming if necessary. Because there is still a chance for you and me if you'd only put on your armor and come do battle with me on the top of the Clerigos Tower in Porto.

But, I have never been a blessed person, and I do not believe in any God that cares to help us. So I fear I shall fail in all these endeavors.

Ah, I almost forgot; I also have one extra goal just for myself, a secret superficial wish which will never come true: I would like to play the guitar as if I were making love — to get that insensate wood vibrating with desire and soaked with the juices that spill from a man when he's really been well loved. Was that how Paganini played the violin? Imagine lifting your instrument and getting the same thrill as when you're thrusting into forbidden shadows. Back and forth goes the bow. Sounds of friction fill the silence. There is only movement and resin and tension and a cadence so loud and sweet that the violin cracks right in half and falls at the Gate of Compassion which kabbalists contemplate and which must exist if we are to have any chance of survival.

António might be able to play the guitar like that someday; he was already close. Did the gods get jealous?

Is that what this is all about?

After giving two guitar lessons that morning, I took a cab to the Santo António Hospital. António had a bed on the second floor.

I don't know why I made myself go to visit him. It wasn't guilt, I don't think, because I didn't make him sick. And it couldn't have been loyalty, because I left behind two friends heading into the ninth inning in New York to move to L.A. and a brother about to step up to the plate in the top of the seventh to move to Portugal. Could it have been the power of beauty being destroyed? It would have been like turning away from the destruction of Sodom and Gomorrah. You know you shouldn't watch, because it's going to break your heart, but you know you must be a witness.

So there I stood at the foot of António's bed as if before an altar, a middle-aged relic paying homage to Michelangelo's David being attacked by viral curses.

António, the angelic prince of Porto, the rightful heir to Segovia, who must live in order to fulfill the destiny in his fingertips.

António, who was lying with an IV plugged into his arm, asleep, blond curls falling toward sunken eyes that may never see the sunrise of age thirty.

António, with the clenched and silent mouth of a child passing judgment on parents who have beat him. I was asking myself: *What does he see when he is asleep? The pyramids of Egypt? The Grand Canyon? Is it only thirst that's making him lick his lips right now?*

Fate. Life. Death. This boy should have been cavorting under a blanket on the beach at Moledo. Or sipping tea at home and eating *pão de ló* like a little pasha.

Surely my thoughts should be enough to cure you, António. If only I could find the right sequence of words as I stand before you, the right combination of letters...

But all the right incantations were lost when the Jews were kicked out of Spain and then converted to Christianity in Portugal. Five centuries ago. *That's* what I should have told Ricardo. We had them, we had the formulas we'd need to save the world, and then Ferdinand

and Isabella ruined everything with their satanic expulsion order.

António's eyes flutter open. "Professor," he says.

"Hi," I say. "Don't you know that you're not allowed to call anyone you've slept with 'professor'."

I'm trying to be funny, of course. It's pathetic, I know, but this boy is already being dressed for the Angel of Death, and I used to be an amusing Jew in a previous life.

The boy sits up. He has bruised eyes shadowed by a future without joy. He asks, "Where's time? Do you know where time it is?"

Let me explain this nonsense speech, dear Carlos. This is not a bad translation of what he actually said in Portuguese. António had the bad luck to be invaded by two diseases at one time: influenza and shingles. For the discomfort, he was taking codeine, and the codeine had made him slightly delirious.

Of course, we still didn't have the results of the test for HIV. My brain kept repeating: *Even normal people with perfectly fine immune systems sometimes get shingles.*

António spoke for a while like a badly translated haiku. From time to time, I jotted down on automatic teller stubs what he said; someone had to note these things for that little old Armenian who's going to dig up the records which we are leaving of our civilization.

His infections were supposed to go away by themselves. He was taking antibiotics to prevent pneumonia.

The way I figured it, after ten days, he'd either be back to normal or be dead. You think that I was exaggerating, don't you?

"How are you feeling?" I asked him.

"Tired."

"Would you like some water?"

He licked his lips to check if he was thirsty. He shook his head.

"You're looking better," I lied.

"The food's no good," he frowned.

"What would you like? I'll smuggle it in for you." António is crazy about sweets. I started to reel of a list of pastries: *ovos moles, pasteis de nata, pasteis de côco, pão de ló...*

"No, nothing," he replied. His eyes closed.

I tried cheeses; he's also a dairy-food lover. He shook his head.

We sat without talking. António's bed was just below an inner window giving out on a hallway. A quiet gray light filtered into the room. There were nine other beds. Across from António was a skeletal old man with a bandage around his wrist. Next to him was a fat man with beads of sweat on his forehead and Coke-bottle glasses. He reminded me of Piggy in *Lord of the Flies*. I was disoriented. I was wondering where exactly we were.

I don't know how long I sit in that hospital room. The memory of when António first let me inside him moves my gaze to the floor tiles. I had never been so gentle with anything, not even the butterflies I used to catch as a child.

Who was it who sealed my António's destiny inside a hospital ward? We don't know for sure. We suspect Sardinha. It's not his real name. But he'd always stored his cocaine and crystal meth in a can of sardines and the name stuck. He used to shoot up behind the Conservatory, in the yard of a vacant house on the Rua da Cedofeita. He was a piano student. They're the worst kind of musician; they don't have to tune any strings, so they begin to think everything should come easy to them. When it doesn't, they get a big shock. Disappointment leads to depression. Then come the melodramatic episodes of self-destruction. If you want to try a musician, stay away from piano players. Go for oboists. They've got lungs like opera singers and big big hearts. They hold their breath like pearl divers.

I've been told that a blow job from an oboist is almost always a feat worthy of the *Guinness Book of Records.*

Dear Carlos, I remember that Henry The Beast — the power forward on our West Village B-ball team — used to say that love in our decade is like a wicked stepmother; it poisons you and makes you die. I'm sure you think he had a point. So maybe you're right to fear me.

6

For no reason I can fathom a sense of calm returned to me on Saturday, May 27th, maybe because I had no lessons to give or simply because the sky was blue and cloudless. A calm comes over me even now thinking of how I stood on Fiama's verandah and looked at the turquoise dome guarding Porto that day.

So I'll risk telling you now what Ricardo the Brazilian suggested to António a couple of weeks ago.

As I mentioned, he, Pedro and I were standing at the foot of António's bed. I introduced everyone. The boy's brain was alert for the moment, and he said he'd just woken from a pleasant dream. He said, "I was high up, like a bird. And I saw a city in a valley. A large city stretching for miles."

"Which city was it?" I asked.

"I don't know. Maybe Madrid. Maybe Paris." He shrugged. "It seemed very big. But, of course, I've never been to those places and couldn't recognize any monuments."

"Have you ever been out of Portugal?" Ricardo asked.

"Never."

"Would you like to travel? See those cities?"

António smiled. "I'd love to. More than anything. But how? There's classes and exams and everything else."

Ricardo looked at me. I knew what he was telling me: *You can do something for someone else and be with him as he decides whether there's still any hope in the world or you can retreat. It's your choice.*

I asked António, "Would you like to go away when you leave the hospital? See Paris? See where I bought you your silk shirts in Madrid?"

António bit his lips. He stared at me like he couldn't understand the language I was speaking. My heart was pounding like it wanted to escape my chest.

I knew his answer was *yes,* but he was afraid to hope for it.

Carlos, I know you're not going to understand this, because you've never known anyone who's been informed they've got a terminal illness. But sometimes the most important moment comes just after they learn their fate. Two paths spread away from their knowledge: one skirts the edge of life, and if they choose it, they remain with us, with the living, fighting to get back to our domain; the other leads straight for darkness, and none of the words addressed to them are ever really received.

True, António's test results hadn't come back yet. But if the worst had happened, he'd have to choose his path. And now that I knew what just might keep him with us, how could I even consider refusing him?

But I did consider it. I folded my arms over my chest. I stared out the window at the dirty green paint in the hallway.

Maybe all is lost, I thought.

I told him I was going to rent a big American car and drive us across Europe.

His brain slipped out of phase, and he asked if the car would have sandals. It was the codeine again. We talked some more about nothing. He closed his eyes in the middle of a sentence. He began snoring.

Ricardo came to me and whispered, "You look like you might faint. We should go sit at a café or something."

I agreed, but I couldn't move. I watched António. It occurred to me that Pedro had told me once he knew one of the guitar teachers at the Paris Conservatory. Was that the real reason I wanted to take the boy away?

Carlos, do you always know for certain your motivations for the crazy things you do? Does anyone?

I turned to Pedro and asked, "Who's that guitar player you know at the Paris Conservatory?"

"José Maria Landero."

"Is he good?"

Pedro tilted his head. "Deutsche Grammophon certainly think so. They're putting out his recordings of Leo Brouwer."

"And would he accept António as a student?"

"What are you talking about?"

I said, "I can only teach him so much. If he's going to ever start giving concerts, he'll need to study with someone better."

"But now, with this? What if...?"

"Especially now. Especially 'if'."

Ricardo said, "And you? Where would that leave you?"

It was a good question. Could I give up António? Determined to do the right thing for a change, I asked Pedro, "So would this Landero give the boy a chance?"

It was settled. António and I would set out for Madrid and Paris. Pedro would call José Maria Landero. And I would try my best to give António up to someone else — if that's what the boy wanted, of course. I wasn't sure I could do it.

But that's not what's worrying you, Carlos. You think I won't be able to resist sleeping with him on the trip, that the Cossacks are certain to get me, too. And by extension, even you. But don't worry, viruses can't cross time warps — at least not yet.

Or maybe my death is what you're hoping for. It would certainly take you off the hook, wouldn't it?

"Who are you?"

I've returned to the hospital, and a man too handsome for his own good is standing next to me. He has graying hair clipped very short, several days' dark stubble on his cheeks, sensitive lips. He has lovely sad brown eyes, and crow's feet spread from them as if he's been squinting for a long time to get a look at the future. His expression is angry and aware. His teeth are clenched, and his jaw is throbbing. He wears a leather jacket, white shirt and jeans.

I stand up. He is several inches shorter than me. "I'm António's guitar teacher," I say.

"Oh," he says. His whole body relaxes. He knocks his hand against his forehead and says, "I'm sorry, Professor." He shakes my hand gratefully, holds it for a long time. There are thick calluses on his palm. "Thank you for visiting my son."

This is Miguel of the Minho, as António and I have always called him. António told me all about him because he used to often fantasize about having sex with him. Yes, with his own father. That, too, apparently, is possible in your lovely backwater country, Carlos.

Or at least children dare to fantasize about it. So I knew that Miguel came from Vila Nova de Cerveira, just across the Minho River from Spain, and...

that he had a sweet resonant voice;

that he worked dawn to dusk as a stone mason, was fundamentally kind and gentle, but also deeply afraid of António's homosexuality;

and that he had a big uncut cock which speared too much extramarital maidenhood for his wife to put up with. They were divorced when the boy was just seven.

António showed me a picture of his father once when he was in his twenties, and they shared the same dirty blond hair. Somewhere on their family tree is at least one well-hung Celt.

Carlos, can you guess yet which of the portraits at the Frick Collection resembles Miguel?

Don't bother looking again. It's Hans Holbein the Younger's painting of Sir Thomas More.

Get it out and you'll see how handsome he is.

Quite a face, no? If António lives to forty-five, he'll grow to look like just like that. Some guys have all the luck, no? Judging by my father at seventy I'm gonna end up resembling a shark with a David Niven mustache.

What is extraordinary is that Sir Thomas More and the youth painted by Titian who looks like António share a family resemblance. Is it possible that this young man was actually related to More? Could he have been his son?

Or is each painter's love for his subject the key to this resemblance? I've always felt that both artists were passionately drawn to the men posing for them.

António snores. We stare at him. I don't want to stay because I'm attracted to Miguel. I fear that I may say or do something considered perverse, and the Portuguese offend easily. So I offer him my chair. He won't sit and offers it back to me. It's a little dance the Portuguese do every time a door opens or a seat comes free. So I sit back down till I can think of an excuse to leave; being a foreigner, I'll be forgiven for not continuing to offer him my place.

We don't say anything for a long time. Miguel whispers, "He looks better." He nods gravely. He is trying to convince himself.

"Yes, he does," I say. Then, I don't know what comes over me because I ask Miguel if he'll come have a beer with me. "We should let him sleep," I say. "There's nothing we can do now."

"You're right." Miguel shuffles next to the bed, bends over and presses his lips gently to António's forehead.

A handsome man kissing his son... Gray light uniting their faces...

If I were Vermeer, it would be this scene which I would paint.

Miguel motions me to walk ahead of him, and we leave the ward. Outside, in the sunlight, Miguel starts to cry silently as we walk to the Praça de Lisboa. I don't want to embarrass him, so I make believe I don't notice. He wipes his eyes and takes out a pack of SG Gigante cigarettes from his coat pocket. He offers me one. I can't refuse a crying man anything. He inhales greedily as he lights up and closes his eyes for a moment. Lighting mine, he says, "I keep telling myself it's a dream. But every morning I wake up and every morning he's still in there."

His words come in a cascading exhale of smoke.

We sit outside at the Café da Praça. It's crowded with college students. I want to confess that I love his son, but he'd probably reach down for a paving stone and try to crack my skull open. Who would blame him? I drink my beer quickly. I look at the rooftops above the rim of the sunken square. Miguel says to me, "If I could find the person who gave him this disease, I would kill him with my own two hands."

His voice is hoarse. His hands tremble as they imitate strangulation.

I say, "It's not certain that he's seropositive. There's a chance."

Miguel dismisses that possibility with a disgusted wave of his hand. He sighs and shakes his head.

I say, "We've got to be calm so we can help him whatever the test results reveal. That's what's important."

I hate myself for speaking in clichés like a concerned Jew. I want to get away from the cowering victim in me who's been splattered with the rain which is falling everywhere. I want to leave Portugal, just as I'd left America.

But I realize I'm stuck — an American insect glued to Portuguese flypaper. Backed up to the Atlantic Ocean with nowhere to go. Or am I? Is that the real reason I want to take António away? A temporary escape into fantasy...? One final escapade before the Cossacks attack and burn my very last refuge to the ground?

7

Sunday, May 28th arrives. We are supposed to have the test results for HIV in twenty-four hours.

I sit in Fiama's room all morning and watch television. I eat three custard apples and six kiwis for lunch.

I do some laundry. I have diarrhea.

I watch the street out my bedroom window. Some kids play

soccer for a while. A wagtail lands right on the window ledge. He has a white face and black gorget. His tail bobs up and down. He stares at me. I try to read. I drink ouzo.

Miguel and I see each other at the hospital. He calls me 'Professor'. I beg him not to, but he insists. António awakes, speaks in haiku again. We have a conversation with him for about an hour that is worthy of Ionescu. Between my Portuguese and his poetry, we are like that old Yiddish joke about the guy who asks his hard-of-hearing friend on the street what he's carrying in his brown paper bag. "Peaches," comes the reply. "That's nice," says the first man. "And how's your family?" The deaf man shrugs and answers, "Squashed."

Lunch arrives: a piece of fried fish, overcooked vegetables and a baked apple. Miguel feeds his son. A pit opens in my stomach as he ladles peas into António's mouth. I remember...

coaxing spoonfuls of Dannon vanilla yoghurt into Henry The Beast's scabbed mouth;

feeding a last baked apple to my brother;

handing my mother a can of Coke with which she can take yet another valium.

I turn away from memory and watch the other people on the ward. A pea falls out of António's mouth onto the bed sheets. Miguel picks it up with his index finger and thumb and puts it back in his son's mouth. I want to say, *Stop that, that's dangerous.* Of course, it isn't really. But a coward like me who can't witness any more death inevitably grows paranoid.

Tender caresses are more intolerable to me than the ugliest scenes of violence, so I tell Miguel I'll meet him in the café for a beer in an hour if he wants.

He's the kind of man who waves as he approaches your table, then bows and asks if he may sit down. He makes me feel important, and I don't like it. When you know you're a frightened worm, feeling important is such a hypocritical emotion that it makes your skin crawl. So I don't wave back, just nod my assent. When he sits down, he thanks me for meeting him. There's nothing to thank me for, I say. He gives me a cigarette and lights it. I buy him a beer. His face turns serious. I notice that the spokes of crow's feet at the corners of his sad eyes have deepened overnight. He asks, "Is António really a good guitar player? Does he have talent?"

"His hands understand the guitar," I reply. "And he understands music, which is more important."

"I'm a stone mason," Miguel says. "I don't know what 'understanding music' means." He leans forward. "I want to know what it means because I want to know my son."

"It means..." I don't know what I say after that. My Portuguese fails me because he is asking me something I care about and which is therefore beyond my verbal capabilities. I make a mess of the conversation, discuss shape and color and other adjectives which normal people don't ascribe to music. He probably thinks me condescending. But he nods at what I say, smokes and drinks his beer.

Just before we go our separate ways, he says, "I want my son to have a life. I want him to continue with the guitar after he gets out of the hospital. Will you help him?"

I want to kiss him on the forehead as gently as I can and tell him I will be sweet to his son because there is no other choice except to be distant and cruel and I have seen so much cruelty and even been cruel myself that I know it is no longer necessary. Sooner or later, I'll have to tell him that I've slept with the boy, however. That knowledge hammers at my rib cage. *When António is better I will tell him,* I think. But I may just leave both father and son to fend for themselves as soon as António is discharged from the hospital. I say, "Your son will always be my student. Nothing can change that."

I hate myself because I say it like I'm pledging my love to a dying swan. Everything is starting over again — the dramas and clichés and friends in black uniting around deathbeds. I promised myself: *never again.* And yet here I am. A fool must command my fate and my heart. But even this fool lets me rush away from Miguel because he looks too much like his son, is simply too handsome, and because I want to kiss him so badly that my guts are burning.

The old jailhouse. A baroque granite tomb. Sixty yards across, four storeys high, with rusted iron grills in all the windows. It's just been refurbished by the government. For what purpose, they don't know; the tail always wags the dog here in Portugal. On the way home from the café, I run into a sad little construction worker there whom I gave a few moments of relief to just after I moved here. His name is Rui. He called me *maricas* in a contemptuous voice as he came, and I told myself I'd never do him a good turn again because there are too many Antónios buried in too many cemeteries to ever be cursed with condescending names in any of the ten thousand living languages still flowering in the land of Babel. This time, he invites me up to the jail cell where he's been working. "Just to talk," he says. It's lunch time. Everyone else is eating. I don't know why I go. Anxiety? So I can have the companionship of a seemingly friendly stranger for a few moments?

Rui wears filthy white painter's pants. When we're alone, he takes his shirt off. He's barefoot. Dark fur glistens with sweat on his chest, and there's a mop of black hair on his head. He's a Moor, this

Rui. A miniature Portuguese Othello.

He reaches down with one of his catcher's mitt hands to scratch his balls. It's the Portuguese signal of need, like a fledgling bird opening its mouth and yapping.

"Not today," I say.

"Doesn't the *maricas* want his treat?" he asks.

I shake my head and start to walk away.

He cups his hand under his bulge and says, "Come on, queer, kneel down and get what you like best."

I'm suddenly enraged. After all, what makes these pathetic closet cases think that they can treat us this way? Do you understand it, Carlos?

I step up to him and say, "Okay, but before I do anything, I've got a question for you."

"What?"

"Isn't it about time that you admitted you're *maricas* too? You're a big boy now. And you might find reality appealing once you become a little more acquainted with it."

He frowns. "I've been married seven years," he replies. "I've got two kids."

Laughing, I say, "I've heard that a hundred times on two different continents. You press yourself down between your wife's legs once a month and close your eyes and pray that you'll come quickly so you don't have to feel her big breasts against your chest, and you think that big sacrifice makes you a normal little Portuguese explorer. A kid pops out of her belly once every couple of years and you think you're a real man. You're *maricas,* my little Rui. Ask your wife, if you think I'm wrong. She knows, she'll tell you if she's got the courage which you don't have." I step closer to him and whisper, "But for now, it's our little secret."

I reach out to shake his hand, because the Portuguese shake hands even after unpleasant conversations like this, and without warning he barrels up into me and knocks me flat on my ass. I think he might have broken the bottom right rib again which Pietro the Italian professor fractured in another lifetime. He stands over me gloating. "Fucking *maricas!*" he calls me. Two other men are now standing at the doorway to the cell, both short and balding, but one with beautiful brown eyes like you, Carlos.

Yes, even when I'm flat on my back and can't get a full breath into my lungs, I notice a man's eyes.

Knowing certain risks I take, I always keep one tool of the trade on my person; a switchblade with an amber handle made in Turkey and purchased from the back of a Korean discount store on Melrose Avenue. It is out and shining before anyone can step toward me. I stand up and hold it toward the men at the door. I grin because I've been in this situation before and know you should always smile when you're trying to save your ass from straight men with thirty years of pent-up anger wound up like a spring in their balls. Virtually all Portuguese are intimidated by foreigners, so I say in English, "You fuck with me, and I'll cut you open!" I motion them out of the doorway.

Rui shouts: "I'm gonna find out where you live, and I'm going to fucking kill you!"

"Move!" I say to the men at the door. They stand aside. I walk by, then run to the stairs and dash out of the jail. No one tries to follow me.

I suddenly wish that just a little of Rui's blood were shining on my knife.

The walls in the apartment I share with Fiama are made out of papier-mâché, and silverfish parade down them at night. Paula next door is watching a Brazilian soap opera. The star of the show screams at her sister, "I can't stand you! I live in fear of seeing you on the street! You're a monster! A whore! And not just me, but everybody hates you!" All this name calling because the poor sister has fallen passionately in love with the star's eldest son, her nephew. From the sound of things, all eight million people in Rio de Janeiro are bent out of shape about it.

It occurs to me that such shouting would never happen in Portugal because — even at their most dramatic moments — the natives here prefer to talk around a subject than enter directly into it. It probably took me longer than most people to understand this. I mean, my usual pick-up line in the States had been, "I think you're really good-looking and would like to sleep with you." Kind of Jimmy Olsenish, I admit, but it has the great advantage of American efficiency. Here, such a line would never work; it is beyond the comprehension of a European, in general, to come to the point. Depending on his level of education, if you want a Portuguese man to get to know you under your sheets, then you've got to discuss with him the weather; politics; soccer results; the latest drought in the Algarve; or, as once happened to me in Lisbon, the semiotics of Alfred Hitchcock's films.

All of this with little comments slipped in to let your target know that there's a little belly dance taking place below the surface of the words. You have to say things like, "The weather's been real hot lately and has been keeping me up at night." Or, "Hey, I would really like to be lying nude right now on a beach, wouldn't you?"

After about an hour of this sort of code, if your mark is still talking with you, then you know you've got him softened up to the point where you can reach right over and grab him through his pants. By then, he's got no resistance. Verbal foreplay saps a Portuguese man's strength — like green kryptonite to Superman.

It's why I know that if I just put the right sequence of words in this letter, I could loosen even you up a bit, dear Carlos.

Remember how hard it was to first get you in the sack? The boring conversations I suffered with you and Monica in order to open your zipper should put me in the Sexual Idiots Hall of Fame. What I want to know even today is how could you stand living month after month with that giant poodle? When I remember her hold on you, I run to the toilet in case I should need to retch. Then I think of her frizzled black hair; the permanent grimace on her wafer-thin face; her she-beast laugh.

I wonder sometimes how your penis didn't just turn right around at the entrance to her cave and run for cover up your ass.

And to think you went out with her for more than two years! The lengths to which a closet case will go to prove his masculinity know no bounds. I suppose I should be awe-struck.

Now that I think of it, Monica is really the opposite of Fiama. Fiama is slow but intelligent. Good-looking. She has a big heart and wants more than anything else to keep her eyesight. And she also wants to be happy — something she'll never be because men are always going to use her and send her home with crabs. As for Monica, my intuition was that the only thing she wanted was to dominate other people. Why else would she have chosen a boyfriend who was a cowardly queer?

How many nights did we go out together to those closet-sized bars in Porto with their clouds of cigarette smoke and their women in latex pants and men with mustaches trying their best to look sophisticated even though they can't put a sentence together that doesn't have something to do with soccer or car racing? It must have been two weeks straight. My cock was atrophying, and I was going insane. How bad was it? I'd begun watching those goddamn Brazilian soap operas when I got home, just so I could forget that there were people like you who didn't know what they wanted and who were going to wreck everyone's life around them because of it.

If I only teach you one thing, Carlos, then remember this: *The biggest bastards in the world are those who can't admit who they are, because they torture everyone else to keep them from finding out.*

Like you, you prick!

And then, when I was no longer sure if I even had a spine, you rang my doorbell wanting to talk. I slithered to the door. In what passes for a macho voice in this European Lilliput you asked if I was trying to steal Monica from you. Did you intend to bloody my nose? Did you think that because I'm an American Jew I wouldn't beat you to a pulp? What a chickenshit liar you were. Or were you really that stupid? Though I refuse to believe that I could fall in love with anyone that dumb.

I told you then that I despised the bitch with all the bile that my metabolism could produce.

Of course, I should have despised you, not her. She probably even loved you in her own way.

You told me I wasn't good enough to have contempt for her. "And don't use the word *cabra* (bitch) when describing her," you warned me.

I said that I respected her for being able to step right onto the neck of anybody who got in her way. And that *cabra*, for me, wasn't a bad word.

Then I offered you a drink. We had a couple of ouzos together and began our seduction conversation. It was about Rosa Mota and her victories in the marathon, as I recall. What a monolithic bore you were before you starting sleeping with men. Are you aware of that? Yeah, you were handsome: Tyrone Power shrunk to the size of a terrier, with tight little buttocks that later squeezed my cock like they were applauding every beat of my heart. But what a snooze! And what a coward! You always thought that a man would eat you up and never let you go, that you hadn't the power to resist his will. But you're not as weak as you think. Are you aware that our arguments always happened after I fucked you? You lost yourself in your pleasure and then blamed me. It scared you being filled with a man. Somewhere in childhood a popular folly entered your brain and spoiled your bowels — the one which said you were less than a person for craving a cock inside you.

Poor is he who spites himself his own pleasure.

Shakespeare didn't say it exactly that way, but he should have.

You know, I don't even know why I want you; I should want António. He takes pleasure in his body, in sex. So why then do I love you passionately and not him? Is he too young? Do I prefer teaching him to making love with him? Wouldn't that be a strange discovery for me to make at age thirty-nine?

Perhaps you're maturing, I hear you say, trying to elude the reflection of yourself you see in my eyes. *Maybe you've even realized you're not gay.*

Don't you believe it for a minute; I'd commit suicide if I found out I was straight.

Sleep did not come to me on the night of the 28th. I sat at my window and listened to dogs barking into the darkness.

8

Fourteen months of sun between Harold's death and this current crisis was all I had, and it wasn't enough. Sometimes, the body and mind need simply to escape a predicament they can't face. We've been taught that fleeing is wrong. But when a tiger opens his jaws and growls after eating your basketball team and half your neighborhood are you going to refuse refuge with the peasants in the hills? Not that there aren't other ways to escape than camouflaging yourself to look like a sane person in an overgrown olive grove like Portugal...

Stevie Rosenthal, our head cheerleader, joined the Peace Corps and is teaching electronics in Sri Lanka;

Pat de Lucca, Henry The Beast's six foot six inch ex-lover, and a man who holds the record for most French fries eaten at Jones Beach, is in Saudi Arabia, designing off-shore oil rigs for Shell;

Manuela Pierce, our Metropolitan Community Church minister from Brazil, got married to a Dutchman and set up a ministry in Saint Martin. When she told me that she was doing great, she noted that Brazilians have a molecule for happiness attached to their DNA that got left off everybody else's double-helixes.

I no longer write to any of them though; there's nothing left for us to say to each other.

On the morning of the 29th, I call in sick to school, drink ouzo and go for a walk by the river. In the afternoon, I circle the Hospital of Saint Antony five times as if performing a kabbalistic ritual designed to save the boy. Then I enter. I find the head nurse before I find António. My heart is beating wildly. She says, "The tests still haven't come back."

"How can that be?" I ask. "It was supposed to be today."

"Tomorrow," she says.

It is the eternal battle cry of the Portuguese and Spanish: *Amanhã*. Tomorrow.

I cannot face António. I head home. I'm so tense that I ask Fiama if she'll rub my back. Her hands are powerful, but have little effect. So she tucks me into her bed and puts two down pillows behind my head. I sip my ouzo and watch television. She makes me turnip soup. The prettiest droplets of olive oil float on the surface.

At eleven that night, I get a call from Miguel, António's father. "Professor, is that you?" he asks in a eager voice.

"It's me."

"I didn't see you at the hospital today."

"I couldn't make it."

"António was asking after you. He's better. He's much stronger. And the shingles are going away."

I haven't the heart to say that this small recovery doesn't matter if the boy turns out to be seropositive. I'm silent.

"Professor?" he asks. "Are you there?"

"I'm here."

"Did you hear what I said. *O rapaz está melhor.* The boy is better." He speaks as if António is *our* boy. My lungs seem to deflate; I can't face the reality of him coming back to the world. The truth is, I know that I'm probably safer with him dying right away in the hospital. I've learned that if a friend's body makes it into the ground before you know about it, you can almost make believe he's still alive, trekking forever in the Himalayas or lost in upstate New York. Anything which isn't confirmed dead can be considered alive.

"I'll talk to you some other time," I say to Miguel. I hang up before he can protest. He doesn't call back. I realize that I should feel like shit for not listening to him. But I'm relieved. I finish my bottle of ouzo.

António is a sprite of light and music, a boy born for the Elizabethan Age. He likes eating sweets and playing soccer and doing handsprings in the middle of the street. You'd hate him, Carlos, because you'd be jealous of his freedom and his life. Even gravely ill in a morbid hospital, he was far more alive than you'll ever be. That's the real tragedy. You were middle-aged the day you were born, and at thirty-four you're already crusted into your final form.

How dark and quiet you always were with me, like an evening forest waiting for wolves to howl. How you brooded about the sacred theories behind your art.

You know, everything between us always returned to the subject of *you*, as if you were a great fascist statue erected at the very center of the world.

Ah, but how gently and completely you made love when you forgot what you had to remember!

On your request, I whipped you once. That you'll surely recall. It was just a small leather tassel that you'd bought in some alleyway in the Bairro Alto in Lisbon. I'm sorry to say it didn't turn me on in the least. You moaned and writhed on your bed, but each crack of leather left me cold. "Give it to me good!" you kept shouting at me. I obeyed because I was in love, but the whole scene seemed theatrical and silly. When you started bleeding, I couldn't continue. Yes, I've got a weak stomach, I admit it.

A little later, after I'd carried you beyond the walls of Sodom, you got angry. "You hurt me with that fucking whip," you said.

"I'm sorry. But it was your idea," I answered.

"Even so, you really hurt me."

"You said it was what you wanted. I didn't mean to do anything... "

"Well, maybe I didn't know what I really wanted!" you interrupted.

"Maybe so." I caressed your cheek, and you pulled away. I said, "Don't be angry with me. We don't have to ever do it again."

After that night, you only wanted to fuck me. It was safer, of course. Because you could hold on to the last shreds of your ancient self-portrait. I'll admit I enjoyed it. I didn't need to screw you to be happy. But then you even got worried about letting a man lie underneath you. Did it make you *maricas*? Could you hold your head up as you walked down the Avenida da Boavista? Would little kids run up to you and tell you that they knew you were queer? It was pathetic — all those provincial worries in an artist who thinks that he's going to be the next (and hopefully last!) Andy Warhol. What a hypocrite you are! You take the leap, but it's off a curb one foot off the ground.

And you expect the rest of us to think you're really daring.

I'll preach at you one more time, my little Picasso: being daring isn't dumping resin and melted lead onto squiggles painted on a wooden pallet. It's walking down the gangplank without flinching. Maybe someday I'll learn how to do it myself. I'll give you a call if you've still got a phone.

That afternoon, I get a letter from my mother. She writes that she's still having nightmares about my brother. "Harold and I were in a king-size bed together, with wrinkled salmon-pink sheets. I knew that they hadn't been ironed... " It's these details which kill me: the *wrinkled, salmon-pink sheets.* Would anyone else take note of such things? She goes on: "...and your brother had turned his head to face a clock on the wall which had blood-red hands. When he looked at me, his skin was translucent, and through him I could see the dark sea as it looked when I was a child in Brooklyn. I felt as if we were trapped on an island together. When I awoke, I needed to vomit. I was so ill that... "

I've received letters like this for over a year now, since the day Harold stopped breathing in room 602 of the Neurology Ward in that factory of death on 59th Street and 9th Avenue called Roosevelt Hospital. My mom still hasn't gotten the idea that I'm not her therapist or rabbi. Or maybe she secretly thinks her letters are great literature and that I'll put all her correspondence together and get them to a publisher who will see in them the makings of a poignant memoir, the Great Jewish-American Lament. In that case, she's got a big surprise coming; no sooner do I read her epistles of doom then I burn them. It's a little ritual I've developed; disposing them into the garbage wouldn't be enough; they're too toxic, too weighted with my brother's illness. So after I read each letter, I calmly fold it over four times, sit it in a glass ashtray with a picture of the Eiffel Tower at the bottom and set it ablaze with a Bic lighter discarded by António when he stopped smoking. If I knew a Hebrew prayer against possession or hauntings, I'd whisper it to myself as the smoke rises. Why?

Because I've got those dreams about Harold, too, of course. Complete with the curse of wrinkled sheets. And that, you see, is why I don't really need her nightmares.

I feel too guilty about my brother not to answer her, of course. So I write little notes which let her know I've not forgotten. But the secret is this: mostly I *do* forget her and Harold. They sit dry and pale and stiff inside a past that will never be changed and which I've managed to sweep inside a room whose door only opens accidentally. I've trained myself that every time I approach the door, I turn away. They're both covered by cobwebs, of course, like modern Miss Havershams left at the altar of life just when things were getting promising. And yet, there are days, when the Portuguese sun is out and my fingers are particularly nimble at the strings of my guitar, when the cobwebs drop from my mother, her face blooms pink and healthy, and she steps away from my brother and comes out of our old family house into the world I inhabit. The trouble is I can hardly remember what she looks like, nor what it feels like to kiss her. Everything that animated her was buried with Harold; she who walked away from his grave was a specter — a ghost dreaming of other ghosts.

After I burn her letter, I call up Salgueiro, the only man I've spent a night with since I split up with you, Carlos; now that António is recovering, my plan for taking the boy to Spain and France is coalescing in my brain, and I'll need a loan to pull it off. Unfortunately, I've only managed to save up twelve hundred dollars over the last year. As for the savings I'd squirreled away in the States, flying back and forth to New York to visit Harold in hospitals ate up most of it. The rest was spent on António's new guitar, which I told him only cost nine hundred bucks and which he's paying back in installments, but which actually set me back nineteen hundred.

You're probably wondering who this Salgueiro is. I met him at Porto's Moinho de Vento bar, maybe six months ago. He was easily the oldest guy there, sixty-four at the time, as I later learned. He had a big head, lovely sad green eyes, white hair that was combed back with water so that it looked like carded silk. In profile, he looked a little like Leonard Bernstein. He was sipping something green and syrupy that looked like mouthwash. "Chartreuse," he explained when I sat next to him. We shook hands, and he held mine for so long that I knew he wanted me. I downed the rest of his chartreuse in a single gulp, and we walked to his apartment. It was in a modern building, with a spectacular view over the Douro River toward the wine cellars in Gaia. The furniture was all expensive antiques. He told me his story. He'd been married forty-two years when his wife died. Before that he'd never so much as touched another man's cock. I didn't believe him, of course. But I don't usually fight illusions. So I nodded a lot. After she passed away, he said, he began to have sex with men. He couldn't get a woman at his age except a prostitute. And he desperately needed companionship at night. Among other things, he'd become afraid of the dark.

As it happens, we only slept together three times; he couldn't get it up, and it didn't seem like much fun just getting myself off. But we became friends right away. It was Salgueiro who told me at my small birthday party two months ago that he was sure António had learned to play the guitar like an angel because the boy and I had been lovers. That made me really happy for the first time since you left me, Carlos; it meant that my cock had been useful for something in this pitiful decade.

Now, when I tell him over the phone about my need for a loan in order to take António to Paris, he asks "How much?" His tone is wary.

"Two thousand dollars," I answer.

He gasps. So I say, "I wanta do it right and get a big American car. It's a fantasy of António's. I know someone in Lisbon who's got an old Thunderbird, but he's a cheap bastard and he's going to charge me a fortune. Listen, if two thousand is too much, I'd really appreciate whatever you can come up with."

Silence; Salgueiro is thinking of what he can get in return. Horny old roosters always negotiate. "It's been a long time between trips to the oasis with you," he says.

"I'm really not in the mood," I reply.

"Just sleep beside me till dawn. You won't do anything you don't want to."

"Okay, but I want two down pillows just for myself."

"Deal."

"I'll be over after dinner," I say.

"I'll have dessert warm and ready."

He pronounces this last line as if he's raising his eyebrows at the same moment. It makes me realize that he's hoping for a plunge

61

into the warm lake of our oasis after all.

Perhaps a passionate little dip will do me some good, too, I think.

When I enter the kitchen to tell Fiama that I'll be spending the night with Salgueiro, I find her dicing onions and singing a sad old song. The chorus goes: *Todos nós temos fado, e quem nasce mal fadado, melhor fado não terá* — all of us have a destiny, and he who is born ill-destined, a better destiny will never have.

Her manly voice drips melancholy. Maybe this despairing androgyny is what I love about her. Or maybe I'm free to love her because I don't sleep with her. In any event, my heart is bursting with fondness. So I tiptoe up behind her and plant a kiss on her neck that in another time and place would have gone to my mother.

Her song stops and she whips around. "Oh it's you," she says, disappointed. "I thought you were back in bed drunk."

I put my arms around her and stare into her eyes. "If only you were a man," I sigh.

"If only *you* were a man!" she retorts.

That makes us both laugh from our bellies.

It's codfish she's making for dinner. She's been soaking the damn thing in a tub of water for three days.

"I won't eat it if it's big pieces," I tell her like a little kid. "It's like trying to swallow a dictionary."

"You know something? You make me tired. You make everyone tired. You're like walking uphill."

"No big pieces," I repeat.

"Little pieces," she agrees. "With onions and eggs. Just like you like it."

"And olive oil."

"And olive oil." She points her knife at me. "Now get out of the kitchen. I'll call you when it's ready."

"Any crabs?" I ask.

She reaches down to scratch herself and shakes her head. "Clean as a baby's bottom."

I need a belly full of cod and eggs if I'm going to give Salgueiro even close to his money's worth in bed, so I eat up Fiama's dinner like a hog and drink half a bottle of cheap red wine. Then I stumble over to his apartment.

He opens his door in his wife's satin dressing gown. It's cobalt blue, edged with white fluff. I don't mind him trying to look like Jean Harlow, but his dentures are already out and his squashed face is disconcerting. He gives me a big toothless smile. We hug. He pats my behind. In a poetic voice, he says, "Speaking of his equipment, he possessed fine horses... "

Salgueiro always gives me a quote to start our escapades, but I don't know the origin of this one, so I say, "I give up."

"You should know it — it's part of your own heritage."

I burp out some codfish and say, "I make it a point never to read anything to do with my own heritage. As a matter of fact, I try very hard not to read at all anymore."

"From the *Canterbury Tales*," he says.

"That's English," I explain. "I'm American."

"Same thing," he observes.

"You might recall that there's an ocean between us."

Salgueiro waves away my objection. He puts his dentures back in his mouth.

We go to his living room and talk for a while about his past; of late, his wife has been coming to him in dreams. She asks him to find lost silverware and punishes him for new scratches on the furniture. When I tell him about my mother's nightmares, he says, "Everybody who has been abandoned lives in the same inner landscape."

He surprises me by making no sexual advances. When we go to bed, he takes out his teeth and puts them in a Chinese cup on his night table, the kind where rice laced in the porcelain leaves transparent dots at the rim when it evaporates in the kiln. He gives me a peck on the cheek, then twists around. He falls asleep like a baby in my arms.

At three in the morning, however, he slides down under the covers and attaches himself to me like a soldier dying of thirst.

About the same time as I realize where I am and who the mound in the blanket is who's ravishing me, he asks me to enter him. "Anything," I groan, "if you'll just let go for a second."

"Sure," he says. "As a matter of fact, I need a moment myself."

He washes his bottom in the bidet, powders himself with talc, then takes a violet-colored hand towel from his dresser and unfolds it carefully on the bed. Positioning himself face-down as if his groin has to be right at its center, he says, "Go for it, son."

This man fucks like it's the Japanese tea ceremony, I think. I put a condom on.

His insides feel like the sea, and we lay together like lovers on a raft. His heartbeat pounds against my chest. His body leaches sweat, and he begins to smell like a young man.

"I want to be on my side," he says, so I turn him. Low and behold, the old bird has a real live hard-on.

"*Caramba,* where'd that come from?" I say. "I think you've got a tumor."

He starts to caress himself, but I offer my hand instead. A few minutes later, when he's completely drained, he begins to sob.

I start to pull out of him, so I can face him and ask what's wrong. But he reaches behind to hold me in place. "Stay," he whispers.

I caress his flanks. I kiss his ears. *What a treat to be able to give an old man some happiness,* I think.

When I pull out of him, he turns over. His face is beet red and sweaty. He wipes his eyes. He says, "It's the first orgasm I've had in maybe five years. I'd forgotten..." His voice grows silent and he starts to cry again.

I kiss his eyes, then clean his cum from his legs. I rub his silvery chest hairs and play with his nipples. I hold his hand. I tell him what a lovely old man he is. He caresses my belly. He says, "I waited these past months without asking for more than friendship because I wanted to be sure... I had myself tested. I'm negative. I want you to be able to make love to me without a condom. I want to feel you inside me. Only you."

"Why me?"

"Because...because I don't know. I just want it." He senses my sudden dread and says, "Don't worry. No commitments." He cups my chin. His eyes are serious. "Listen, more importantly, is your António going to be okay?" he asks. "I dreamt about him, too, and it wasn't good."

"Don't know. The results of his tests will be in tomorrow."

"Youth is precious," he says, starting to cry again. "And life is cruel. You must be very nice to him."

In the morning, while I'm dressing, he writes me a check for the money I need to rent the T-Bird. Naked, he holds it behind his back and steps up to me with a coy look. "I'll give it to you if you hug me."

I wrap my arms around him and reply, "A handsome friend to hug and lots of money — maybe things are looking up for me."

He takes his dentures out, and we kiss for a long time. It's like being eaten alive by a warm bullfrog. As he hands me the check, he says in English, "No loan. Is a gift." He takes my head in both his hands like he's my mother and says very carefully: "Make Antonio happy." Then he holds his index finger to his lips.

A man like Salgueiro can almost restore your faith in the world. Almost, because when I tell Ramalho the next morning that I do indeed need the last two weeks of school off, he tells me to forget about it.

"But I'll get Pedro to cover for me," I insist.

"No way."

"But I told you my father was ill. I could just leave, you know, with an excuse like that, and no one would blame me. I've already done thirty weeks of teaching without missing a class."

"If you take off, there won't be a job waiting for you when you get back."

"Ask the students what a good job I've done this year. You wouldn't want to lose me."

"Fuck the students! I know you're lying about your father. I found out that he died a long time ago!"

I realize that there's a part of Ramalho that despises me my freedom, my having an American cock that didn't grow up constrained by Catholic doctrine and a mouth liberated of the need to eat every last vegetable so it could get a woman for dessert. For a moment, I consider telling him the truth just to bring him into reality. But since his mind only understands petty lies, he would think I was a Martian. Sitting there with the bastard, another thing was revealed to me clearly: *The longer I lived in Portugal the better liar I'd become.*

"If you don't have anything more to say, you can leave my office," he says. "I've work to do."

"Can't I think a minute? I have to decide whether to tell you the truth or not. I don't know if I can trust you."

This was the first step in my new plan: weaken his defenses by faking intimacy.

"You don't know if you can trust me? I've put up with more shit from you in the last four years than Mother Teresa would have."

"Screw you!"

"Screw you, too!"

Now that I had him incensed at an *intimate* colleague, I could hook him completely. I said, "Look, it's my girlfriend. She's in Lisbon, has to have an operation. Her ovaries. They're rotten."

"You never mentioned a girlfriend." He takes out his Marlboro Lights and gold lighter and nods at me as if he's intrigued. "Some of us were beginning to think you were queer, you know."

"Fuck you," I say.

"Okay, you've a right to be angry. But I still don't see why your girlfriend's rotten ovaries means you need time off."

"The operation's going to be in Lisbon. I need to be there with her. I promised. And it can't wait. Look, if it goes wrong, she'll never be able to fuck again with any sort of pleasure, so for us it's kind of important."

If he had a brain, he'd have asked what her ovary had to do with lovemaking, but I was counting on the well-known fact that Portuguese straight men know even less about women's anatomy than any queer I've ever met. They think it's a sin taking a good look at a pussy; might turn them to salt or something. Or the damn thing might turn out to look like a turtle's ass.

Ramalho lit his cigarette while considering his options. It was time to press my advantage. I said, "I've already gotten Pedro to agree to cover for me."

"Pedro's got enough classes of his own."

"That's his problem. He knows it'll be two weeks of hell, but he's agreed."

That was a lie, of course. "There's only one other problem," I continued. "If I go away, it'll mean having to give up that newspaper interview. If you want, I could ask if you can cover for me."

"What interview?"

"A reporter at *O Publico* wanted to do a piece on me. An American guitarist in Porto. Foreigners bringing modern skills to The Land That Time Forgot, that sort of crap. It was to be Friday of this week. I'll suggest that he talk to you about foreign music teachers in general. You can talk about me and Pedro and all the rest you've hired over the years. Discuss our strengths and weaknesses."

"You think he'll buy it?" he asked.

Ramalho's the kind of cloistered beast who loves vulgarity in the service of his minuscule ego. So I replied, "Journalism's like fucking — it's all about filling up space. He's got a big fat hole he needs to fill up in the Culture Section and from what I hear you've got the right size cock to fill it."

He inhaled deeply on his cigarette and winked at me. What a specimen of obscene ego he was. If you could tie a brown paper bag over his head, you could package and sell him as cheap pornography.

At four o'clock in the afternoon, after giving lessons to three satanically ungifted students, I head to the hospital. The results still aren't in. "Tomorrow," the head nurse tells me. I reply that that is unacceptable.

She walks away from me.

"Unacceptable!" I call after her.

I look in on António. He's asleep. From a distance, he doesn't appear dangerous.

I slip away.

I pass another sleepless night in my flannel Macy's pajamas. I'd bought a new bottle of ouzo, and I sip it out of a blue ceramic soup bowl. I listen to dogs barking again.

And all the worry, all the secret prayer, all the alcohol is worthless. Wednesday morning, Miguel leaves a message on my machine: "António is seropositive. He's very depressed. He will not talk. Professor, will you help me with him? Are you there? Will you call me back? Are you there?"

Part II

9

Harold, my brother, showed symptoms of the approach of Death for six years before the unavoidable confrontation. First, back in 1987, his chest erupted with shingles. Then the lymph nodes in his groin and underarms grew to the size of quail eggs. Next, his brain was attacked by toxoplasmosis. After sulfa drugs liberated him from that protozoan encampment, he started losing sensation in his hands, feet and vocal chords. The doctors called it neuropathy. They speculated that the HIV viruses themselves were clinging to his nerve-endings and dampening their electric signaling. But neither the name of this particular condition nor any theorizing about its cause were of any use; there was no cure. Toward the end, Harold lay like a goat-ribbed castaway in his hospital bed and used his hands like seal flippers. His vocal chords were numbed, as well, and he talked in a hoarse whisper, like Marlon Brando in *The Godfather.* Any schmuck with even half a brain would have known for certain he'd reached the ninth inning and that the count was two strikes, right? Yet when he took a last strike down the center of the plate, it was such a shock to me that I couldn't get out of bed for two weeks.

The moral of the story is that you are never as prepared as you think.

There are two important things to guard against when you're suffering from the first wave of disbelief that washes over you when you learn of the grave illness of a loved one. First, watch out for friends who simply slink away from you when they smell your thoughts about death. Clothed in cobwebs of fear, they are convinced that life is all about having fun. Death is not fun. Nor is illness.

Can you recall how you spent my convalescence in bed hiding at your studio, Carlos?

Ah, but there are those bitter souls who will not just slink away but also seek to injure you. Why? Because they know that you will suffer so much more in your fragile state. Let me tell you a simple story to illustrate my point. When my brother died, my boyhood friend Bernie happened to be in Salamanca for an international meeting of biophysicists. I never told you about this, Carlos. I was feeling completely isolated because you were already moving away from me. I desperately wanted Bernie to come to Porto to talk with me; he'd known my brother well, and I needed someone around me with whom I could discuss our family history. I considered his presence in Salamanca at that moment a gift from God — proof, I suppose, that grief had clouded my vision. I told him I'd pay his way to Porto and put him up at our flat or any hotel in town, that it was only three hours by car. Do you know what he told me? That he had only one day in Salamanca free for shopping and couldn't come. He wanted to buy some *wacky* t-shirts for the kids; a leather bag for his wife; and *something really pretty* for his younger sister, Sandra, who was getting remarried to a dental surgeon with *wax for a brain.* I offered to help him find all these things in Porto. Or I'd even rent a car and drive to Salamanca myself. He was silent for a moment and then, as if I hadn't made even one desperate proposal, asked if I had any suggestions for what to buy Sandra. "No," I replied, numb.

"You never were much for shopping," he observed. He added that if I wanted to meet him at the Madrid airport just before his flight off, I could come. He spoke with a patronizing twist in his voice, as if he were grudgingly conceding a minor point to a persistent lab technician. When I said, "What about Harold?" he sighed and answered, "It happens, pal. Life goes on."

He actually called me *pal.* As if life were a television sitcom, and in the next episode, we were all going find out that the last six months had been a bad dream, that Harold was actually alive and well and living in a Holiday Inn in San Juan with amnesia.

Life goes on, he told me. What do you say to that?

I said, "Fuck you, you prick!" It was one of my few moments of eloquence in this world.

Carlos, you're cut from the same mold as Bernie, of course. After all, you ducked out on me only three months after Harold died and wrote in your goodbye letter that I was just a *foreign faggot whose whole family was damned.* In closing, you called me an *oversexed pervert without any balls!*

Paradoxical, of course, but inquisitors have never been concerned with logic. Were you able to rationalize somehow that saying such things evidenced compassion?

The second thing to watch out for is closer to hand: self-loathing. If you listen to the sermons of your own guilt, you'll spend your days guzzling cheap Greek liqueurs or mainlining valium and ranting at everyone you meet as if they had personally invited the Angel of Death to your room. Or maybe, if you're really a cowardly shit, you'll even move to some backwater encrustation at the edge of Europe. So if drunken exile in The Land That Time Forgot is not how you want to spend your life, then you better tie a gag around your guilt, attach a block of cement to its foot and dump it in the nearest body of water. If only I could. Not that I would return to America, now. No, that's over. God save me if I had to face assholes like Bernie and their cheerful new sitcoms every September. But if I could loose myself from remorse, at least this epistle to you, dear Carlos, would get burned in the sacred ashtray which receives my mother's letters. And then I could get on with my life.

But why do you still feel guilty? I hear you ask.

For any number of reasons. And maybe the most important is for simply surviving.

I'll tell you a secret now, dear Carlos: my love for you may very well be nothing more than my guilt at not helping my brother enough. Let me make what I'm saying even clearer. On his death-bed, Harold told me that he had only one regret. Of course, I thought he was going to say that it was lying face-down underneath the son of a bitch who ejaculated a million invisible Cossacks inside him. But that wasn't it. He opened his eyes wide, slipped his right flipper in my hand and croaked, "I wasted too much time cloistered in a closet and blaming everyone for it — even you. Because you were out and free. And now the time is all gone. I've never even fallen in love." He waved his seal flippers in the air like a magician showing his audience that his white rabbit had been made to disappear. His lips were trembling. He smiled bitterly and whispered, "All gone." Then he shouted it as best he could and kept honking it with his disappearing voice...

all gone
all gone
all gone...

until a nurse ran in wearing surgical gloves and a face mask and shot him full of something that made him go to sleep.

I never got to speak to Harold again; the next morning, I had my flight back to Portugal.

He couldn't talk on the phone.

I wrote three more letters. He received one.

Why didn't I work harder to pull him out of his closet when he was well, when I had the chance? There are lots of answers. He was a rude and selfish bastard. And like he admitted, he begrudged me my freedom. The only thing you need to know, Carlos, is that all the answers lead right to you; because you're just like him in those respects. You see, maybe the real reason why you have this over-grown letter in your hands is that I've got some sort of savior complex. All these words are aimed at simply preventing you from wasting your life.

Are my motives also selfish? Of course.

You are, after all, my second chance.

After Miguel left his message on my machine about António, I called in sick again at school and headed to the park behind the Porto's Museum of Modern Art. I thought a lot of my brother as I walked around the pond watching the gliding ducks and admiring the pampas grass. I dropped down under the shade of a broad magnolia. I could see Harold sitting there with me, white and stiff, a momentary exile from that room of the past which I try my best never to enter. Then it started to drizzle. When it really began to pour, I let myself get soaked as if that might help me awaken into another reality in which António was just a boy worrying about soccer results. With my clothes fully saturated and rain dripping in a shredded curtain from my hair, I returned home on the 78 bus.

There are few things more foul smelling than a herd of wet Portuguese wearing sopping woolen sweaters.

At home, I took off my clothes and threw them in the bathtub. Three of Fiama's black bras were hanging from the shower rod. She washes them by hand, then leaves them there like sleeping fruit bats. So I ripped them down and threw them in the toilet. I flushed and flushed, but they wouldn't go down the drain.

Portuguese plumbing isn't worth shit.

After I slipped on my sweatpants, I called the American in Lisbon who owns the Thunderbird I wanted. His name's Bob, and I knew him because he supplied our Australian cello teacher with hashish. I'd only spoken to him once before in passing. He answered the phone with a drowsy voice, said that he'd just gotten back from Boise, Idaho, of all places.

"How does someone from Idaho wind up in Portugal?" I asked.

He replied, "The short version is that I was a lonely university student at Idaho State and met a Portuguese girl with the loveliest eyes I'd ever seen. We married. Her mother was dying. We moved to Portugal. End of story."

I should have known he could have only gotten here through love or death; they're the only things that get people moving.

I explained why I was calling. Sure enough, he still owned the T-Bird. He said that he'd purchased it nearly a decade earlier from a Portuguese immigrant from New Bedford who'd had the car shipped here for a summer of fun back in '86, then sold it when he faced up to the fact that he and his kids hated the Old Country. Bob snorted and said, "Imagine being an American kid and finding out your parents were from this weird place where people eat squid?"

He told me he would let me have the T-Bird for $200 per five hundred miles to pay for wear and tear on the engine. I bargained him down to $150. But I'd have to pick the car up in Lisbon and leave a $750 deposit.

"I just want to warn you the heap only gets about eleven miles to the gallon," he said.

"What color is it?" I asked.

"Black."

"Sounds like a hearse."

"Looks more like the Batmobile."

A comic-book car kicking up dust across the Castilian plateau into old Madrid sounded perfect to me. We agreed that I'd show up at his place at four in the afternoon the next day, Thursday, to pick it up. When I hung up, I began to pace around the room. I was thinking, *two weeks on the road with António.* I guzzled some Cointreau while leaning against the refrigerator; ouzo was beginning to make me nauseous. I brought the bottle over the phone with me. By the time I dialed the boy's number, my emotions had slipped through my head into the room. I could see myself from above. My hand was trembling. My face looked green. My lips tasted like turpentine. When Miguel answered, I'd half lifted the bottle up to my lips again. I spilled the syrupy gook all over myself. "Oh shit!" I said.

"Who is this?"

"It's me, António's guitar teacher. Sorry about the profanity, I just had an accident."

"Professor, I've been calling and calling," he replied. His voice was grainy and dry.

"I got your messages, but I couldn't talk."

"Then you know about the boy."

"Yeah."

"Will you keep giving him lessons?"

"Of course," I said.

Miguel burst into sobs. I'd heard so many people crying into phones over the past decade that it no longer seemed unusual. Long ago I'd gotten over the idea of wanting people to stop bawling on my account. But his tears were useless to me. So I held the phone down on my lap and drank some more.

The Portuguese love to be sorry for displays of emotion, so when he stopped crying, he apologized.

"No reason to be sorry," I assured him.

"I'm really sorry," he continued.

"It's okay."

"I'm *really, really* sorry."

I responded a sigh. Miguel said, "António told me he doesn't want to continue with lessons. You'll have to speak to him. He won't talk with me."

"I will. But listen, I've a proposal to make. I know there's still two weeks of school left, but I want to take António to Madrid and Paris. I'll make sure he gets incompletes in his courses and that he can do final exams in September. There'll be no problems."

"How? I mean, you and he will go together?"

"Would you mind? I think it will do him good to get away and see other places. He said in the hospital he wanted to go away. If you're worried about the guitar lessons, I could continue them on the road."

"But your other classes?"

"Forget 'em."

"But why would you do this for him?"

"Because he wants to go."

Silence.

I said, "Look, don't try to understand anything for now. Things will become clearer later. Just decide whether you'll let him go away for two weeks or not."

"I'll have to think about it. And I'd have to discuss it with his mother."

"Can you call her tonight?"

"Sure."

"Then call me after you've spoken to her. Now please put António on."

"I'll see if he'll come to the phone."

As I waited, I realized I'd take António away with me even if his parents didn't want him to go; Miguel could send the police after us for all I cared. It would be an even greater pleasure to have the Spanish Civil Guards after us as we sailed toward Madrid in our Batmobile.

"He won't talk to you," Miguel said.

"Tell him that if he doesn't get on the phone right now I'm going to come over and step on his guitar and make him sing like Edith Piaf."

"Step on his guitar?"

"He'll understand. Just tell him."

When António got on the phone, he said, "I'm listening, what do you want?" His voice was full of irritation.

"So, are you ready for our little excursion?" I asked cheerfully.

"What are you talking about?"

"Our trip to Madrid and Paris."

"Why?"

"In the hospital... You talked about seeing them. I said I'd take you." I considered letting him know about his chance to study with José Maria Landero at the Paris Conservatory, but decided to only tell him that at the last minute. Right now, it would only give him one more excuse for not going.

"I'd prefer not to," he replied.

"But Paris. We'll walk the streets. See the Eiffel Tower. The pastries are the best in the world. And the cheeses are wonderful. It'll be good to get away."

In English, he repeated, "I'd prefer not to."

One night in bed, I'd made the mistake of reading him Melville's

'Bartleby the Scrivener', and this dry expression of refusal was how he was going to punish me. "António, listen," I said, but I couldn't finish the sentence because I made a vow never to give anybody a pep talk ever again. So I said, "Do you want to finish your classes and then go?"

"I'm not finishing any classes."

"Look, I'm going to Paris in two days. Via Madrid. I'm going to pick up the car in Lisbon tomorrow, and we leave the morning after that. You're coming. So pack some things. And we'll bring my guitar. It's better than yours and we won't need both."

"The last thing I want to do is play the damn guitar."

"You love the guitar."

Silence. I said, "It's something you do beautifully, a gift, but it requires practice."

That was a stupid thing to say, of course, because it made reference to the future. António was silent. I cursed myself for getting out of practice talking to the doomed. And it was becoming ever clearer that in Portuguese my conversational skills were totally inadequate. Carlos, maybe you don't understand. But there's a whole vocabulary you have to develop to talk with people who are confronting their own death. It is absolutely obligatory to avoid certain grammatical tenses.

I wanted valium so bad at that moment that I could feel a little phantom pill melting on my tongue. The Cointreau would make it slide deliciously down my gullet. And maybe I could speak Portuguese without grammatical errors if I were drunk and drugged at the same time. "Do you want me to come over?" I asked.

"No!"

"Listen António, you don't have to shut me out."

Silence again. The little bastard was going to roast me with unspoken contempt. I said, "This is important... What I'm going to say is important." But I had no idea what I was going to say. I crossed myself like I used to when Harold would fly into rages at me.

"So say it!" António shouted.

"I want to be with you... More than anything I want to be with you. To hold you. To be with you and hold you. But I'm afraid. Because I don't know how you're going to react. And I don't know if I can take it. I'm weak, António. Once I was strong. Years ago, I could have helped you more. But now I'm weak. I've no foundation left."

He hung up without saying a word. I guzzled more Cointreau, then called back. Miguel answered and said António had run to his room and locked the door. "I'm sorry, Professor," he said.

"That's okay," I replied. "Just call me later to tell me what you and your wife have decided."

Miguel didn't call that evening. I clipped my hair off in tufts and sat by my window. I went back to ouzo because the Cointreau was too sickly sweet. I waited up for Fiama till one in the morning because I wanted her to give me another back rub. When she didn't come home, I went to bed resolved to take the train to Lisbon the next day to pick up the T-Bird. The phone woke me at two-thirty in the morning. It was Miguel. He sounded desperate and drunk. "Can I come over?" he asked. "I need to talk to you. I can't stay here alone. I can't."

"Where's António?"

"Sleeping at his mother's."

"Why do you want to come over here?"

"It's dark here."

"What kind of answer is that?"

"It's too dark."

"It's dark here, too. The sun's gone down. It happens like that."

"I'm alone."

Fiama was standing next to me now, naked. She began mouthing, *"Está tudo bem?"* She was squinting at my chopped hair.

I nodded that things were under control and said into the receiver, "Okay, come over. You know where I live?"

"I know."

He hung up. Fiama said, "Who the hell was that?"

"Miguel, António's father." I explained about the test results. She sat on my bed and held my hand. "So that's why my bras were in the toilet," she sighed. "And your hair... What did you do to it? You look like you were attacked in a chain-saw movie."

I reached up and felt my hand over her breasts. She pushed it away. "What are you doing?"

"There are times when I could almost imagine making love to you."

She held her hands over her chest and said, "You stink from ouzo."

"Thank you," I nodded.

She slipped on her bathrobe and got a scissors from the bathroom. She began straightening out the mess I'd made of my hair while we waited for Miguel. I'd say she's a saint, but she's much better than that. So I asked her advice about what to do for António.

"What did you do for the others?" she asked.

"It's always different. And the same."

"So what did you do?"

"I don't know. You have to wait and listen for them to tell you what they need. Listening seems to be the most important thing."

"Just what most people can't do."

I let her clip away for a while, then said, "I ended up doing a lot of listening over the last twelve years. But there comes a point when they stop talking. Henry The Beast sat rigidly in a chair for the last three months of his life. He wouldn't talk or move. He got sores on his rear end and a tumor in his throat and still he wouldn't move. He was like one of those wild animals at the zoo that they put in a cage alone and they get so depressed that they just stop. Stop everything. They call a strike. They stare at you with accusing eyes. Then they die."

"António won't do that." She grabbed my head and angled it down. "Look at the floor so I can cut the top better."

"How do you know he won't clam up?"

"He just won't. My vision is still twenty-twenty."

Miguel showed up a half-hour later. He was wearing a blue dress-shirt stained with something yellow on the collar and buttoned wrong. He stank of alcohol, tobacco and sweat. Dark stubble contoured his cheeks, and his hair was an oily gray. His eyes were wild and unfocused. Fiama helped me lead him to the couch. His hand fell against my ass as we walked. "You've got me all wrong, mister," I said in a manly voice, knowing that he couldn't understand my English.

Fiama understood because she works in a travel agency and needs to know other languages. She told me I was an idiot.

"What did you say?" Miguel asked.

"Just lie down and stop wondering what it would be like to break some taboos."

"Sshhh," Fiama told me.

He raised his hand as if he wanted to make a Shakespearean speech, then let it fall. "I need to sleep," he announced. "But I'm thirsty. So thirsty." He grabbed my arm. "I'm really thirsty."

Fiama went off for water. After she handed me the glass, I raised Miguel's head and helped him get a few good sips before spilling the rest on his shirt. Unperturbed, he raised his hand and flapped it in Fiama's direction. "Who's that?" he asked in a surprised voice. "Your wife? Have I disturbed your wife, too?"

"I'm just a friend," Fiama answered.

"Your wife?" he questioned again, looking through me.

"A friend, *meu porquinho*, my little pig. A friend!"

"Your wife..." he whispered. He sighed, exhausted with the effort to remain conscious. He groaned once, licked his lips, then passed out.

As if she'd only reached an obvious conclusion after decades of building toward it, Fiama nodded gravely and said in a poet's voice, "You know, men are the loveliest and also the most repulsive things in the world." She pointed toward Miguel, "If only someone would invent a dildo with that face..."

"What about women?" I asked.

"What about them?"

"Don't you think women are lovely and repulsive, too?"

"They're little marigolds — easily trampled, hardly seen. But men..." She flapped her hand at Miguel. "Men are great big hibiscus flowers. But if you get too close, you realize their petals are poisonous to the touch."

"Not all men," I observed.

"No?" Fiama shrugged, scratched the stubble growing back in her Bermuda triangle, blew me a kiss and went to her room.

I sat listening to Miguel snore. Drunk, looking like a slob, I didn't find him the least bit attractive. I turned off the lights.

10

I awoke at close to five in the morning, fully awake. I slipped on pajama bottoms and walked to the living room. Miguel was still asleep, but somewhere along the line, he'd taken off his shirt and jeans. He wore white boxer shorts of all things. It was stuffy in the house. I slipped on a sweater and went to the verandah. Out past the plane trees guarding the other side of the street I could see the Crystal Palace, a giant lime-green dome of copper and concrete used for sporting events. It looked to me like a flying saucer which had landed on the top of a ravine. A couple of hundred feet below was the dark river. A breeze chilled my newly shorn head.

Behind me, I suddenly heard footsteps. Miguel was coming out to meet me. He'd put on his jeans, but was still barechested. He was a furry little thing, muscular. "Hi," he said, and he shook my hand. "I guess I fell asleep."

"You passed out," I observed.

"You cut your hair," he said.

I rubbed my hand across the bristle that remained. "I suppose it looks like I joined the army," I said.

"No, it looks fine. Don't worry." He rubbed his belly. "Man, I drank too much."

"Really? I hadn't noticed," I smiled.

He grinned. "Listen, I'm sorry to have done this. I must be crazy."

"It's no problem. I understand."

We stared at each other. There was a lot to say about António, but neither of us wanted to begin. Miguel lit a cigarette, got it going with a couple of puffs, then handed it to me. He lit another for himself. We went to the railing and stood there smoking. I wanted to pat his back and feel his solidity. He said, "I was the one who prevented António from going to the Conservatory."

"Meaning?"

He took a greedy inhale on his cigarette, then pointed to the green dome in the distance. "Ever see pictures of the building which they tore down to build that monstrosity?"

I nodded; it had been all iron and glass — a real Crystal Palace modeled on the building of the same name in London.

"Lovely, wasn't it?" he asked.

"Very."

"People do crazy things and then something beautiful is gone forever. All we have are postcards."

He stuck his cigarette in his mouth and gripped the metal railing of the verandah with both hands. He pulled on it as if testing its strength. "I used to do gymnastics, you know," he said. "Time was when I wouldn't have been afraid to do a handstand on this railing."

"Don't do one now or I might have to peel you up off the pavement."

He rubbed his cheeks as if dissatisfied with himself. "No, now I'm old. Some things are only good when you're young. Then it's over."

We stood together watching the night passing toward day. He said, "António came to me when he was eighteen and asked if he could go to music school. I said, 'no'. You know why?"

I shook my head.

"I thought it was because we were too good for music. I mean, I told myself that music was for a whole different class of people, snobbish people, people not like us. António was meant to be a stone mason like me. That was good work. A man's work. Do you know what I mean?"

I nodded.

"But that wasn't the real reason." Miguel gripped the railing again like he might press up into the handstand he threatened to try earlier. He turned to me. In an exhale of smoke, he said, "The real reason was that I was jealous of him and wanted him to be nothing more than me. You understand what I'm saying? I stopped him from doing what he wanted because I was a jealous bastard. He was better than me, had a gift, and I knew it. But I didn't want him to have it." He flicked his cigarette up over the railing. It fell with sparks on the pavement below. "I'm a jealous bastard," he said.

"António told me that he didn't come to school earlier because you didn't have the money."

"He told you that?!"

I nodded.

"That wasn't it! The kid was protecting me."

"So what made you change your mind?"

"Before I answer that, there's one other thing," he said. "I don't know if you've figured it out yet, but António is a homosexual."

Miguel pronounced the last word as if it were very powerful.

I smiled. "I've known for a long time."

"And it doesn't bother you?"

"I'm the last person it would bother."

"What do you mean?"

I was suddenly afraid to tell him, so I said, "I'm from New York. There, it's not so very important."

"I guess it's more common in the States."

"No, just less hidden. It's pretty common everywhere."

"I always knew about him, I think. Little things, when he was young... And I thought that somehow if I prevented him from doing what he wanted, he'd change. I mean, if I told him straight out that I didn't approve of what he wanted to be, what he was, that it would be like telling him that he had to change." He was silent for a while, looked up at the stars, then turned to me and said, "You see why I'm really a bastard."

"António is a wonderful kid," I said. "And he was able to do what he wanted. He came to school. You're not as big a bastard as you think."

"After three wasted years... I made him waste those years. Gone. And now..." His voice faded. He lit another cigarette. He turned to me and said, "I used to be real close to him. He's my son. You know him. You know what he's like. When he was growing up I felt blessed to have him. We all did. And then this Conservatory thing... The arguments. And finding out for sure that he was gay. It was like somebody was separating the two of us behind fences. I shouted at him all the time. I hit him once you know. Really hit him. Punched him right in the face when I found out he'd slept with a boy at our house when his mother and I were gone. 'In my house!' I shouted. Like it wasn't his house, too. Like having sex wasn't something natural for him. Like it would have been better had he fucked on the street like some animal."

I didn't know what to say, so we both leaned against the railing. Finally, I noticed I was cold and said, "Maybe we should go inside."

He reached for my hand. "I want to know my boy," he said. "I want to know my boy." Every word was clenched. "I want to know him before...before he dies." He grabbed both of my hands. "Professor, is it too much to ask to know my boy?"

"No."

"I want to go with you. I want to know António like you know him."

He spoke again as if António belonged to us both. Did he know

I was gay? Was he just testing me? "You want to go with us?" I asked.

"You're going to take the boy to Madrid and Paris. I want to come. Will you do that for me? Will you help me?"

"I'm not so sure it would be a good idea."

"It's the only way. I may not have another chance to reach him." He shrugged regretfully at his own insistence.

"If António agrees, then it's fine with me," I said.

"He won't agree. You've got to decide."

"I don't know. I don't think I can."

"I want to know him. You understand what I mean?"

"I'll talk to him. I'll see what I can do. We'll work it out."

As soon as I agreed to intercede, I realized I'd made a mistake. We walked back inside and said goodbye. I rationalized that if Miguel came along we'd at least get one side benefit; he could find out what regime of medications, if any, António needed to follow on the trip and be the one responsible for making sure he kept on schedule. The last thing I wanted to do was be in the position of managing someone's HIV infection ever again.

I couldn't get back to sleep that night because people long buried kept assaulting me with sunken, supernatural stares. I slipped into my jeans and a t-shirt, swathed myself in a woolen scarf, draped my L.A. Dodgers jacket over my shoulders and headed out to make the seven a.m. train to Lisbon. The air was cool and crisp and shaded a misty purple. On the horizon, the Arrabida bridge was a gray rainbow protecting the black river. Porto seemed to me then to be a city with a dream landscape, a city of hills like the flanks of a human body falling toward a river filled with night;

of shamed thoughts and desires given form as alleyways and hidden courtyards;

of death wishes become windows lit with the single flicker of a harsh red light bulb.

Like a dream, Porto was a city which never presented an easy face. It welcomed the tourist not with the pat on the back of Lisbon, but with a cold hard stare. The Swedish campers, British birdwatchers and French intellectuals who wandered into Porto all left the city muttering, "What the hell was that place all about?"

Huddled in my baseball jacket, I cut past the ancient sycamores bordering Martyrs Of The Nation Park. Ahead was Clerigos Tower. Lit in arresting orange tones by floodlights, it looked like a giant granite pagoda. I cut right toward the Praça da Liberdade, Porto's central square. The dusky streets were windblown and empty, and maybe because of that I suddenly knew that all cities were the stuff of fear — conglomerations of foundlings glued together by collective panic. All these people huddled in their beds at the fortieth parallel in the north of Portugal had come together to deny the overwhelming emptiness of the wild dark hills to the east and the open ocean to the west — the symmetrical abysses of a world where men and women are always isolated and unable to reach one another and straining to flee the inevitable end. And with all that collective fear stored in one place, I also knew that cities were the stuff of nearly limitless potential — Pandora's boxes waiting for dawn to spill open their seeds and sparklers. In the great metropolises, London, São Paulo, New York, whole circuses and villages were hidden in these boxes for the night. Entire histories flowered in the morning. But my nerves could no longer take the commotion, the productions, the choice of roads to follow in these swollen capitals. I no longer had the resilience it took to bear the deracinated waifs fumbling for syringes, the go-getters barking stock prices, the brown snow in winter and sweating air conditioners in summer. I needed a city the size of Porto, a city poorer and less anxious, a city willing to stumble about in the twentieth century and let the fast trains and faster people pass by.

Even modern, brightly lit Porto was a city that watched and pointed toward the United States, then emulated what it could import, gave it a Portuguese twist by painting it mauve and white, or by scenting it with cod and tripe. Old Porto didn't even compromise that much with the outside world. Underneath the gloss of the street lamps, beyond the mirrored discos and pubs, was still the nineteenth-century Porto of old peasants with furry stubble in the caves of their cheeks, stumbling along in soiled gray pants with broken zippers, slipping their callused cocks out and peeing smelly and brown against the side of a collapsing building; the Porto of cackling old grannies with puckered sunburnt faces, dressed in black and smelling of wax, their sex as dry and wrinkled as elephant skin. It was this hump-backed Porto laden with the dead weight of dingy five-story townhouses and a population of gawking illiterates that attracted me first to the city. I loved the cracking plaster and chipped yellow tile, craved the very idea of a city which could bear in its bowels the carcasses of splintered wooden staircases and broken sinks and bedbugs. It was the Porto of backed-up sewage on medieval streets paved with dark lichenous cobbles and running with tubercular spittle that I saw when I closed my eyes at night — a city of oil-streaked windows hung with bug-eyed goat carcasses; of pastry shops and cafés with endless trays of caramel-smelling sweets made with only egg yolks and sugar the way they've made them for centuries; of legless shoeshine men wheeling their carts into smoky cafés where children were chasing one another and cats were scratching at fleas and dogs licking the scent glands under their friends' tails. It was a city made for a Kurt Weill musical, a place where Elisa Doolittle would have been happy to sell her violets and the Artful Dodger overjoyed to confound the police.

As I stared admiringly at the turrets of the neo-classic buildings of the main square, as I walked through the eastern districts, as I watched doors opening and women in aprons sweeping the sidewalks in front of their stores, as dawn came up and the town's clock began to beat, I realized that Porto, like all cities, was a fortress where men and women could bump into each other and eat like pigs and complain about the weather and build houses of cards under blankets and wash off the dirt of the world and avoid the single truth...

The truth that mortality was waiting for them just at the edge of town.

But every now and then, I thought, there comes to us that sudden silence — the silence after a bird's sharp screech or fog horn's bellow. It is in that moment that we detect the footsteps of a giant a long ways off. We look inwards and we think: *The Angel of Death is pacing in the wilderness beyond the city's outermost districts. And He is waiting for me.*

António was the progenitor of much of these thoughts, of course, and on the train to Lisbon my chest began to feel as if it were being squeezed in a vise. I wanted valium so bad that I actually hunted in vain in the recesses of my wallet in case an extra pill stored for emergencies had survived. I went to the bar, drank juice mixed with mineral water so that the bubbles would relieve the pressure building around my heart. I smoked a cigarette which I bummed from a ruddy-faced businessman wearing a black rug on his head who proceeded to talk to me about a gas pipeline that would come all the way up from Morocco to Porto by the year 2000. I don't trust the Portuguese behind the wheel of a car, so how could I trust them with a thousand-kilometer pipeline of combustible fuel? When I mentioned this preoccupation and pointed to the possibility that we might all end up as barbecued beef, he smiled and told me that *there was absolutely no risk involved.*

"No risk?" I replied. "A pipeline laid down by the Portuguese carrying highly volatile fuel, and you don't think we should already be planning our escape routes?!"

"It's just like everything else," he said. "It's all in God's hands." He nodded to reassure himself and added, "I always feel that if we do things the way we should, He'll make sure that nothing bad happens."

He didn't wear glasses, but Fiama would have said his eyesight was totally shot.

11

In Lisbon, there was a major commotion in the Rossio when I arrived because Julio Iglesias was in town for two concerts at the Estoril Casino, and it was rumored that he was eating in one of the outdoor cafés in the central square. As you know, the Portuguese are crazy about forming crowds and have a wide-eyed curiosity of anything foreign or ghastly. Julio Iglesias was foreign, of course, and was generally regarded as ghastly, so it was doubly interesting to them. The only thing better than seeing a pop star with a permanent tan and perfect teeth would have been seeing a few people killed in a big car wreck.

I didn't have to be at Bob's place to pick up the T-Bird until four o'clock and it was only ten in the morning, so I elbowed a few old ladies in black out of the way and made my way up to the Alfama district. I cashed Salgueiro's check at a branch of the Banco Nacional Ultramarino across the street from the Magdalena Church and took out an extra five hundred dollars from my account. It took awhile because they had to verify my signature over fax with my branch in Porto, but I eventually received eighty-four five-thousand escudo notes and placed them securely in an envelope in the breast pocket of my coat. From there, I continued along the route of the trolley cars to the Graça neighborhood to visit Barabas. He'd lived in Paris for several years, and I thought I'd quiz him about hotels for my trip.

Barabas is another of my friends whom you refused to meet, Carlos. He's only four feet two inches tall. He says he's a dwarf and maybe he is, but what's particularly encouraging is that he's a dwarf with *attitude*. He's got jet black hair cut into Mr Spock bangs just above his eyebrows and an earring in blood-red enamel of an elephant rearing up on his hind legs.

After we got some coffee together that morning, I asked him if his earring had any special significance. He replied, "An elephant never forgets."

"In this case, what doesn't he forget?" I asked.

He gave me an explanation which made quite an impression on me. He said, "When they were excavating some nineteenth-century houses by the river in Porto, they found tiny skeletons buried in the plaster of the walls. Most were aborted fetuses. But some were babies that had been born already. They discovered that the buried babies had been cripples and hunchbacks and dwarfs. I guess they knew from their bones. I learned then that I come from a race against which genocide has been practiced throughout the centuries. So I don't forget those babies."

Not just gays and Jews, I began thinking.

Barabas listened to my philosophical ravings about the cruelty of Man for a while, then said, "It was my mother and father who told me about those discoveries of dead babies in Porto. They showed me an article in the newspaper about it. My father looked me right in the eye... He was a stout and silent man, with the loveliest brown eyes. And he said, 'It's what we shoulda done when you was born, son.'"

"Why'd he say a thing like that?"

"Around my village the people said I was brought by the Devil. Kids used to call me *o anão do diabo,* 'the devil's dwarf'. People were always looking for my horns. Until I was thirteen, I really thought they'd sprout from my forehead one day. I used to look in mirror all the time." He suddenly lifted off his turtleneck. Deep scars crisscrossed his back. "My father used to beat me when he drank. I was a humiliation to him."

"What a fucking bastard," I said. "Is he still alive?"

"Still back in the village. I haven't seen him in years."

As Barabas slipped his shirt back on, I asked him if he knew the myth of Chronus. He shook his head. I said, "He was a Titan, the father of Zeus, Poseidon, Demeter and Hera. He started to eat his own children because he was fated to be overthrown by them. Some escaped. Including Zeus. Eventually, he took over Chronus' spot as King of the Gods."

"So?"

"People eat their kids out of jealousy sometimes. Like Miguel and António." I explained how the situation applied to them.

Barabas squinted. "And you think that my father was really jealous of me, too?"

"He must have known that despite everything you were intelligent and talented, that you'd get out of the village, get to Lisbon, Paris. He never got anywhere."

Barabas shrugged. "Maybe," he sighed. He made us tea, and I told him that I needed a nice but inexpensive hotel in Paris. He penned the name *Jean Floris* and a phone number on a used bus ticket. "He owns the Hotel Greco on the Place Saint-Sulpice," Barabas explained. "And he's on our team."

He meant that Floris was gay.

We sat at his kitchen table and talked about books for a while. I told him of my theory that magic healing incantations had been once known by Jewish kabbalists, but that they'd all been lost. He told me that there never had been any magic at all... Never.

When I left his flat, he came outside for a moment and kissed me on the lips.

Nobody stared. Nobody called us names. The ground didn't open up and swallow us.

You see, Carlos, it really isn't such a big deal.

After I left him, I walked to the top of a nearby hill for the view over central Lisbon — from here, a wide valley of orange rooftops ending at the Tagus River. I headed on to the Moorish Castle, sat on a bench and thought about things which you never think about when you're inside a house. Like the sky. And wind. And the attempts of composers to capture nature's beauty and turn it into a melody for flute...

or violin;

or voice;

or even guitar.

12

Bob, the Idaho expatriate who owned the T-Bird which I'd agreed to rent, lived in one of the new sections of Lisbon near the airport. It was a land of utilitarian concrete apartment houses painted bright pink and blue and yellow because that was some city planner's idea of how to keep things cheerful. I took a taxi. The driver was a black man from Mozambique who told me I looked unhappy. I said I was. He recommended a beach vacation and grilled shrimp.

When I rang the bell at Bob's apartment, a tall weedy guy with long brown hair answered the door. He was all smiles. He remembered me. I assured him that I remembered him as well, though I didn't. He wore high-top black sneakers, sweatpants and an Idaho State t-shirt. I figured he had gotten dressed for my visit, but he said that's what he always wore. His teeth were so white and large that they looked fake. He had tiny pimples all over his forehead. He looked like he lived on junk food. "Come on in, pal," he said, shaking my hand. "I'd offer you something, but I'm on my way out. We better get down to business."

I took out a wad of twenty-five five-thousand escudo notes, the equivalent of seven hundred and fifty bucks.

"So, what brought you to Portugal?" he asked as he counted the deposit. He was the kind of person who held the bills in one hand, licked his thumb and popped off each of the notes.

"Sex and death," I replied.

He tilted his head and nodded like I was a smart aleck and said, "But what really got you here?"

"The beaches."

"I hear you," he agreed.

While he counted the last of the bills, I glanced at the apartment. The place was a little nugget of the USA, complete with an Idaho State pennant and Idaho license plate on the wall above a dirty white couch. On the purple shag rug at the center of living room was a pyramid of Diet Coke cans. Everywhere was clothing and clutter and overflowing ashtrays. The place smelled like old cheese.

"It's all here," he said. He tossed me two keys on a ring. "The short one is the trunk, the other's the ignition. The insurance card is in the glove compartment. If she has trouble starting up in the morning, push the pedal all the way down twice, then start 'er up. She won't flood. Baby guzzles gas. She's in the lot to the left as you go out. Can't miss her."

Bob led me to the door and shook my hand firmly. "One last thing. There's a switch under the driver's seat. Just reach straight between your feet and you'll hit it. When it's flipped down, the whole electric system is shut off. Prevents robberies. Just flip it up to start the car. Got it?"

I nodded.

"Now when did you say you'd be back?"

"Two weeks, more or less."

"Goin' to Paris?"

"Exactly."

"I been to Paris twice," he said proudly.

"Mazeltov," I said.

"What?"

"Parabéns."

"You talking Portuguese?"

"Sort of."

"I been here ten years, but my Portuguese still isn't so hot. I guess I should be ashamed." He laughed.

"No big deal. I was just congratulating you on your adventuresome spirit. It's not every American who would risk a trip from Lisbon all the way to Paris."

"You know what they say. If you don't take any risks in life..."

"You won't get any snacks," I said, finishing his thought.

"That's not it," he frowned.

"That's the Portuguese version," I explained. "He who takes no risks, gets no snacks."

"You shittin' me?"

I crossed my heart and started away. He shouted, "You treat her right, now! And have a good safe trip!"

I turned and waved. Looking at him made me so grateful not to be in America that I started singing old fado songs that Fiama had taught me.

The T-Bird was black and immense and gorgeous. But filthy. And it stunk like old cigarettes. So the first thing I did was pull in to a car wash on the Avenida dos Estados Unidos da América. The guy who vacuumed the inside of the car wore a green uniform. He was real skinny and had large black eyes. He looked like he'd stepped out of a Martin Scorcese film. He discovered three eight-track tapes in the glove compartment — John Denver *Live*, Frank Sinatra's *September of My Years*, and Glen Campbell's *By the Time I Get to Phoenix*. When he'd finished his work, he offered me the equivalent of fourteen dollars a piece.

"You really want them?" I asked.

He held them up and smiled. "You kidding? They're collector's items."

"Sorry, I can't," I said. "It's not my car."

"Twenty bucks then."

I decided to sell him one to pay for the wash and wax. He took the John Denver tape. "My lucky day," he beamed.

The T-Bird had black bucket seats and a dashboard like an airplane — round dials everywhere. A bar from zero to 120 miles per hour recorded the speed. The tape player no longer worked. The AM radio got pretty good reception. The seat belts were blue and locked you into place.

I drove at ninety miles an hour on the freeway because the car hit its stride at that speed. It had so much inertia that it seemed as if you could coast a couple of miles once you got it going.

It took three hours to get from Lisbon to Porto because I stopped for a half-hour at the Mealhada rest area and got a dinner of roast pork and mashed potatoes. Eating just off the freeway, with the T-Bird waiting for me in the parking lot, gave me quite an appetite. I felt like I'd entered the Twilight Zone. I sang John Denver songs the rest of the way home.

It was hard finding a parking space in Porto because they just don't make spaces for Batmobiles in Europe. I finally had to create one by climbing up a curb on the Passeio das Virtudes and leaving it on the sidewalk.

When I got to the door of our apartment house, I found a graffito painted crudely on the door in white paint: *"Vou matar o paneleiro que vive aqui"* — "I'm going to kill the faggot who lives here."

I stared at it for a while, then I thought: *My little Moorish fruitcake, Rui, has paid me a visit.*

Apparently he'd found out where I lived. "What an asshole," I whispered to myself.

Inside, Fiama was in her powder-blue nightgown with the ink stains on the sleeves. "The prodigal son returns," she said. We kissed cheeks. "Know anything about the message below?" she asked.

"It's a Moor from the Algarve whom I misjudged completely. He doesn't like the fact that he's gay. Sorry. I don't know how he found out I live here. What a drag."

"Must've followed you. The Portuguese do that sort of thing. Anyway, listen. The whole world has been calling you and leaving messages on the machine. That drunken hunk who was here last night apologized for about five minutes; Salgueiro called to wish you interesting adventures on your trip; Ramalho wants you to call about Pedro's covering for your lessons at school; and Pedro wants to know why you didn't tell him that you wanted him to take over your classes. And António called, too. He just left his name and said for you to call him."

"That's all he said?"

She nodded.

"Did you save the message?"

She shook her head. "All he said was that he wanted to speak with you."

"How'd he sound?"

"Tired. Dry. Like he'd swallowed sand."

"How long ago?"

"A few hours maybe." She shrugged. "You eaten?"

"I stopped at a rest area on the way up from Lisbon."

"You went down to Lisbon?"

"I was picking up the car for our trip."

She frowned. "I would've made you something, you know."

Fiama is going to make a great mother someday. "You're sweet," I said.

"Some tea?"

"Nothing, thanks."

I was nervous because António had called, so Fiama held my shoulders while I dialed his number. Miguel answered. "It's me," I said.

"Professor, António's gone."

"Gone?"

"Gone. I had to go out to buy some things at the pharmacy. For him. And he just disappeared. I mean he wasn't here when I got back."

António had a concealed operatic personality, and I envisioned him jumping off the Dom Luis bridge downtown, two hundred feet to his death.

I realized I was catastrophizing but my heart was pounding wildly. "He'll come back," I said.

"I'm going insane," Miguel confessed. He started to cry again. I handed the phone to Fiama and said, "Try to comfort Miguel, I've got to go out."

I took a taxi to the Conservatory, figuring António would be in one of the practice rooms with his guitar, trying to keep depression at bay. When he wasn't there, I grew frantic. The muscles in my legs were knotted with desperation. I wanted to sit on the ground and cry. I walked to the city's main square. If I'd passed a pharmacy, I would have seen it as an omen from God and bought valium and eaten a half a dozen without any hesitation. Instead, I drank an espresso and a whiskey at the Café Majestic and bummed a cigarette from a man reading the sporting newspaper *Bola*. My heart was pumping as if it were trying to fill the whole place with blood.

Night was descending over Porto. I decided to walk to the Dom Luis bridge, after all; so much experience with death has not given me any faith in God, but it has convinced me that moments of impossible intuition occur. As I passed the Cathedral and Bishop's Palace, I decided to check there, too. I'd once given António a blowjob on the path below the Palace. Afterward, he'd said that if he keeled over then and there, he would die happy.

No sign of him. And he wasn't on the bridge. So I trudged home. Low and behold, he was sitting right in front of my apartment, at the center of one of the benches overlooking the great cavern below the Passeio das Virtudes. His back was to me. As I walked to him, I began singing 'Les Trois Cloches'.

He didn't turn.

I kissed the top of his head and put my hands on his shoulders.

He whispered, "I'm going to die very soon."

I walked around the bench, squatted down and held his head in my hands. I whispered, "Continue forward one day at a time."

He turned to me. His face was gray and drawn. He surveyed my haircut, then sighed. "None of it matters now."

"Why?"

"It's all nothing. Nothing."

I sat next to him on the bench. After a few minutes of silence, I said, "How can I help you?"

He shrugged.

It's amazing how one's fears are subdued by love. Looking at António, wanting to kiss his eyes, I wasn't afraid to die. I only didn't want him to suffer. In a few moments, I grew frightened again. But if I could have taken on his disease during those few moments of unqualified life and freed him, I would have. I put my hands on his thighs and made him look at me. "I will help you any way I can," I said. "If you need me to listen, I will sit in silence while you talk. If you need to hear someone else's voice, I will tell you stories or read to you. If you need me to hold you, I will hold you. And if you need me to make love, you can have me anytime you want."

He nodded. But I could see that there was an opaque wall in him through which my words would not be able to penetrate for some time. "My brother had shingles, too," I said. "And he lived for six years after that. Good years. Henry The Beast had eight years after his first infection. With any luck, we'll both live to see the year 2000. And by then, there may be better drugs. Meanwhile, we've got work to do. Your Cello Suite is a mess. If it's going to..."

"No music," António whispered.

I despised myself for having started to give him a pep talk. So we sat in silence. I was watching the sky, trying to distance myself from my emotions so I didn't melt like a puddle before him.

"Why don't you go?" he suddenly said. "I don't want to talk."

"I'll stay if you don't mind."

We sat without speaking for a while once again, then he turned to me and said, "Listen. I'm going to be horrible these next few weeks. I feel it in me. I'm going to scream at you and tell you you're a perverse faggot and that I don't want you in my life. I'm going to be a living hell for my father. I don't know why, but it's as if a demon is inside me and soon it's going to come out. Because I hate you. I hate that you're going to live and I'm going to die. I hate him for that too."

I started to protest and he got angry. "Just shut up!" he snapped. "I hate you both. And I can't forgive you or him. But what I want to say is that none of it is true. Or that there's more to it. I don't want you to leave. I want to play guitar more than anything. But I can't talk about that now, so don't make me. Let me hate you."

I nodded. I was thinking of my brother and his contempt for me. Having withstood that hurricane, I was confident that I could weather António's storms.

"But maybe it's not the best time to go away," he continued.

"On the contrary, I think it is. Now, while all this is new."

"Maybe."

"You know your father wants to go, too."

"He told me already."

"You want him along?"

He shrugged. He looked away for a moment. "Aren't you afraid of me?" he asked. I could rape you and give you Aids."

"I wouldn't let you rape me. I might let you make love to me, but never rape me."

"There's no difference between rape and making love when you've got what I've got."

"Sometimes, dear boy, you don't think straight. You wouldn't know how to rape a man because you don't hate anything enough. I've been raped more than once, and I can tell you that it's not what you think."

"You never mentioned that you'd been raped!"

So I told him about you, Carlos. When you were drunk and came to see me in the middle of the night just after my brother had died. "Oh, it's you, thank God," I'd said, half asleep. Remember? Because you had my key then and had let yourself in. So you slipped into bed beside me. And I snuggled back against you.

I smelled the alcohol on you and should have realized something was wrong.

You took out a knife and jabbed it into my earlobe.

I turned the scar to António, and he felt it between his thumb and forefinger. He said, "So it wasn't from an earring somebody tugged on?"

"Carlos did it. And he said, 'I never want you in my ass ever again. You're the faggot. Not me. I'm the man, you're the woman.' He proceeded to stick his ugly little cock up my behind and fuck me as if he wanted to kill me, all the time whispering hateful little things to me like, 'Take that in your pussy, you little whore,' and 'You're the woman and I'm the man.' I let him go on even though I could have thrown him off because I knew it would free me from him. Our relationship was already a disaster. But I needed this to free me. Because I'm the kind of person who will get depressed and put up with too much. I need to get totally enraged to free myself."

"You should've killed him."

"If I were to start offing people, I might never stop. Even today, every time I see a photo of Ronald Reagan, I think that being a serial killer in Washington DC would be kind of fun — certainly a job you could take pride in."

The boy rolled his eyes. "So that's what finally broke you and Carlos up?"

"More or less. I told him to get out. He apologized profusely. Brought me flowers. Gave me a wedding band. Made of petrified venom, as it turned out. We stayed together for a few weeks more. The strange thing is that I still loved him. And still do. But I know that I can't be with him until he accepts that he likes lying underneath a man. It's a small thing, really, but it's just too much for him."

"Strange guy," António said in English.

"Me or him?"

"Him. You, you're not strange." He switched back to Portuguese. "You're a bit daft, of course, but you're not strange. You're the most normal person I know."

I laughed at that. António showed the traces of a smile. We hugged. I held him to me and kissed his cheeks. I prayed so hard that he wouldn't die before I did that I began to shiver. Then I asked him a question for which I'd never gotten a satisfactory answer from you, Carlos: "Why is it that Portuguese men are so frightened of enjoying someone inside them?"

"They were told it was a sin."

"But it doesn't bother *you*. You never thought it was a sin, did you?"

"My sense is that anything I find so pleasurable can't be wrong."

"I admit it, I'm stumped."

"It's like Carlos said, they think it makes them a woman."

"I'll never understand that."

António shrugged. "Some things are cultural. You'll never understand them if you weren't born here. Like those big chunks of codfish you hate which we all love."

"But apparently you don't understand it either."

"I'm not wholly Portuguese."

"No?"

"No."

"What are you then?" I asked.

"Don't know. Don't care. An extra-terrestrial living temporarily in Porto."

We sat holding hands and looking at the stars. I began searching for António's home planet. "You know, they say there are 350 ways to prepare codfish in Portugal," I observed. "It's the most beautiful testament to human perversity I can think of."

I sat pondering cod, till António said, "My mother told me that she never wanted to see me again." He spoke dryly, without emotion.

"When?"

"I stayed over at her apartment last night. This morning, I told her about me. She flipped out."

"She'll change her mind."

"I don't think so. She said horrible things. She was crazy."

"Such as?"

"Such as, 'No son of mine could be *maricas*. It's genetically impossible.'"

"Genetically impossible? What's your mother know about genetics?"

"She works as a secretary in a biochemistry lab on the Campo Alegre. She hears words. She collects them and thinks she knows what they mean. She's not a bad person. She's just got these weird ideas." Like it explained everything, he said, "She's from a little town in the Minho."

"Some people think our way of loving is somehow different — all dark and sinister. Like we're vampires."

"I hope so," António said. He shrugged. "Vampires live forever."

We didn't talk again for a while. The boy broke the silence: "You know, I'm sure my mother must have sucked my father's cock and done all the rest. So she must know what it's all about."

"You would think so. Give her a little time."

António looked down. I could see him thinking that time was the one thing he wasn't sure of. I said, "Can we call your father? He's really worried about you."

"My father can go bore himself to death with his own lectures. Count me out."

"Then can we just go inside? I've had a long day. I'll make some tea. Maybe Fiama will sing us some fado. You can stay the night if you want."

"You wouldn't be afraid to sleep with someone like me?"

"You're still António. I'm still me. Nothing has changed that."

"Everything's changed. Even my name."

I shrugged casually, but a sudden constriction in my chest made me cough. "Everything, it's true," I said. "And me... I want desperately for nothing to have changed. It's funny how our hopes have so little to do with reality sometimes. Listen António, you gave me a warning about you. Now I'll give you one about me. Two warnings, in fact. The first is that I have a tendency to give encouraging wisdom at times like this. Just tell me to go back to New York if you see the edges of my yarmulke."

"Your what?"

"The hat Jews wear. Never mind. Doesn't matter. The other thing is that I sometimes try to make believe that things aren't the way they are. Remind me. Gently if you can. If not, then brutally. It doesn't really matter so much how you do it. I desperately want to live in the real world. So don't let me escape."

I'm not sure he understood what I was talking about, but he nodded his agreement. As we walked back to the apartment, he asked, "So what made you cut your hair like that?"

"I got sick of it."

He shrugged. "It's just hair. It'll grow back."

He read the graffito left by Rui on the townhouse door informing the world how he was going to kill the faggot who lived there. "What's that about?" he asked.

"Some asshole wants to get revenge because I was the little bird who whispered in his ear that he's gay. It's nothing that needs to concern us."

"You'd better watch out. Portuguese men get into fist fights and things all the time. He might really show up one day while you're here."

"If he does, he does. I'm not going to fight." We walked inside. "I'll let Fiama strangle him with one of her French bras."

António gripped my arm and said, "I'm not joking."

"Neither am I. She's become very protective of me."

As he walked ahead of me, I put my hands on his shoulders and steered him up the stairs to my apartment. Fiama was reading the Portuguese edition of *Cosmopolitan* while lying on the couch. They kissed cheeks. Fiama offered to make tea for everyone. Meanwhile I took António to my room. He sat on the end of my bed. He picked up a copy of the *Independent* Sunday magazine, flipped some pages, then said with casual, deadly aim, "You know, if it weren't for you, I wouldn't have Aids."

I was stunned to silence. I stared at him.

He looked up from his magazine with a contemptuous face. "Nothing to say?" he challenged.

"António, I didn't give you Aids. What am I talking about? You don't even have Aids — you're just seropositive."

"Well, whatever I have, you might as well have given it to me," he declared.

"What are you talking about?"

"Before I met you, I didn't even sleep with men."

"Don't lie! You'd slept with boys before. You told me that. You were hardly a virgin."

"With men, I said! Not boys!" he shouted.

"Boys, men — what's the difference?"

"The difference is that I wasn't sure I was gay till I met you. Maybe I'm not. Maybe loving you changed me."

My hands were suddenly trembling. A bloodcurdling scream was stuck in my chest and needed to get out. I ran to the kitchen and vomited into the sink.

Fiama said, "What's wrong? What'd they feed you at the rest stop?"

"Water!" I gagged.

She gave me a glass. As I was drinking, I heard footsteps. I made it to the living room in time to see the door closing. I ran to the verandah, and when he came through the front door of our building, I called to him. He wouldn't look up, just kept walking away.

I thought: *That boy's got deadlier aim than even my brother.*

13

I drank myself into a stupor that night and passed out sometime after the bells of São Bento Church tolled midnight. First thing in the morning, I dropped by Pedro's flat on the Rua de Dom Carlos de Castro to apologize for not discussing with him his need to substitute for me at the Conservatory of Music. His apartment was too bright. I kept shading my eyes. He gave me cup after cup of bitter maté tea and chided me for *poisoning my body with alcohol.* I hated the brew but his sharp, motherly words were soothing. We sat opposite each other on his black-and-white checked rug in the living room. He dropped down into the lotus position like a holy man. I leaned back against his couch with my legs out like a kid playing with blocks. He said, "It's not the extra work that bothers me, but you really should have given me some more notice."

"I know. I'm sorry. It's all been rather sudden. I seem to have lost my ability to predict my own behavior. Things happen to me. Like they used to happen to characters in Greek myths. Maybe I'm losing my mind."

"You're not losing your mind," he assured me. "You're just out of control."

"Same thing," I replied.

"Totally different."

"So will you substitute me?"

He frowned. "That was never the issue."

I took from my briefcase the music for the pieces which my guitar students were working on. I explained the difficulties each of them was having. When we finished, he said with South American gallantry, "Okay, that's decided. Now how are you going to survive two weeks on the road in the state you're in?"

"We'll see." I looked out his window. He's got the loveliest view of the gardens of the Museum of Modern Art. The lemon trees were bursting with yellow fruit. "Did you call up Landero at the Paris Conservatory yet?" I asked.

"No. I'm waiting to see if you really go."

"Just tell him to expect us in a week or ten days. Use your Uruguayan charm."

Pedro laughed. "What if I can't reach him? Or what if he's not going to be there? He does concerts out of town, I'm sure."

I shrugged. "I guess we'll wait for him. No point in coming back till we know."

He tapped my foot with his. "Treat yourself well," he said.

In the early morning, I tend to mimic my mother, and I said, "You're an angel." Pedro laughed at that and poured us more tea.

Later, as he walked me to his door, I remembered António's evil tone of voice when he accused me of having given him Aids. My discomfort must have shown on my face. Pedro asked me what was wrong. When I told him, he said, "Want some advice?"

"As long as it's not another lecture about doing evil to my liver with ouzo."

"I want you to spend enough time alone so that you have the strength to be with him."

I was surprised and grateful. He said in an excited tone, "Hey, remember my Brazilian friend Ricardo?"

"Sure."

"I got a call from him from Belmonte. He met up with that poet you know who wants to get a thousand tortured people on a mountain chanting toward Jerusalem. He's most impressed. He says that the guy doesn't make any sense at all, but that maybe that was the point. He also said to tell you that he's also been learning how to kiss like a kabbalist from a half-Jewish law student named Maria-Teresa. The secret is in your *lingua*," he told me.

The English translation for *lingua* could either be *language* or *tongue*, so I asked which he meant.

He shrugged. "Don't know. I'm quoting Ricardo. Maybe he wanted to keep the interpretation open."

We hugged goodbye. I asked, "You want anything from Spain or France?"

He shook his head.

"Clothing...? Wine...? There must be something... Some Julio Iglesias records? He's in Lisbon, you know."

Pedro made a gagging sound. "Maybe some books. I never get to read in Spanish anymore. See if there's any new novels from any Uruguayan authors."

"I thought you were through with Uruguay."

"May its leaders all drown in the Río de la Plata," he sneered. He reached up and cupped my chin in his hand. His black eyes fixed me in place. "But I can't give up on my *lingua*, can I?"

Back at home, I packed my canvas suitcase and yellow daypack, then got some sandpaper from Fiama's tool chest, slipped it over the spine of my *1994 World Almanac* and sanded the hateful graffito off the door to our apartment house. I took a hot shower. At five to eleven, I called Miguel and told him I was coming by for him and António. He said that neither he nor his son were ready yet. That wasn't a big surprise; the Portuguese are the world's most accomplished procrastinators.

"Look Professor," he said, "I don't know if this is going to work.

António...the boy..."

His words faded, and I thought that he might start sobbing again. I said, "Just don't panic."

"My heart won't stop racing."

"Trust me. All will go well."

"It won't."

"It will. Trust me."

I don't know what else I said, but I managed to get Miguel off the phone before he burst into tears. I left Fiama a note, doused it with counterfeit Polo aftershave which she'd given me as a gift and left her twenty thousand escudos in case any bills came that needed to be paid right away.

It took a half-hour to get to Miguel and António's house; it's way on the east side of the city by the Campanhã train station. Number 57, Rua Ferreira Cardoso. It was square and somber, looked as if it was haunted by nineteenth-century ghosts. Dark green tiles cut like brick decorated the outside. It had two upstairs windows fronted by a thin concrete verandah with a black metal railing. I double parked and rang the bell. The wooden door was painted cobalt blue. A transom of smoky glass was covered by a metal grill.

Miguel answered. He wore jeans and a yellow t-shirt. The hairs on his chest were peeking over his collar. He hadn't shaved. We shook hands. "Come in," he said.

"I'm double parked," I observed. "Let's get going if we can."

"I think I'm ready, but António... I'm afraid he's holed up in his room."

He spoke as if he was counting on me to coax the boy out. I stepped into the foyer. The walls were whitewashed. To my right was a wooden staircase that led to a second-floor gallery. I just kept staring at it like it meant something.

"He won't come down," Miguel repeated.

"If you want, I'll get him," I said.

"When you get to the top, turn right. The door at the end is his. The ugly one...the one that he spilled all different colors of paint on to make it look like some artist or other had done it."

I exhaled a mild laugh at Miguel's frown. I could see he wanted to smile, but he was at the stage where humor seemed a betrayal of his son. It would be a while before he would allow himself to relax. Years perhaps. And then, if António died... Carlos, I've learned that there are people who survive their dead children only in body: zombie parents of cursed queers buried in their youth. Life has begun to resemble a bad horror film from the 'fifties, hasn't it? In the last scene, all we see are pale fathers and mothers sleepwalking through their days and standing by their windows at night, taking advantage of the faint moonlight to stare at their children's photographs.

Miguel looked like a solid candidate for such a future.

António's door was splattered with spider webs of pink, yellow and black paint — an experiment he'd tried a couple years ago after discovering Jackson Pollock in my catalogue from the Museum of Modern Art in New York. I crossed myself twice for protection, a habit I'd gotten into when about to face my brother. I looked skyward, then knocked. No answer. I knocked again and feigned a gruff voice: "Open up, it's the thought police." When he didn't answer, I opened the door a crack. It was dark inside; the blinds had been drawn and curtains closed. António was lying face down on his bed, his head buried in a pillow. There was a tiny green glass bottle on his night table and for a moment I thought: *He's downed a dozen sleeping pills and killed himself.*

A small weak part of me would not have been sorry.

"Confucius say, time has come for Marco Polo to leave for the East," I announced.

Nothing.

I looked absently around the room, figuring that a kiss or any show of care would elicit another dart of vengeance from him.

He didn't utter a peep. I kicked a leg of the bed. "Hey you, time to go. We've got a date with some trendy cafés in Madrid."

He wasn't about to get up, so I walked to the window and opened the curtains. Light streamed in.

Imagine seeing a recurring dream open in front of you.

He was lying on the black-and-white striped quilt which we'd bought a year earlier at a store for Chinese and Japanese imports on the Rua de Santa Catarina.

The walls were painted olive green, the ceiling bright pink, exactly as he'd seen in Pedro's book on Mexican design.

The wicker hamper which we'd bought at the flea market in Espinho was under his desk.

On the bookshelf above his night table were all the American and British books in translation we'd found at the Livraria Bertrand: *Light in August, Portnoy's Complaint, My Dog Tulip, Songlines, Sirius, Tropic of Cancer...*

Spangled dust was suddenly billowing into an amphora around my head, and I was dizzy, as if the world were revolving slowly around me. António turned over and righted everything. His eyes were glassy and distant. "I don't want to go with my father," he said in English. His voice was crusted with hopelessness.

"Why?"

In Portuguese, he replied, "I hate him."

He looked at me as if he wanted me to challenge his answer. I closed the door so Miguel wouldn't hear and said, "That's a pretty good reason. But let's just give it a try anyway."

"No."

"Okay, then tell him you don't want him to come."

"You tell him. This was your idea."

"But I want him to come."

"Why?"

"Because he wants to — desperately. These days I try to give people what they want."

"What he *wants* is to keep track of me!" António raised himself on his elbows. His eyes opened wide. "He wants to keep track of you, too. He doesn't trust you with me. That's the only reason he wants to come. Don't let him fool you."

"Did you tell him about us?"

António sneered. "Worried, Professor?"

"Did you tell him?"

"No, I thought *you* were going to. The liberated American in The Land That Time Forgot, and all that other bullshit."

"I was planning on it. But I got chicken at the last minute."

"And you're supposed to be the guy who isn't ashamed of playing guard on the national basketball team of Sodom? That's a joke." He lay back down, stared up at the ceiling.

"Listen António, all the shame was kicked out of me by the Cossacks long ago. But I'm not stupid. At first, I thought he might bash my head in with the nearest cobblestone. Then... Look, he's fragile right now. I didn't want..."

"You didn't want to risk it for yourself. It's got nothing to do with my father. Be honest."

"Oh, so now you know me better than I do?"

"Someone's got to," he declared.

"And where did you amass all this wealth of psychological knowledge?"

He raised himself up again and leaned back against the wall. "From you, Dr Frankenstein."

"You're hardly a monster, and I'm no mad scientist."

He raised his eyebrows threateningly and said, "Wait and see what I turn into. You've even got me talking like you do."

I said, "If you don't want him to come, just tell him. You owe him that at least."

"You don't know shit!" he yelled. "I don't owe him one damn thing!"

"Who paid for your guitar lessons?"

"Money," he sneered. "That's always what it comes down to for Jews."

"That's beneath you," I said.

"Beneath me is where you always liked to be. So don't make believe you're upset. Take it like a man."

"Being clever only goes so far."

"'So far' is all I'll ever get to go. So go ahead and tell him we don't want him to come. You do it. You started all this."

"I already told you — if you want to plunge that knife in, you'll have to do it yourself."

"You don't think I will, do you?"

"On the contrary, I've learned recently that you're capable of saying anything. No matter how hurtful or untrue."

António turned away and licked his lips as if he were trying to look bored.

"You warned me," I observed. "And you're living up to your warning. But let's just have a break in this game for a moment. You're going to need your father's help to get through this..."

"There's nothing to get through. It's over."

I sat at the foot of the bed. "Now I see where you've erred. You're just beginning, my prince. It's a long slow war. It will help to have your father by your side. Maybe more than having me with you. And whether you like it or not, he loves you."

António puffed out his cheeks like a blowfish and shook his head like I was being an idiot.

I said, "And I also know...because you told me so...that you love him — desperately."

"That was a year ago when I told you that!"

"So...?"

"So, times change."

It was my turn to shake my head. "I'm not stupid."

Silence. António kicked his feet over the side of the bed, gave me his best glare and marched out. His footsteps slapped angrily on the wooden stairs. Downstairs, he shouted at Miguel: "It's you who's killed me, you know! You did it! If it weren't for you, I wouldn't be the way I am!"

There are moments of silence which one hopes will never end. But António slapped the stairs again and marched back into the room. He slammed the door. Avoiding my gaze, he lay down on the bed. He put his hands behind his head like he used to after we'd made love and looked up at the ceiling. He said, "Go ahead and tell me how disappointed you are in me."

"I'm not disappointed. I'm upset. And there's something I have to tell you."

"You promised me no pep talks or lectures, you asshole," he said in a voice so contemptuous of me that I could never have expected it from him. He seemed to be trying on a new personality. He said, "So shut up and get the car ready. I'll be down in a few minutes."

I stood up and kicked the side of the bed. "People are fragile, you little bastard! Me in particular. You hit people too hard, they break. Then you can't pick up the pieces. So be careful! And I've seen too many people die...people just as good and lovely and talented as you in their own ways...to put up with your attacks!"

António's arm swung over his eyes. I stood there listening to him whimper for a while, absent from my body, then sat on the bed and curled my fingers around his arm. He was trembling. "Don't you touch me!" he said with a painful cry.

"Shut up!" I yelled.

I curled up behind him on the bed. He resisted at first, but I hugged him and held him fast.

"If you touch me, you'll get it," he moaned.

"Shush. Let's just forget everything for a few minutes. Sometimes forgetting is the best thing." I squeezed him against me. He tucked his rear back into my lap and went limp. The bed became our nest.

After a while, the urge to flee Porto and never give another guitar lesson surged so strongly in me that I held him as hard as I could. I wanted to disappear into him, to cease to exist. "Think of Madrid," I said. "Think of Paris. We'll have an adventure."

I was talking to myself, of course.

When his crying subsided, he turned around. His breath came warm against my eyes as he told me he was scared. I caressed his hair, and he told me his when-I-first-realized-I-was-gay story. He said, "I was with my father in his home town. In Vila Nova de Cerveira. We were taking the ferry across the Minho River to Spain. I couldn't have been more than six or seven. He lifted me up over the railing for the view and put me on his shoulders. The river was lovely, black, reflective... Like a mirror made of night. But mostly I remember his powerful hands gripping my ankles, the feel of the hair at the back of his head against my belly. When he lifted me down, I looked up at him like I was looking at the Clerigos Tower. I remember thinking: *He's so tall and handsome and strong, and I would like to sleep with him at night.* I guess it was partly because my parents were having problems even then. I mean, I was scared all the time and needed his protection. But it was then that I knew that there was something different about me, that I was attracted to the shape of his mouth, his whiskers — above all, his hands."

"Did you ever tell him?"

"I started to once, just after I started sleeping with boys. But he got frightened, and he began telling me that I had to try to find the right path in life. He wouldn't even mention the word *homosexuality*. He said that a wrong path is like an addiction, and the farther I walked down it the harder it would be to get back to where I needed to be. He must have said the word *path* a hundred times during the whole drawn-out sermon. It was like an incantation. It was weird."

I told António another of the poisonous sentences in your farewell letter to me, how you said that if I would just try a woman, you were sure I would begin to understand what *real men* feel.

You know what my little Segovia said? "Sounds like one of Pavlov's dogs trying to convince a friend to salivate with him when the bell goes off."

It's not that he's necessarily brighter than you, Carlos, though he certainly is, but simply that he's far more honest.

Then I told the boy how I learned at the Bronx Zoo that I was gay. I was twelve, because it happened on a field trip we took in seventh grade. And I remember Karen Roberts being sent home because she was wearing pants and the school still had a dress code penned by some macho Puritan in the 1950s saying girls had to wear dresses. Anyway, a giraffe was responsible. He had the most elegant and powerful legs you've ever seen. If you'd have slipped black lace stockings on him, the whole seventh grade of Woodfield Junior High would have come in their bell-bottoms. What caught my eye was that the calf muscle of his right leg had spasms every now and then. His whole leg would shimmy. I'm not sure why this tripped a switch in my brain, but the next thing you know I was looking at the legs of all the boys in the class, and the powerful thighs of a particular gray-haired zoo keeper in khaki shorts with his shirt off whose shoulders were so attractively sweaty that I nearly swooned and who was looking down into the moat separating the giraffes from the public as if he'd lost something.

I realized all of a sudden that there was some magnet in me that had been pointing all my life toward that man.

"So what are we going to do about your father?" I asked António when I'd finished my tale.

He snorted and replied, "He'll just get in the way."

"Is it that, or are you afraid to have him see you twenty-four hours a day? Afraid of what you might show him?"

"Don't know."

I began combing António's hair with the back of my hand because he looked so lovely and vulnerable, and I wanted to see what he'd look like with bangs. I daydreamed about taking him to the barber as a child. All was well. Then, for no seeming reason, my heart suddenly went wild. I sat up and started heaving to try to get oxygen into my lungs.

"What is it?" António shouted.

It was an anxiety attack. A 7.0 on the Richter scale — the first real big one I'd had since my brother's death. I'd forgotten how they shook my ribs and clenched my gut.

valium, I thought. *I've got to have a valium!*

António brought me water and held my hand. I lay face-down into his pillow to escape into darkness.

When I was calm enough to turn back over, he brought me a warm towel to wipe the sweat from my face and neck. I sat up. He asked, "What happened? You scared me."

"It's no big deal. It's a symptom of battle fatigue. My heart gets pretensions of being a kettledrum. No matter, twenty minutes later I'm ready for action again."

But I was lying; it was a big deal. Why? Because I realized that what caused this particular internal earthquake was the simple daydream that António was a kid in need of a haircut. I wanted him to be my son, you see. And that seemed to change everything.

"So what should we do about my father?" he asked.

"My intuition says that he should come," I replied.

Did I now want Miguel along so that the reality of António being just my student could be maintained?

The boy closed his eyes. "I'm afraid of him," he whispered.

I rubbed his cheek. "Why?"

"That he'll have an explosion of anger, and I won't be able to take it. I can't take his sermons anymore. Not now. You don't know what they're like."

"I'm sure he won't be making any for a while. He told me the other night that he realized he was at fault in not letting you come to the Conservatory, that he was jealous of you."

"Jealous?"

"That you could be so much more than he is, that you have talent, that you won't be just a stone mason. I don't know what he was like before, but I think he's already changed quite a bit." I kissed António's forehead and sat all the way up. "Sometimes parents have to evolve to keep up with their kids, you know. If they don't evolve, they lose them. He doesn't want to lose you. More than anything else he wants to know you. He told me that that's why he wants to come."

"I'm not so sure. He's not as simple as he lets on." António winked like he does when he's discovered a scheme or secret — his right eyelid trembles like a canopy in the wind and his left eyebrow lifts into a circumflex. "He's cunning," the boy said. "Know what my mother calls him? 'The wolf in sheep's clothing.' He may be fooling you. You know you do have a weakness for believing anything a handsome man tells you. If the Pope were Sean Connery, you'd race to the baptism font."

I laughed. "All right, so maybe he also wants to keep an eye on us. But that's natural, too. Would you prefer that he didn't want to look after you at this moment in your life?"

"No, but it's all so complicated. You don't understand."

"I'm sure I don't. Only you can."

António shook his head and frowned. "I guess I should go downstairs and apologize."

"If you want. Or just tell him that you want him to come. He'll understand the rest."

The boy stood up, shuffled around the bed to the door like a kid forced into doing a chore, then reached out and held the frame with both his hands. He turned around. His expression was grave. "I don't want to die, you know. That's why I... I..."

"I know," I said.

"You won't leave me?"

"I'll be with you." I reached out my hand. He gripped it hard. We stared at each other. There was too much to say. I said, "When my brother was sick, he told me something I've always remembered that may help. He was religious, had converted to Catholicism. One day, I was in his hospital room and he quoted to me a line from Psalm Twenty-Three which says something like, *Though I walk through the valley of the shadow of death, I will fear no evil...* You know it?"

Antonio shook his head. "I never read the Bible," he said. "I prefer non-fiction."

I smiled. "No matter. I'd always thought of the *shadow of death* part as the most significant image in that line — when I first heard it, I pictured a caped figure standing in the desert and casting a frigid shadow. But Harold said that for him the important thing was the simple act of walking. 'If you're going to die, you don't want to run,' he told me. 'But you don't want to stop either. In spite of what's facing you, you walk... You just walk.' I'm not sure why it was so important, but it was."

António shrugged and dropped my hand. "Doesn't mean anything to me."

"Yes," I said. I'd forgotten that for him disbelief was stronger than fear at the moment. Later, perhaps, the simple act of walking through one day at a time would mean something to him. Or maybe not. People are different and need different things. The only thing they share, I've found, is a need to be heard. So I said, "I promise to listen." He nodded. Then he left me alone in the room.

14

It was my mother, a child of Jewish peasant immigrants from Lodz, who told me that you can tell a lot about people in the modern world from their luggage. This was just before she gave me a present of an enormous Gucci leather suitcase back in September 1971, the week before I was to leave for college at NYU. I rolled my eyes and told her, "Thanks a lot, Mom. With this, my roommate'll be able to tell I'm an asshole right away." My mother has shrunk since, but she was a feisty five foot one at the time. She raised herself up and pointed a stiff finger toward my nose and said, "Wait and see... Your roommate will be jealous." As the casual coup de grace, she said, "Oh, and your father and I have decided that we're dropping you at the dorm." That was the last thing I wanted, and I brokered a deal which she eventually accepted: *I'll use the new suitcase you bought me if you let me take the railroad into Manhattan and sneak into my room like an orphan.* Moral of the story: I get to my dorm and my first freshman roommate, Bob 'Jerkoff' Birkoff, the stamp-collecting Grand Funk Railroad freak from Princeton, New Jersey, takes off his reflective sunglasses and ogles my Gucci suitcase like it's come through a time warp. On his bed is one of those indestructible American Tourister suitcases with a metallic rim that they used to give away on game shows like *Let's Make a Deal.* Open, it looked like a giant clam. Out of it had spilled the first polo shirts and Jordache jeans I'd ever seen. Bob confessed to me right away that he was *green with envy* over my luggage. He was the most precious heterosexual I have ever known, and since that time, I've had to accept that my mother is more in tune with modern psychology than I am.

Naturally enough I heard my mother tapping her judgmental foot beside me as I watched António and Miguel load their things into the T-Bird. Miguel lugged out a large red plaid suitcase which looked like it had just been vacuumed clean after thirty years at the bottom of a closet. My mother was telling me: *Poor szlub — it's the same suitcase he brought with him to Porto from his hometown thirty years ago. Probably still smells of the sausage and cheese his saintly mother was kind enough to pack for him.* António had one of those utilitarian nylon bags that are sold at flea markets all over Portugal. But he'd slipped some extra things into a yellowing pillowcase, then tied a piece of twine around the top. He dropped it into the gaping trunk of the car with a thud. "An extra pair of sneakers," he explained.

My mother whispered to me: *Be a good boy and buy him some Italian shoes in Madrid.*

António hadn't commented on the T-Bird, so I said, "What d'ya think?"

"It's okay," he answered.

"Okay?"

"Yeah, okay."

I patted the hood. "It looks like the Batmobile. Haven't you noticed?"

"So?"

"Never mind. Did you bring your sheet music?"

"I told you, I don't want to play my damn guitar!"

"No matter, I've got the Bach," I said with a dismissive wave. "We'll work on that." I figured he would play the Cello Suite in C for his audition in Paris.

The secret of our mission warmed me.

"You don't let go," António said, shaking his head.

"No. Never. It's one of my endearing qualities."

He frowned like I was a dead weight around his neck, which was exactly my intention, and then slipped into the passenger seat. "This car door must weigh a ton," he said in disgust.

I turned to Miguel. "You all ready?" He nodded as he took the last puff of his cigarette. He opened the back door and got in head first. I dropped into the driver seat. I sensed myself having just walked on stage in some play Eugene O'Neill never wrote but should have, and that I'd forgotten to memorize my lines. My heart was pumping like a metronome on *scherzo,* and I was convinced that its springs were going to break at any moment. "Where's the nearest pharmacy?" I asked.

"What do you need, Professor, maybe I got it," said Miguel gallantly.

A courteous heterosexual father spying on his son's queer teacher was not exactly what I needed just then. I eyed him in the rearview mirror and answered "valium" without bothering to give it a Portuguese pronunciation.

António pointed straight ahead and said, "I'll show you. It's up there."

I started up the Batmobile. Miguel asked, "What's valium?"

I turned around to face him. I should have been impressed that there was someone left in the world who hadn't yet heard of God's incarnation on Earth, but I was pissed off. He was sitting with his hands between his legs, as if he were chilled. His graying hair was unkempt, and he still hadn't shaved. The skin around his eyes was wrinkled like he hadn't slept in weeks. Looking at him, I realized that António might have been right. Maybe he'd fooled me with his heroic admissions of jealousy and guilt. He simply wanted to keep an eye on the homo from America and his protégé as they rocketed their way into Old Castile and the heart of Gallic Europe. I was insane for allowing myself to get trapped like this. "You can have one yourself and see," I said, suddenly desiring to corrupt him. Shifting into drive, I had a momentary fantasy about Miguel passed out in the back seat of the Batmobile as we crossed the Estremaduran plain — two mad gay terrorists and their heterosexual hostage.

When we got to the pharmacy, I told myself I'd keep the tranquilizers in my pocket *just in case*.

The typical addict's excuse, of course.

The pharmacy was one of those ancient places with little wooden drawers lining the walls and a balance for weighing yourself in the corner. The marble counter smelled as if someone had spilled Vick's Vapo-Rub just a few moments earlier. Three tiny women in white smocks smiled at António and me as we entered. I pronounced the magic name of the only deity I've ever been convinced exists — *valium*. And I thought: *Maybe this time, He'll lower me gently into the underworld and I can give up the struggle.*

Behind the counter were five white ceramic jars glazed with blue names: Noz Vomica, Flor Cinae, Belladonna, Ung. Populeum and Arnica Montana. While we waited for a pharmacist with frosted blond hair to bring out God to me from the back room, I asked António if people still ordered such things.

"Before tranquilizers people had other ways of slipping away," he replied.

God turned out to be housed in the old familiar green and white box. The brand name was Victan. I remembered it well; it had been my first purchase after moving to Portugal. Like the old addict I am, I checked right away the lettering indicating that there were still sixty pills inside — a full month of ministering in the doses I needed.

Miguel had waited for us back at the double-parked T-Bird, was sitting with his legs out the door, puffing away like his life depended on nicotine. António snapped, "I told you, I don't want you smoking in the car. Don't be so inconsiderate."

Like most ex-smokers, the boy was vehement in his contempt for tobacco.

"Sorry," Miguel said. He tossed his vice away.

António marched over to it and stubbed it out with his sneaker. He turned back to his father and glared. "You think people want to breathe that shit in the street?!"

Miguel's eyes had gone glassy. I thought: *Two aging masochists and a kid whose dials are set on RAGE; this is going to be a fun trip.*

"Everybody back in the car, and not another word!" I told them.

We drove in angry silence to the freeway, the Victan safe in my shirt pocket. I was really glad to get the Batmobile up to 120 kilometers per hour, the speed at which she started to coast under her own weight. "Now leaving Porto at Warp seven-point-five," I said cheerfully. No one replied. Maybe they'd never even seen *Star Trek*, though that seemed impossible. Miguel read the soccer results in *Bola*. António sat with his hands between his legs — exactly like his father, as it turned out — and watched the scenery with a stiff expression. He looked so pale and hard that I began fantasizing about working on our tans in Madrid's Retiro Park like a couple of Central Park homos. After a while, I began to notice that the broom bushes along the side of the road and in the center strip were all in bloom — wild and harsh and absolutely festooned with flowers like canary yellow popcorn. "Pretty," I said to António, pointing. He nodded. I said, "You want music, we got a radio." I turned it on. Phil Collins was singing some song I'd never heard. "That guy's everywhere," I said innocently. António snapped it off. He leaned his head against the glass like some forlorn alien dreaming of his home planet a thousand light-years away. I looked in the rearview mirror and found Miguel with the newspaper over his face. Very carefully, I slipped my hand onto António's thigh and squeezed. He didn't look at me. After a while, I withdrew my touch.

I wanted to take a valium so badly that my legs were trembling.

We got on the IP5 at Aveiro and started heading east. The sun was high in the blue sky, and everything looked wonderfully clear. There's a part of the road where you rise up over some scruffy hills and get a panoramic look back at the coast before you disappear into the Caramulo mountains. I pulled over to the side of the road. My legs were so tense by now that they were aching, and I wanted to stretch them. António had seen me go through my ritual before, so he didn't laugh or stare. But Miguel was fascinated. He let the smoke curl out of his nose as he stared at me. As you may recall, Carlos, the ritual goes as follows: I first sit down and take off my sneakers. Then, with my right hand, I grab the heel of my right foot and stretch my leg straight over my head and maintain it stretched for a count of sixty. I can actually feel the muscles unclenching. Then I do the same with the left leg. Symmetry is the rule for such things. I learned this from a ballet dancer I'd made love with once in his dorm at the North Carolina School of the Arts in Winston-Salem and who had muscles in places where normal people just have skin and tendons. I say this because Miguel asked where I'd learned these exercises, and I didn't lie. I said, "From a ballet dancer I slept with in the States." I used the masculine form of the word for ballet dancer, *bailerino*. António looked between us as if he was waiting for a bomb to go off. But I figured that if Miguel didn't like my being gay, he could...

a) go fuck himself, and

b) walk home to Porto before we got too far away.

Miguel simply took a greedy inhale on his cigarette and nodded. He said, "We used to do similar exercises for gymnastics. There was a time when I could do a split, you know."

I pictured Miguel's buttocks parting like the Red Sea and me, an exiled Israelite, hoping to jump inside. Before I had to hide my expanding covenant with Elohim, I said, "Time to get going again," and slunk into the driver's seat.

I was thinking: *So now Miguel knows. Or does he? Maybe he just thinks I made a mistake in Portuguese and that I meant 'bailerina'. Or is he biding his time? Maybe he'll sneak up on me in our hotel room tonight and choke me to death, all the time spitting curses at me for having perverted his son.*

The violence which I sensed in him was there all right, as I found out a little later. At the time, however, I figured that I was just over-dramatizing; ever since the viral eclipse over homosexuality, I have tended to believe that worst-case scenarios are the only ones that come true.

As I look at it, dear Carlos, a modern-day Cassandra needs no special powers to see into the future; just half a brain and the good eyesight Fiama so cherishes.

António started munching on his cuticles as he slouched in the car; fingernails are off limits to classical guitarists, so the next best thing are those sweet little crescents of delicious skin.

Miguel sat with his hands under his legs. I understood now it was to keep from reaching for a cigarette. Apparently, we each had our constrictions here on our trip. I, for instance, couldn't use certain words — supplicating verbs like want, need, hope and wish. They had gripped their talons into my chest, but I dared not utter them to António. So I watched the broom bushes on both sides of the road as they dazzled their way like a thousand yellow chandeliers up the hillsides — hillsides we first approached, then climbed, then left behind with the sound of wind. We were in the Caramulo mountains, latitude 40.39 north, longitude 8.24 west. Here, it was easy to forget Porto, the Conservatory, my mother, the past, you, dear Carlos, even António's illness. Tension loosed its hold on me. It was as if bandages long wrapped around my body were slipping away. The past and present were only shades here, nothing more than far-off scents from a future century unable to haunt the sunlit June of a landscape which Van Gogh might have painted had he kept the colors of his famous sunflowers on his palette: orange, yellow, the pink of apple blossoms, a dewy verdigris, and the silver-green of the ancient olive tree.

Take a fresh canvas out, Carlos, paint a landscape with those colors and maybe you'll be able to see where we are. Try to imagine you're painting by numbers and don't leave out the...

towering eucalyptus trees guarding the sides of our road;

the pines looking up at them;

the ferns sprouting from the forest floor;

and the broom bushes, still yellow, still ribboning the hills.

There's a black and white dog chained to an *espiguero,* too. What's the word for that in English? A *granary*, that's it. Paint the black and white mutt chained to the granary with his furious snout wide open, a bark caught in time and muffled by my window.

Here in the hinterlands of Portugal, where orange-roofed houses sit like unchallenged monopoly pieces in valleys draped with grape vines, Aids did not exist. How could it? How could a virus just a thousand angstroms in length — hardly more than a few tinker-toy molecules joined at a microscopic hip — appear from out of nowhere during the last quarter of the twentieth century? How could they curl up inside scrotums and vulvas across the planet and cause so much unhappiness?

How would you paint this disease, Carlos? What color is an Aids virus? Has no one ever asked you? Have you never thought of it? Then perhaps you've never known anyone who's died of it, and I envy you. But it would be something heroic for you to put on your canvas: The Color of Aids.

Carlos, maybe your ancestors are even from these hills, from that little hamlet of sad little houses nestled into that sloping hillside up ahead which hasn't changed its Aztec's-nose contours since the Druids sent their ships from Ireland south to Portugal looking for... For what? The sun of lower latitudes? God? The last, fatal corner to a flat world? I have only to squint a bit and I can see them clearly, setting up camp just ahead in a serpentine twist in a rivulet. Yes, even crazed old Druids draped in white linen robes, slumping a bit under the weight of their iron jewelry, are more alive in this outback than Aids. Here, at the very edge of Europe, in an Appalachia where nobody speaks English, the calamities have never changed and they aren't viruses. Here, it's the gray winter storms sent by Zeus and — even worse — the summer sun of Hera. She stares down at the fields, sets over the sea where centuries earlier sons left with da Gama for India and never came home. Heat rises from baked earth. The edges of leaves brown and curl like ancient manuscripts. Flowers, sick of the struggle, wither and drop. In town cafés hung with posters for bullfights fought forty years ago by grandfathers long buried, men who've never had X-rays penetrating their leathery skin down glasses of sour green wine and talk of drought as if it were their parasitic uncle who comes back each year to eat them out of house and home. Here, it's almost logical to believe in the ancient deities, even the Grand Old Tyrant of the Torah. It's easy to imagine that God hasn't died after all, that He's been exiled from the capitals of our world to these countrysides like some silly second cousin who never should have left the farm in the first place and who, in the cities, just gets lost standing on street corners singing rap music in a voice so out-of-tune with our century that you just have to shut your ears to it and hope He'll go away.

And so, António is not ill, after all. He's safe here. We're safe. And we are driving to Madrid to drink *horchata de chufa* mixed with rum and pineapple juice in celebration of having entered another century.

These are the thoughts I have, dear Carlos, because neither António nor Miguel will talk to me, and my hands are stuck on the two-and-ten position on the black steering wheel and my mind refuses to believe that the worst has happened. Call my denial a relapse, if you want. The crazy whore who took two steps forward has now taken one back. Or maybe it's simple cowardice, *cobardia*. You who were always creative in the service of contempt can probably come up with an even better word for me in Portuguese.

15

Just outside of Viseu we pulled in to a British Petroleum rest stop, everything painted garish green and yellow. We'd been on the road for two hours. António didn't look like he was going to budge from his seat. He had the face of a kid determined not to have a good time because the one thing he really wanted has been denied him. But he hadn't been a kid in a long time, of course, and the one thing denied him I couldn't give him, so I chirped, "Time for lunch," like I was my mother and I'd just prepared tuna-fish salad sandwiches.

"Not interested," he replied.

"You want anything from inside...yoghurt, candy, something to read...?"

"Not unless they sell cocaine," he said with an open look of possibility.

I glanced back at his father. Did Miguel know that his boy's constantly runny nose three years back wasn't just a lingering flu? Apparently so. He stepped out of the car without a moment's hesitation and stood by the passenger side door. He lit a cigarette.

António had mentioned cocaine to provoke another argument, of course. But I simply said, "Then you don't want anything?"

"Nope."

"We'll be quick," I assured him.

"Take as long as you want," he replied, and he turned away from me.

Miguel and I walked to the restaurant. "You want a cigarette?" he asked. He was calm. Was he getting used to the snapping turtle with the terminal illness that had become his son?

"No, thanks," I replied.

Miguel halted suddenly and looked around the parking lot as if searching for something lost. He settled his gaze on me like he was trying to figure me out. "Is he still on something?" he asked.

His jaw was throbbing, and I realized he was a teeth grinder, like my brother.

"You mean drugs?" I questioned, as if I didn't know perfectly well what he'd meant.

"He mentioned cocaine just now."

"Oh, that... He was never really addicted. It was mostly before I knew him. I'm sure he doesn't take anything anymore."

"Just like you were sure he wasn't sleeping with any dangerous boys... And sure about this Aids thing inside him."

"I never said that."

"No, you never did, did you? But you must have thought that or you would have done something, right?"

This was the side of Miguel which António had warned me about. "What are you trying to say?" I asked.

"Nothing." He licked his lips, and we started walking again. I could hear him thinking: *Not just a faggot, but cocaine too.* I imagined him repeating those words to himself like prayers counted on a rosary, and each repetition making him grind his teeth a little bit harder. By the time we got back to Porto, we'd need to fit him for a full set of dentures.

At the door to the restaurant, I said, "I told him frequently only to have safe sex." I took a newspaper clipping from a few years back from my wallet. The headline was: *'Preservativos: 60% sem qualidade'* — 'Condoms: 60% Unfit for Use'. I read the article to Miguel. Fourteen condom brands available in Portugal had been subjected to strength tests. Eight had been classified as totally unfit for use. Harmony Normal was the only one classified as *muito bom,* very good.

"What's the point?" he asked impatiently.

"I read this same article to António when I found out he was sleeping with other young men, and we went to the pharmacy together to buy him his first dozen Harmony Norals. I used to look in his wallet to make sure he was using only this brand. I couldn't watch him every minute, but I was going to make sure that he used a condom that would protect him."

Miguel nodded like he was too tired to argue about being lied to. I said, "Maybe you're the one who should have told him more about sex and life and death before it was too late."

His jaw started throbbing again. He held the door for me and said, "After you, Professor."

We sat at a counter. It was like an American truck stop. A balding waiter in a dirty white shirt came to take our order. Miguel got fried sardines. I ordered soup and salad. We didn't talk. Miguel lit another cigarette and let the smoke curl out through his nose like he does.

"Can we start over?" I asked.

"Start over?"

"If we're going to get along on this trip, we've got to trust each other."

"I don't really know you," he confessed.

"True. And yet you just implied that I didn't do enough for António."

He started fidgeting with the top button of his t-shirt and swiveled around to face the parking lot. As he looked at me again, he said, "When I was young, I used to stare at myself in the mirror a lot. People said I was vain. My father used to tell me over and over what a conceited asshole I was. But they didn't get it. I thought I was ugly and scrawny. I simply couldn't believe that during my one lifetime, I'd been sentenced to live with an ugly face and body. Before my father's stroke, he was really strong, you see — a real man. Handsome, too. That's one of the reasons I started gymnastics. To get muscles. Anyway, I used to call other people names a lot. I tried to believe that they were the ugly ones. But later, when I got older, when I left my father's house, I started thinking other people weren't so ugly after all. Women were suddenly pretty. Inside his house I was one thing, away from it another. It was like magic." He put his hand on my shoulder. "I didn't mean you, just now, when I said what I said. I meant me. Me." He was fidgeting with his button again, and it popped off his shirt, landed on the tile floor. I started to get off my chair to retrieve it, but his hand gripped my shoulder. We stared at each other for a while. The ash was curling on the end of his cigarette, and he was holding me like he wanted to pull me to him. My heart was pounding out a code which said: *Take the leap and reach for him.* He said, "Forget the button. When I broke up with my last girlfriend, I stopped buying clothes. Everything I own is disintegrating. I hope they all crumble to nothing." Ash dropped from his cigarette to his jeans. "Shit," he said. He took his hand from my shoulder and looked down at himself. He brushed himself roughly. "These jeans, this shirt," he said, "I bought them both on a trip to Lisbon. In some old store downtown. I remember buying them so well. It was years ago. But these last few days, I can't seem to recall a thing. I think I've got amnesia. I don't even know who I am." He stared at me again. "You know, I can forgive António for everything but hurting himself."

"He loves you dearly."

"You think so?"

"He's always loved you. He used to fantasize about you."

Miguel stubbed out his cigarette angrily. "That's no good."

"Why?"

"You don't fantasize about your father."

As he said that, I began to suspect that Miguel had dreamed of sleeping with his father, too. He'd called him *handsome — a real man.* Our trip together hadn't become some Eugene O'Neill play after all, but a South American epic novel beating with unspoken desires passed down from generation to generation.

I said, "I'm gay, you know."

"I've known for a while."

"So you were testing me on the verandah of my apartment when you confessed to me that António was gay?"

"I was seeing how you'd react."

"And you know, of course, that I slept with him for about a year. When we first met."

"I'm not a professor, but I'm not stupid."

"No. That you're not. It doesn't bother you?"

He shrugged. "There's nothing I can do about it."

"If there was something you could do, would you do it?"

"I can't say I don't wish António weren't gay. But wishing won't make it so."

"António's fine being gay," I said.

"Is he? Is he really?!" He leaned toward me and whisper-screamed, "Tell me what's so fine about being sick with this Aids thing!"

"That's caused by a virus, not by his being gay," I replied.

Miguel frowned as if that weren't the correct reply.

I watched a woman dragging her son through the parking lot for a while, then said, "Tell me more about your father and mother. Tell me about your childhood."

"Why do you want to know about my parents?"

My soup came. I said, "When I was little, my mother and father used to read me Doctor Doolittle books. Since then, I've always liked to hear stories."

"There's not much to say. My father was a stone mason. My mother..."

I slurped my soup and didn't look up at him, because I'd begun to realize that Miguel didn't like being watched.

"My mother... I don't know her well. She's silent. I grew up mainly with my father." He lifted his hands. "I've inherited these from him. That's all I got. He gave the farm to my older brother."

"But what do you remember about him?"

"He liked to sit in front of the fireplace and drink brandy and fall asleep. He was bow-legged and waddled when he walked. He was strong. The strongest man I've ever known. He liked dogs, but he played with them roughly and never took them to the vet. When they got sick, he let them die in a shed we had. They would howl and howl. His face was hard, dark, like coal. You couldn't tell what he was thinking. He passed judgment like God. Once, he told me that he wanted to go to Brazil to see tropical fish. He said there was no color in our lives in Portugal. After that, he slapped me across the face and said, 'Don't ever tell anyone I told you that.'"

I continued eating my soup. Miguel said, "What's it like?"

"Tasty, but a little too salty," I replied.

"I mean, what's *it* like?"

"What's what like?"

"Being gay."

I was tempted to say something amusing, but Miguel was gravely serious, so I replied, "It's like being straight. No different. Didn't you ever consider sleeping with a man?"

"No." But then he said, "A friend on our gymnastics squad once asked me. We were drunk. For a moment, I considered what it would be like. But I knew it was wrong. For me, I mean. It just seemed..."

I didn't face him, so as not to frighten him, but he didn't explain any further. He said, "I want to understand António. I want to know what makes it right for him. What he feels. I want your help in understanding him."

"Okay. But my first concern has to be him."

He squinted at me. "You know something, I can see sometimes why António likes you so much."

"My good looks or my personality?" I smiled.

He shrugged and said, "His doctors say that his blood counts are still good."

That was a subject I wanted to avoid. I grunted an acknowledgment and checked for the valium in my pocket. He said, "You're okay, aren't you? I mean... I mean your blood, with the..."

"My tests are all negative. I'm fine."

We were silent for a while. My salad and his sardines arrived. I ordered a toasted ham-and-cheese sandwich for António. "He's bound to get hungry sooner or later," I explained.

"He trusts you, you know," Miguel observed.

"I'm glad for that."

"He doesn't trust me."

"I don't know. I don't know anything. I can't find all the things I used to be sure of."

Miguel shoveled the food into his mouth as if trying to win a race, then downed two espressos and smoked two more cigarettes. We went together to the bathroom. As he peed, he said, "God, that feels good." I wanted to investigate the source of this pleasure; by now, it's become an automatic response to the sound of running water. "I'll meet you outside," he said, finishing up. He zipped himself and patted my shoulder.

Miguel was waiting for me just outside the door to the restaurant, his hands thrust deep into his front pockets. We sauntered together back to the car like two doomed men gathering their courage for the gallows. I slid into the driver's seat and handed the bag with the grilled ham and cheese sandwich to António. He stared at it with a puzzled face and sniffed. "What is it?" he asked. When I told him, he chucked it onto the back seat and said, "Did you get me something to drink?"

"No — you said you didn't want anything."

"But you got me the food. What did you expect me to wash it down with?"

"I'll go back and get him something," Miguel offered.

"No you won't!" I said.

I lifted my hand to António's shoulder. He knocked it away. "Don't touch me!" he shouted.

"I don't mind going back," Miguel said.

"He wants to go, so let him go," António ordered.

I got out of the car. I was furious. My hands were trembling, and my chest was so tight that I had to kneel to keep breathing. I fumbled the package of valium in my hands and gulped one down, then ran to the gravel embankment to the side of the parking lot and sat down on like a kid settling into a sandbox. I hid my head in my hands. The darkness behind my eyelids gave me refuge. When I opened them again, Miguel was walking back to the restaurant. António was sitting in the car. I vowed to stay put until the drug started working inside me because I simply couldn't imagine going any further without being sedated. I etched lines in a pebble with my switchblade. I started to make stick figures. I talked to myself. What I said was that I wanted to make an incision in António's arm.

I wanted to cut him open and suck the poison from his blood.

Bloodletting fantasies — I get them when I'm upset and enraged. I've spoken to lots of friends about this. It's more common than you'd think.

Miguel came to see me after he handed a can of Lipton ice tea to António through his window. He stood before me with his hands in his pockets. I said, "In spite of what you said inside about thinking yourself ugly, you've got to know by now that you're a really handsome guy."

He nodded. "Why don't you come back to the car?"

I surprised myself and replied, "Usually I do whatever a good-looking man tells me, but I'm not coming back till the valium starts working."

"You took a pill?"

"Sure did."

"What's it do?" he asked.

"It unwraps the bandages from around my chest till I can breathe freely again. I handed him the package. "Take one. It'll help you stop smoking."

"I don't want to stop smoking," Miguel replied.

"I mean, it'll help you while you're in the car."

"Really?"

I didn't know if that was true, but I said *yes* because I wanted to corrupt him and it didn't seem so terribly important and he deserved to relax, too. Miguel swallowed a pill. I said, "Give one to António if you like."

"Should I?"

"It's just a tranquilizer. We all deserve a break. Otherwise we might end up killing one another. Three dead bodies in a rest stop outside Viseu... It would make a nice mystery. But they don't write mysteries in Portugal and nobody'd care."

Miguel went back to the car and offered the pills to António. He spread *Bola* on the hood of the T-Bird and began to read. When the valium kicked in, I thought: *Gee, if I'd have remembered how nice it was to feel like I was sitting on a warm sand dune, I'd have never quit taking these little pink beauties.* Because it was really the biggest relief in the world feeling my lungs filling with sweet-smelling air for the first time in ages and watching the cloudless blue sky like it was distilled from turquoise. It was like coming home after years of exile. I started singing 'Penny Lane' as I walked to the car. By now, Miguel was curled in the back seat, sound asleep. António stared at me like I had food on my face. I looked in the rearview mirror, but I was clean. "What is it?" I asked.

"You told me you'd never take valium again."

"I lied." I put my hand on his thigh. "Don't be disappointed. I've already been disappointed enough in my life for the both of us."

"Clever," he said

"That wasn't my intent. I was telling the truth. How about being encouraging? I've rented a Batmobile, a car I thought you'd love. We're going to Spain. Can't we have an adventure?"

"What do you want me to say?"

"Say you're glad to be traveling."

In a monotone, he said, "I'm glad to be traveling."

"I see you didn't take your pill."

"No."

He handed me back the Victan box. I slipped it into my shirt pocket. "Look, why don't you sing?" I said. "Sing anything. Piaf... the national anthem...anything."

"I don't feel like it."

"Okay, then don't sing. Just hold my hand." I reached for him, but he pulled his hands between his legs and turned to look out the window. I shrugged and started up the Batmobile, eased out of the parking lot. Driving seemed like a game. I was so unused to feeling valium's presence inside me that I was really in a kind of trance. Of course, I shouldn't have been behind the wheel at all. But I had my hands glued to the two-and-ten position and it felt good and I wasn't about to move them.

After a while, António put his hand on my thigh and nodded at me. "Hello," he mouthed.

"Hi," I answered.

He sighed.

"I'm scared, too," I said in English, so Miguel wouldn't understand. "Why not take your pill and we'll all be tranquilized together."

He did as I told him.

After a half-hour, he was asleep. He and his father were out for a couple of hours. All the way up the flanks of the Serra da Estrela. Miguel even snored. It was really lovely, like having two hard-working men lying beside you in bed. I laughed out loud once because it seemed so incongruous with the scenery. The mountains were rocky, harsh, born of a severe climate, looked something like the Black Hills of South Dakota which I'd visited once with my brother. The broom bushes were so exuberant here that they had no leaves, only garlands of canary yellow. Wherever boulders and escarpments left room for roots, there sprouted violet sprays of Spanish lavender and red poppies. It was as if the rocks themselves were blooming at their edges. Far in the distance, in the scooped out valleys, hid clusters of stone houses hugging each other.

I was happy.

When the mountains ended, we reached the cragged plateau that extends across from the easternmost districts of Portugal into Spain. I couldn't keep my eyes open any longer, and when I saw the sign for a Pousada hotel in Almeida along with another indicating *Spain 3 Kilometers,* I stopped the car.

The border also seemed to portend danger. Here, in Portugal, we were home. There, in Spain, people wouldn't even know how to pronounce our names.

I decided to head to the hotel for the night. It was three-fifteen in the afternoon. As I pulled into the parking lot, António sat up and yawned; he must have sensed the Batmobile coming to a halt. "Where are we?" he asked. I explained, then added, "I'll go in and make sure there are rooms. Wake up your father."

Behind the reception desk was a pale young woman with a prudish white blouse buttoned to her neck. She had auburn hair parted in the middle and a gold cross around her neck.

She informed me that there were rooms available.

"There are three of us," I said. "Do you have something with three beds?"

"I'm afraid not. But all our double rooms have two double beds."

"How much are they?"

"Sixteen thousand escudos."

It was a hundred dollars, more expensive than I thought it would cost. It didn't seem rational to pay for two rooms just because Miguel and António were feuding. The valium was clearly circumventing my reasoning. I signed the reception card for a room with two double beds and handed the girl my passport. "I'll get my friends," I told her.

António and Miguel had already taken everything out of the trunk. It had gotten overcast and a little chilly, and Miguel had gooseflesh on his arms. António said, "So do they have rooms?"

I knew then that I'd made a mistake; my old ability to anticipate arguments was coming back to me. I knew, for instance, that António was going to say he didn't want to share a room with his father. When pressed, he was going to complain about him smoking. And that's just what happened. In English, he said to me, "I told you, I'm up to here with his damn cigarettes."

My libido had been swept away by the friendly god curled up inside my valium, and I replied, "The cheese stands alone. I'll sleep with your father."

António shook his head. Continuing in English, he said, "It is a terrible error."

"Why not just give it a chance," I pleaded.

Miguel couldn't understand anything but Portuguese and asked, "What are you two arguing about?"

"António doesn't think you and I should share a bed," I replied.

"Then I'll sleep with him."

"No, he wants to sleep alone."

"So we'll get two rooms." He looked at António, who agreed with a nod.

"Too expensive," I said.

Miguel lifted up his suitcase and said, "I'll pay."

"It's ridiculous. Paying a hundred bucks for a bed." I looked at the both of them. "What is the big deal? We're in this together, aren't we? Isn't this the land of explorers and adventurers?"

António rolled his eyes. "It's a land of shit," he said. *"Um país de merda."*

"What would the prime minister say if he heard that?" I inquired.

"The prime minister is a robot with a suntan and closet full of Italian suits."

"António..." Miguel exclaimed, like he shouldn't say such things.

"It's okay," I said. "The boy's right."

Miguel shook his head like we were nuts. That's just what I wanted him to think. It made me comfortable adopting my usual posture as a crazy whore.

António picked up his suitcase and headed inside. Miguel, gallant as ever, waited for me. I locked up the car and led him to our room. It was on the second floor. It was lovely, with dark wood everywhere and a bathroom of polished white marble, and I was inexplicably happy. António claimed the bed nearest the windows. Miguel headed for the bathroom. I got on my blue flannel pajamas.

"What are you doing?" António asked, staring at them.

"You slept for the past two hours. Now it's my turn."

"But those...?"

"Haven't you ever heard of discretion?" I inquired.

"You?"

"Me!"

"No one wears pajamas in this day and age," he asserted.

I slipped my cock out my fly. "You want to see my equipment, now you've seen it! Now leave me alone."

"Sometimes you're really rude," he noted.

I got under the covers. "Kiss me goodnight," I suggested.

"What am I supposed to do while you sleep?"

"Practice guitar outside. Read a book. Or go for a walk with your father. Sniff the receptionist's underwear. I don't care. I'm not your mother."

He looked around the room. "I can't believe we're here."

"Me neither. Now kiss me goodnight."

We kissed cheeks, and I held him to me and whispered that I loved him. Before he could complain, I turned onto my side and huddled into the fetal position.

António told something to his father which I didn't get, then left. A minute or so passed and Miguel said, "I'm going out too, Professor."

After that I slept. I woke an hour later and lay in bed remembering my dream. I was back in New York and my brother was alive and was playing something by Beethoven on his piano. I couldn't get the tune out of my head when I opened my eyes. It took me forever to feel as if I could move my limbs, and I remembered the down side of valium. It was as if my body were a sack of potatoes. Dragging myself to the bathroom, I got into the shower. The hot water seeped into my bones and helped. I got back into bed and started a novel called *Life With a Star*. It was about a Jew in Prague trying to escape the Nazi ovens.

Sometime later, Miguel returned. He was all sweaty. He sat on the end of the other bed. He had the saddest, most honest eyes I'd ever seen. But my libido was still back in Porto, so I didn't get excited. I said, "What you been doing?"

"Walking. I went for a long walk. I haven't walked in the country for so long. It was like being a boy up in Vila Nova de Cerveira."

I put my book down. "Did you like living up there?"

"I loved it. I really loved it."

"Then why did you come to Porto?"

Miguel slid the tips of his fingers against his thumb to indicate money in Portuguese sign language.

"Where's António?" I asked.

Miguel shrugged. "Walking too, I guess."

I went back to my book. Miguel showered. He came out of the bathroom with a white towel wrapped around his waist. Looking at his swirl of chest hair I realized that my valium was wearing off and that if I didn't take another one that night I'd never be able to sleep in the same bed with him without begging him to violate me. So I got up and slipped on my clothes and escaped outside with a lame excuse about loving the scent of late afternoon in the country. The sky had cleared again, and the sun was high in the western sky. Tubular purple flowers on long stiff stalks sprouted around my feet.

Medieval battlements of dark, ash-colored stone formed a twelve-pointed star around the town. Walking around this perimeter, I was struck by the sense of wide open space, of cragged farmland slipping endlessly away to a hazy horizon. I almost believed I was in America, on the South Dakota plains. I thought of prairie dogs with their noses up, sniffing at the wind; of buffalo grazing in tall grasses; of tourists in sunglasses taking photos. I thought of those happy places I'd visited with Harold during the summer after my sophomore year when he proposed that we get to know America. It ended in arguments, but we had had some good experiences. Now, the air was dry and calm. Harold could have been happy sitting and reading here. I thought: *Wouldn't it have been better to die sitting in the sun, surrounded by flowers?*

So I continued walking and found António standing in one of the rook-shaped guard towers jutting out from the corners of the battlements. I entered his shadowed space. He half-smiled at me, as if he was fighting tears. We were about fifty feet above the plains around the town. "Europe's problem is that everybody is always at each other's elbows," I said. "If only it was all small towns built of lichenous stones." He was looking out at the horizon. Searching. I squeezed his hand. "How are you?" I asked.

"Okay."

I questioned him about his thoughts, but he didn't want to talk. So we walked through the town and came to a little house which stopped us both. It was one-storey, rectangular, whitewashed on the outside. Between the door and window rose a tangled vine of ivory roses. Its outermost filaments curled around the blue drainpipe at the side of the house as if they were fingers reaching out for anchor. At the base of the drainpipe was a proud red geranium. The door to the house was open, and the position of the sun made the first four steps of an unvarnished wooden staircase shine like gold. The contrast of the gilded stairs with the darkness behind and the roses was moving. I was seized by an emotion of transcendence. I wished that you were there with us, Carlos. I began to tremble. António was very sweet. He hugged me and told me over and over that he was going to be all right. A small long-haired dog came out of the house and faced us, its nails clicking on the cobbles. It had sleepy brown eyes. It was black, with a white heart-shaped patch on its chest. Two lower fangs curled into its upper lip so that it looked like a malevolent barracuda. We laughed, and António observed that we'd better leave before it started barking. As we headed off, he said, "I found the graveyard, you know."

"Swell."

"I want to show you something," he said.

The cemetery looked like a set for a Vincent Price movie, complete with a rusted gate and cypress trees, unkempt hedges and overturned stones. But I'd been to so many funerals that all my associations with ghouls had been drowned out long ago by real terror. "Look at this headstone," António said, slapping a Doric marble column about four feet high.

It was topped by a granite lamb with a metal cross around its neck. "Home-grown surrealism," I observed.

"Look down," he said.

What I'd at first taken for weeds were cherry-tomato plants. Orange and red fruit dangled from scruffy foliage. The tomatoes looked like the balls we'd played jacks with as kids, and they were ready to be harvested. António pointed to the headstone. It read:

Manuel Correia Pinto Bastos
1902—1974
Um bom pai e jardineiro

I whispered the inscription to myself to hear its sound: A good father and gardener.

"You suppose his children have planted the tomatoes in his honor?" António asked.

"I wouldn't be surprised."

"A week ago I would have been touched," he observed.

"And now?"

"I've got a confession to make."

"What?"

He shrugged. "Maybe I did this on purpose."

"Did what on purpose?"

"Made myself sick."

"Why would you do that?"

"Revenge."

"On who?"

"My father. My parents. You. Me."

"You don't have that sort of personality. You may have wanted to take some risks, but you didn't want to get sick. I know you."

"Are you sure? You say you know me, but do you? One new fact, and nothing is the same. I can't even remember what it was like to play guitar without what's tainting my blood sitting in the back of my mind spoiling everything. And you... I can't remember what it's like to look at you without being jealous that you're not ill." His eyes grew misty, and he turned away.

"It's all still so new," I said. "These doubts, they'll go away. You'll remember who you are. Trust me. It's all there, it's just covered with something so overwhelming and opaque that you can't see through it."

António bent over and picked one of the cherry tomatoes, held it up to me. "But I don't even remember simple things," he said, "like whether I really ever liked these things." He tossed it away, then locked his hands behind his neck and looked at me desperately. "What kind of person can't remember whether he liked the flavor of a tomato?"

Part III

16

It was dark in our hotel room, and António was whimpering. I sat up. I closed my eyes to gather my thoughts. I whispered his name and asked if he was okay, but he didn't reply. The wind was battering the windows. I brought the covers up to my chin and turned to look at Miguel. Facing away from me, he was breathing softly. I went and sat by António. He was curled at the edge of his mattress with the sheets in his fists. When I caressed his hair, he turned on his stomach and buried his head in his pillow. I tiptoed around the foot of the bed, lifted the covers and got in next to him. His back and behind were frigid, his skin coarse with goosepimples. To warm him, I took my pajama bottoms off and snuggled up against him. I gripped his right shoulder and coaxed him onto his left side so that we fitted snugly. He put one of his pillows over his head and started to sob soundlessly. I pressed my lips to his neck and kept them there. After a while, he rolled on his back and whispered, "You shouldn't touch me, you'll get Aids."

I took his hand from his thigh and brought it to my lips. I kissed it, then put it over my face like a mask. The scent of him mixing with my breathing was comforting.

"You shouldn't..." he said.

I placed his hand down to his stomach and pushed him gently on his side again. I said, "Go to sleep with me holding you. You need to sleep."

He sat up roughly and said, "Please don't."

"Sshhh, I'll tell you a bedtime story."

"No, go back to your bed."

Cuddling up next to him like a child, I drew my knees in and pressed against his hip. I played with the hairs on his chest. He closed his eyes. When I felt for his cock, it was half erect.

He pushed my hand away. "Please don't," he begged.

"It's okay," I replied.

"No, I'm contagious."

"I'll be careful."

"You can't be careful enough."

"I can."

"My father's in the other bed."

Miguel was still breathing softly. I whispered, "Let me just get you off. Then you'll go right to sleep."

"You're such an idiot," he said. He pushed my hand away.

I flipped to my other side. The curtains were open a crack. A beacon of light threaded through the darkness to my eyes. I imagined a lonely farmhouse housing peasants who never spoke to one another. After a while, António lay back down. I turned over and held him. "I'm sorry," I said.

He finally slept.

He woke and cried three times during the night.

Once, he grabbed onto me so tight that my old fractured rib started to ache.

Miguel never roused from sleep. Or so I thought.

The next morning, Saturday, António's right leg was over my left thigh and his arm was under my head. The sun was shining happily through the breaks in the dark drapes. Freeing myself from the boy, I sat up. I was dead tired. My legs ached as if I'd been running in the night. I stretched them over my head. Miguel was lying on his stomach. His back was uncovered. His spine was a shadowed river running between sheer palisades of muscle. I imagined the feel of him. António was still sleeping soundly. His eyes were crusted with sleep.

Do tears summon the Sandman? Does he sit for hours by the side of doomed children and sprinkle his powders in their eyes to dim their vision of the future?

In a vertical sliver of window unobstructed by curtain, green and gold plains glistened in the oblique light. I dressed without the others stirring. I got the map of Spain from my suitcase, peed and went to breakfast.

A fire in the night had burned fifty acres near Evora. The newspapers were full of warnings about the forests of Portugal because May had been so dry. I read some of *Life With a Star*. The central character, a Jewish young man residing in a broken-down shack in Prague during the Nazi occupation, was holding imaginary conversations with his missing — and very possibly dead — girlfriend. I sipped my tea and ate my rolls.

Miguel joined me maybe twenty minutes later. He wore one of those brushed silk bomber jackets that had become popular of late — emerald green in color. His washed-out jeans were impeccably clean and ironed, but his white sneakers were filthy. His hair was wet and slicked back. He hadn't shaved. His face looked pale and depleted. "Good morning," he said. He lit a cigarette with exact movements. "Got to smoke before António gets down. You want one, Professor?"

I shook my head. The waitress, a stocky young woman with thick eyebrows, took his order.

"You sleep well?" he asked me.

"Not really."

"Why's that?"

I sighed. "António was up most of the night."

"Yes, I heard. When he'd cry as a baby I always woke up. You don't forget."

Miguel buttered his bread and smoothed on spoonfuls of apricot jam. I said, "António inherited his sweet tooth from you."

He smiled automatically. He read the *Publico* newspaper, drank two cups of coffee. He was a man of large appetites and long silences. When he pushed his plate away, he lit another cigarette. "You know, I saw what happened last night," he said. "I just want you to know."

"I'm glad you're attentive."

He stood up abruptly. "I guess I'll go for a walk."

He sounded as if he wanted to get away from me, so I said, "You didn't like me getting into bed with him, did you?"

"It's one thing to help the boy, another to indulge him every time he cries."

"Indulge him?!"

"Exactly."

"It's not indulging António to hold him when he needs help."

Miguel looked away and smoked.

"You don't indulge someone falling from a cliff by offering him your hand," I told him.

He nodded as if I were ranting. He said, "I'm going for a walk."

He started away, but I stood up. I asked, "What happened to the man who just wanted to know his son?"

He lifted his eyebrows as if surprised, then left me without a word. I sat back down and opened my book. But I couldn't read. I stared out the window at the orange rooftops of Almeida. I took a valium.

António came down to breakfast wearing a billowy rose-colored silk shirt I'd bought him. His hair was mussed up. His eyes were sunken and deeply shadowed. He looked gray to me, as if fear were taking the very color from him. He looked like his father.

I called the waitress over. He ordered coffee and I got some tea. He stared at the cigarette butt in the ashtray. "Where's our neighborhood chimney?" he asked with a frown.

"Walking."

"Right, he was always a big walker. When I was a kid, he used to walk miles showing me off around the community."

"Times have changed it seems."

António nodded. "I've been a disappointment."

"Quite the opposite. You're too much competition for him. He'd like to be like you."

"I don't think so. And certainly not now."

"Your father is a mystery," I shrugged. "Anyway, how are you feeling?"

"Better. You?"

"Okay."

He buttered a roll and coated it with apricot jam. "Looks cloudy today," he observed.

I looked out the window. The sky had become white and still. "Rain, I think."

He ate ferociously. I kicked back my chair and watched him.

"What are you looking at?" he asked.

"I like looking at you when you act like you. You'll understand when you're older."

Big mistake, of course; I'd gotten out of practice eliminating the future tense from my grammar.

António gulped down his coffee. "Maybe we should just head back to Porto," he said. "This isn't going to work."

"If Jason had said that, he'd have never gotten the Golden Fleece."

"As I recall, things didn't turn out too well for Jason," he observed.

"You're not going to make the mistake of getting married, then cheating on your wife."

"No," he replied, wiping his mouth with his napkin. "No, I made a much bigger mistake." He turned and stared out blankly at Almeida as though made of plaster. From time to time, he broke his pose by licking his lips. He had quit the present and was focusing on either the past or future. "You know," he said, facing me again, "I really didn't think I could get it." He passed a hand in front of his face as if to block his eyesight. "I was insane. And so incredibly blind."

If I had a wish for every time I'd heard someone say exactly that, each and every buried friend I had would have gotten the one and only second chance for survival they'd have needed.

I stood up and spread out my map of Spain on the table in front of him. I held his shoulder and pointed to the road we were going to take. "It's going to be a nice drive today," I said. "We'll cross the border and head to Salamanca. You'll love the main square. We'll stay there if we're in the mood. If not, we can head on to Avila."

"My father was watching, you know," he said. He looked up at me and twisted his lips wryly, as if to say, *We're running a risk...*

"How'd you discover that?" I asked.

"I can see his eyes in the dark. They light up like an owl's."

I sat back down next to the boy, where Miguel had been seated. António made an ugly face and said, "Doesn't the idea of him seeing us in bed together give you the creeps?"

"No. It's his problem if he doesn't like it."

"Easy for you to say."

"Look, you can't take away his problems," I said. I reached across the table and held his hand. António looked around to see who was watching. I said, "If he makes trouble, I'll kick him out the car and make him find his own way back to Porto. But I don't think he will. He knows his limits."

The boy slipped his hand from mine and crossed his arms. "He'll beat the shit out of you if it comes down to that." He spoke with a perverse pride in his voice.

At the time, I thought he was kidding.

Why is it that I never believe that men I know are capable of physical violence? Even today, I sometimes wonder if my memory is playing tricks on me when I think of how you raped me, Carlos, with your knife at my cheek. Then I look in a mirror and see the scar on my ear...

Will I ever be able to forgive you?

So it was with a bit of what I considered harmless bravado that I said to António, "Your father can beat the shit out of me but he's still not going to ride in the Batmobile if I don't want him to."

"We shall see," the boy replied.

I finished my tea. In the teacherly voice I adopt to let António know I'm really serious, I said, "When we get to Salamanca, I want you to sit somewhere for an hour and practice the Bach Cello Suite in C."

"No way."

"You can sit in the hotel room or in a parking lot or find a shady spot under a tree. I don't care. But you *are* going to practice."

He started to protest. I put my hands over my ears.

Miguel insisted on splitting the hotel bill with me. He fixed me with an angry look and said, "I'm not going to have *you* pay for me or my son."

It was a matter of pride, of course. His teeth were grinding again. Maybe I should've realized from the emphasis of his words that he was on the edge of something crazy.

We crossed the border at Vilar Formoso. An overweight Spanish guard with a wrinkled brow ogled the Batmobile. "What year?" he asked.

"Sixty-five."

He whistled and took off his cap. He scratched his sweaty scalp. "She still goes?"

"Like a dream."

He handed me back my passport. "You want to sell her, you come back to me."

Carpets of poppies unfurled from the road. At Ciudad Rodrigo the sky cleared. A white stork was sitting in its nest at the top of a brick church. Nobody cared but me. "Did you see that thing?" I kept saying, but nobody looked back. Nobody talked. It was like we'd passed through a mist of gloom without my noticing it. No matter. I sang revolutionary Irish ballads because the valium was working and I didn't care what anybody thought. Occasionally, I looked in the rearview mirror. Miguel stared back at me each time.

Sorrowful dark eyes.

Crow's feet.

Angry stubble on his cheeks.

It took an hour and a half to get to Salamanca. My legs were heavy, and I knew I was going to want a siesta after lunch, so we parked at the back of the Gran Hotel. In the lobby, we had an argument about how many rooms to get. It all started because António wanted to stay alone. I didn't think that that was such a good idea and said so.

"I'll stay with him," Miguel offered. "The Professor should have his own room, anyway."

"I wanta be alone," António insisted.

"What if you get upset again?" I asked.

"I've got to sleep alone sooner or later."

"Later is better than sooner."

He rolled his eyes and said, "So what do you propose?"

"That we share a room and your father gets his own."

"No way," Miguel said. "I can't let you two take a room together."

"Why not?" I asked.

"Professor, we've already discussed this," he said.

"We have? I can't recall when."

"I'll stay with the boy," he declared.

António glared at him and crossed his arms over his chest. It was the boy's battle stance. "You won't," he said.

I'd had enough by then and told the girl behind the desk that we wanted a suite.

The room had three beds — two doubles and a single. Miguel tossed his plaid suitcase on the single like he wanted to crush the life out of his poor pillow. I was happily tranquilized, so I didn't care. "Who wants lunch?" I asked.

António raised his hand.

Miguel went to the bathroom without responding.

António flapped his hand in that direction and said, "Forget about him, let's go."

"You want a valium?" I asked. "It's really good."

"Later maybe."

I handed my guitar case to him. "After lunch, you play. The Cello Suite is inside."

We headed off to the central square. I bounced as I walked because the sky was blue and the buildings were made of beautiful sand-colored stone. António munched on his cuticles like a Central Park squirrel as we stood staring at the cathedral. As we set off again, he said, "It was like I was drowning last night. The fear was rushing into my lungs. It came in waves, like a tide." He stopped and looked around, stood the guitar case in front of him like a shield. He gripped the stone column of an archway in front of a newsstand. "And now, here I am. In Spain. The walls are solid." He breathed in. "It's hard to believe I'm me. It's hard to believe I'm sick." He stared at me. "There's no evidence but a piece of paper which says so."

The evidence will come later, I thought. *It will erupt on your skin and spill steaming from your bowels.* I said, "We're going to have lots of adventures. I'll be your Sancho Panza."

"What are you talking about?"

The boy hadn't read *Don Quixote.* I was appalled. I made groaning noises and hid my eyes from him. We sat an outdoor café in the main square. He called me a cultural snob. I decided to play the fuddy-duddy professor for all it was worth; it was nice having a safe role to play for a change. "Why am I a snob?" I asked. "Because I think you should read? Is reading only for some intellectual aristocracy?"

"Because you think you know *what* I should read," he replied indignantly.

"*Don Quixote* is a classic."

He laughed from his belly at me.

"What's so funny?" I asked.

"Calling it a classic doesn't make it good. I've seen lots of *classic* Portuguese films and they're all shit."

"So now *Don Quixote* isn't any good? Is that what you're saying?"

"I don't know. And I don't care."

"That's your problem — not only are you ignorant, but it doesn't bother you."

The irony in all this was that I'd never read *Don Quixote* either, though I'd started it on three different occasions.

The waiter came to take our order. He was about fifty, had thinning hair and bad teeth. In my pidgin Spanish, I said, "This young man here has never read *Don Quixote*."

"It's a masterpiece — *una obra masetra*," he replied. His back stiffened and he raised the tip of his pen. His eyes sought greatness on the rim of the square and, seeming to find it, he declared in resonant Spanish, "Most happy and most fortunate were those times when that boldest of knights, Don Quixote de la Mancha, came into the world..."

He continued to quote Cervantes for a few moments. Only one phrase registered inside me: *an age lacking in merry entertainment.*

I understood that description of the author's era quite easily, almost intuitively.

The poetic lift of the waiter's arm relaxed suddenly, and he leaned toward me. He was a humble servant again. We shared a smile. He whispered, "You know, some people think Spain's national book is the Bible. But it's *Don Quixote*." To António, he said, "You really must read it."

"If I can find it back home," he replied in Portuguese.

"You can find it in every city, in every language. In China, Russia, Greece." He winked. "Even in Portugal where you hate us."

"Don't worry, I've got a copy," I said. "He's trapped."

We laughed. But I stared too long at António's smile and spoiled it.

We ordered two vegetable soups and a large mixed salad. A small dead fly was smeared to a piece of lettuce. In America, this would be enough to provoke great shows of indignation — maybe even a stroke.

António simply lifted the leaf in question and dropped it upside-down on his bread plate.

Thank God for you Portuguese, Carlos; you're still convinced that food is just food and not some sacred means to perfect health.

We sat sipping our coffee and belching for a bit, then I left António to take my siesta.

"What am I supposed to do?" he asked.

"It's Spain. You always wanted to come here. Segovia's from here. Explore. Find a tree with lots of shade. Sit like the Buddha and chant the word *Salamanca* over and over. When it stops denoting a city and loses its meaning, start practicing the Cello Suite."

"I need you to tell me what I'm doing wrong."

I rolled my eyes. "You've got a better ear than me. I'm only good for spanking you when you're lazy." I raised my eyebrows like an old lecher and said, "I do love to spank you, you know."

I left him sitting in the café. He watched me leave with such panicked eyes that I almost went back to him.

Fear comes in waves.

17

I woke from my siesta under the sensation that I was traveling alone and had forgotten to give my brother a check-in call.

Then I remembered where he was.

As I showered, I recalled my dream:

My brother was being kept alive at my mother's house. Plastic tubes led from his mouth and nose to machines covered with the metallic dials of the Thunderbird dashboard. His vulturine head was centered like a still life on his Spiderman pillow. I was sitting with him.

His sheets were white but still wrinkled.

The water in the shower scalded my skin before I realized it was too hot. I hopped out and stared at myself in the mirror for a good long time. I couldn't find Harold at all — not in my nose or eyes, not even in my hair. I took another tranquilizer. I sat on the toilet and counted floor tiles. When the drug began to pull me away from myself, I wiped beads of perspiration from my face, dressed and went for a walk. It was late afternoon and very warm. The streets were full of Spaniards eating nuts and chewing gum and smoking.

A man without something in his mouth cannot possibly be a Spaniard. Cervantes never said that, but he should have, because the entire culture has never left the oral stage of development.

And yes, Carlos, I've met several Spaniards in my time who've never left the anal stage either.

I strolled around for a while, got some more tea, then headed back to the hotel. On the way, I spotted António. He was playing guitar in Santa Justa square. The square was enclosed on three sides and was centered by a circle cut by two intersecting gravel pathways forming a cross. In each of the quadrants were proud little flowerbeds of marigolds and purple pansies. Red benches lined the pathways. António was seated on a blue water bucket turned upside-down at the perimeter of the circle. The light gleamed off his guitar.

When I first spotted the boy, twenty-three people were gathered in front of him, listening. I counted.

I stood across the one traffic street passing the square, behind the thick trunk of an old chestnut tree. To impress the Spanish, he was giving them their own composers. He played...

Rumores de la Caleta by Albéniz;

Variations on a theme from 'The Magic Flute' by Sor;

Recuerdos de la Alhambra by Tárrega.

Two young boys, maybe twelve years old, with New York Yankees baseball caps on backwards, sat at his feet.

An old woman in a black shawl without any teeth, chomping on her gums as if she'd just eaten something tasty, was watching from a high window. She had a square red rag on her head to protect her from the sun.

People clapped after each piece. Of course, they smoked and ate their pine nuts, too.

The Spanish are hard to please when it comes to soccer, sex and guitar. They were right in their assessment of the artist, however; his rendition of *Recuerdos* was particularly lovely. It's because he has the best tremolo stroke I've ever heard. He makes the melody sound as if it were played on a mandolin.

I've seen Narciso Yepes four times, Andrés Segovia three times and Julian Bream twice. I've seen Christopher Parkening, John Williams and Pepe Romero... I've seen all the best guitarists in the world play *Recuerdos*. António took the individual notes and strung them into a more shimmering necklace than any of them.

I was thinking that maybe that was what he should play for his audition in Paris.

Except if he gets nervous, it'll sound like shredded wheat, I thought.

I had to kneel down to the packed earth at the base of my chestnut tree because my legs were beginning to tremble. I faced away from him and caught my breath. I considered the question of what he should practice for Paris as if it were a riddle asked by a malevolent sphinx who hated gay people, as if he had to pick the right piece for guitar or...

Or he'd die.

I was crazy with fear suddenly. I wanted to run and not stop till I was too far to be called back. I stood up and backed against the tree. I hid my head in my hands. I pictured myself playing basketball. Receiving a pass at the foul line. Pivoting around. Faking right, driving left. Stopping at the baseline for a jumper.

The ball hit the front rim and careened to the ground with a dull thud. It just sat there. Empty of air. Crushed by its own weight.

António had started *Prelude No. 1* by Villa-Lobos. I looked up and saw something across the street that blocked out sound. It was as if my head were trapped in a ceramic jug.

Miguel was standing at the corner of a three-story building, watching his son, crying his eyes out. His hands were pressed at arm's length into the sand-colored rim of stone. The tendons stood out dangerously on his neck.

He, António and I formed a triangle in space.

Yet in the geography of our hearts, the boy was between us.

After a minute, Miguel spotted me. He lowered his arms and raised his head back in fear, like a whipped horse. He turned and started away.

I crossed the street and ran to catch up with him. I called his name. He stopped and sighed regretfully. He wiped his eyes. "You shouldn't see me like this," he said.

"Let me buy you a drink."

Miguel stared at me with sad puzzlement. "I can't decide whether I hate you or not," he said. He spoke matter-of-factly, as if it were an everyday confession.

"Come, let me buy you a drink."

"I hate you," he said. "Don't you understand what I'm saying?"

"I understand. What would you have me say?"

"Go fuck yourself!" He flapped his hand at me. "Just go fuck yourself, you American bastard!" he shouted. He formed fists. He shook them at me. Spittle had collected at the sides of his mouth. "I hate you!" he repeated. He started walking again, tensely, as if stalking. I followed from about twenty feet behind. When we reached our hotel, I called out, "Come with me to get a drink and we'll talk."

He turned. "You wanta talk? Talk! To me!" He laughed caustically — the laugh of the theatrical villain.

"I want to talk about António."

"I've nothing to say to you. You! You're the one who should have prevented this!"

"We need to talk."

"What about? I don't want to talk to you about the boy."

"Other things. Anything."

"What other things are there? You're a professor, you tell me. What other things are there for a twenty-four-year-old than his life? Tell me? Philosophy? Psychology? Music? Is that what there is? Classical music?! Go fuck yourself with your damn guitar!"

He was shaking a fist a me and foaming at the mouth.

I was silent for a while, then said, "Listen, I know a bar just down the street. It's dark. Nobody will bother us."

He looked away down where I was pointing. "Fucking Spain," he said. "Nothing good comes from this land of shit."

"Come on." I walked around him and continued slowly up the street. His footsteps followed me.

Churchill's was a gay bar on the Gran Via where I'd been once before in a previous lifetime — the one I'd enjoyed before the invisible Cossacks launched their first offensive. Nobody was there but the potted ferns. I ordered Miguel a double whiskey and got an ouzo for myself. He drank in gulps. He lit a cigarette.

"Can I have one?" I asked.

"You want one of my cigarettes?"

I nodded. He threw the pack at my chest. "Take them all." He faced away.

I took one and put the pack back by his drink. He lit my cigarette without my asking. He faced away from me again. His jaw was throbbing.

I called the waiter over and got another double whiskey and ouzo. He downed his in two gulps, licked his lips like a cat and said, "They got a bathroom here?"

"Don't know."

"Don't queers need bathrooms? Or do you just drink each other's piss?"

I rolled my eyes.

Miguel asked the bartender, then came back to the table. He stubbed out his cigarette, then took mine from my hand and stubbed it out as well. "I want you to come with me, Professor," he said.

"Why?"

"I said for you to come with me. I want you to see something."

I got up. "Walk ahead of me," he told me. We headed down a corridor at the back of the bar. It was painted green and it smelled of beer. We came to a wooden door with black letters spelling *Caballeros*. I turned around. "Go in," he nodded. I went in. Two white urinals, two stalls without any doors.

I suddenly flew forward. I saved myself from falling by reaching out for the black and yellow wall tiles. Miguel had pushed me. I turned around and said, "Give me a break."

He stepped up to me. I figured he was going to start yelling because his teeth were grinding. No such luck; before I could react, he punched me so hard in the stomach that I lost all my wind.

I fell down and doubled over. I didn't think I'd ever breathe again.

It felt like someone had strapped a rope around my ribs and pulled it so tight that my lungs couldn't expand.

I gasped for air. I raised myself to my knees.

Liquid of some sort dripped from my nose.

I fought for breath. A crack of air opened around my lungs. At the first heaving inhale, I took a shit in my pants.

Then I was sick. I crawled to the toilet. I vomited ouzo mixed with salad. Miguel began patting my back. "Water," I begged.

He left the bathroom and came back with the glass of mineral water with a blue plastic straw and wedge of lemon.

I wanted to laugh, but I was covered with spittle and vomit. I sat on the toilet floor. Tears welled in my eyes. I wiped them hard, then let them fall.

I wasn't sad; I was hollow. There was a raw pit in my stomach like I'd been screaming for days on end and only just stopped. My chest felt like someone had scraped it with sandpaper. My bowels ached, and when I felt my behind, I realized what had happened. I cursed.

I'd forgotten what one good punch in the solar plexus can do.

I'd never been hit so hard in my life, not even when my Italian professor cracked my rib with his dictionary.

Miguel stood back and just stared at me with his mouth open. Like a little kid watching a scissors of lightning cutting the sky.

"Go away," I told him.

"I can't leave you here," he said.

"I've been beaten up in bathrooms before. Just go." I wiped some vomit from my mouth with my shirt.

"I can't."

I tossed what was left of the mineral water in my glass at him. The lemon wedge bounced off his jeans and fell on the floor. "Go away," I sighed. "This isn't anything special."

He wouldn't leave.

"It's nothing new," I said impatiently. "Don't you listen? Every queer in the world's been clobbered by an asshole in a toilet. You're nothing special. You're just some dumb schmuck who doesn't know what he wants. Go away."

"You want more water?" he asked.

I closed my eyes. I sighed and hung my head.

"You've got to get up," he said.

I had no force in my legs. My body was a sack of smelly manure. I felt my forehead. It was freezing. I realized I was going to faint. It would have been a relief, but I asked for a wet towel.

He handed it to me. I wiped my brow and laid down on the toilet floor.

After a while, he took my elbow and tried to lift me up. I didn't move. I don't remember what happened after that. I suppose I fainted after all.

Then I was sitting up. His hand was touching my shoulder. "Wake up," he was saying.

I leaned back and rested against the toilet bowl. "Just leave me here," I said. "Go home and leave me be."

The bartender entered the bathroom. He stared at me. "Jesus," he said, "what happened to you?"

Looking up from a bathroom floor makes you feel tiny and idiotic. I was thinking: *A child must feel this helplessness all the time.* A great tenderness welled inside me for the brutalized children nearly all of us queers had been.

"Something I ate," I whispered.

The bartender put his hands on his hips. He pointed a knowing finger and said, "Spoiled seafood, I bet. I never trust a clam."

I tried to laugh, but all I could do was nod.

He pursed his lips and raised his eyebrows in Miguel's direction. He said, "And I thought you two were playing with each other's turnips. Well, come on up outta here." He grabbed one arm and Miguel grabbed the other. They walked me out with my legs dragging and sat me at our table in the bar. "Have you got a hotel room?" he asked.

"Just down the block," Miguel said in Portuguese.

"What was that?" asked the bartender, scrunching up his nose like a rabbit scenting predators.

"El Gran Hotel," I said.

I sat for a while sipping some camomile tea which our host was kind enough to make for me. "Always works for me," he observed.

Gastric juices kept rising up and stinging my nose. The bartender and Miguel walked me back to the hotel. I threw my soiled underwear in the toilet and washed my tush in the bidet. I got in the shower. I sat down. I let the water spray over me like warm rain.

Then I got under the covers.

Miguel stood by his bed for a while and watched me with the worried brow of a punished dog. He scratched the stubble on his cheeks, ran his hands nervously back through his hair. He paced. I wasn't going to make it easy for him and closed my eyes. Then, summoning his courage, he sat next to me. I felt his gentleness in the slow bowing of the bed. He put his hand on my forehead. "I'm sorry," he whispered.

I was silent. I was exhausted and almost fell asleep with his hand guarding me. Then he said, "I'm really sorry."

"That's the last time," I whispered. "No second chances for Portuguese queerbashers."

"I won't do it again."

I raised my hand. He took it.

I fell asleep inside his grip.

I woke up when it was dark. Miguel was sitting by the window, staring out at the street. I was thinking of you, Carlos, wondering what you were doing at that exact moment:

Slapping paint on a canvas?

Sleeping peacefully under your Chinese quilt?

Embracing someone else? A woman?

To my surprise, I realized then that I would have preferred you being with another man; it would have meant that something of what we'd experienced together had remained with you.

"Where's António?" I asked Miguel.

He came and sat next to me. "You're up. Are you feeling okay?"

"Tired. Where's the boy?"

He handed me a glass of water from the nighttable. "He just went to dinner. We can join him if you want. I know where he went."

I drank the whole glass. "I can't eat," I said.

"Nausea?"

"Just not hungry."

"Maybe some coffee and dessert?"

"Maybe coffee. Or tea."

I slipped out of the sheets and stood up. I stretched. My body was warm. My arms and legs were sore, like I'd had the flu. I was naked. Miguel looked me up and down.

"I know, I'm flabby," I said. "It happened one night a few years ago in L.A. While I was asleep, someone replaced all the muscles in my chest and stomach with fruit compote. The one clue the police found were empty jam jars in the garbage. Strangely enough, they all had my fingerprints on them. So I think it must have been an inside job."

Miguel waited till I finished my attempts at humor and said, "I was just checking for bruises. But I don't see any."

"Don't worry, you didn't break anything that wasn't already partially fractured."

He shook his head. "What a son of a bitch I am!" He turned away. Then he furrowed his brow and said, "I've been thinking."

"Any conclusions?"

"What I said was true... I want to know my boy. But..." He shrugged. He stuck a cigarette in his mouth and lit it.

"But what?"

"But I'm also afraid." He took a long inhale. He let the smoke curl out through his nose and licked his lips.

"Of?"

"Of him."

We were silent for a while. I watched the scenery out the window, but every time I looked back, Miguel was staring at me with his bloodshot eyes.

I pointed to my suitcase by the door. "Can you bring it over here? I need new pants."

"Wait." He stubbed out his cigarette. He took off his shirt. He rubbed his arms like he was cold, then unbuckled his pants and stepped out of them. He wasn't wearing underwear. He was partially erect and handsomely endowed.

"I want to know my son," he said.

We stared at each other without resorting to language.

After a while, I walked to him. I dropped to my knees. "No," he said. He took my arms and lifted me. We stood an inch apart. Our chest hairs were tickling together. He caressed his hands up my thighs and played his fingertips into the shadows of my behind. He pressed his palm to my stomach where he'd punched me. "I'm frightened," he said.

He was leaning over, sniffing my chest. I stepped my fingers across his back. "God, you're a beautiful man," I whispered. I rubbed his powerful shoulders.

He knelt. When he took me in his mouth, I thought I might pass out.

He gagged a few times. Afterward, he swallowed hard and gargled in the bathroom. I thought he might wretch. He sat on the toilet with his head between his legs. "Just dizzy," he said. He reached out his hand. I took it.

After a while, he said, "Taste's bitter. I never expected."

"It grows on you," I observed.

He shrugged and put his head back between his legs.

I thought he would be aloof afterward, but when he left the bathroom, he came up to me and kissed me on the lips. "Thank you for that," he said.

We hugged. I had my chin over his shoulder. He was holding my ass, and we did a slow, swaying dance across the floor. His longing began to press hard against my thigh. We began kissing as if hunting for each other's secrets. The stubble on his chin burned over my neck.

He held me at arm's length. "Do I kiss all right?" he inquired eagerly.

I tilted my head. "Come on. Don't ask such questions."

He looked down as he collected his thoughts. "As good as António?"

"It's not a contest."

"But I want to learn how to kiss a man," he said. "It's...it's something I want to learn."

I reached my hand to his chest. "Just close your eyes. Imagine I'm a woman if it helps. You can fantasize anything you want."

"No, I want to think of you. I want to be here. In the room. It's important."

We kissed for a while, and he held my face in his hands. He moved me to the bed. We lay side by side kissing, our desires pressed between us. When he reached into the crack of my behind again, I knew what he wanted. I put a condom on him, flipped around and curled into his belly. One hand gripped my hip, the other my shoul-

138

der. "I want you, Professor, but how do we do it?" he asked.

I lubricated myself and moved back so that we fit together. "Slow," I said. "Much as you'd like it to be, it's not a vagina."

"I've had my wife this way," he said.

"Then you know."

"But she was different. A different shape."

"Because of a single chromosome. Think of it."

"Think of what?"

I didn't reply; he'd popped inside me. I twisted away because it stung. "I'm hurting you," he said with an anguished face. "We should stop."

"Here, this'll make it easier." I got on my back and put my legs over his shoulders.

"Okay?" he asked when his hips were pressed to me.

I nodded.

"You know, some people say this is against nature," he observed.

"At a time like this you want to argue philosophy?"

"But maybe it is."

"You have a choice. You can ask the Pope for his take on the subject or you can ask your own cock. Personally, I think that what's inside me is a far more eloquent and intelligent spokesman for God and nature." I tugged on his nipples. "Go ahead and ask it what it thinks."

He leaned over me and plunged in as far as he could. Shit!" he shouted, pulling out. The condom was hanging loose. He pulled it off. He spurted all over the sheets. "I haven't fucked in months," he explained. "What a mess, Professor."

"It's the one drawback of being gay — somehow, despite the best laid plans of mice and men, the sheets are always filthy afterward. There are Chinese laundries in New York that make a living just cleaning semen and shit off gay men's sheets."

He sighed. "I'm sorry," he said.

I caressed his cheek encouragingly.

"You know, my wife once took a dump right in our bed," he said. He laughed from the belly, shaking, like someone who'd been close to tears. "She thought she was farting and out came a turd. It was great. I loved her for that."

We told shit stories for a while — our biggest, hardest and soupiest. He claimed he'd had one two feet long after getting over the flu just this past year. It curled around and around the toilet bowl like a snake. I told him of an Australian friend desperate with constipation in Florence who deposited three days' worth of stored pasta into the bidet of her hotel room by mistake. Out of embarrassment, she transferred it all to the toilet with a teflon cooking spatula she'd just bought for $22 and which she never dared use again.

We cleaned up Miguel's exuberant mess with hand towels. He lit a cigarette and lay back in bed. "How many times have you done that?" he asked.

"What? Clean a bed?"

"Fuck with a man."

"Thousands. I stopped counting after a while because I realized I wasn't going to find my prince. I'm a masochist, it's true. But keeping a record seemed unnecessarily indulgent."

I sat next to him. I rubbed the hair gracing his inner thighs. We curled our feet together. He put his arm behind my neck. "Thank you," he said.

"Stop saying that. It makes it sound like I'm doing you a favor."

"You are."

"I'm not. I don't even know what we did."

"You think I'm handsome?" he asked. "You said that."

I turned on my side and took the bud of his sex in my hand. I kissed his shoulder. He smelled just like his son. Was that why I was proceeding so carelessly down this dead end? Or was it simple testosterone buildup?

"You think I'm handsome?" he repeated.

"Did your wife have to answer so many questions?"

"Yes."

"Okay, you're very handsome."

"How many times with my son?" he asked.

"I told you, I don't count."

"But for about a year you slept together?"

"Yes."

"Once a week? Twice?"

"Maybe four times. We didn't sign any contract, though. He isn't Jackie Kennedy and I'm too tall and poor to be Aristotle Onassis."

"Four times fifty-two... Two hundred and eight."

"But we didn't always fuck," I pointed out.

"What else did you do?"

"Everything. But cunnilingus, of course. You want an alphabetical list? Latin, Portuguese or English?"

"No, but when you fucked... I mean, who...who fucked who?"

"We fucked each other. We sucked each other. We sat on each other, blew each other's noses, cleaned each other's toenails and fell asleep imagining we were each other."

"So he fucked you?"

"You don't give up!" I noted.

Miguel shook his head with childlike determination.

"He fucked me all the time. He likes to fuck. He's got a healthy libido."

"And you fucked him?"

"That's what I'm telling you."

He lay back smoking and considering this information. After a while, his cock began to swell in my hand. I started sucking him. He played with my ears. I pushed him back on the bed and moved his hands out to the side like a victim of crucifixion. I lowered myself down on him. His head kicked back. He gripped my hips and closed his eyes. He didn't open them again till he came.

I figured that he was picturing a woman.

I only found out some days later in Paris what he was really thinking.

18

I thought that even if Miguel and I didn't mention our awkward but strangely tender coupling, it would right all the harsh angles in our little triangle; he would draw close to his son, even become playful with him. The boy would discover in his father's tearful embrace that he was well and truly loved. After a few more days driving down the pathway leading from that love into the heart of a new country, António would learn that he still had a chance for a future.

Love teaches; maybe that's its greatest gift.

And what about hope? Was the pathway leading from love into the boy's future paved with the hope which everyone in our passionless decade was constantly losing?

The question now seemed to be, *How do you get hope back when the very word has shed its meaning and become nothing more than four meaningless letters arranged in a random order?*

opeh, peho, ehop...

And yet it must have been hope which was animating my daydreams; I pictured the three of us as a happy family with the relationships all pleasantly confused.

No matter how much I might have wanted it, however, my life wasn't a TV movie directed by some major Hollywood has-been and featuring a retinue of B-actors as Miguel, António, me, my brother's frolicsome ghost and even you, Carlos. So that's not how it happened.

António jumped out of his bed on Sunday morning and took a shower. When he came back into the room, Miguel was up. In a resentful voice, the boy told him that he didn't appreciate the *stink* of tobacco when he got back from dinner the night before. He began dressing like he was in a rush.

"Sorry," Miguel said. He was sitting up in bed and scratching his underarms.

I was standing in my pajama bottoms by the window, watching people going to work on the street below. António's voice exhausted me. I sat on the end of my bed, wanting to say something to him but not knowing what. He glared down at me. "From now on, I get my own room," he announced.

I chose cheerfulness for a strategy. "How about if we discuss all this over breakfast? Aren't you hungry?"

"I'm not eating with you. I met someone," he said.

"Who?" I asked.

"Someone."

Miguel said, "António, you have to be careful. You have to..."

"Who said I was sleeping with him? Who said it's even a *him?* Mind your own business." He turned toward me. "Oh, and I've decided we're staying today in Salamanca. We can go to Avila tomorrow."

He grabbed my guitar case and walked out. I expected him to slam the door. Probably to disappoint me, he didn't.

Miguel covered his face with his blanket and slipped deep under the covers. He didn't peek out.

I ate breakfast alone and went for a walk. It was a warm morning and the sky was blue. There was that vague sense of dust about which meant that it was going to be a scorcher. I got a cappuccino in the main square and was served by the same waiter as the day before. "Hey, where's your son?" he asked.

"Is it that easy to tell we're related?" I asked.

He pointed to his eyes with two fingers, as if to poke them. "I can tell when people are in the same family." He twisted his hand. "They have the same expressions. You and he smile the same way. It's your lips."

"My *hijo* went for a walk," I told him. "He was restless."

Calling António my son made my pulse stop for a moment. It was only a word in Spanish. But it didn't feel harmless.

The waiter nodded and brought his hands into a position of prayer. "To be young again," he sighed.

I passed the square where António had been playing guitar and kept on going. I figured that I had a lot to consider, what with António having a secret encounter to hide and Miguel shedding vestigial layers of his personality in front of me. But the truth is I wasn't thinking about any of it. I was thinking about how detached I felt when walking with no destination. I was kicking stones. I could've kept kicking them right to Istanbul. And in between kicking them I

142

was thinking that when I died I would leave no legacy behind:

no paintings of my lovers;

no unpublished manuscripts for my ex-agent Libby to discover and send to a small but highly prestigious press for publication;

no crocheted scarves draped around the necks of my friends;

no ceramic ashtrays I'd made on a potter's wheel for my mom;

no witty letters from famous gay friends which could be excerpted in *The James White Review*;

nothing.

The only thing I had that seemed of any value was my guitar. If António outlived me, I'd leave it to him. If not, I'd request that gay terrorists use it to clobber New York's Cardinal O'Connor.

I ended up on the road to Valladolid. One asphalt lane in each direction. I passed some utilitarian concrete apartment blocks, then some chipped stucco hovels with barking dogs. Spanish cities end rather suddenly, and pretty soon I was in the country. I was wearing a blue woolen cardigan sweater my mother had bought for me on sale at Macy's in Roosevelt Field and which was decidedly too hot for the day. I took it off and curled it around the foot of a speed-limit signpost — 80 kilometers per hour. I was figuring that I'd pick it up on the way back. The horizon was a long ways off and hazy brown. I set off for it following the gravel shoulder of the road. Cars whizzed past. Two huge buses filled with old ladies went by in the opposite direction. A sparrow-hawk watched me suspiciously from a fence post. Warm breezes swept over my face as if trying to calm me.

A short time later, I came to a miserable village without sidewalks. It was like something in a Mexican hinterland. In a dark café with a linoleum floor littered with cigarette butts and opened sugar packs, I ordered mineral water. Two old men with grizzled faces were playing dominos in the corner. A game show blared from the television on a shelf above them. On the counter, flies buzzed around prosciutto sandwiches stacked on a white porcelain plate. The prosciutto stuck out between the slices of bread like bloody tongues. The elderly woman who served me my water watched the television with her arms crossed. Now and then she picked her nose with her fat pinky. She wore a floral dress and had bad breath.

"How long you lived here?" I asked during a commercial.

"Here?"

"Sí."

Four times she flashed all her fingers at me like I was an idiot. "Forty years," she said.

She scratched her behind then went back to picking her nose.

The place smelled of depression, so I left. About a mile down the road, a young woman wearing thick red lipstick pulled over in a white Toyota and rolled down her window. She asked me directions to a place called Cañizal. "Never heard of it," I said in Portuguese, because I'd forgotten the verb *to hear* in Spanish.

"Lisbon?" she asked.

"Porto," I nodded.

"Viva Porto!" she exclaimed. Her tires screeched as she zoomed off.

I came to a path to the right, south, leading through an olive grove. The dry brown earth around the trees was newly plowed and lumpy. The path itself was rocky and laced with purple wildflowers on long stiff stalks. I walked for a half-hour or so and came to a whitewashed rectangular house with a red tile roof. It had an old diesel Mercedes out front and a yellow satellite dish marked *Astra* sticking up at the back. A big brown dog in a fenced yard was barking snappishly at me. A tall weedy man appeared at the front door. He was eating an apple and had a knife in his hand.

"Can I get some water?" I asked as best I could in Spanish.

"American?" he replied in English.

"Yes."

He waved me over. He was tall, balding and sweaty. He'd slit the sides of his white shirt to allow the air to reach his armpits. He wore leather sandals and pressed gray slacks. His feet were long and bony. We shook hands. He had vibrant brown eyes. His name was Angel Llorca. "No, I'm not related to the playwright," he told me without my asking.

"How do you know English?" I asked.

"I studied in Edinburgh for a while."

He invited me inside. All the inner walls had been knocked down so that it was one giant rectangular room. The vaulted ceiling, crossed by two reinforced wooden beams, was a good twenty feet high at its central axis. Two triangular stained-glass windows glowed at both ends. One was of a blue-and-green harlequin dancing a jig and wearing a red snout; the other was an orange-and-red snake twining up a blue-and-violet tree.

It was warm in the room. The glowing space made me quiet.

"It often has that effect," Angel told me later.

A kilim in chestnut brown and bright fuchsia covered sandy floor tiles. *Whoever designed this house was relying on color for help in something,* I was thinking.

We sat at a wooden dining table. He gave me tap water in a ceramic mug. I drank most of it, then sprinkled the rest on my neck and hair. He asked what I was doing in Spain, and I told him the truth minus António's illness. When I asked what he did, he told me he taught psychology at the University of Salamanca. The dog was still barking outside, and he went to get her. "To show her you're not dangerous," he smiled.

She came waddling over to me, her head bent, one ear up, one down. She was shaggy and brown, had clear blue eyes. I petted her neck and she turned her back to me. When I scratched her rump, her long tail swung up and away. She rubbed against my leg.

"She's in heat," he said. "All you have to do is touch her and she shows herself. She's a big furry ball of need." He called her from me. Her name was Limosa, *muddy*, he explained, because she was born in December and loved to flop around in the winter puddles like a hippo. She slumped down and put her head on his foot. She looked up curiously at me.

Angel had an upright piano by his unmade bed. "May I?" I asked. He nodded.

I played the first chords to 'Pictures at an Exhibition'. The piano needed to be tuned, but I didn't say so.

"You play well," he commented.

"Enough to teach harmony classes. But I never liked piano. I like an instrument you can carry."

"It was my wife's."

He got up and took a framed photo from a bookshelf.

A woman with short stiff hair had her arm around Angel. She wore a blue tank-top and had a man's shirt tied around her waist. She had a lovely smile.

"A year before she died," he said. "We were in Italy together. I had a conference in Bologna."

"How long have you been alone?"

"Two years." We sat back down. We were silent for a while. Angel picked at something crusted on the table top with a letter opener. He got me another mug of water. "Two years," he repeated, slumping back in his chair and petting Limosa's behind. "Sometimes it seems like five minutes, sometimes a lifetime." He looked around. "This was Isa's place. She designed it. She taught art history at the university. She was from Salamanca. Her parents are still there. We see each other every other Sunday for lunch. They don't like me, but I'm a connection to Isa. I don't like them either, but otherwise I never see anyone but my students."

I sipped my water. Everyone I was meeting lately seemed to have been left behind.

"Have I made you unhappy?" Angel asked.

"No," I said. "It's not your fault." I explained about António.

He said, "I lost my best friend five years before Isa died. We grew up together. He was a doctor in Madrid. A surgeon. We spoke on the phone every day toward the end of his life. His voice kept fading and fading until it was finally nothing at all. I had these phone calls that were just monologues — me talking, him listening. Finally I had the idea to read him stories. I ended up reading him *A Hundred Years of Solitude*. Ten pages every Saturday afternoon for half a year. My phone bills... Jesus. He said my voice was soothing. For a while after he died I had these urges to pick up the phone and make believe he was on the other end. I talked over the phone to nobody, but as if it were him. Isa called them 'phantom conversations'. She said I was like those people who've lost a hand or foot and still feel it itching or hurting for a year afterward." He shook his head. "Without my knowing anything about it, she adapted my monologues into a play. She tried to get it performed at the university before she died, but the theater director didn't like it." He shrugged. "Some people can turn death into art. Or at least give the empty space we inherit some form. And some people can't. I'm one of those who can't."

"So what do you do here alone?"

"I keep reading. To myself now." He pointed to the bookshelves. "I just want to read now. Nothing else."

"About anything in particular?"

"No. Novels mostly. I prefer other people's lives to my own." He laughed. "God, I hope that doesn't sound pathetic. You mustn't think of me as feeling sorry for myself. I'm glad to be here, glad I have the freedom to read. There's nothing else I'd rather be doing. I'm lucky." He stood up. "Let me show you something," he said.

He took me out back. Five rosebushes were in bloom; two had white flowers, one pink and two orange with red tips. "My friend, the one who died in Madrid, gave me an idea. He said that when someone we love dies, we should plant something. So far, five rosebushes. He pointed to the orange ones, "Those are Coriolano — that was my friend's name — and his lover. And that pink one, that's Isa." He pulled off one of her blooms and handed it to me. "It doesn't help at all," he said. "But the flowers are pretty, don't you think?"

Angel locked Limosa in the house and gave me a ride back to Salamanca in his old Mercedes. "A present from Isa's father," he explained. "It used to be a taxi. He drove it for twelve years. He's retired now. He watches soccer games and thinks up mean things to tell me every other Sunday." He shrugged. "People need to be angry at something."

We stopped on the way to pick up my sweater. He said, "Sometimes I wish I'd been born in the Middle Ages. You wouldn't know then what causes disease. You'd believe in God."

"But the doctors would use leeches on you and your teeth would be shit," I replied.

He smiled. "I could live with that."

"You'd smell, too. And there'd be no hot water. You'd have to spray yourself with perfume from morning till night just to stand your own stink."

"To believe in a Creator, I'd smell like a garlic stalk."

"Not me. I like to be clean. Besides, I'm Jewish and gay. God didn't like people like me in the Middle Ages."

"He still doesn't."

"Maybe, but He doesn't matter so much anymore. People prefer watching television. It's not much of an improvement, but it's at least a start."

Angel smiled. "It's really good to talk English again," he said. "Spanish is such a ridiculous language. After a while, it makes you start thinking that you're trapped in a very weak picaresque novel. The most absurd things occur when you think in Spanish. It's this country, I think. Like you running into me by accident in the middle of an olive field and both of us being people left behind. In Spain, those things are normal. Lines meet that shouldn't. Stories cross. And you begin thinking in these circuitous, long-winded ways. I like English more. English is far more direct and sensible. English is a nice neat path through a sensible garden. Spanish is a vine bridge skirting a swamp."

He dropped me at my hotel. We shook hands. I said, "Listen, if you want to eat dinner with us tonight..."

"No," he said, "It's better to go our separate ways while we like each other. Pretty soon you'd see there's nothing left to me but lines from other people's novels."

I ate a delicious potato soup at the Café Sillín, a trendy little place with brass handrails on Zamora Street, then wandered around looking for António and Miguel. I was admiring the weathered carvings of saints crowning the main entrance of a small Romanesque church just up from the Tormes river when I heard the popping sound of a bouncing basketball. Out back of the church was a small blacktop court. Three teenagers were shooting around. I watched for a few minutes. They noticed me and started talking amongst themselves. They laughed. I shivered, thinking they were making fun of me. I was about to leave when one called out, "*Quier jugar?* Want to play?"

I replied, *"No hablo español."*

"No importa, doesn't matter," he called back.

"Soy viejo, I'm old," I said.

He laughed good-naturedly. *"No importa."* He waved me over.

He had long hair tied into a ponytail, the scruffy beginnings of his first beard. His eyes were almond-shaped, almost Asian. His name was Paco. He and his friends were juniors in high school. The others were Roberto and René. "René's mother is French," Paco explained.

We shook hands. I was going to play on the same side as Paco because he was the best. Roberto, who was only about five foot five and skinny, was going to cover me. I thought I'd have it easy. But he stole the ball from me every time I dribbled. He was like a ferret turned human. So Paco, who was a generous teammate, kept giving me picks. To my great surprise, I could still shoot well from about twelve feet in. Paco drove strongly to both sides and had a soft jump shot. We won the game by three baskets. Everybody laughed about that. But I was disheartened that I was so terrible. What would my old West Village teammates have thought? I was panting like a dog. Roberto and René wanted a rematch, but I said I was too tired. *"Muy viejo e muy malo,"* I explained.

No, no, they lied. We shook hands.

On my way home, I was thinking that you should have known me when I was young, Carlos, when I smiled easily, when I didn't know yet that our lives would be filled with departures ending in hollow silences. Maybe there's just not enough left of me to have a relationship with anybody. Maybe I should give up on trying to find a man who will hold my hand till death do us part and limit myself to teaching fingerings on guitar concerti.

Once, you hinted at it my diminished capacities for love, as I recall. You said, "Sometimes I feel it's useless trying to get the attention of a man who's listening with one ear for signals from beyond the grave."

It made me furious at the time. But there must have been moments when you were absolutely right.

Perhaps I had a good deal more to do with our failure than I originally thought. The more I put in this letter, the more I'm willing to believe that I must have really hurt you at times. Again, I apologize.

Proof that I still haven't learned to let the ghosts go, Carlos, is that before I got to our hotel I stopped at the cathedral to light some candles for my friends and for Nancy the Border Collie. It was cold and dimly lit and depressing. I got out fast.

Nobody had gotten back to our room yet. I was scared at being alone and dropped a valium. I showered. When I got out, Miguel was sitting on the end of our bed. He'd shaved. "You got rid of your stubble," I observed.

And I noticed that he hadn't done a spot just below his nose, like António.

He nodded, and I was thinking: *Now he's going to tell me that what happened between us was a terrible mistake that can never be repeated or even revealed.*

He rubbed his cheek with his palm. "I don't want to scratch you when we kiss," he said. He stood up and faced me.

I was wondering if I'd understood his use of the present tense correctly. "Any sign of your son?" I asked.

"Nothing. I don't know what he's up to." He came up to me and peeled away my towel. His hand cradled my balls. He held my behind. We kissed. He tasted deliciously of wine and tobacco. And something else. Lack of sleep?

It's easy now to say that I should have guessed that Miguel had an ulterior motive behind these seductions, but at the time I didn't scent anything more unusual on his neck and ears and fingertips than the need for some compassion.

Maybe my blind acceptance was due to the tranquilizers.

Or perhaps it was my understanding that men like Miguel, who marched straight through life without any deviations whatsoever, might suddenly detour to the other side of the street if hit hard enough by trauma.

It was Henry The Beast who said, "People either fly out of the closet when hit by personal disaster or lock the door with an extra dead-bolt."

One of my hidden thoughts was that any man whose chromosomes had helped create António had to be at least a little bit gay.

I considered all these reasons only afterward; the feel of my naked skin against his jeans and t-shirt seemed to preclude all rational thought except one: I said, "Let me get a condom."

"But you're negative, right?" he asked.

I nodded.

"And I had a blood test after a girl I knew got hepatitis a year ago. I'm negative. So we don't need one." He paused for a moment, biting his lip. He said, "Though if you used one with António..."

"Yes," I said. "All the time. It's become a habit. Like putting your seat belt on."

After we were both covered, he said, "I'll tell you what. Just tell me what makes you feel good." He knelt before me and looked up for my reply.

In his eyes, I saw that one of the reasons I wanted to make love with him was because I was a little like Angel Llorca; I wanted to cling to Miguel's story, his life — to make his past a little bit my own.

Miguel asked so many questions that it was hard to enjoy his gallant effort. Finally, I just told him to please be quiet and do whatever he wanted under the theory that even having your cock bitten raw by an inexperienced stone mason might feel good if you were excited enough.

I was right.

For some reason, he insisted on taking off my condom just before I came.

He gargled in the bathroom afterward. He drank a can of Coke he'd had the good sense to buy. He sat on the toilet with his head between his legs again.

I told him, "If you're not enjoying it, you shouldn't do it. I don't even know why we're doing it. If I weren't so crazed about all this..."

"I am enjoying it. But it must be an acquired taste. Like beer. Don't worry about it, the Coke takes most of the bitterness away."

"Their marketing men would think that was a great selling point. 'Hi, my name is Miguel. I'm a stone mason. I put in a hard day's work. And after I give my man a blowjob, Coke's the refreshment I need.' You should write them. I'm sure they'd be interested."

He smiled weakly. I said, "You don't have to swallow it, you know."

He looked up, puzzled.

"No," I assured him. "Lots of guys don't. You can spit it out or have me come outside your mouth."

"My wife swallowed it."

"Good for her. But you're not in competition with her. This isn't a test of strength."

"So it's okay not to? Gay people don't mind that?"

"No."

"Did my son mind if you didn't swallow it?"

"What a question!"

"Did he?"

"Of course not! And even if he did, if I didn't want to, I wouldn't."

"No?"

"No."

I kissed him on the forehead, left him sitting in the bathroom. As I was just getting back into *Life With a Star*, there was a knock on the door. "It's me," António announced. Miguel closed the bathroom door. I let the boy in. I was standing in my towel. "What's going on?" he asked.

"Let's see... I just took a shower. And today it's your father's turn to have Montezuma's revenge. He's on the toilet."

He put my guitar case on his bed. "I need to shower," he said.

"I'll be out in a minute," Miguel called.

The boy started to undress.

"Did you have a nice day?" I asked.

"Okay. I like Spain more and more."

"What'd you do?"

"I'll tell you at dinner. I just want to shower."

His clothes were sopped with sweat. They exuded the smell of a boy who'd been using his body. When he got his underwear off, I asked for them. I lifted them to my nose and inhaled deeply.

"You're crazy," he said.

"That's old news." I threw his underwear at him and hit him in the head.

He grumbled and tossed them on the floor.

"Have you been exercising?" I asked.

"No."

"Beating up old ladies for spare change?"

He rolled his eyes.

"Bungee-jumping from the top of the cathedral?"

He stepped out of his clothes. He knocked on the bathroom door. "Can I come in?" he asked.

Miguel opened the door and emerged with his hair slicked back with water. He stank of aftershave.

"You look pale," António said.

"I'm okay," Miguel replied.

"He looks pale because he shaved," I commented. "The sun hasn't hit his cheeks in a week."

"No, he looks sick," António insisted. "Are you nauseous? Was it seafood?"

"I'm fine," he said.

"It's that scent he put on that's making it worse," I noted. "Spanish aftershave is toxic. It's all made from recycled motor oil and powdered castanets."

"It's American aftershave," Miguel noted dryly.

António said, "You should drink some warm milk. You need something in your stomach."

Miguel shared a look with me.

On the road, time is divided by meals not hours. We ate dinner at a restaurant with carnations in crystal vases. It had a view of the cathedral and signed photographs of North African landscapes on the salmon-pink walls — camels and sand dunes and Bedouins, that sort of thing. I was wearing my blue linen sport coat and a yellow t-shirt. I hoped I looked elegant in a *Miami Vice* sort of way. António told me I looked like a stuffed animal, but then squeezed my hand

and smiled. "You look handsome," he said. Miguel agreed.

I thanked them both for lying so graciously.

The boy wouldn't tell us what he'd been doing, but he was in a good mood, so I didn't care. He said, "I want it to be a surprise."

During the meal, António would neither look at his father nor talk to him, however. Out of default, he and I ended up talking about the Bach Cello Suite. Miguel played with his olives, then his fork, then picked his teeth with toothpicks. He wolfed down his flan and left without having coffee. He said he wanted to go to bed, but I think he just wanted to go to a café and smoke in peace.

António leaned toward me. "Has he told you what he really thinks of you yet?"

"He can't decide whether he hates me or not."

"Really?"

"That's what he said."

The boy frowned. "I'm sure he didn't like it the other night when you got in bed with me."

"No, I don't think he did."

"What'd he say?"

I sighed.

"What did he say?!" the boy insisted.

"He said just that, that he didn't like it."

"Did he threaten you?"

"No."

"That's a surprise. Maybe he's growing up."

I leaned forward in a conspiratorial sort of way. "Listen, he's frightened of you."

"Frightened...? Oh, you mean of getting it."

"No, that's not it. You know you really should talk to him about all this. I don't want to be in the middle."

"Me on top, my father on bottom, you in the middle. Why would you complain about that?"

I sighed again; I realized that I didn't like it all that much when the boy sounded like me.

"Don't deny it," he told me. "I see the way you look at his ass."

"He's attractive. So what."

"You'd fall on your knees and swallow his cock any time he asked."

I leaned toward him again and whispered, "Why don't you talk a little louder so everyone in the restaurant can hear you?!"

"It's not a crime. Besides, we're in Spain now. We cross a border and presto, we're beyond the restrictions of Portugal. It's like time travel."

"António, before you brought down the level of this conversation I was saying that you should talk to him."

"No more sermons. Those days are over."

"Fine. Have it your way."

António sipped his coffee. "Have you noticed him spying?"

"He doesn't spy."

"Oh please, don't you see the way he looks at you and me? Like he wants to catch us off guard. He's probably following you around the city. He could be disguised as a nun, for all we know."

"Maybe you're misinterpreting his motives."

"No, there's something he's concealing," he said in a voice of certainty. "One of these days, he'll pounce on you. Or me. Then we'll know. If we survive."

"You make him sound dangerous."

The boy raised his eyebrows as if that were obvious and downed the last of his coffee.

19

António woke me up at two in the morning on Monday. He was standing next to my bed. I sat up. "What's wrong?" I whispered.

"It comes in waves," he replied.

I walked him to his bed and got him back under the covers. As if afraid even to hope for my kindness, he said in a tiny voice, "Would you please sit with me?"

He fell asleep with me holding his hand. I climbed back into bed. When I woke an hour later, he was standing over me again, this time with a pillow over his chest. His forehead was beaded with sweat and his clothes were damp. I thought: *Night sweats so soon; it can't be.*

"I had a nightmare," he explained.

"Step out of your clothes."

He didn't move. He was trembling and his teeth were chattering.

I tugged the pillow out of his hands. I led him into the bathroom and took off his clothes. I covered him with a towel and rubbed his hair. He sat on the edge of the bathtub. He said he was being buried alive in his dream. He started to sob. I hugged him. I closed the door so as not to wake his father. But after a little while, Miguel poked his head in.

"Get out!" António yelled at him.

Miguel stepped forward into the doorway and reached out to touch the boy. António pushed his hand away.

Miguel scratched his cheek. He backed away. He closed the door gently behind him. A few minutes later, I heard the latch on the door open and close. When António and I entered the room again, he was gone.

In the morning, I turned over and found António reading a Spanish guitar magazine. "Hi," he said. He eyed me. I turned back over because I sensed he was about to say something abominable. I was wrong; he slapped my behind playfully and popped out of bed, laughing, before I could hit him back. He went to the bathroom.

Miguel hadn't returned.

I heard the boy shaving. My bladder wouldn't wait. I trudged to the toilet. "Don't come in!" he shouted.

"I need to pee."

"Go away."

I opened the door. He'd nicked himself on the chin and was dabbing at it with toilet paper.

"Don't come near me!" he shouted.

"It's just a cut."

"It's not just a cut. It's what it's got inside. Stay away!"

"António, you're not going to explode and spray me with blood. You stay there and tend to your face and I'll walk around you to tend to my bladder. If we don't panic, the two will never meet and everything will be fine."

I peed. My underwear from the day before was still at the bottom of the toilet. I flushed twice but it wouldn't go down. António said, "Now get out."

I left. I took a tranquilizer for him out of my pack. I peeked inside and said, "I'm leaving a valium on your nighttable. Take it. Then come to breakfast. We leave for Avila this morning — before noon."

"And if my father's not back?"

Neither António nor Miguel showed up at breakfast. I shopped for a bit in the new part of town, bought myself a pair of blue-and-white striped bikini underwear to make up for the soiled one that I'd leave behind as my gift to the sewers of Salamanca. It was eleven when I got back to the hotel. Miguel had packed, was sitting by the window staring at the street. No sign of António.

"Where'd you go last night?" I asked.

"For a walk."

"All night?"

"All night."

"You mustn't let him treat you like that," I said.

He shrugged.

"It's not helping him or you."

"You don't know that," he said. "You don't know that at all."

"You need to talk with him."

"In a few days," he replied. "Maybe in Madrid I'll know enough."

"Know enough?"

"Yeah."

"About what?"

"About everything."

I started packing. "Ever been to Avila?" I asked.

"No. I don't like Spain. It's pretty, but it's just not right."

"Not right?"

"It's upside-down. It makes me nervous. It's like I'm going to spill out."

I zipped up my bag. Miguel walked to me and gripped my thigh with his legs like a dog. He undid my pants. I got a condom on him.

I thought he might push my bowel straight up through my mouth. It was over in less than a minute. Afterward, he kissed my neck for a time as if he were trying to press whispers into my body. When he went to the bathroom, tears came to me. For two reasons:

the sheer sexual power of this man was inducing memories in me again of a time long gone when sensual love was not covered with the rusty armor of illness and death;

and because, when I got really excited, I began fantasizing that I was lying with you, Carlos.

Do you understand the significance of what I'm saying? Probably not, so listen up...

I could have chosen to imagine anyone from Sam Shepard to Sholom Aleichem, and I chose a frightened little painter who thinks I'm a pervert!

It proved to me that I was still a little touched. And still very much in love.

And I knew that I couldn't go forward into my future without telling you that in this letter.

Does such an admission make you fear me again? Or are you even now painting over that all-too-colorful emotion with alternating layers of white indifference and black derision?

A warm day; tranquilizers coursing my veins; the clean hollow left behind by a man.

It was as if I'd been blessed.

I farted an entire fanfare in the car. If António had been paying attention, he'd have guessed. But he was humming to himself. As I eased the Batmobile out of the parking lot, he turned with an enthusiastic face. "Sing this melody," he said. He sang for me. I couldn't repeat it because it:

was in five-four time;

shifted between a major scale and whole-tone scale;

and had a pair of chromatic triplets right in the middle like two big speed bumps.

I was heading passed congested intersections and weaving around double-parked cars. I told him, "Driving and staying awake are all I can do. Singing in five-four time is one thing too many."

"You sing the harmony," he said. He sang another tune which wasn't much easier.

"I can't," I said.

"You're not fucking trying!"

"You're right. I don't have your talent. I can't do it."

"You're an idiot, *um burro.*"

I wasn't the least bit hurt at his comparing me to a donkey, but I felt I should be, so I said, "Don't talk to me like that."

"I'll talk to you any way I want. You're the one who forced me on this trip."

I spotted a road sign for Avila. I was relieved. I said, "No one forced you."

From the back seat, Miguel sang the first seven notes of the original melody. He had a lovely baritone. He leaned forward between our bucket seats. He faced his son and said, "Teach me the rest."

I told Miguel, "I didn't know you could sing."

He shrugged. It was hot, and he was sweating profusely, his powder-blue t-shirt stained darkly under the arms. I gripped the wet material and put my fingers to my nose.

"What are you doing?" António asked me.

"Isn't it obvious?"

"You're perverse."

"Leave the Professor alone," Miguel told his son.

I found it curious that he could defend me but not himself. "A knight comes to the aid of the..." I stopped because I didn't know how to say *damsel in distress* in Portuguese.

It made no difference; António snapped at his father right away. "Don't tell me what to do! I hate that. I really hate that."

We were about to have one of our arguments, so I said to Miguel, "When was the last time you sang anything?"

"I always give it a go in the shower," he replied. "And sometimes in bed. Only when I'm alone. When I was young, I wanted to be a singer. You'll laugh. I wanted to study opera."

Nobody laughed.

"Who cares?" António said. He faced forward and folded his arms over his chest.

I shared a look with Miguel. To António, I said, "Your sweat smells like your father's."

He rolled his eyes.

"Teach him the melody," I said. I rubbed the boy's thigh in encouragement. "Go ahead and teach him. What've you got to lose?"

"All right." He kneeled on his seat to face his father. "Move back, you idiot, you're too close," he said. António spoke with such acid in his voice that I hit his shoulder. He glared at me. I entered the freeway. Miguel sat back in his seat. "It goes like this," the boy said. He sang the first melody again.

Miguel had trouble with the rhythm on the triplets, but he sang the melody note for note. It was a miracle.

"Teach him the harmony," I said.

Miguel sang that melody back perfectly, too. I looked over at António. He wasn't surprised. He made an impatient face. "What?" he said. "You think I just happened from out of nowhere? It's genetics. Didn't you study any science in that capitalist wasteland of yours? Pea plants? Mendel? Does any of this ring a bell?" He turned to his father. "Okay, now you sing the harmony — the second melody — at the same time I sing the first."

He was exhibiting the pride in his father that an animal trainer might show for a terrier who could dance around on its back legs with a party hat on its head.

I watched Miguel in the rearview mirror. He had his hands pinned under his legs where they couldn't reach for a cigarette. He sat up, eager to follow his son's orders.

"One, two, three..." the boy said, marking the tempo.

They sang.

Two handsome men sitting next to you and singing a dissonant melody as valium slides through your circulatory system and you guide a '65 T-Bird through the Castilian countryside at eighty miles per hour. Life doesn't get much sweeter and stranger than that.

António tapped my leg. "Well?" he said.

"Well what?" I asked.

"What do you think?"

"I don't know what it's supposed to be."

"Just tell me what you think," he insisted.

"I don't know what to make of it because I don't know what it's supposed to be. The *Messiah* is fine for a chorus and an orchestra, but I don't think any of the songs would be right for a beer commercial."

"You just don't want to say that you hate it," he declared angrily.

"It's just too strange for one hearing. What is it, a piece you heard in Salamanca? A transcription you're doing?"

"You'll see. It's a surprise. For myself, even if no one else likes it."

"I liked it," Miguel chirped.

António turned to him and frowned contemptuously.

My mother pops out of my mouth at the weirdest moments, and I said, "Make that face too often and it'll freeze on you permanently!"

Thankfully, the boy was used to it and ignored me. We sat in silence, then Miguel said, "Remember when we used to sing together?"

António watched the scenery out his window.

"You've done that sort of thing before?" I asked.

"Who do you think taught me music?" the boy snapped. "It wasn't just you. You came later. You didn't teach me everything I know, you know."

I said, "I never thought so."

"Sure you did! You thought you made me. What a talented teacher you are, right?" The boy laughed at me like a bad actor. He winked.

He's suddenly become an incompetent Iago pandering to an audience, I thought. *Why else that cruel wink? This is all for Miguel's benefit.*

Dread soaked into my gut like a black dye. I was quiet.

"You probably even slowed me down," he continued. "I could've gone faster without all those scales and all those silly studies — those things by Sor. Remember? Day after day, that music for children you made me learn. You know, if you were a better guitarist, I could have learned much faster. Imagine if you were Leo Brouwer or Christopher Parkening...? Imagine where I'd be? Or even somebody not quite that good but who had performance experience himself. I'd already be giving concerts instead of driving with you and my father through a desert in the middle of nowhere.... In the middle of nowhere in fucking Spain!"

I must have looked like a baby seal clobbered on the head for its pelt — dazed, confused and one blow from unconsciousness.

I gripped the steering wheel hard. I told myself that none of this was happening. It was a bad dream that would soon end.

"Shut up, António!" Miguel shouted. "Shut up now!"

"No, you shut up!" the boy yelled back. "If it weren't for you, none of us would be here. You're the biggest coward of us all! So don't you tell me what to do! Don't you ever...!"

They yelled at each other for a few minutes. I struggled in vain to unlearn Portuguese.

When they were both quiet and both looking out their windows, I reached into my pocket. As I downed another tranquilizer, I thought: *I've got to give him credit; he's scored at least two direct hits into my heart without any hesitation. But how many more will there be?*

Miguel finished up the drive to Avila because a slight overdose of God in my little pink pills had dragged me down into a cave of depression. I curled up in the back seat and tried to tuck myself into the black vinyl. We stopped at the *parador* just inside the high fortifications of the city. Miguel and António got their bags from the trunk. I told them I'd join them inside the hotel in a minute. I needed to sit alone. I needed to think. If I could only think enough, I could figure out what to do. But I couldn't.

Thoughts formed, then dissipated. Smoke — my brain had become smoke.

António took his own room. The receptionist told me my room number and said that my *brother-in-law* was already there. She asked for my passport.

Miguel was sitting on the end of a bed when I entered. His head hung down. He was scratching the stubble again sprouting on his cheeks. He looked up. "The boy didn't mean what he was saying," he told me.

I dropped my luggage and sat on the empty bed. "I've got to lie down. And I've got to be alone."

He looked at me with those helpless eyes of his.

I stared back, so empty that I didn't care if he saw all the way through me and found nothing.

"You'll be okay?" he asked.

I said, "Don't worry, I'm not the operatic type. No suicide attempts or broken glass. Go and enjoy Avila."

With his fingers gripping the door handle, he asked, "You need anything from the stores?"

"Families are jigsaw puzzles," I replied.

"What?"

"Jigsaw puzzles. Only every time we think we've completed the picture we realize we've left out whole areas. It's like a universe that keeps expanding. We can't catch up."

"You've lost me, Professor," he replied.

"I've lost myself. Doesn't matter. I'm just babbling. It's what I do when my brain doesn't function."

"You want anything from the outside world?"

"If you find the ghost of Santa Teresa, ask her about the importance of hope for me. Ask how you get it back. If she says anything reasonably intelligent, then come right back and tell me. If not, just take your time and bring me back a can of Coke."

I slept a dreamless sleep. Maybe because of that, I daydreamed vividly when I woke.

Henry The Beast used to say that our waking fantasies are opalescent tropical birds which we keep inside sacks, and that we're afraid to let them out lest they fly off and get lost.

But Henry didn't live long enough to know that in our decade of dread they've become more like rattlesnakes which we're afraid to look at too long lest they be tempted to eat us alive.

I began picturing myself in the Batmobile, driving like a demon through the gates of Avila, leaving António and Miguel far behind in a cloud of medieval dust. I zoomed passed Madrid to Barcelona, boarded a rusted freighter flying the Liberian flag, drank myself into an ouzo stupor inside the arms of a bearded Greek sailor and ended up in Izmir. I ate fresh figs on the beach and threw their purple skins to sea gulls. I was young and handsome again, had a full head of silky hair curled into ringlets and smelling of Herbal Essence shampoo. I made money by selling my body in the marketplace, right next to the cucumber sellers; there was no need to be subtle. And why was I able to do all this so freely?

Because there were no invisible Cossacks to chop off my head, of course.

Anything can happen in a daydream.

I even pictured you there, Carlos, walking into the marketplace dressed in white Arabian robes, making eyes at me and offering me a small fortune to come home with you. I told you, *If you'll kiss me right here in front of everyone you won't even have to pay.*

And what a kiss it was! The cucumber sellers and barbers and spice dealers and fortune tellers all stood up and applauded.

Then I pictured myself really sick. I was in a ward for plague victims in a filthy hospital. The sheets were covered with spittle and crusted blood. I wrote heartbreaking goodbye letters to Fiama and my mother. I was in agony, but I wrote: *Don't be sad for me; I had a good life.*

Heroic prose. What a joke.

The key turned in the door. "I'm taking you to dinner," Miguel said as he entered the room. His eyes were bright, his manner excited. "We're going to eat caviar and drink champagne! So get your clothes on, Professor."

"Any particular reason for the champagne?" I asked.

"Because I feel like it!"

"But why?"

"I just do." He clapped his hands. "Come on, let's get going."

It's nice sometimes to follow orders. I showered quickly and chose a special outfit: a pink silk shirt with a counterfeit Giorgio Armani label and gray woolen pants. I draped my blue linen jacket over my shoulders like Marcello Mastroianni.

We walked toward the cathedral without talking. I was waiting for a compliment that never came.

After a while, when depression began clinging to me again, I wished my feet were made of fur so I could make no noise. I wanted to be smaller than the smallest memory; only if you can escape everyone's remembrance of you, can you really escape.

"There's one thing I need to ask you to do for me," Miguel said.

"What?"

"I'll tell you tonight."

"Another secret? What is it about you two? You and your son are like squirrels."

"Squirrels?"

"Storing things for winter."

"We test the waters before we jump," he replied.

"Be careful, squirrels don't swim very well," I observed.

"I don't get it."

"Doesn't matter. Anyway, do you know where the boy is?"

"Probably playing guitar somewhere."

Miguel stopped, looked at me pensively, then told me a story about his father. He, too, had been a stone mason. Once, when he was ill for more than a month, he had to sell the little fishing boat which he used on the Minho river every weekend. He never got another one. He made enough money, he just never bought one. When Miguel asked him why, he didn't answer. For a year he didn't reply. Then one day, apropos of nothing, he pulled the boy aside and said, "I haven't bought another boat because I never really liked fishing."

The story seemed important to Miguel. He said, "António is just like my father."

"How?"

"He just is. I can't explain. They wait. They scream. Then wait some more. They don't trust people. They want to do everything themselves because they think that no one else can be counted on for help."

"And your mother?"

"My mother... She's still alive. She's like a castle. Cold but powerful. With secret rooms and dungeons and great fires burning that are never quite enough. Then sometimes she's like a little girl. It makes no sense. She confuses me." He shrugged. "Sorry," he said. "I'm talking to much."

"I like it when you talk." I admitted. "Though I like you when you're silent, too."

"You say things other people don't," he observed.

"I ditched my censor during the war," I replied.

"What war?"

"There's always a war. There's one on right now, as a matter of fact. It's a weird war though because even the enemy doesn't know he's fighting. It's like something only a madman would dream up."

He shrugged. He thought I was nuts. But he didn't really care. He even liked me for it.

The restaurant which Miguel had discovered was on the Calle de la Dama. It was called La Coruña and was right across the street from the convent of Santa Teresa, a high stone fortress glowing golden in the evening light. It reminded me of another of my daydreams. "Samson tore down the building that was his prison," I told Miguel. "Just tore it right down to the ground."

He nodded and opened the restaurant's glass door for me. He didn't have a clue what I was talking about.

"The thing is," I said, "He could see his prison. You can destroy what you can see. But I don't see anything. It's dispersed throughout my body, throughout all our bodies."

Miguel said to the maître d', *"Dos persones,"* in his Portuguese-accented Spanish.

We were led to a table by windows looking out on a garden. A tall palm tree was fronted by oleander bushes. Behind it, climbing up a far wall, was a red bougainvillea just beginning to flower.

Inside the restaurant, the floor was wood parquet. The table-cloths and walls were white.

I was in one of those moods where I couldn't let go of something that seemed meaningful. "Invisible," I said to Miguel.

"What?"

"All my enemies."

"Except my son," he nodded.

I agreed. But I was suddenly unspeakably sad, as if I were homesick for a land beyond my reach. I wanted to disappear again. "Order the wine," I said.

"Champagne," he corrected. "We're celebrating."

"What could we possibly celebrate?"

"For one thing, we've escaped Portugal. And then..." He reached out and held my hand.

My heart skipped a beat. But our connection just made me sadder; it was only temporary, and it would never be enough.

"For another," he continued, "we've gotten to know each other. I always wanted to know you. All the stories António told." He squeezed my hand once, then leaned back and started buttering his bread. "Most importantly, we're having champagne because António yelled at me — really, really yelled at me. It's the first time since we started the trip."

"That's good?"

"Very. You don't know the boy like I do. He's got to spit all his anger out. Then I can try to talk to him. Then I can get another chance. He's just like my father."

"There's one thing you're forgetting," I pointed out. "Young people who are told they're going to die... They have so much anger that sometimes they can never spit it all out. They're bottomless."

20

We got back to the hotel around eleven in the evening. We were smashed. We asked at the reception desk whether António had gotten back. He had, an hour before.

I paused in front of his door. Number 17. The lights were off. Miguel shook his head.

"What if he wakes up in the night and we're not there?" I asked.

Miguel opened our door. He waved me in.

He showered, then got into bed with me. I was nearly asleep. His body was very warm. The hairs on his legs were soft. It was good to lie in bed with a man. I cuddled into him as into a nest.

When I was almost in dreamland again, he took me in his mouth. Then he slipped a condom on me.

He turned around and positioned my sex at his opening. He whispered, "This is the favor I wanted to ask you — be very gentle."

I reached around his hip. His heartbeat was banging against my chest. His penis, however, was an acorn. It wanted to turn around and hide inside his balls.

I was drunk and couldn't talk. I rested. Then I whispered, "Why are we going to do this?"

"I want to."

"I only want to do those things that make you happy." I rubbed my hand over his chest and kissed the top of his head. I breathed in the scent of him.

He said, "I really want to."

I tugged playfully on the end of his penis. "Then why is it like this?"

"I'm frightened. I told you. Just be gentle." He lubricated me with spittle.

His opening was stitched tight. When the seams came out, he was going to scream from his gut. I couldn't keep my erection thinking about it.

He blew me again, then turned around. "Now!" he said. "Put it in now, Professor!"

"It's going to hurt you."

"Shut up!" He tugged me toward him. I pushed. But it was no good.

"Wait," I said.

I loosened him with my fingers. He hissed with pain. I stopped. "Why are we doing this?" I asked again.

"Shut up!" He coaxed me back up with his mouth. He stroked my behind. "Give it to me," he said.

He grunted as my tip broke his stitching. "It stings," he said.

I pulled right out. I rolled on my back. "I'm too tired. Let's just go to sleep."

He turned on the light and straddled me. He spit on his cock and jerked himself erect. "You said I was handsome."

I turned away.

He caressed my cheek. "Look at me," he begged. "Look at my cock. You can do anything you want to me."

I held his hips. "Fine," I said, "but I don't want to fuck you."

"I'm a virgin. You can have me."

"Read my lips," I said. "I don't want you — not this way. And virginity means nothing to me. I don't even remember what it means."

"Don't be so kind."

"I'm not being kind. I can't get an erection if I know I'm going to hurt you. Believe me, it's been a liability in the past. I'm not proud of it."

"You're not going to hurt me." He lubricated his behind, then played with me to make me hard. He sat down harshly on my cock. He grimaced and clenched his teeth. He shook his head.

"Stop this," I begged. I twisted to my side to get away from him.

He leaned forward and gripped my shoulders hard. He pinned me to the mattress. "Don't move!" he ordered. He impaled himself down inch by inch as if he were a knight putting a sword into his own gut to pay for an unforgivable humiliation he'd given his king.

"Why are you doing this?" I asked.

He didn't reply. When I was fully inside him, he kicked his head back and breathed deeply. His behind felt like a feathered vise.

I thought he might faint. I was afraid to move.

"Let me pull out of you," I said. "It'll hurt less when I put it in again."

He knew what I was up to and replied, "If I let you out, I'll never get you back in. Now fuck me!"

I lay motionless. Why would I want to be the instrument of any man's penance?

I shrunk to nothing. I twisted away. His shoulders sagged hopelessly and he rolled off of me. He moaned once in anguish. He punched the mattress. He curled up like a ball. He faced away from me. His ass was bleeding.

Blood sluicing across a raw behind is a paralyzing sight.

As if I were talking to every man I'd ever met who liked to take out his frustrations in bed, including you, dear Carlos, I said, "This isn't what fucking is about."

I went to the bathroom and ran a hand towel under hot water. I stared at myself in the mirror. Did I always look so old? My hair wasn't growing back well at a spot right in the middle of my head. I fluffed it up with my hand, but I was obviously going bald. *Drugged, depressed, practically impotent and a head like Friar Tuck,* I whispered to myself. *It's gonna be a swell last five years to this century!*

I climbed up on the bed and pressed the towel softly to Miguel's wounded stitching. He started, then moved slowly back to soak up its warmth. I rubbed his legs with my free hand. "Don't ever do that again," I said. "Your body is sacred. What is a blessed act for some people is a crime for others. We are each of a different nature."

He sobbed like a baby.

The next morning was Tuesday, May the 30th. I started the day by smearing antibiotic cream on Miguel's behind. "What were you thinking of?" I inquired.

"I was drunk," he replied. "Champagne does strange things to me."

"That wasn't it."

He shrugged.

"So many secrets you have."

We went to breakfast. António had already eaten. He met us in the lobby. His things were packed. "What a dump this town is," he announced in English.

"So?" I asked.

"Do you mind if we leave right away?"

"I guess not." I looked at Miguel.

"Okay with me," he said.

"Just let us eat breakfast," I told the boy. "Come sit with us."

The receptionist watched his bags while we sat together in the dining room. António faced sideways and looked out the window.

"Have you been practicing?" I asked him.

He nodded.

Miguel guzzled his coffee and wolfed down bread, butter and jam; he wanted to smoke and couldn't with António at the table. "I'm going to pack," he said. He nodded to us both, stuck a cigarette in his mouth and left.

The boy leaned toward me. "You get anything more out of him?"

"I'm not trying to get anything out of him," I replied.

"But what's he said?"

"Nothing."

"He must have said something."

"He said that his father was a lot like you."

António's face was incredulous. "Grandpa Zé?"

"I guess."

"That old bugger had a screw loose."

"Why?"

"He just did." The boy looked away for a bit, then said, "He was originally from Galicia. That's where our Celtic blood comes from. He even played a Galician bagpipe. After he had his stroke, he was like someone in a comic strip. One of his eyes drooped and was always red. The other was half closed. He looked like the Hunchback of Notre Dame."

I was going to say, *Don't be so mean; illness does ugly things to people,* but didn't. I nodded.

"He didn't even speak Portuguese," António continued. "He spoke in Galician dialect to me. I didn't understand a word. What a lunatic!"

"I don't speak Portuguese either. Does that make me crazy?"

"You speak Portuguese. Incorrectly, of course, but you speak it."

"Forget it. Listen, I want to talk about what you said yesterday. About you being able to go faster with a more qualified teacher. I just wanted to say..."

I was going to tell him that we were going to Paris to get him an audition with José Luis Landero, the prominent instructor he deserved. He interrupted me and said, "I don't want to talk about that."

"We have to talk about it."

"I don't want to." He stood up. "Give me the car keys and I'll start loading up the trunk." He held out his hand and tried to look bored.

I reached into my pocket. As I handed him the keys, I told him, "What you said was true."

"It wasn't."

"It was. How you said it was unnecessarily cruel. We'll talk about

166

that some other time if it becomes necessary. But what you said was right. I've been selfish. I've known for some time that I had nothing more to teach you but kept you as my student. That was wrong."

"But Pedro couldn't teach me any more either," he replied.

"No, but there are other people."

"Not in Porto."

"No, not in Porto. But..."

"Not in Lisbon either."

"The world is bigger than Portugal," I observed.

"I'm not leaving Portugal."

"You've already left. We're in Spain."

His face whitened. He rushed away.

I never got to see any of Santa Teresa's relics. By nine-thirty, we were on a dusty road, headed toward the rising sun. By ten, we were cruising at eighty miles an hour on the freeway to Madrid. I thought it would keep António busy to have him drive, so he took over. He got excited about being behind the wheel in a foreign country, but wasn't about to say anything to boost my spirits.

The countryside turns to pine-covered mountains about half-way to Madrid: green bodies with wide hips reclining in the sun-light.

The city comes up suddenly. You descend off the flanks of the mountains, go through a few miles of desert scrub, pass some sub-urbs reminiscent of Phoenix or Santa Fe, then hit the traffic pour-ing into the city. You pass a big park with the zoo, then you're there. The brick towers of the skyline rise up.

I took the wheel and asked António to guide me to the hotel.

Right, left, right, another right, no not there, *there, there!!!*

You get the type of conversation we had, Carlos. The kind that makes everybody anxious. I dodged in and out of traffic, waited for double-parked trucks, cruised up the Alcalá, ducked past the Puerta del Sol and found our hotel. It would have taken a cabby ten min-utes; it took me forty-five.

I chose my old standby, the Hotel Cortezo, because it has a parking garage.

My underarms were dripping sweat and my back was stuck to the car seat.

I was excited to be in a big city. I wanted to walk fast, go shop-ping in expensive stores, walk up wide, tree-lined boulevards. I wanted to eat grilled octopus and drink *horchata de chufa* in clut-tered cafés till I could sit my distended stomach down on the table in front of me.

António said he was going right away to the Prado.

Suddenly, I wanted to show him so many things. I wanted to stand in front of Ribera's paintings with him. I'd drape my arm over his shoulder. We'd stare at the brushstrokes forming the shadowed cavity beneath Saint Jerome's collarbone, come up close to see the reflection of seventeenth-century varnish over his faithful eyes. The boy would smile the smile of discovery. *Incrível,* he'd whisper. Just incredible.

I wanted to watch him gaping before Jesus' ivory whiteness in Cano's *The Dead Christ Supported by an Angel.*

And sneak up behind him as he studied Titian's self-portrait.

He sensed these excited daydreams ricocheting through me and went for the kill. "I want to see the museum *alone,*" he said.

He landed on that last word with both his feet.

I went to my room and tried to release the bindings around my chest by downing two tranquilizers. I shouldn't have, of course. But I successfully summoned that old addict's standby: *Just this once.*

I considered flying back to Porto. Then, I thought, *No, when I can breathe freely again I'll sit by the man-made lake in the Retiro Park and feel sorry for myself. I'll sleep in the grass, and if someone robs me, so much the better.*

I told Miguel we'd walk together to the park. He brushed my shoulder with his hand and went to take a shower.

I'd forgotten how treacherous tranquilizers make me. I slipped out of the room like a cat burglar. He never heard a thing. Walking east on Atocha, I pictured António in the Prado. I thought of him surrounded by the works of El Greco.

A terrified boy circled by a hagiology in blue and black.

I remembered what my brother told me once, that when El Greco was at the height of his powers, plague was making the cemeteries of Spain overflow with death.

Half a million people died in the outbreak from 1596 to 1602 alone.

Harold told me that art critics maintained that the gaunt whiteness of El Greco's figures and their pallid features symbolically represented the softening that had taken place in the aristocracy of Spain.

Maybe so.

But El Greco was surrounded everywhere by withering misery. Who are the gaunt fire-lit figures of his paintings if not his Toledo neighbors? Look at his St Francis. Is he not a hooded plague victim?

As I came to the Plaza of Emperor Carlos V, I wondered what the old master would have been working on today.

Would he not have been painting my António?

I slept in the park, just as I'd predicted — on a cool lawn next to an empty 7-Up can, under the shade of a chestnut tree where someone had carved the initials AQ and RZ. No one robbed me. No one even looked at me. I had succeeded in disappearing from sight. I thought gratefully, *Just one more tranquilizer than usual has given me these valuable extra powers.*

I awoke with a bad headache. The sun, high in the western sky, was making my eyes tear. I drank two *horchatas* at a café with gray metal chairs and watched boys with earrings roller-blading in front of the lake. I asked for aspirin from my waiter. He had a nasty lump under his ear and walked with a limp. He brought me two with a smile. I ate a bag of potato chips manufactured in Bilbao. I got another. A beggar woman in a blue sweater came up and thrust her filthy hand under my nose. I gave her a hundred-peseta coin. She kept her hand out. I gave her the rest of my bag of chips. She grumbled something about God, but I didn't get it. The waiter shooed her away. He said something to me. I didn't get that either.

It was a relief not understanding everything people were saying. I'd forgotten how lovely it was to keep your distance.

As I walked back to the hotel, I stopped for real food at a restaurant. I stood at the counter with two businessmen either discussing...

a bad fall in the stock market;

a lady who had had her leather bag stolen;

or a pocket with a hole in it.

My Spanish was disintegrating. I ate grilled octopus and peppers. I ate sautéed mushrooms with whole cloves of roasted garlic. I ate a prosciutto sandwich. The bartender admired my appetite. He wore a white shirt and black bow-tie. He had a mustache. He looked like Velázquez's portrait of Mars. Or maybe he didn't look like that at all. I glanced around for the first time. Crystal chandeliers dangled from a flaking ceiling. Wilted orange lilies centered each of the wooden tables. The floor was black tile.

I went back to my sandwich. I ordered tea.

"Tea?" the waiter asked.

I pointed at myself. "English," I explained. *"Yo soy inglés."*

He smiled. He had one golden tooth.

As he steamed water from the espresso machine into a little white teapot, I asked if he didn't, by chance, have any English water he could make it with. "Always tastes better with British water," I explained. *"Siempre sabe mejor con agua britanica."*

He laughed.

My meal cost $32.

Maybe they ripped me off. No matter; it was comforting to play the fool in a big city where I didn't understand a thing with certainty.

I spent the rest of that day entertaining shopkeepers with my American-accented chatter. In a little store in the Chueca district, I bought a pirate shirt in turquoise blue from Ecuador; a striped vest in fuchsia, yellow, orange and pink from Guatemala; and a brown woolen hat with white llamas circling the rim knitted by hand in Bolivia. Next door, I bought a t-shirt which said *Viva el Rey! Viva el Preservativo!* in bright pink lettering on a blue background. Long Live the King! Long Live the Condom!

Yes, I was shopping in the gay section of town. And yes, Madrid has gotten queerer than ever in the last few years. Strangely enough, blond hair seemed to be in fashion. I counted five fair-haired members of the congregation with black roots in one three-block stretch along Hortaleza.

Apparently, the first thing you did after flying out of a Spanish closet was go Scandinavian.

At the Casa del Libro on the Gran Vía, I bought Pedro a collection of short stories by the Uruguayan writer Horacio Quiroga entitled *La Gallina Degollada,* The Decapitated Chicken. *Psychological tales of suspense,* the blurb read. Just across the street was a sporting goods store where I bought Salgueiro blue sweat pants to match his wife's robe. In a silver store just off the Plaza Mayor, I bought Fiama long filigree earrings.

I was finished buying presents.

In the evening, I sat in the Retiro Park again and drank some more *horchata.* I was beginning to be able to think rationally and found I could do simple algebra in my head, so I popped two more tranquilizers. I walked north out of the park and managed to find a street with several musty, shadowy restaurants where smoked hams hung from the ceilings. It was positively raining pig carcasses in Madrid.

Everybody but me was just snacking because it was only eight-thirty. Standing at the counter, I ate...

octopus with the consistency of rubber erasers;

cooked spinach which tasted like wet toilet paper;

potatoes and peppers which felt in my mouth like soft oily leather.

The restaurant was very noisy. I just pointed to what I wanted. I drank water like I'd been lost in the desert.

I wondered what was going on with the blandness and chewy textures of the food till I realized I couldn't taste *anything.*

My tea was simply hot water. When I added two packets of sugar, a hint of sweetness seeped through.

With my second cup of tea, I tried my joke about English water again. The waiter couldn't hear me. He cupped his hand around his ear, but it was too late.

I trudged on to an outdoor café in the Paseo de la Castellana with red and yellow metal chairs. A cold wind had come up from God knows where, and I slipped on my pirate shirt and vest. A woman with frizzled hair so black that she looked like a marble statue with a raven on her head asked me for a light. "Me no smoke," I said in English.

She smiled with thick red lips that frightened me. She backed away like I was dangerous.

Had I spoken too loud?

The sun went down. I sipped more tea. I kept my hands in my Bolivian woolen hat and bent to sip the liquid like an animal at a wading pool. I looked at the cover of my Horacio Quiroga anthology.

I was happy.

I wondered again why I'd ever given up drugs.

A tall and distinguished old gentleman in a gray herring-bone vest and pale yellow shirt came up to me. His hair was combed in a swirl of silver. He had a stern chin and assured eyes.

I thought he looked like Bellini's portrait of the Doge Leonardo Leredan.

"You need a place to stay?" he asked in Spanish.

"No, I'm okay," I replied.

"Americano?"

I nodded.

"May I sit down?" He spoke heavily accented English.

In all the weeks I'd spent at various times in Madrid, this was the first time that anyone had invited himself to sit with me. I wondered if I was bewitched.

He leaned across and whispered to me, "You need money?"

It came out like *Jew neet mowney,* so I laughed and replied, "No, this Jew is really okay." He knitted his brows and looked at me gravely, so I added politely, "I have a hotel room and everything. A good hotel room. Thank you."

"I'm sorry," he said. "I misunderstand. You look..." He made a graceful continental gesture that could have been interpreted a million ways.

I took it to mean I looked like shit. But I wanted to make sure. "I look how?" I asked.

"Jew look... *Jew* look not so very well sleeping."

I thought it might be fun seeing myself. I asked, "You don't have a hand mirror by any chance?"

"Excuse me..."

"Tiene espejo?"

"No, I'm sorry."

He stared at me. His foot knocked against mine. "You will stay in Madrid several days?" he asked.

"Maybe. I don't know."

He knocked again.

Apparently, this was a Spanish pick-up technique, because then he said, "I would like to show you around if you don't mind. It is a big city for one all alone."

I pulled my feet back underneath my chair and leaned across to him. I said, "You look like a very nice man. And I like to think I'm nice, too. But I have to say that I can't sleep with you."

"I just want to look at you," he whispered. "Look, no touch."

"What exactly do you mean?"

He gestured to his eyes and smiled sweetly. He had crooked yellow teeth.

American men don't have stained teeth anymore. It's something I admire in Europeans.

"Can we just sit here and talk?" he asked. "I let my eyes move across you."

I nodded. His name was Juan. He'd studied ornithology at Cambridge in the 1950s, had taught at Madrid University, was now retired. His daughter, an artist, lived in Barcelona. He had a calm, elegant way of talking, and I enjoyed his accent.

When I started to tell him about my life, I talked about you, Carlos.

Juan nodded and said, "I understand him perfectly. I was like him. Exactly equal. Frightened of what the other people would think if they knew."

I leaned toward him and asked, "And how did you get beyond your fears?"

He showed me a puzzled face. "Beyond?"

"Overcome them," I explained. "Find hope and love despite them."

"Oh, love," he said. He flapped his hand. "I never did." He pointed to his eyes. "But I'm old now. It's okay. I like to just look."

21

When I got back to the hotel, Miguel was lying on his stomach, his nose squashed to the side of his pillow. He was snoring. I kicked off my shoes and took another valium. I sat for a minute to end a sudden dizzy spell and passed out in my clothes. I slept straight through till Wednesday morning.

As I lay in bed trying to make believe I hadn't woken yet, Miguel said, "You left me here all alone yesterday."

I kept my eyes safely closed.

"I waited for you to come back. I thought you'd just stepped out for a few minutes to get something. I don't know. Soap or cigarettes or something."

"I don't smoke," I whispered.

"What?"

"I don't smoke. It wouldn't have been cigarettes."

Silence, then he said hopelessly: "I don't know why you left me."

"You're like a bulldog," I said. I sighed theatrically. He was silent. I opened one eye. He was standing in front of my bed. He looked pained. He frowned.

"Don't try to make me feel guilty," I said.

Miguel knew nothing about employing psychobabble in an argument. He said, "What the hell are you talking about?"

I patted the bed next to me. "Sit," I said.

He sat. He stared down at me like a wounded child. I thought: *I mustn't forget that inside of him is a boy still feeling the humiliation left by a colorless father.* "How's your rear end doing?" I asked.

"A little sore, but fine."

"That's what happens when you try to stick a camel through the eye of a needle."

"Professor, you're hardly the size of a camel," he observed.

I smiled. He wanted to, but didn't.

"Where's our little prince?" I asked.

"He's already out. He was playing guitar early this morning. That melody he was teaching us. And then..."

"Teaching *you*..." I interrupted.

"What?"

"He was teaching you, not *us*."

"Whatever. Didn't you hear him playing this morning?"

"No."

"You should take a shower," he said.

"Do I stink?"

"Yes, and you look like you're covered with dust."

When I stood up, the room started spinning. I reached out for the wall. I thought I might vomit. It was too many tranquilizers, of course.

"What's wrong?" he asked.

"Nothing," I said. "You'll wait around for me while I shower?"

He nodded.

"You won't skip out on me as vengeance?"

"No."

I turned on the water and let it get hot. I stripped off my clothes. I went out to Miguel again. I enjoyed him seeing me naked. Sensing myself protected by his glance, I dared to say, "This trip hasn't turned out anything like I thought it would."

"Nothing ever turns out like you think it will," he observed.

"Come on, not *nothing.*"

"What then?"

I tried to think. I stood in that doorway a long while. I realized that the answer was *death. The death of a loved one turns out pretty much like you think it will.*

I went back into the bathroom without saying a word.

As I dried off, Miguel asked me what I wanted to do and I told the truth.

"You won't want me to come along," he observed. "I've never been to an art museum before."

"What you're really saying is you don't want to go."

"No, I do want go, but I...I don't know about places like that."

"There's nothing to know. You go in. You look at art. You make fun of some paintings. You admire some of the others. You try to figure out why you like what you like from time to time. You remember things about your own life. You look at people. If you're lucky, you get a blowjob from a guard in the staff bathroom. Then you go home."

He accepted my explanation with a nod. He grabbed a towel and dried my porcupine hairdo without my asking. What a feeling it was to have my head shaken by those two magnificent hands! I considered not taking a tranquilizer, but decided to *just in case...*

We went to the Thyssen-Bornemisza collection. I'd never been there before.

As we passed the palms in front of the entranceway, I began wishing that you were there with us, Carlos. Don't you think it's a shame that we never made any of the art pilgrimages we'd planned? Or have you already erased them from memory? Are my words even reaching you? Perhaps this entire letter has already been tossed in your garbage, this page stained with kiwi peelings and coffee grounds.

Somewhere along the line, Miguel had acquired the notion that art should be an attempt to record what things look like to the naked eye. He walked around the museum for a while without saying anything. Then, in front of Francis Bacon's 'Portrait of George Dyer in a Mirror', he blurted out, "I just don't get it." He shook his head at me. "I told you that you wouldn't want to come with me —

I just don't understand any of it."

Like an old rabbi, I said, "What's to get? I told you... You look. You see things you like. You make fun of some of it..."

He pointed angrily to the canvas and said, "This! I don't get this."

I took a closer look. In Bacon's painting, it's as if space itself has been smudged. His subject's body is trying to re-contour itself to fit a cockeyed reality. His face in the mirror is broken in two.

"Why is it important to understand it?" I asked.

"I want to figure out what it's a picture of. I want to figure it out, goddammit!"

"George Dyer. It's a picture of him. You can read that on the title." I pointed to the sign.

He frowned and rubbed his cheeks. He drew his hands back through his hair roughly. "But nobody looks like that," he blurted out.

I explained my theory about smudged space as best I could in Portuguese because I didn't know the verb *to smudge*. Miguel listened attentively, then squinted at me and said, "Maybe," as if he really meant, *I don't think so*.

As we walked together around the museum, he continued to point out paintings he couldn't fathom. I gave him my theories.

In front of a Klee, I told him to imagine a house made of a paper being unfolded. "It's about the simplicity of a child constructing a home out of orange and yellow paper. Remember how it felt to do that? Remember the smell of the paste and its coarse stickiness when it got on your fingers... Those tiny scissors our teachers would give us that were so dull that they could barely cut the paper?"

He rubbed his cheeks and shrugged.

I pointed to the painting. "Didn't it feel anything like that, all pretty and happy and colorful?"

He squinted at me again. "Maybe," he repeated skeptically. But I sensed that I was making myself understood; this time, he meant, *You might just be right.*

He stopped in front of Kandinsky's 'Painting with Three Forms' and said, "Well?"

"Tell me what you see," I replied.

"Red and green stripes."

I shook my head. "Not good enough. Tell me what you imagine is there."

"I don't know."

"Try harder."

"I see a witch on the right pointing with her left arm toward an upside-down rabbit. See the eyes?" He stepped right up to the canvas and indicated a form in the left corner with arms and legs raised up.

"I see them," I said. "What's the witch doing to him...doing to the rabbit?"

"She's poisoning him," he said. He stared back at the Kandinsky. He licked his lips. "She's shooting venom into him." He stared at me with frightened eyes. "And she's giving him a disease he'll never get over."

We didn't talk much after that, but we spent two more hours at the museum. I ended up waiting for him in the cafeteria. I bought a postcard of Lucian Freud's self-portrait and addressed it to my mother because he was one of her favorite artists. I wrote, 'Having a restful time in Madrid. The food is scrumptious. Hope New York hasn't gotten too hot and muggy.'

Scrumptious and *muggy* were my mother's favorite adjectives. I wanted to make sure she knew I hadn't forgotten the cadence of her speech.

When Miguel reached my table, he smoked a cigarette and downed a double espresso. He'd bought some postcards, too. On the back of a playful Klee painting, he started writing to his wife.

"You're divorced and you still write to her when you're away?" I inquired.

"Well, on a trip like this... She's worried about the boy. I've called her a couple of times, too."

"I bet you were a dutiful husband. Despite the affairs, I mean. Or maybe because of them. And a dutiful son to your parents."

"Dutiful?" he asked.

I'd used the Portuguese word *obediente*. I explained what I meant: "You did what your mother and father asked of you. Same with your wife. You probably didn't show any enthusiasm, but you did what was required — chores, homework, marital duties in the bedroom. You always kept your resentment to yourself. And you sought to hide your affairs and anything that might give anyone cause to feel shame or doubt."

"I tried to be polite and conscientious, if that's what you're saying. Is there any crime in that?"

"No, but didn't you ever want to just unburden yourself of all that goodness? I mean, when did you think you were going to get to do what *you* wanted to do? In the next lifetime? Listen Miguel, there is no next lifetime."

He lit another cigarette. He thought for a while, then said, "I think my father was ashamed of me."

"How so?"

"I wasn't like him."

"No?"

"No." He shook his head and repressed a smile. "We had a fist fight once. I broke his nose."

He went back to his postcard. When he'd finished, he stared at me as if he wanted to say something momentous but was afraid to.

"What?" I asked.

"I think I'm throwing it all away," he replied. "By being here, I mean. I had to choose. And I chose to come. António's more important than all the rest."

"More important than even your fear?" I asked.

"Yes, that's right," he nodded. He took my hand. "Look, do you mind waiting a little while longer? I want to look at some paintings again."

An hour later, on the walk back to our hotel, he said, "I didn't want you to get into bed with António because I was jealous of your ease with him."

I nodded.

"I realized that that was what I was feeling while standing in front of that painting by Francis Bacon — the smudged one. The painting is about jealousy. A man coming apart because of it."

"Maybe so."

"No, it is," he insisted.

I nodded.

He wanted to confess more, but after a few moments of trying to put his thoughts into words, he shook his head and said that it didn't matter. Miguel thrust his hands in his pockets and kicked garbage and stones for half a mile up Alcalá toward the Puerta del Sol. In front of the Sevilla metro station, where we had to turn left to get to our hotel, he took my arm. People were passing by like they were all in a rush. He said, "I can't bear the thought that he'll die before me. I don't know what I'll do if he does."

What could I reply?

Should I have mentioned that I'd heard his panicked confession so many times before that my ears couldn't bleed anymore and that what surviving parents end up doing is just dragging themselves forward toward the next calendar year, and the next and the next... It's a kind of inverse metamorphosis; after enough of your loved ones die, you turn from a butterfly into a caterpillar and just get through your days crawling and eating.

I told Miguel that I understood. He generously accepted that assertion with a nod of solidarity, but who knows if I did understand? After all, António wasn't really my son. Even in Spanish. I hadn't changed his diapers or taught him to tie his shoes or told him about the birds and the bees, or even warned him about the mating rites of *Homo frequently erectus.*

Miguel said he couldn't take the chance of running into António at the hotel just yet. I led him to the Pastelería de Cebada, a bakery and café I knew at the corner of Sevilla and Arlabán. It smelled of warm yeast. To the side of the hulking metallic cash register was a display case of fruit tarts and cakes with colorful icing. Serving customers behind the case were ladies with eager faces wearing pink aprons with lacy white stitching. Plump loafs of bread sat in bins behind them. We dropped down at a circular wooden table in the café section and faced the window. We watched people rushing by. I longed to be one of them.

"I'm coming apart," Miguel said. He held his head in his hands.

A young waitress in a pink apron with a red bow in her hair came to our table. I ordered him a brandy and me a *horchata.*

"We don't have any liquor," she said.

"The owner must have some whiskey or something. Anything." I handed her a thousand-peseta note. "Whatever you can find. *Es la hora dela desesperación.* It's desperation time," I tried to say.

She shrugged and replied, "I'll see what there is."

Miguel began to cry soundlessly. He was shaking.

I told myself that I'd witnessed so many slow-motion endings that maybe one more wouldn't matter so much.

He suddenly made a sound like he was gagging. He wiped his mouth and nose roughly with his sleeve. His eyes were so red they looked like they were bleeding. He held his head again in his hands.

Our waitress returned with my *horchata* and something amber-colored in a tall glass.

"Whiskey," she said.

I fed Miguel his drink. He held my knee under the table like he was in danger of falling. I put my hand on his and squeezed.

The touch of one person reminds you of others. I let the present slip away and felt my fingers...

massaging Henry The Beast's sister's back outside his hospital room;

combing my brother's hair so that when the nurse came in to change his plasma he wouldn't be embarrassed;

gripping the arm of my mother's raincoat as I led her across Central Park West toward my brother's apartment in order to inventory his possessions for dispersal among his friends.

Nothing has distinct borders when you've lived long enough. We are all connected in memory.

I said to Miguel, "Maybe António being ill doesn't matter enough to me."

He turned to me squinting. His eyes were deranged. Reaching

into my shirt pocket, he snatched my foil pack of tranquilizers. He stood up. "I'll be back," he said.

I grabbed his arm fearfully. "What are you going to do with them?"

"Maybe I'll throw them out."

"Don't joke about these things. This is serious."

He shook his head and sat back down. He held the pack out to me, then dodged it cruelly around my snapping hand.

"Give them back!" I ordered.

He took one for himself, then handed them to me. He put the pill on his tongue and downed it with the last gulp of his whiskey. He licked his lips. "Now, go ahead and tell me again that he doesn't mean enough to you," he challenged.

We knocked at António's door, but he wasn't in. I sat on my bed. Miguel stood by the window. I watched the TV news:

corruption at the highest levels in the Madrid government;

fighting in Bosnia;

Barbara Streisand boutiques opening in Los Angeles and New York.

I drifted to sleep.

Next thing I knew, I was on my side and my pants were down around my ankles.

"Don't worry," Miguel was whispering in my ear. "I've got a condom on. I bought some yesterday. Spanish ones. The best latex. Okay?"

I nodded.

"How did António...? I mean how did he like to...?"

I lay flat on my stomach. "Like this," I said. "Your son made up for his lack of imagination with stamina. It was like being run over by a railroad train."

Afterward, Miguel spooned up behind me and breathed warm at my neck. I thought he'd fallen asleep till he whispered, "Sex is a funny thing."

"Why's that?" I asked.

He sat up and rubbed my shoulders as if to keep me warm. He said, "You've been through a lot, haven't you?"

I nodded. He took my hands and brought them to his lips. "The older I get, the more affection I seem to want," he said. "Is that possible?"

"I guess our needs change as we age," I replied.

He kissed my fingertips one at a time. It made me happy. He whispered, "I feel strange being with you."

"Why?"

"Fragile," he replied. "Like I've left a window open and I don't know what's going to come inside."

He got up then and smoked at the window. I lay in bed and watched him for a while, feeling free of time, as if our room were all that was left on the planet. Then I propped *Life With a Star* up on my chest and began to read.

A little while later, when António's door opened and closed, Miguel looked at me for a moment, alarmed, like an animal caught in the headlights of a speeding car. Then he turned back to watch the street.

I slipped out of bed. As I got dressed, I told him, "I want to try talking again to your son."

He shrugged indifferently. He lit another cigarette.

I knocked at António's room and said, "It's just me."

The door opened. The boy looked wan and exhausted.

"Can I come in?" I asked.

"Why?"

"I just want to sit with you and hold your hand."

"I'd rather not," he said. "Not just now."

"António," I said, "I can't seem to climb over the fence you're building around yourself. I'm not as agile as I once was."

"I have to guard myself," he said.

"From me? Why?"

"I just do."

"But why?"

"Because if I don't, then I get angry at you. And I say mean things."

"Can I sit in your room without talking?"

"No."

I walked past him and dropped down on the end of his bed. He closed the door. I smiled up at him. "I'm here now. Too late."

I was trying to be cute. António punished me for it. "You should have known," he said.

"Known what?"

"That I'd get it. That's what I get angry about."

"I didn't even know you were sleeping with anybody. I told you all about safe sex. I read you my famous list of condoms over and over. I made you a copy. I even bet you still have it in your wallet!"

"Not enough. You had a responsibility and you didn't fulfill it. In a way, this is your fault."

In a tone of warning, I replied, "I told you once before that I'd seen too many people die...good people...to be brutalized by you. And I meant it."

"Then go. If I can't say what I want to, then go."

But I didn't leave.

He walked to the window and stared out. When he turned around he said, "I want you to promise me something."

I nodded.

"If it comes down to it, you'll poison me. You'll give me something."

"Comes down to what?"

"Don't act dumb. You know what I mean."

"I think I do. But I want to make sure we understand each other perfectly. You don't get second chances with poisoning people. You won't come back from the grave with Jimmy Hendrix's electric guitar strapped around your neck."

"If I'm in too much pain. If I'm in a hospital and there's no chance and I can't take it anymore. You'll poison me. I want you to promise."

"Okay," I said.

"I need to hear you promise. I need to hear those words."

"I promise I'll poison you."

He tossed up his hands and sighed. He hung his head. "I don't believe you. You're not taking me seriously."

"António, I am taking you seriously."

"You sound so matter-of-fact about it."

"You want me to scream about it? Would that help?"

"It might."

"António, I'm on megadoses of valium because of this. I can't scream. I can't get an erection. I can't taste my food. I'm deep below an armor made of chemicals. I can't even think half the time."

"Then whatever you say I can't believe. It's not you. It's some drug talking. A drug with legs and arms."

"It is me. I'm here. I'm camouflaged, but I'm here."

He stared out the window again.

I told him a story I'd never dared tell anyone.

"I had a friend named Carlo Foggia. He was the other guard on that basketball team I told you about. He asked me to promise to give him some poisons if necessary. I said, *no*. So he asked another of our friends, Bob Jenkins. The black guy who played center for us. Anyway, he got ill, Carlo I mean. He was in Mt Sinai hospital. He had all these things wrong with him. He couldn't swallow anymore because he had sores up and down his esophagus that made it too painful. He gargled viscous xylocaine milkshakes to numb his throat. Percodan took some more of the pain away, but not enough. He couldn't walk. He couldn't read. So he wanted to die. Bob, who'd promised to kill him, remember, said he couldn't do it. He thought he could, but he couldn't. It's harder than you think. So I did it."

"You did it?"

"Yeah."

"You did it how?"

"Before it got so bad, Carlo was really upset and wanted tranquilizers, but he couldn't take any because his breathing was so weak. His doctor told me that even one valium might kill him. I've always wondered if he told me that on purpose because he knew I was taking them myself. Anyway, when nobody was in the room, I held his head in my hands and I asked him if he wanted to die. He said, *Yes.* I said, *I had to be sure, did he really mean it?* He said, *Please* and balled his hands into fists. He didn't want to get delirious, you see. That's what he was most afraid of. So I fed him four valium on a spoon, one after another. He ate them with a smile on his face like they were chocolates. When he was done, he leaned his head back into his pillow and let out a sigh. He gripped my hand. He stared into my eyes like people do who have to say goodbye for the last time and said, 'Thank you, you've saved my life.' It was a strange thing to say, I thought at the time. Because I hadn't had much experience yet with pain. We held hands.

"His mother and father arrived. I understood then why it had to be now. His father had to get back to Santa Fe because he had big problems with his lungs and could hardly breathe in New York. His mother and father held one hand together, I held the other. I wanted to tell them to say goodbye. My heart was aching to say, *Tell him now that you love him and that you'll always, always remember him.* But Carlo and I exchanged a look and he shook his head. He told them he was okay. His father told him he'd be back in a week and not to worry. Carlo fell asleep. That was it. We kept holding his hands. Then we dropped them and began whispering about his father's plans to get to Kennedy Airport by taxi and how much it should cost. Carlo stopped breathing. His mother noticed it first. We looked at each other. His chest wasn't going up and down. His mother stepped to him and held the back of her hand to his mouth. She shook her head and closed her eyes. No one shouted for a nurse. We didn't talk. You see, he just fell asleep forever. So they collected his body and did an autopsy because they gave this story to his parents that what they found might help them with other patients. Some test or other revealed, of course, that he'd gotten a hold of some valium. A man from Mt Sinai administration called me up one day and accused me of having killed Carlo. *You were the only one there,* he said. He told me he was sending the case to the New York City prosecutor's office. At first I thought it was a joke. Then I got a call from the prosecutor's office asking for the name of my lawyer. I was scared shitless. Carlo's mother saved the day. She told everyone she gave the valium to her son. They didn't dare charge her. The love of a gay friend they were willing to put on trial. They wanted to, in fact. But not the love of a mother. She called me up when everything was settled. I was afraid she was going to scream at me but she said, *God bless you.* A week later, I got in the mail an eight-by-ten inch photograph of me and Carlo standing arm in arm on the Sixth Avenue basketball court where we used to play. His father wrote on the card, 'My son always said you were the best defensive player on the team.'"

António faced away from me so I couldn't see his expression.

I said, "So when the time comes, if you tell me to, I'll kill you."

I used the verb *matar* in Portuguese. He turned back to me and frowned. "Can't you use another word?"

"If you give me one, I'll use it."

"And what if I can't speak when the time comes?"

"I won't let you suffer."

"You promise?"

I nodded.

He came and sat next to me. I asked if I could hold his hand. He nodded. I stroked his fingers for a good long time, then put them over my face and breathed.

Sometime later, he took out a piece of sheet music from a folder and asked me to play the melody which he'd written out. I didn't think I could play anything, but my hands had a life of their own.

I watched my left hand pouncing at the frets like it was a cartoon. I began to laugh.

"You're losing it," António told me.

I played the melody again. It was similar to the ones he'd asked us to sing in the car — rushed, dissonant, endlessly falling, then suddenly rising.

"Did you transcribe this?" I asked.

"Sort of."

"Bartok?"

"I'll tell you when I'm done."

"Why not now?"

He rolled his eyes. "You've no patience," he said.

I was angry beyond all reason. "On the contrary, for the important things I've got more patience than anyone I know."

"Sorry," he said.

"Apology accepted. Can we go to dinner together tonight?"

He nodded. As he walked to the window, I noticed how gaunt he looked. "What have you been eating?" I asked.

"Nothing." He shrugged. "I don't have any appetite."

"You must eat."

"I can't."

"You want a valium?"

"Maybe one," he said.

"I should give you two, you'd be less trouble."

"Let's just stick with one. You never know how drugs are going to affect a member of our particular sub-species. Though you might be tempted to force the whole bottle down my throat the way I've been acting."

I made exaggerated nods, like a puppet.

He fought off a smile.

As we left the room, he said, "When I die, I'm going to haunt you. I'm going to make a point of it. But I won't be mean. I'll just be a pleasant nuisance."

I hugged him from behind. "With any luck, my prince, I'll already be long dead and beyond your reach."

Dinner was easy. The calm before the storm?

We ate shish kebab outside on the Plaza Santa Ana, one of my favorite squares in Madrid. We talked about our impressions of the city.

Miguel said it was dirty, but he liked the shade trees on the streets and the cafés. In general, he thought Spanish men were too dark, fat and hairy.

"And the women?" I asked.

"Too much make-up. They look like sluts."

"And what's wrong with that?" I inquired.

"Dad, you have to understand," António said happily, "all of his best friends have always been sluts."

Miguel smiled. The first real smile I think I'd ever seen on him.

He reached out to take his son's hands. António let him touch him for only a moment. He pulled them back safely between his legs.

"All my friends have always been sluts with the exception of those here gathered," I observed.

Miguel said, "Nothing wrong with looking like a whore, I suppose. I just don't find it attractive."

The boy said, "I think the people of Madrid are very generous."

I thought that was a strange remark till he took out five thousand-peseta notes neither Miguel nor I had given him — the equivalent of forty dollars. He grinned. "Not bad, eh?"

"Where'd you get those?" Miguel asked suspiciously.

I thought he was going to accuse the boy of selling himself. "Sshhh," I said, rather too aggressively. "Let him explain."

"Four hours in the Retiro Park," António said. "In front of the lake. I was playing."

"Good for you!" I said.

"I never knew playing guitar could be so lucrative," Miguel added.

"Me neither," António smiled.

It was the first time they'd agreed on anything on our trip. I would've proposed a toast, but I didn't want to draw attention to this minor miracle. I've discovered that it's better not to test God.

So António and Miguel were relaxed with each other that night. Why? I'd given them both valium. Could it simply have been drugs?

Or were they both saving their fury for later?

Tropical storms begin as breezes, drift lazily over thousands of miles, then begin to pick up speed as they near land.

I figured we were two days away from the touchdown of Hurricane António on our little mobile island.

Turns out, I guessed just about right.

22

The past decade has taught me that miracles occur, but that they're not at all what we're taught to believe. We expect them to evidence hope and resurgence and union — to lift us up like a magic carpet and bring us face to face with holiness. Instead, they reveal more clearly than anything else our utter hopelessness and separation from transcendence. They take our hand and lead us down dark stairs to the Underworld.

An example, Carlos, one of many that I never dared mention:

Henry The Beast once told me of a friend of his named Anny, a young woman in Düsseldorf suffering with Aids. She'd been confined to a bed in her parents' apartment for a year. She hadn't the strength to...

go to the bathroom herself;

plant her tulip bulbs;

lift a gardening magazine;

hold a fork.

Then one day, her parents had to leave the house for some reason. It was the first time she'd been alone in months. It was then that the miracle occurred:

Anny found the strength to get up from her bed, write a goodbye note, open the window of their eighth-floor apartment, stand on the ledge and jump.

The next morning was Thursday. The news item I liked most in *El Pais* was a brief story noting that King Juan Carlos of Spain had had a normal shit after a bad case of diarrhea contracted in France. The exact words were: *un excremento bien normal,* a perfectly normal bowel movement.

Had we progressed at all since the Middle Ages? It was the last decade of the twentieth century and the health of the Spanish nation still rested on whether or not their monarch was having a tough time at the toilet.

António confessed over breakfast that he hadn't visited the Prado two days before after all. He, Miguel and I resolved to go that morning. I went up to our room quickly to brush my teeth and down two tranquilizers *just in case.*

It was another day of glorious sun. I bounced down the street singing Irish revolutionary ballads as if we were off to the Emerald City.

At the museum, Miguel was fascinated by the classical Spanish and Dutch paintings. António passed them by without saying a word. I stood him in front of Riberas and Goyas and El Grecos, and he showed no interest.

I was saving Bosch's work for last. But the boy simply nodded his acknowledgment as if they were dull acquaintances passed in the street.

"António," I said, "don't you have any comments at all?"

"Not yet."

He hooked his arm in mine and prompted me forward into a circular room for sculpture, so I didn't pursue the matter further.

Miguel fell behind. He studied each painting as if it might be a clue to something lost.

The ground floor of the Prado is dedicated to Flemish and Spanish painting. When we'd finished, António said, "Now I want to go back through it all alone."

There I was again, that stunned baby seal with the blood on his fur. But I was better equipped this time and said, "You're trying to hurt me, aren't you?"

"I'm sorry, I just can't concentrate with you staring at me, expecting things."

I realized with a thud how heavy my hopes were for him. "I guess I wasn't thinking about that," I said.

"Listen," he smiled, "the third time through I'll show you the ones I like and the ones I hate."

"Fair enough."

I waited on a wooden bench for Miguel. "Well?" I said, when he dropped down next to me.

"Did you see 'Christ Embracing Saint Bernard?'" he asked.

"We passed by," I replied. "António didn't want to pause."

Miguel nodded pensively. He looked like he wanted to speak, but didn't say anything.

We sat in silence for a while, then he said, "I understand now that it's symbolic. He's not really with Christ. The idea of Christ is his support."

"Like water in the desert," I said.

"No. Like the certainty while walking through the desert that water is awaiting you."

"Yes, that's better."

I stared admiringly at this handsome, intelligent creature beside me. António was right — there was a genetic connection. If Miguel had been given half a chance in life, what beautiful things he might have created with his powerful hands or his baritone voice.

Then again, he had created one transcendently beautiful thing with his seed, hadn't he...

"I don't believe in him," he said.

"Him who?"

"Him God."

"You don't?"

"No," he said definitively.

"Why don't you believe in Him?"

"I don't think any God has been watching over my son." He patted my leg. "But I don't begrudge the artist his faith. It's a good painting. Makes you think." He said he was going to continue on. We'd meet up in the cafeteria in a couple hours if we didn't see each other sooner.

He patted my leg again and left.

António came to me a while later and said, "Ready for my tour?"

He stood me in front of Cano's drawing of the Annunciation and said, "He's done so much with so few lines and almost no color. It's amazing."

The sketch did little for me. I realized that we can't always predict what will move even those we love.

He grabbed my hand and took me like a child leading a parent to treasure to Goya's drawing of a man wearing a dunce cap in a courtroom and surrounded by a jeering crowd. "You see?" he asked.

"See what?"

"You see how he's created a scene of pure humiliation and injustice without extra detail?"

I began to understand that what moved António was economy of expression — the single gesture which stood for an entire story.

Later, out of curiosity, I took him to see 'Christ Embracing Saint Bernard'. He said, "I can't stand this painting."

"No?"

He spit out a cuticle he'd been gnawing. "Awful."

"Why?"

"It's so false. So invented. As if to convince the artist and everyone else of a lie. After all, we know most of the saints were bastards. It's seventeenth-century propaganda. The equivalent of a commercial promising you health if you buy their multivitamins. Christ was the vitamin supplement back then."

I said that I thought he was being too hard on the artist.

"Not at all," he replied, and he underlined his words with a fervent shake of his head.

When we're young, we're so sure of things.

We walked upstairs to the rooms of Italian Renaissance art and stood for a good long time in front of Raphael's 'Portrait of a Cardinal'.

He's a young man in red robes with sad eyes. He looks as if he wished he could be anywhere but where he was — stuck posing in front of a perfectionist painter.

"I think he was gay," António chirped.

"Why?"

"Something about him being trapped in a world he didn't want."

After that, we made a game of spotting queers and lesbians on canvases. António fixed on the Virgin Mary in Tiepolo's 'Immaculate Conception'; she wore a long-sleeved, tawny-colored robe clearly designed to hide all feminine contours.

I suggested that it simply implied *modesty and chastity.*

But the boy theorized that the virgin birth was really only the first case of a lesbian wanting a baby but unwilling to taint herself with a real live man to get it.

After a snack of French fries and Coke at the museum café, we started back to the hotel. I began seeing Renaissance portraits in the faces of people walking in the streets. Among others, I saw Van Eyck's 'Man in a Turban' carrying a black briefcase and waiting for a bus at the north end of the Plaza Canovas del Castillo. He had the exact same pale, irritated, feminine face. I saw one of van Reymerswael's 'Tax Gatherers' limping just behind us on San Jerónimo; those troubled lines ribbing his forehead were unmistakable. And who else could have had an upper lip lifted in a permanent snarl, revealing a ruin of brown-edged teeth?

I nodded at this unfortunate man to show that I knew his true identity. He frowned; he didn't want his cover blown.

The elderly gentleman who sold me *El Pais* from a green metal kiosk was the Duke of Urbino as painted by della Francesca. Who could mistake those goldfish eyes and three moles on his left cheek?

After a few minutes of this I began to suspect that I was hallucinating. This had happened to me before on valium, so I wasn't too upset. I asked Miguel and António if we might stop a moment. I drank two glasses of water at a café behind the Teatro Español in order to flush the drug from my body. I ate a grilled ham and cheese sandwich for the hell of it.

Neither the food nor drink did much good in the short term; our waiter looked like the Venetian Doge Niccolò Marcello as painted by Titian. "He's got the same bulbous nose and jowls," I confided to my two companions. "Do you think it's really him?"

"Him who?" António inquired.

"Isn't it obvious?"

"No."

I explained. Miguel furrowed his eyebrows. He was looking more and more like Sir Thomas More every minute. "Are you okay, Professor?" he asked.

"Just great," I said. I saw no reason to upset anyone other than myself.

Back at the hotel, the young woman handing me my key from behind the desk showed me the unscrupulous smile of Beatrix van der Laen as painted by Hals.

What was taking place was evidently one of those weird 1990s miracles; I'd seen almost all of these people painstakingly reproduced on canvas that very day, and here they were in the flesh — alive and reasonably well and living in Madrid.

Very calmly, I said to António and his father, "I think I'd better lie down. I believe that I may be having a slight psychotic episode."

Pequeno episódio psicotico was what I actually said. It wasn't perfect Portuguese. They looked at me strangely, whether for that or for some other reason I was unable to tell.

The experience of perfect strangers looking like familiar Renaissance portraits or even being those very people in disguise didn't leave me the least bit anguished. It was comforting to believe that reincarnation actually took place and that finally, after so much suffering, there was no need to bow one's head to the finality of death.

Miguel and António spoke to me with gentle voices on the elevator up to our third-floor rooms. But I was wondering whom I resembled and whom I might be the reincarnation of, and I didn't pay any attention.

Miguel helped me into my pajamas, and I slipped into bed. When António brought me a glass of water, I asked him whom I looked like.

"What do you mean?"

"I mean, who do I resemble?"

"You look like you." He sat next to me and felt my forehead. He turned to his father and said, "He doesn't have a fever."

"But who else, besides me I mean?" I asked.

"Besides you? No one."

Miguel said, "Maybe we'd better ask the hotel manager to call a doctor."

"I must look like someone," I insisted. "Everyone looks like someone. If you'll just tell me whom I look like, everything will be fine."

"I better call the desk," Miguel said.

"No doctors!" I ordered.

António said, "You should see someone."

"No. Just tell me who the hell I look like!"

But they wouldn't tell me. They looked at each other and faced me with concerned expressions that were utterly useless.

Miguel and António took turns watching me. I hounded them to tell me who I might have been in a past life, but they still wouldn't say. I finally gave up, turned on my side and fell asleep. When I awoke it was dusk outside, and I no longer cared whom I looked like. I had a headache, and I was very thirsty.

"Apple juice," I whispered. I said it to myself, because I was wondering if I had a voice and was convinced at this point that I was alone and living in Los Angeles.

A light came on. Miguel walked to me from the window. It seemed normal that he was in L.A. with me. "Are you feeling better?" he asked.

"Can you get me some water?" I requested.

He went to the bathroom, brought back a full glass and held it out to me. "Are you feeling better?"

I sat up and took his offering. "Miguel?"

"Yes? What is it?"

It was suddenly clear that I was not in the States. Was I in Porto? Lisbon? The water seemed more important. I downed it all in one gulp.

Madrid, I thought. It all came back to me, like air rushing in to a previously sealed cave.

"Are we still in Madrid?" I asked.

"Yes."

There was something furry on my head. It was a brown woolen cap with white llamas on it. I took it off.

"I didn't want you to get cold," he explained. "People always used to wear nightcaps, you know. My father and mother did."

He didn't look all that much like Sir Thomas More any longer. His nose was all wrong.

I suddenly recalled sitting with him on a bench at the Prado, how nice it had been to discover that he was so similar to António.

"Where's your son?" I asked.

"In his room. I'll call him."

"No!" I caught his arm. My heart was racing. "He'll just yell at me."

"He won't."

"He will."

Miguel sat next to me. He put his hand on my chest. "Calm down," he said. "He'll want to make sure you're okay."

"Yes, it's what they do," I said.

"What who does?"

"They rip you to shreds. Then they give you time to recover. And then they rip you up again. I know all about it. There's probably some Greek myth about it if you look hard enough. The Harpies, that's it. They're Harpies!"

"Who are these Harpies? What's this about?"

"Everyone."

"Sshhh. You're not making sense."

Miguel left and brought back his son. António sat on my left side, Miguel on my right. I felt like Dorothy in the last scene of *The Wizard of Oz*.

You were there, and you and you...

Only I didn't make any jokes about it because there was this terrible constriction in my chest, and I was having difficulty getting air into me. It was like a shutter had closed in my throat.

"I promise I'll be nice to you now," António said like a little boy.

My lungs felt brittle, like they were made of splintered wood. I was cold, and I was frightened for my life. I replied, "I don't want you to be nice." I rubbed my hand over my chest. "I just want to be alone."

I sensed that if I could spend enough time by myself in a dark room, the pain would go away.

"What I want to say is that I won't say things I don't mean," the boy added with heavy regret.

"You will. We all do. Besides, you meant some of the things you said. But it's fine. Just let me be."

He sighed. He said, "You're not easy to apologize to, you know."

"You don't need to apologize to me." I considered lying and telling him that I knew what I was getting myself into when I proposed this trip. But I didn't want to lie. I wanted him to leave. His face — his handsome youthful face — was absorbing all the air and warmth in the room.

He said, "Why won't you just let me say I'm sorry?"

"Because it's not important. Go back to your room and practice. That's what's important."

"You don't understand everything, you know. It's important that I apologize *for me.*"

"Okay, I accept your apology. It's all settled."

"Let me say it."

I nodded.

Very carefully, he said, "I'm sorry."

"Thank you. Now let me be still for a bit."

He stood up. "Can I get you anything?"

"Yes, a tranquilizer. I don't know where they are. Look in my shirt pocket."

"Forget it!" said Miguel threateningly. He turned to his son. "They're no good for him. You're not to buy him any more."

I waved to get the boy's attention. "They're in my shirt pocket. Pay no attention to your father."

The boy went to the chair on which I'd tossed my shirt and searched it. "They're not here."

I faced Miguel. "You took them!"

"Yes, Professor."

"I want them back. They're not yours."

"Too late. I've gotten rid of them."

"Asshole," I said in English.

"We'll all go eat," Miguel announced. "You need food."

I squinted and asked, "You're not a Jewish mother in drag, are you?"

"What?"

"I need a tranquilizer, you pig." I repeated my words in English.

"Come on, let's get your clothes on," António said.

"I don't want to put my clothes on. Can't you see I'm about to have a heart attack! I want a tranquilizer!"

"No," Miguel said.

I considered begging. But my well of pride hadn't been completely drained, and I didn't want to appear too abject in front of António. "It doesn't matter," I said cheerfully. "I'll just go to a pharmacy and get more."

"Not tonight you won't," Miguel announced. "They're all closed."

"It's a big city — four million people. You really think that I'm the only queer having an anxiety fit? Let me tell you something... Right at this moment, in this very neighborhood, there have got to be at least twenty queers going berserk with some despairing drama. There's always a pharmacy open. If I have to I'll go to a hospital.

The American Hospital. Americans understand valium."

António brought me my underwear, jeans and shirt. He pulled the covers off me. I sat up. My chest was thumping and I couldn't get enough oxygen into my rickety lungs. The room was wheeling slowly around me. I said to the boy, "Why won't you help me?"

He turned to his father and said, "I'm going to go out and get him a tranquilizer. They probably have some right at the desk downstairs."

"Stay right here!" Miguel ordered.

"Why are you being so tyrannical?" the boy asked.

"I'm not being tyrannical. Those pills were making him sick. And they're going to make him sicker if you give him any more."

If I'd have had a razor, I'd have given Miguel the operatic spectacle his heroic effort deserved, despite my claims to be little inclined toward melodrama. I'd have slit my wrists and dripped blood all over him before collapsing at his feet in a heap of self-pity. But I hadn't anything sharp within arm's reach.

I wanted to make a witty-bitchy reply. I wanted to cry. I didn't do either.

Miguel said, "António, run the bath."

The boy didn't move. He hid his eyes with a nervous hand.

"You heard me!" his father shouted, "Run a hot bath. Now!"

"I'm not Blanche DuBois," I noted. "A hot bath isn't going to stave off my collapse."

"What would stave it off?" António asked.

"A little pink pill with God inside it."

"Run the bath!" Miguel said.

"Just one more," I pleaded.

The boy went into the bathroom. The water came on. It was so loud that I held my hands over my ears.

Miguel sat next to me. With António out of the room, I was free to really beg. "One more," I said. "Just one. Then I'll stop. I promise. Just one."

He shook his head.

"Go away, you asshole," I grumbled in English.

He reached for me, but I pushed his hand away.

"Asshole!" I said. "Asshole, asshole, asshole!"

He frowned. His eyes were angry.

"What are you going to do, punch me again?" I asked in Portuguese.

He closed his eyes. He puffed out his cheeks. Then he kneeled on the floor, placed one hand on each of my thighs and put his head in my lap.

It was as if I were an executioner and he was offering me his life.

Or like he was St Bernard giving himself over to Christ in the flesh.

It gave me goosebumps to see him and feel him. And it was the first time I realized that he mimicked what he saw — in art and in the people around him.

Maybe he had disregarded his own instincts for so long that he needed other people to give him cues to appropriate behavior.

Or maybe he couldn't express himself well enough in words and was looking for another way.

Dear Carlos, was that why you took up painting? What were you trying to tell me with all those squiggles and splashes of color?

You know, there's a good many things about you that I must have failed completely to understand.

In any event, I was taken aback because it seemed as though art could change Miguel. It *had* changed him — or at least given him a way of expressing that alteration.

I realized that I didn't know who he was. António didn't either. And that we had to be gentle with him. Why? Because I was beginning to think that he was more receptive than either of us. Maybe the most fragile beings need the thickest armor? Is that possible?

I began to rub his head. His hair was soft. The stubble on his chin scratched against my thighs. I couldn't figure out what I should do.

Miguel stood up again. He held out his hands. Still sitting, I hugged him and buried my head in his stomach. I wanted to push my head into him and never come out.

After a few seconds, I heard him say to António, "Come, help me get him in the bath."

I was standing up. The room was leaning at a crazy angle, like it might fall. I thought I was going to faint. My pajamas were coming off.

They eased me down into the warmth of the water. I closed my eyes and let the steam fog up my thinking. Miguel sat on the bathtub rim. The boy stood in the doorway. He was no longer using up my air. I waved to him. He smiled back.

Afterward, he and Miguel lay me on the bed naked, face down.

For a moment, I thought that they were both going to take advantage of my incapacity.

This was not an unhappy thought. I considered that maybe they could open a deep path to my anxiety and let it bleed out of me.

Miguel straddled me and started to rub my back. He swept up from my buttocks to my shoulder blades and over my arms in long powerful strokes. He said, "When I was on the gymnastics team, we used to massage each other after practice."

"You must have had a gay coach," I opined, my face crushed at a crazy angle against my pillow.

"He just thought it was a good idea. To relax us."

"That's what Zeus said to Ganymede. Next thing the poor boy knew, he was a waiter in the world's biggest gay resort."

"I can't hear you," Miguel said. "You're mumbling."

"You know, you're the worst audience I've ever had. Bar none."

Two familiar hands started kneading my right foot.

"António, stop!" I cried sharply. "You might hurt your fingers."

I was thinking of his audition in Paris, of course.

"You should cut your toenails," the boy replied calmly.

Miguel pushed my head down to the pillow. To myself, I whispered, "Then as long as you're down there you can bite them if you like."

"Sshhh," Miguel said.

My shoulder muscles were so knotted that the pressure of Miguel's fingers was exquisitely painful.

It made me think that fucking is just an acute form of massage.

When Miguel put his hands under my belly and lifted me from my rib cage a couple inches above the mattress, I started to cry. I was not sad. I had no idea why.

He kept lifting and the tears kept coming. It was as if I were shedding something.

Stones with dew on them in the early morning. Stones crying at the loss of night. That's what I thought of.

And it occurred to me that maybe he was touching a spot which had never been touched before. But that seemed impossible.

23

When I was dressed for dinner, I stared at Miguel as if seeing him for the first time.

"What is it?" he asked.

"You're just not what I thought," I replied.

"I suppose that's good."

"You're a chameleon," I observed. "Or a parrot. Or a chameleon with a parrot's head."

"What are you talking about?"

I shrugged and smiled. "Anyway, whatever you are, whoever you are, I appreciate what you did."

António was standing by the window. He looked at his father tenderly. I thought he might reveal this devoted side of his heart. But when Miguel turned to face him, the boy's expression grayed and hardened.

Clay that has been baking too long in an angry kiln cannot regain its pliant form, I thought.

Yet maybe this brief rapprochement made the tropical storm touch down in our little world sooner than it would have otherwise. Who can tell?

Not that either of them cured me of my desire to be drugged senseless, however. At dinner that night, as a matter of fact, I wanted a pill so bad that I excused myself to go to the bathroom and asked instead at the bar if there was a pharmacy open nearby. We were at that Greek restaurant around the corner from our hotel where we'd eaten shish kebab.

"Not around here," the bartender replied. He was tall and geeky-looking. His hair was parted in the middle.

"You wouldn't have a tranquilizer by any chance?" I tried.

"How about aspirin," he suggested.

I shook my head. "I guess people don't take tranquilizers in Madrid."

"They drink," he observed. "Have a whiskey."

"No thanks."

"On the house," he smiled.

I nodded. He handed me a glass of Jack Daniel's. "Straight from your homeland," he said.

It calmed me at dinner and for a little while afterward. Even so, I couldn't cross the border to dreamland that night. You can't withdraw from valium and sleep at the same time. It's a law of nature.

I was nervous and hot.

It was like I was going to have to march behind a casket at another funeral.

Or like I was going to have to perform a guitar piece far beyond my means.

I searched through my medicine bag for pink crumbs that might have dropped off a pill.

Nothing.

Miguel had confessed at dinner that he'd flushed my stash down the toilet, so I got down on my hands and knees to see if any pills were still floating in the bowl or had fallen on the floor.

Not a speck of help in sight.

I looked through the garbage under the sink and found the foil pack. Empty. I shook it for powder. Dust from God fell on my palm. I licked it.

I watched the hours passing on the luminous dial on Miguel's watch. One in the morning.

Two.

Three.

I hated him for putting me through this. I considered killing him in his sleep by wrapping the phone cord around his neck. I fantasized about the headlines in the morning newspapers: *Portuguese Stonemason Strangled by American Lover — Horrified Son Discovers Body Hidden in Closet.*

I paced. I ran in place in the bathroom. I thrashed about in bed. Past humiliations trapped me inside intricate plans of vengeance against schoolmates.

At four in the morning, I put on my woolen hat with the llamas to see if it would help.

Five.

Six.

Friday's sun came up. I hadn't slept a wink. But I was happy because I was going to slip out of the room and wait with my tongue hanging out against the window of the first pharmacy I came to. Spanish tranquilizers would be large and blue and lovely. They'd taste like Pez and smell like Constant Comment tea. I'd hide a few of them in the tip of my Dentagard toothpaste in case Miguel found them in my medicine bag.

After all, a handsome bisexual man can only be trusted so far.

But I'd act normal around him. He wouldn't suspect a thing.

I was daydreaming about all this while kneeling by my bag and hunting for a fresh pair of underwear.

All through my thrashing about Miguel had slept. Now he woke. Maybe my mother was communicating with him telepathically.

"What's wrong?" he asked.

"Sorry. Go back to bed."

He sat up and rubbed his cheeks. He looked at his watch. "It's too early even for bakeries to be open. What are you doing?"

I found my underwear. I stood up and held them in front of my sex. "I'll just be gone a little while. I need to walk, get my legs moving."

He stood up. He was naked. He yawned and scratched his balls. He came to me and took my underwear. He threw them back in the bag.

Cupping my balls in his hand, he knelt and squinted up at me.

A few minutes later, he paused in his assault and asked, "Am I doing better than last time?"

I was panting like a dog. I nodded.

He stood up. "Now show me how my son likes it." I got a condom and sat him on the end of the bed. I did everything the boy liked.

When I was done, he said, "Thank you, Professor." I lay down to get myself off. He turned me over on my side. He got behind me. I thought that he was going to fuck me. But he reached between my legs and shook my cock in his fist till I came all over the sheets. "Nothing wrong with you now," he said.

He massaged my legs and feet for a few minutes, then crawled up beside me.

I slept with his arm over my back and his face against my shoulder. The sound of his breathing was like water passing over sand. *A few more days of this and maybe all my ghosts will begin to give me some peace again,* I thought.

At ten in the morning, I woke. I had a bad headache again.

"The color is back in your face," Miguel said.

"Is that good or bad?" I asked.

"Good. You *are* feeling better, aren't you?"

"My head is pounding."

"You want aspirin?"

"Keep going."

"Aspirin is all you're going to get." He brought me two and a glass of water. "Sometimes sex makes you feel worse," he observed.

"No, that was fine."

"I really think I'm improving, you know."

I downed the pills. "Anytime you want to practice some more, feel free. My cock is your cock."

He stuck a cigarette in his mouth and fixed me with a grave look. "Do you think you have a soul?" he asked.

"What brought this on?"

"I just want to know." He lit his cigarette.

"Do I have a soul? I doubt it. But maybe some people do. Maybe mine just got left out. Or maybe it was taken away when I visited Sodom for the first time. Like giving the border guard your passport. I'll tell you one thing though, I haven't missed it."

"I don't think I've got one either," he said. "Or maybe it's in the wrong place and I can't find it."

"A soul that can't be found... I don't think that's the idea. I mean you don't misplace a soul. Either it's there or it isn't."

"It could be hidden."

"Yeah, it could hidden inside your balls. And every time you have an orgasm, it comes out and tries to reach somebody else's soul."

He shrugged. "You know, I like lying next to a man," he said, as if it were a conclusion he'd only just reached after thirty years of hard struggle.

That's probably just what it was, of course.

"But I like being with women, too," he added.

"I suppose a few unlucky people can't make up their minds," I observed.

"No, I've made up my mind," he said. "I like everything."

"Almost everything. Your bottom didn't fare so well the other day as I recall."

"It's just a question of practice."

I got out of bed to go pee. "You can't really like the taste of pussy," I commented.

He rolled his cigarette between his thumb and fingers like Bogart while considering his reply. He lifted it to his lips, took a draw with squinted eyes, then licked his lips as the smoke cascaded out. "I do. I love it. I love pussy."

From the bathroom, I told him that I thought it tasted like a postage stamp. He replied, "You know, mostly a pussy tastes just like a woman."

I knew then that he really did like sex with women because he didn't need any metaphors.

He and António had already eaten breakfast in the hotel, and the dining room was closed until lunch. Miguel proposed that we go to a café in the Plaza Mayor. He stubbed out his cigarette. We collected António, who kissed me good morning on both cheeks.

Something new seemed to be animating him.

Miguel brought our maps, so I knew something was up with him as well. António hummed as we walked. He hopped on and off curbs like he does when he wants to show off for me. I would have said he was happy, but I was not about to risk optimism.

It was a warm morning. Big billowy clouds floated lazily in the blue sky. After I'd downed a cappuccino and picked on the fresher sections of a day-old croissant, Miguel said, "My son and I were thinking that we should head to the countryside today. Not too far because you're sure to be tired."

I rubbed my temples. "You've been conspiring against me."

António replied, "You're not going to ask me who you look like, are you?"

"You never did answer. I still want to know."

The boy rolled his eyes.

"The countryside," Miguel repeated.

"Let me guess, you think the city is a bad influence on me."

"Too many museums with old paintings. You need fresh air."

Miguel was communicating telepathically with my mother again. I needed to find a jamming device. As if to shock her back in her Long Island retreat, I whispered, "What I really need is to get fucked by both of you every day for a year." I downed the last bitter dregs of coffee. "What I need is a desert island with pumpkin cheesecake growing wild and Sean Connery in a thong bathing suit climbing up palms to pick me coconuts."

António replied, "How about some requests that are within the realm of the possible?"

Maybe he wasn't shocked that I'd mentioned sex and Miguel in the same breath because he'd already guessed about us. But I figured that it was far more likely that he thought I was simply playing the crazy whore again.

"Madrid doesn't just have old museums," I pointed out. "We could buy a few gold chains and go disco dancing tonight." I did a brief imitation of John Travolta in *Saturday Night Fever*. Nobody smiled.

"Or we could go to a zarzuela concert," I proposed, "and see how long we can last before we pass out."

"The countryside," Miguel repeated.

"You really are a bulldog."

"First I was a chameleon, then a parrot, now a bulldog."

"Noah's ark in a single body."

"I don't get it."

"I mean, you're very persistent."

"A gymnast has to practice a routine a thousand times to get it right. Persistence, not just talent."

"That's certainly been my motto. And look how far it's gotten me. Stuck on the plains of Spain with two Portuguese animal trainers."

He pulled out the Michelin map he'd brought along. "I'm proposing we stop somewhere outside Burgos. When we get bored we can go to town and see a movie or something."

I snorted. "A Spanish movie? When did you ever see a Spanish movie you enjoyed?"

"Lot's of times," he replied.

António said, "Name one."

"All those films with Maria Felix," he observed. "She was great."

"She was Mexican," António said. "She made Mexican films. And all she had going for her were big breasts — big Mexican breasts."

He showed us what he meant with cupped hands about a foot from his chest.

"That's two more talents than Anthony Quinn had," I pointed out.

Nobody picked up on that theme.

Miguel faced me and said, "Burgos it is."

I looked at António. He nodded.

"One of you is going to have to drive," I said.

António held out his hand and said, "Keys, Batman."

So that's how we ended up at the *parador* in Santo Domingo de la Calzada, a broken-down town of flaking stucco and stone surrounded by vineyards about twenty miles east of Burgos. And that was where all hell broke loose.

Trouble started at about two in the afternoon. António invited us to his room. He announced he had a surprise. He raised his eyebrows up and down like Groucho.

Oh shit, I thought. *What now?*

In his room, he handed me my guitar and the sheet music I'd played earlier. "I've made a few changes. Practice it for a minute." He turned to Miguel. "Dad, you come with me."

He took his father into the bathroom.

While I practiced, António taught his father the second of the melodies he'd sung for us in the car. It had words now, and the words were taken from the last verse of Whitman's 'Song of Myself'. Shortly after we'd met, António and I had read together the bilingual edition published in 1992 by Assírio & Alvim:

> I bequeath myself to the dirt to grow from the grass I love,
> If you want me again look for me under your boot-soles.
>
> You will hardly know who I am or what I mean,
> But I shall be good health to you nevertheless,
> And filter and fibre your blood.
>
> Failing to fetch me at first keep encouraged,
> Missing me one place search another,
> I stop somewhere waiting for you.

He must have memorized the Portuguese version because that's what he was teaching Miguel:

> Entrego-me ao húmus para crescer da erva que amo,
> Se me queres ter de novo, procura-me debaixo da sola das
> > > > > > > tuas botas.
>
> Dificilmente saberas quem sou ou o que significo,
> Todavia dar-te-ei saúde,
> E filtrando o teu sangue dar-tei-ei vigor.
>
> Se à primeira não me encontrares, não desanimes,
> Se não estiver num lugar, procura-me noutro,
> Algures estarei à tua espera.

The idea of the dead wishing the living well had always touched me. And that they were waiting for us...

When António and Miguel came back into the room, the boy said, "Ready?" His eyes were expectant. He gnawed at a cuticle on his thumb.

"Tell me what to do," I said.

He tapped his foot. "That's the tempo. The first three measures you play solo, then we come in." He turned to his father. "Got it?"

Miguel said, "Can I smoke half a cigarette first?"

António made a face. He tapped his foot again. I started the piece. Sixteenth notes racing down staircases.

They joined in.

I didn't listen closely to their harmonies because I was concentrating on my playing. But what I heard I didn't like. It was a relentless motet, and the voices reduced the guitar to near silence.

António's shoulders sagged. "It doesn't sound like I thought it would," he sighed.

"It was interesting," Miguel tried. "Who wrote it?"

António rolled his eyes at him again.

"It's got to be all the same instrument," I observed. "Three violins or something. If you want to keep the words, then it has to be three voices."

Miguel took my shoulder. "Think you can sing your part?"

"Maybe if we slow down the tempo to a crawl."

António said belligerently, "If we crawl, it won't work!"

"Let him try," Miguel said.

"Write down the Portuguese words for me," I told António.

He scribbled them on the inside back cover of *Life With a Star* as if he were doing drudge work. He was about to tear it away from the book, but I shrieked. I held out my hand. "It's a sin ripping a book apart."

He handed it to me. "Start whenever you want."

I stood up and began singing at half speed. The melody descended a gentle staircase, rose up in jubilant ascent, then met the two other voices. Together, we bounced down a jagged slope, hurdled three fences, tripped over a stone, picked ourselves up, raced for a bit, then slowed and rolled to a stop.

I made two mistakes when both of them were singing Es and I had to sing the D just below. Naturally enough, I wanted to join them on E and ended up floating somewhere around Eb.

Three travelers side by side, moving apart, coming together, stopping and looking at one another. They don't know what to do with each other. They're afraid to achieve consonance but even more afraid to move permanently apart.

That's what I was thinking about the melodies. Miguel must have been thinking it too, because he sat with his head in his hands.

A knot lodged in my throat and I nodded at António. I was proud of him. He shrugged. "It's such a small thing," he said, "and not at all what I thought."

I whispered, "No, it never is."

António told us he'd started the piece in Salamanca. The day he'd spent performing on Santa Justa square he'd met a young guitar player named Monica. She'd invited him to her parents' apartment. They played duets at her house for five hours on Sunday. A Catalan friend came by who was studying voice. He sang popular songs to their accompaniment, mostly standards which everybody knew. António got the idea of writing a series of pieces for two guitars and voice, one based on a folk tune from Portugal, the next from Salamanca, the last from Catalonia. The original melody for this piece had come from a folk song from Miguel's home province called, *'O Marinheiro Noivo',* The Sailor Groom.

"Yes," Miguel said. "I can hear it now."

Miguel told me that he had taught António that song as a boy. "It was lovely, son," he added. "I'm proud of you."

Good for you, I thought. *Now tell him you love him.*

The boy didn't acknowledge his father's words. He took my guitar and put it back in its case. He snapped the latches roughly and lifted it. "I'm going out to practice," he announced.

"Don't be disappointed," I said. "Something that moves from your head down to a piece of paper and up into your voice has to change. You wouldn't want it to be the same as you originally conceived it."

"Leave me alone."

"Why are you disappointed?" Miguel asked.

"Forget it. Let him be," I said.

"No, I want to know why."

António glared at Miguel. "You want to know why? Because of you. I don't want to sing with you. I don't want anything to do with you. The whole thing is a lie. What I wrote is a lie! That's what I learned when I heard it. That I'd written a lie!"

He marched out. This time, he didn't forget to slam the door.

Miguel was the next to leave. He said, "I'm going to get some coffee and maybe a brandy, want to come?"

He was just asking to be polite. I shook my head. "I've some things to do."

The cathedral was just across the street. I lit a handful of candles at the foot of a large sculpture of the Virgin fronted by a crystal vase of salmon-colored gladiolus.

A young woman with short black hair came to me as I was placing the last one in its holder. "So many?" she asked in Spanish.

I shrugged as if to excuse myself. *"Soy duna isla de los muertos."* I didn't know if that was really Spanish, but it was close enough.

"Where is this island of the dead — America?" she asked in English.

"Yes."

"My English no very good," she said. She smiled girlishly.

In Spanish, I said, "I can understand you if you speak slowly."

"I've had lots of friends disappear, too," she said.

We walked outside together. "My name is Claudia." We shook hands. Hers was cold and tiny. "I used to paint scenery at the National Ballet," she added.

"And now?"

"Now I cook for my husband and my son." She smiled. "And I go to the cathedral every day. You don't forget."

She buttoned her leather jacket. We kissed cheeks. "It was nice to meet you," she said. "Have a nice stay in town. If you're here tomorrow, I'll see you at the cathedral. Same time. I'm in a hurry or we could talk some more."

Claudia made me recall that when you first walk through a hospital room to visit a friend dying of Aids, you enter a worldwide sect.

There is no place of pilgrimage, no holy center.

The axis of the sect is wherever you meet another member.

Claudia strode across the square. After she disappeared, I hunted through town for António like a madman because I suddenly had to tell him something. When I couldn't find him, I grew desperate. I trudged back to the cathedral. I sat for a while, defeated and hollow. I went back to the hotel.

In the hallway, I heard the boy playing the Prelude from the Bach Cello Suite in his room. I knocked. He let me in without a struggle. We sat on the end of his bed like weary warriors. I held his hand. "What are you thinking?" I asked.

"That what I wrote was no good."

I said, "That's what I came to talk about. What you wrote was too good. You got scared by it."

"It wasn't what I expected," he repeated.

"Because it wasn't just music. It was something else. Something you wanted to stage, I think. That's what I came to tell you. You were looking for a way of putting you and your father together. You did. You found it. And that's what scared you. The closer you get to him the more frightened you get. You've just got to keep moving toward him no matter what. You're almost there."

He was silent. Doubts crept into my mind; maybe my reasoning was all wrong. I said, "You know, you and your father sing real well. It was lovely to hear your voices together."

Silence.

"I'm afraid I missed a few notes. My sight-singing is rusty."

He took back his hand. "It wasn't your fault that it wasn't music. Stop assuming responsibility all the time."

"Just the other day you were making me responsible for everything," I pointed out.

"And now I'm not!"

"I wasn't criticizing. I was just noting how things change."

"Well stop it."

"Talk to me nicely. I'm fragile. You're fragile."

He stood up and crossed his arms. "I knew what could happen," he said. "I just didn't think it would. I was stupid." He picked up a pillow and covered his head. He paced.

"Let's go for a walk," I said.

"No."

"It sometimes helps to do something someone else wants. The specific request doesn't matter. It's the ceding of will."

"You know, you're the one I want to find me," he said. "From the Whitman poem. After I'm gone. I'll want you to find me."

"I can't really find anything," I said. "You mean someone else. And I think you mean for him to find you long before you get buried under the soil."

"Who?" he asked.

I shrugged; he didn't need me to tell him. I said, "Let's just go for a walk."

24

We started east on the road to Ezcaray. On our map, it was a dot down a thin white line. As it turned out, it was lucky we chose that destination or I'd never have gotten to meet Doña Margarita.

The sky was blue. The sun was hot. Tiny green grapes the size of currants dangled from the vines bordering the road.

The scent of the hot gravel beneath our feet was comforting.

"What should we talk about?" I asked the boy.

"Anything but music or my father or me or you or illness."

We were silent all the way to Ezcaray. The countryside was pretty, so it was enough to fill me. I noticed him watching me, but I didn't feel up to asking why.

The dot on the map turned out to be a jumble of scruffy streets and a stone church. We found the Café Carlito, however, a single dingy room with six wooden tables and a blue linoleum counter. On the wall behind this counter were a couple dozen postcards attached with yellowing tape to a chipped mirror. I recognized the Leaning Tower of Pisa and the Roman Coliseum. We were the only people there. Doña Margarita served us Coca-Colas poured from cans into tall glasses stamped with the Pepsi logo. She was plump and had hennaed hair like straw. Her eyes were made up like two black doughnuts. She fluttered a fan with red roses under her droopy neck.

"She looks like a Giant Tortoise," António whispered in Portuguese.

I knew that Margarita was her name because ancient black-and-white photographs were taped at random over the moldy green walls of the café. The captions underneath them had been typed on manual typewriter on which the lower-case 'r' and "o" both jumped:

'D°ña Marga^{r}ita with Rafael Och°a.'
'D°ña Marga^{r}ita with C°mad^{r}eja.'
'D°ña Marga^{r}ita with Miguel Quim^{6}n.'

After António looked at them, he made a face as if he'd eaten something spoiled. "What a garbage heap!" he said in English.

I gave him a smile. "This is what I love about Spain."

He rolled his eyes and sipped his Coke.

Judging from the images, Doña Margarita had always been plump. But she used to shine like a porcelain doll. And she had evidenced a certain antiquated style — high heels, pendulous filigree earrings and dark, lacy stockings. In the photo with Comadreja, she wore a fox stole complete with head. The poor animal looked like a furry planarian.

As for the men, they were young and skinny. They wore pin-striped three-piece suits. A few of them had pencil-thin mustaches. Many had their hair greased back. They looked like gangsters.

I called António over. "Who could they all be?" I asked him.

"Local celebrities. Minor bullfighters, that sort of thing."

"Her lovers?"

"Maybe."

She was wiping her counter with a dishrag. We looked at her from a corner of the café, Cokes in our hands, trying to figure out how many of these men had curled her hennaed hair in their fingers. She began dialing a black telephone at the end of the counter. She had long red fingernails.

"She must have been the local whore," António whispered. "One of her clients left her the café."

"Or she bought it with the money she earned."

He smiled. "If only you'd charged when you were young. We could buy half of Spain."

"I don't want half of Spain. Just that desert island with Sean Connery and the coconut palms."

We finished our Cokes at the counter. Doña Margarita said, "You like the photographs?"

"Mucho!" I gushed. *"La señora era muy hermosa."*

"Gracias." She fluttered her fan and nodded gracefully.

"Who are the men?" I asked. *"Los hombres?"*

"Mostly bullfighters," she said.

António took a little bow for having guessed correctly.

Doña Margarita said, "Wait here. I've something to show you and your son."

There was that treacherous word again, *hijo.*

How dangerous it was to look at António and imagine...

There was a back room hidden by a curtain of brown and pink beads. Our hostess walked toward it, then stopped suddenly. She pointed. "American?" she asked.

"Sí."

"No Communistas?"

She must not have heard that all eleven Communists in America owned revolutionary bookstores and hadn't the time to visit Europe. I shook my head. In English, I said, "International Sodomite Party. We've got orifices in every major city on the planet."

She nodded like what I said made sense. "Okay. Just a moment."

"I think she stuffed one of those poor bullfighters in the photos," speculated António happily. "She's going to carry him out here stiff as a board."

She emerged with a photograph in a golden frame. In it, Doña Margarita was no more than twenty. She glistened proudly in her fox stole, pill-box hat and high heels. She was standing next to a little wrinkled man in a military uniform.

There was no caption.

"'You know who it is?" she asked. Her breath smelled of stale beer.

António said in English: "The world's shortest retired bullfighter in his military uniform."

She made a puzzled face.

I tilted my head and looked again. I didn't want to believe it.

"El Caudillo," she announced with a grin.

"General Franco?" I asked.

She raised a single finger in correction. *"Generalissimo* Franco," she said. She studied the photograph. "In Burgos. My father fought with him in the battle for Madrid." She turned a proud and satisfied face to us.

"*Muy bonita,*" I said.

"Ah, how the world changes," she sighed, admiring her own image. With a shrug, she took the photo back to its secret place of honor in her storeroom.

António dropped two hundred-peseta coins to the counter. "Let's get out before she comes back," he whispered.

Her meaty arms were already spreading the beads, however. She waddled up to us. She fluttered her fan and made a righteous face. In English, she said, "Spain no good no more. Communists. Socialists. Corrupt." With a single angry wave of her fan, she wiped out all of them.

I nodded and said, "*Demasiado maricones.* Too many queers."

She took my arm in excited agreement. "They're judges now," she said in an appalled voice. "And ministers!"

"Yes, in Franco's time they were just bullfighters," António nodded.

Indignantly, she replied, "My bullfighters were real men. They had balls." She made a fist. "*Cojones!*" She snapped her fan to attention and stood erect.

"How many thousand did you sleep with?" António inquired in his most innocent voice.

"*Como?*" she asked, as if she couldn't believe she'd heard correctly.

He repeated his question. Only this time, he ended it with the words, "*Mi pequeña puta fascista,* my little fascist whore."

You don't call someone a *puta* in Spain without expecting a fight — even a real prostitute. But when one is young, one doesn't mind confrontations like this.

Spittle flew out of her mouth. We heard her curses for a hundred yards down the street.

António's peals of laughter in reply made me uncomfortable. I only dared to relax when we were safely out of town. It was scorching, at least ninety degrees. After a couple of miles, I sat down on the shoulder of the road and refused to go on.

Coming down off valium is like having bad jet lag; all of a sudden, you're exhausted and dehydrated. You dream about napping, even in the most inappropriate places.

I lay down with my arm under my head. Flowerless proletarian weeds sprouted around me. It was surprisingly comfortable.

António called me names in jest...

pig;
fruitcake;
lazy slob;

American capitalist;
Jewish sponge cake.

"You're in a good mood," I said.

"When I can forget, I feel better," he noted. "I'm me again. I have my name back and everything."

He started holding out his thumb to hitchhike. A hundred cars whizzed by. To my great surprise, after about a twenty minutes, when I was just about ready to turn over and grill the other half of my body, a blue BMW stopped for us.

The explanation was simple enough; even on the outback road from Ezcaray to Santo Domingo de la Calzada a Spanish vampire would drive by from time to time.

This particular one rolled down his window to reveal a large hooked nose. His eyes were dark and somber. If life were a Shakespeare play, he'd have been cast as Shylock. But life is life, of course, and he was just a well-to-do lonely queer out for a drive in the middle of nowhere who was thinking that maybe he'd spotted his Prince Charming.

Unfortunately for him, the Portuguese Prince Charming was saddled with an exhausted American chaperone.

"Is he all right?" he asked the boy, pointing to me as if I couldn't answer for myself.

I was sitting up at this point, licking my salty lips.

"Just tired," António said. "We've been walking a while."

"Portuguese?"

"I am. He's American."

I stood up.

"You want a lift?" he asked.

In English I replied, "No, we're actually Jehovah's Witnesses and wanted to know if you've received the Word yet."

"What?" he asked.

"A ride would be really great," I admitted.

"Ah," he said, raising his eyebrows, "you speak Spanish too!"

António got in front with him. I lounged in back. The BMW had black leather seats. He looked over at the boy far more often than most men would consider appropriate. That's how I knew for sure that he was on our team.

He turned on the radio. "Music," he said, as if we couldn't figure that out.

"Yes." António smiled.

It was a harsh Arabic melody shouted by a group of men. They didn't sound pleased.

"You like sevillanas?" he asked the boy. His hand was tapping up and down on the black knob of the gear shift.

"They're okay," António replied.

"My name is Ramón," he said. António told him his name, and they shook hands. He held my ward's hand for too long. He turned to me for a moment, "Father and son?"

"More or less," I replied with a doubtful twist to my hand.

"*Si,*" António nodded definitively. "My dad's just shy." We shared an amused get-us-out-of-here look.

"Are you staying in Santo Domingo?" our host inquired.

"No," I jumped in. "We've got friends there. We're just visiting them."

The last thing we needed was a Castilian chicken hawk with the chicken's address in his pocket.

He and the boy talked some more. Ramón was a lawyer. He worked in Burgos. He was visiting his elder sister. She had a vineyard a couple miles east of Ezcaray. She had trouble finding good workers.

Unemployment in Spain was more than twenty percent at the time. I didn't understand why his sister couldn't find someone to help.

"No one wants to work on a farm," Ramón explained. "It's peasant work. You ever read Cervantes?"

"*Don Quixote* twice," I lied.

"Then you know that all Spaniards want to be taken for noblemen."

"I do?"

"*Si.* It's in the book."

"You know Doña Margarita?" António asked.

He shook his head. "Who's she?"

"The lady at the Café Carlito," the boy explained.

"Oh her, yeah sure. I've been there a couple of times."

"Do you know what her story is?"

He shrugged. "The rumor is that she's fallen aristocracy. The daughter of a citrus fruit exporter from Valencia who ran away with a bullfighter named Comadreja. They say he dumped her in Burgos." He winked. "I think she's the one who started that story though. Believe you me, *viejas putas contan grandes mentiras,* old whores tell big stories."

When we were safely out of Ramón's car, António shook his head and said, "She was some moldy old hag, that Doña Margarita!"

I realized then what made me so uncomfortable. I stood him in front of me and said, "Listen, when we get older, we try to make sense out of our lives. We try to understand why we went one way and not another. We remember things. We do a lot of sitting and remembering. If I could put pictures of some of the men I've loved on my wall, maybe I would. But I have no photos. I threw them out when I moved to Europe. So be kind to her. She's silly and ugly and maybe she's done some evil in her life, but she's got nothing left. She sits in an old café and wants to show people she's had a life. Don't begrudge her that."

When we got back to the hotel, I took a siesta. I awoke to shouting.

A few days later, I learned what provoked this argument. As a matter of fact, I heard two different versions.

Now, Miguel was screaming, "You think I got what I wanted?! Is that what you think? Because if it's what you think, you're very mistaken!"

António shouted, "Don't give me that bullshit! You don't care what I think. You never cared! All you cared about was yourself! I don't think you ever even saw me. Or Mom. We were props for you. Remember the presents you used to give me? Soccer balls and sneakers. Fishing rods. Fucking fishing rods! All things for you. Not me. You gave yourself presents."

"Don't lecture me about your mother! Your mother and I... You don't know what went on between us."

"Listen, I don't want to see you. I don't want to hear you!" At the top of his lungs, he screamed, "I don't even want to smell you! Your stink of old cigarettes and old lies. All you care about is me not doing something to embarrass you. God forbid you should ever get embarrassed. Or ever really show yourself."

"Show myself? What am I? Go ahead, tell me!"

"You? I don't know. I only know you're not what you appear to be. You're like a ghost. An impostor, an hallucination. I don't know what you are, but I wish you'd just disappear!"

We had silence for a bit, then Miguel said, "You've become merciless. I never thought I'd live to see the day."

He wasn't shouting now, but the walls were thin and you couldn't have peeled my ear from the plaster.

The boy replied, "If I am cruel, it's because you made me this way."

More silence. António added, as if it were just an afterthought, "It's you who caused this, you know. If you'd have been a father when I needed you..."

Miguel didn't reply. I imagined him sitting with his head in his hands. I went out and stood in the hall thinking. I rapped on António's door and said, "It's me."

A hesitant crack of doorway opened. The boy glared at me as if I were an added burden. Miguel was facing out the window. I pushed past António and stood between them. I said, "Something I need to say to both of you."

Miguel turned to me. He looked shipwrecked. My courage waned. I faced António. He had enraged eyes. I said to him, "Listen to me, this virus in you... It doesn't know your name. It doesn't know you play guitar. It doesn't know you're Portuguese. It doesn't know your father or mother or me. It doesn't know how your hair is cut or that you nibble on your cuticles when you're anxious or that you cross your arms when you're angry like you're doing now. It doesn't know anything. Do you understand what I'm saying?"

He showed me the silence of a scared boy trying to look bored.

"António, can you honestly say that you wouldn't have led the life you've led even if Miguel had been the father of your dreams?"

"I don't know. Maybe."

"Look, if you think you're gay because of your father's lack of courage or distance or jealousy or anything else, I think you're wrong. I don't believe it. And you don't either."

"But I do believe it," he replied defiantly.

I knew he was lying. I was so furious at him at that moment I wanted to hit him.

Miguel opened the window wide and leaned out.

We were at that point where people test how far they can venture into their own particular wasteland of cruelty without getting forever lost. How deeply, too, they could wound their enemies. I sat on the end of the bed and looked down because I realized I'd made a mistake by coming in.

António shouted at us, "That's it, turn away. Both of you. Because you can. I can't. And you know why? Because it's in me! That's why! I can't fucking turn away!"

25

Miguel ended up leaving the room first, saying that he needed to smoke. I didn't look for him. I sat in the bar of the hotel and drank port wine. I normally hate the syrupy stuff, but I was homesick and the ruby color was pretty against the light of the crystal chandelier hanging threateningly above my head.

António... He locked the door behind him when I left. I didn't care that he was alone. Or frightened. I thought of Pedro's advice to me before I left and realized that I needed to save myself.

I got *Life With a Star* from my room and read about thirty pages. I got drunk.

In the morning, I didn't remember a single sentence.

Miguel never came back that night.

I'd already eaten Saturday breakfast before I realized that he'd taken my car keys from my pocket. The Batmobile was already gone. *Great,* I thought, *he's stranded me in the middle of nowhere. I'll end my days taped to a wall in Doña Margarita's café.*

António hadn't come out of his room. He wasn't playing guitar. I imagined him lying in a pool of blood in the bathtub.

I'd have cried, of course, if it had been true, but I'd have also been relieved.

There was nothing to do in Santo Domingo de la Calzada, so I sat in the cathedral and re-read the parts of *Life With a Star* I'd missed the night before. It was cool and empty, and there was just enough light filtering in through the grilled windows of the nave to make out words. I didn't retain anything of what I read, but holding a book was comforting. It gave me an illusion of control, the knowledge that I could at least escape into someone else's story.

Mostly, I was thinking about how many churches and synagogues I'd been in in the last decade. Only one mosque. In Brooklyn, of all places, just off Avenue J.

And I was thinking of you, Carlos, of how you'd never been to the funeral of a friend. I was jealous. But curiously enough, I also felt sorry for you. It was as if you'd missed a vital experience and would never have another chance.

After about an hour in the church, Claudia called to me. She shuffled eagerly into the pew in front of mine. We kissed cheeks. She smelled of lavender. Carlo Foggia's mother always smelled of lavender. Carlo himself used to wear Polo aftershave. He used to stink up the basketball court.

"I didn't think you'd be here today," Claudia whispered. She smiled. She said that she was pleased to see me. It was a welcome change.

I said, "The people I'm staying with are fighting." I told her a bit about António and Miguel.

"You shouldn't have embarked on a trip," she replied.

The last thing I needed was a stranger's judgment about something that couldn't be changed. I looked away.

"Sorry," she apologized. She took my hand. "What a stupid thing to say! The things you say when you don't know how to respond..."

I nodded.

"Want to come to my house?" she asked.

I wanted to say, *Maybe you could talk to António,* because I was thinking, *the sound of a woman's voice might help.*

At desperate times, I imagine that magic — if it does exist —must reside in a woman's voice.

I replied, "You don't have any valium, by any chance?"

"No."

"Do you know a pharmacy?"

"Of course."

"Take me there."

The town pharmacy was also a barbershop. A big leather chair was propped on a metal pole. Claudia told a lady in a white smock what I wanted. She came back with a green box marked Tractan. I stared at it and thought, *Don't buy it.*

I bought two boxes of thirty pills each just in case Miguel discovered one.

As I was contemplating asking for Percodan or Demerol, Claudia said, "Let's go to a café." I downed my first tranquilizer with tea. She started to tell me a story in careful Spanish. Her hands circled in front of her face as she spoke. Her eyes grew passionate. The story itself concerned a woman ballet dancer who died of ovarian cancer. I held out as best I could, but then told her not to continue. "I'm sorry," I said, "I need a happy ending right now."

She wasn't annoyed. She bent her head to sip her cappuccino. The story she came up with was short, but perfect for my mood.

Her Uncle Javier used to beat his wife and children. Aunt Soledad was blind in one eye because of it. Their three kids cowered like vagrant dogs. This went on for years. Claudia was told by her mother, Javier's sister, that poor Aunt Soledad was very prone to accidents, a clutz of world-class proportions: she hit her head on fenceposts, burned herself on ranges, dropped bricks on her fingers. Nothing could be done for such a woman. As for the broken bones and mangled noses of the terrified children, Claudia was told that her cousins played too roughly. Then one day, six years ago, Uncle Javier was run over by a truck carrying cantaloupes to Madrid. Claudia shrugged. "He died on the spot."

Claudia said that Uncle Javier's body had to be buried in pieces *as if he'd been nothing but meat all along.* She laughed so freely about it that I had to smile. As if to prove my point about the nature of miracles in our era, she moved her hands into a position of prayer and said, "I like to think that God sent that truck. I eat cantaloupe at every opportunity to thank Him."

Miguel came back with the Batmobile that afternoon. His hands were filthy, his fingernails crescented with soil. Dust powdered the stubble on his cheeks. The crow's feet around his eyes had become spokes on dark wheels.

I put down my book when he entered the room. "What happened?" I asked.

He didn't answer. He took off his clothes and went into the

shower.

When he came out, he got under the covers. He turned away from my stare and fell asleep.

None of this seemed troubling because my tranquilizers were working again.

I'd stashed one of the foil packs in the bottom compartment of my medicine bag and the other in my pants pocket. Six pills were stuffed into my toothpaste and there were another three in my wallet.

Let him try to stop me, I was thinking defiantly.

While he slept, I walked around and around the town. My legs were pleasantly heavy and my thoughts evaporated as they formed. It was warm out, and I was comfortable.

I got back just before dinner time. Miguel and António were arguing again, this time in my room. I stood outside in the hallway. They were being mean in the way people are when they think they've been betrayed for years. Then the boy surprised me. He said, "You should have this, not me! That would be justice!"

"Maybe so," Miguel replied. There was silence for a while, then he said, "I'll never forgive you for doing this to yourself. Never! Not as long as I live. How could you?!"

"You! You did it! You did it!"

Miguel came out of the room. We acknowledged each other's presence. He swept his hands roughly back through his hair. He licked his lips. As he walked away, he paused for a moment to look in a mirror hung above a wooden desk in the hallway. He glared at what he saw. He looked back at me. He crossed his hands over his chest to form an X. His hands were splayed like fans straining to cut his neck.

He walked away.

I never did place that gesture, but I suspected that it meant that he was being faced with something he didn't understand and couldn't control.

He was forming a shield.

It was as I stood in the hallway thinking about Miguel's gesture that António must have punched his right hand through the door of the hotel's wooden dresser. I heard it, but I thought he'd slammed a drawer.

I ate dinner alone, which was fine with me. I was a man without: libido;

worries;

or taste buds.

I was hollow once again. Warm. Like a carved pumpkin with two small candles behind his eyes. I slept peacefully.

On Sunday morning, I woke to see Miguel sitting in bed, smoking. He said, "Maybe I should go back to Porto."

"Why?"

"One of us should go. Either me or António."

"We'll drive to France today," I said. I was half asleep and was convinced that crossing a border would help us all.

Miguel frowned. He stood up. He stubbed out his cigarette and started slipping on his clothes.

"The food is better in France," I said.

"You're not listening to what I'm saying," he observed.

"That's right, I'm not. It's a new policy of mine."

"What new policy?"

"I've decided not to listen to anything that might upset me."

"You won't get very far with my son."

I sat up. "I'll buy headphones."

"He'll rip them off you."

"Then you can drip wax in my ears."

He zipped up his jeans and slipped on a blue t-shirt. He said, "I know that you're back taking your tranquilizers."

"I wouldn't want us to have any secrets from each other," I replied happily.

"They're no good for you."

"On the contrary, they'd be excellent for you, too."

"No thanks."

"I wasn't offering. You'll have to buy your own. I'm not going to be generous with a man who flushed my last stash down the toilet."

"Do you always get clever when you're high?"

"I can't get aroused, I might as well get clever. It's the only substitute I've got."

"Swell."

"It isn't very civilized to begrudge a cripple his crutch," I pointed out. I yawned and drank some water from my glass.

"Stop feeling sorry for yourself."

"Wrong! That's the last thing I feel. I've been lucky. More lucky than you'd dare ever imagine!"

"You're hardly a cripple."

"Why? Because I can walk without limping? Look at me as if I were a painting. What do you see?"

"Not this again. You're crazy!"

"Look at me!" I stood up. I was naked. I held the folds from my belly in my hands. I smiled. I looked like Lucian Freud in his self-portraits. Was that why I'd sent one to my mom? I said, "If I were a painting, what would you say about me?"

He tucked his shirt in his pants. "I don't know."

"At least tell me what my title be? 'Over-the-Hill Jester?' 'The Waif Grown Up?'"

He slipped a black leather belt through his loops.

"I'm talking to you," I said. "Look at me! You've sucked my cock, the least you could do is look at me when I'm talking to you."

He stood with his hands on his hips and frowned. He stuck a cigarette in his mouth and lit it.

I said, "I know you're not having sex with me because you find me so damn attractive. Maybe it's out of pity. Maybe pure perversity."

I didn't say what I was really thinking, however — that he was sleeping with me out of his need to get close to António.

Maybe all my thoughts were proof of how wrong you can be when you search underneath a simple pattern for an intricate design!

Angrily, he said to me, "I don't pity you."

"So then what's my fucking title?" I asked.

He looked like he wanted to punch me again. "Used merchandise," he said. "The man with too many fingerprints on him."

My cheeks burned. I thought: *it's another genetic similarity — he and António are both excellent marksmen!*

After Miguel left, I reached out to the wall with both my hands.

Carlos, old friend, you haunted me as I stood alone in my room. I even looked for a time at the scar you made on my ear. I should have known I was going a little mad, because I was thinking that it might be nice to have nicks on my body from everyone I'd ever loved — tattoos testifying to either my loyalty or masochism or sheer stupefying idiocy, depending on your point of view.

I also began to believe that it was of some occult significance that you were the only lover I'd ever had who left me with a reminder of his presence that could be seen by everyone.

Of course, drugs are good for destroyed pride, as well. So in a half-hour, I was ready to face Miguel again. He was smoking at a breakfast table by the window. Two cigarettes were already stubbed in the ashtray. "We're going to France today," I told him. "So pack your things."

I didn't wait for his reply. I wheeled around, walked down the hallway and knocked on António's door. No answer. I knocked louder and called his name. He opened the door a crack. He was in his underwear. His hair was mussed. There was a crease in his cheek. "I was sleeping," he said.

I told him to pack for our trip. "Is my father going?" he asked.

"Look, I absolutely refuse to leave him here in this nowhere land," I replied.

"No, I want him to come," the boy said. "I'll be ready in a half-hour." He closed the door.

I couldn't figure it out, and I didn't want to. I just wanted to get closer to Paris. It was such a big city that I figured I'd be able to find a dark corner into which I could escape.

We loaded our things in the Batmobile. That's when I noticed the scabs on António's knuckles. It was his right hand, the one that would have to play the tremolo stroke on *Recuerdos*. I didn't ask what happened. Neither did Miguel.

I was thinking, *If he can't play guitar for his audition then I'll just leave them there to fend for themselves and continue driving to Prague. It should be nice this time of year, and I've always wanted to see the Jewish Quarter.*

I drove north to get to the freeway, then headed east. The world looks surprisingly sympathetic when you're drugged and going eighty miles per hour in an old T-Bird. No one spoke. Miguel watched the scenery and bit his nails. António kept his hands between his legs and leaned against his window.

I caught myself humming a few times, mostly the Marseillaise, but a few of my Irish ballads crept in as well.

We crossed the border at Hendaye and kept on going on the N10 toward Bordeaux. I began to construct words out of the letters on license plates. I squeezed my hands on the steering wheel in rhythm to the beating of my heart. The notion gripped me that I had to stay in Saintes, a town I'd been in maybe twenty years before. I was petrified that something terrible would happen if we didn't stay there that night.

We stopped for lunch at a roadside restaurant outside Labouheyre. It was a Swiss chalet in the middle of a pine forest. We seemed to have entered a German fairy tale. "The Brothers Grimm," I said to António as we walked to the entrance.

He nodded. He held the door open for me as if being polite was all we had left between us.

Our waiter had bangs and a dull face. He described the soup of the day in a cheerful voice: potato with leek and a dash of dill.

I translated for Miguel because he knew no French. He picked at his teeth with a toothpick and swallowed whatever he found.

It's hard to sit at a lunch table waiting for food to come without saying a single word. The pressure began to mount like a flood tide. So I went to the bathroom and dropped my second valium of the day. Strictly out of a sense of self-preservation, I resolved to attempt a conversation with my Portuguese albatrosses. When I returned to the table, I said to Miguel, "What was your best event in gymnastics?"

"The parallel bars."

"And the best you ever scored on them?"

"Eight point seventy-five."

"That's pretty good. And you, António?"

"What?"

"What was your best event?"

"I didn't have any 'best event'. I just joined the team to please other people."

"Me, you mean," noted Miguel.

"Who else could I mean? The Queen of England?"

Silence. I excused myself again and went to hide in the bathroom. Mostly I stared at my face. My lips were badly chapped. My hairline was looking more and more sparse. I got up close to the mirror and tried to count the number of hairs in a square inch. I kept losing my count. When I came out, I stood with my back pressed against the bathroom door watching our table. No one noticed me.

My soup arrived without me.

Miguel and António hadn't ordered any because I had. Spite is a strong emotion in dysfunctional families.

The soup was warm and wet. I liked it.

We didn't talk any more at lunch. I played basketball games in my head. I was young, and I was able to dunk.

I'd forgotten to change money. I paid with a credit card. Miguel started making a list of what he owed me.

Outside, I asked if one of them would mind driving. Miguel held out his hand, and I tossed him the keys. "You're in charge," I said. I sat up front with him. I showed him the route passed Bordeaux to Saintes. "It's got a lovely view of the Alps," I explained. The Alps were five hundred miles away, but neither he nor António questioned my reasoning.

As he drove, I stared at words in *Life With a Star*. I sang along with the radio from time to time. I had the feeling that Pandora's box was in the back seat, so I didn't turn around once.

We arrived at six that evening. We pulled into the parking lot of the Hotel Cognac, the ivy-covered four-story townhouse on the west bank of the Charente where I'd stayed once before. A men's clothing store was just next door. Golf clubs and argyll socks were displayed in the cheerful window. I was so relieved to reach Saintes that I wanted to kiss the ground. António must have sensed that and said, "I don't know why we don't just turn around and go home."

I dared to face him and smiled falsely, "Are you enjoying France yet?"

"No. And I'm not going to either!"

Miguel stared at me to see what I'd reply.

I said, "Then the least you could do is shut up."

"Fuck you!" the boy shouted.

I don't know how I managed rage in my subdued state, but I did. I turned completely around in my seat and said, "No, fuck you. Fuck you!" I was suddenly shouting at the top of my voice in ungrammatical Portuguese, "You're doing your best to ruin this trip! And maybe you'll succeed. But I've reached my limit!"

"And I've reached mine!" he screamed back.

Miguel was looking down and away from me. His hands were gripping the steering wheel.

"No you haven't," I said. "You've got years to go. I've seen people who've reached their limit and you're not even close. You're not throwing up into the books you're reading. You haven't got a purple face and bug eyes. Your clothes still fucking fit you. You hear me! You're not even close! I'll tell you when you're fucking close! You'll know when you're fucking close because you won't even remember when you were healthy and could still shout at the top of your lungs like a fucking human being. You'll know you're close when your bones stick out like you're one big elbow and you don't remember what it was like to sit without a bone threatening to pierce like an arrow through your skin. Then you'll be fucking close! And then you'll have reached your limit."

He turned bright red in shock. He reached for the door handle.

"I'm not through yet!" I said. "Don't you move! Don't you dare move!"

He glared at me and crossed his arms.

"Tell me everything now! Because after this, I'm not going to listen to any more blame. If you start, if you say so much as one word of blame after this, I'm going to walk out on you. So tell me what more I've done to you."

Silence.

"Tell me what more I've done to you, goddammit! You owe me at least that."

"You didn't do anything," he frowned.

"Not good enough. That's just to avoid my yelling." I lowered my voice. "How have I injured you? What injustice have I done?"

"Nothing."

"No, no. I tried to teach you. No teacher does everything right. And I slept with you. No lover does everything right. So what did I do wrong? Was it too many scales? If I'd given you less scales to do would you never have slept with Sardinha? Is that it? Which scale

220

was it? C major? D major? No it must have been a minor scale. Which one? E minor? Tell me which one!"

He hung his head.

Miguel touched my shoulder. "That's enough," he said. "Leave the boy alone."

I threw his hand off me. "What are you going to do if I don't stop? Hit me again? Go ahead!" I pushed his chest hard. "Go ahead and hit me!"

António said, "You hit him?"

"Shut up!" I told him. "It's none of your business what happens between me and your father." I faced Miguel. "So are you going to hit me? Because if not then you'd better just shut the fuck up!"

"No," he said. "I'm not going to hit you." He put his hands back on the steering wheel and looked down.

I faced António. "So I want to know, if it wasn't a scale, what was it? Those studies by Sor? Was that what made you sleep with a junkie? Was that what made a virus find you? Was that it? A guitar study by an eighteenth-century Catalonian told a twentieth-century virus to crawl up your ass! Was that it? Did it crawl from the sheet music directly into you? Tell me!"

"Stop," he whispered. He was about to burst into tears.

"No," I said. "Don't you cry! Was it sleeping with you? Was that it? Was it my cock or my ass? Which one was it?"

He rubbed his misty eyes and breathed deeply. He looked away.

"Or maybe my mouth? One blowjob too many? Or was it a kiss? That's the hardest of all, isn't it? Was it that? If I hadn't loved you as much as I did... If I didn't love you, would that save you? Tell me! Tell me! Is love the culprit?! Is *that* what this is all about — you blaming love?"

"I don't know." He held his head in his hands. His palms covered his eyes. He was shaking. "I don't know anything anymore," he whispered. "Everything I knew has disappeared."

I stepped out of the car and got in the back seat with him. I didn't touch him. As gently as I've ever spoken to anyone, I said, "I'm sorry for any wrong I've done to you."

He nodded. "You haven't hurt me. Just let me be alone a bit. I need to think."

I put my arms around him. He hugged me back and started to heave with sobs. I said, "What I said before was a lie. I'll never abandon you."

He hugged me as hard as he could. He cried for a long time. When he could talk again, he said, "It's in me. I can't get used to it. I want it out of me." He shivered and wriggled inside my grip. "I want it out of me so bad I want to peel my skin off."

26

Saintes was lovely that evening. It's a town of gray churches and golden spires. With a peaceful river unfurling like a silver ribbon between watchful townhouses.

Bathed in light, the town seems to levitate above the countryside.

We were blessed by the coming of the summer solstice, and the sun remained with us until nearly eleven. We went from church to church, admiring the stained-glass windows and stone towers. We were three wanderers looking at metaphorical spaceships to God from the fourteenth century.

We sat on green public benches facing the cathedral. An ancient oak guarded us from behind.

Exhaustion is a gift; we couldn't fight anymore.

We ate venison and drank a local red wine from a ceramic carafe in a small restaurant with a vaulted ceiling held up by great wooden beams. Miguel went to bed. When he bid us goodnight, he said to António, "I love you, son."

António nodded his acknowledgment. But he closed his eyes and leaned away when Miguel brushed his cheek with his hand.

I'd expected António's savagery, but not this quiet indomitable resistance.

As part of a Saturday-night series through the summer, there was an organ concert that night at midnight.

I was thinking: *So that's why I had to come to Saintes!*

A small woman with blue-gray hair and stiff posture showered the stone inside the cathedral with notes.

She played:

Frescobaldi's *Ricercar dopo il Credo;*

Pachelbel's *Toccata in E Minor;*

and Bach's chorale prelude *For Christ Lay in the Bonds of Death.*

Guitarists are always envious of organists because with a single touch they can rattle your ribs. António and I shared a smile over that. We held hands. We closed our eyes and were squeezed together in the arms of sound.

That night, walking back along the river to our hotel, he asked when his father had hit me.

"In Salamanca," I replied. "No big deal."

He asked me to spend the night in his room. He said, "I'm frightened of my father. I don't want to sleep alone."

"Why are you frightened of him?"

"I think he wants to kill me."

"Kill you? Why?"

"Not consciously. But I'm his worst fear. Killing me would be a relief for him."

"Antonio, he loves you," I said.

"He *wants* to love me," António corrected. "It's different. He doesn't know what love is. He never learned."

"So what exactly do you think he's most frightened of?"

"Of giving in... I mean, of letting himself go. He's frightened it will have terrible consequences. And I'm proof of that. What's happened to me might happen to him."

"What exactly do you mean, 'letting himself go'?"

"You know what I mean."

"You mean, having sex with a man."

António stopped and looked at the dark water cutting through the town. "That. And other things. I don't really know. But really loving someone is part of it. Just kissing someone on the cheek and really meaning it. Not doing it because he's seen other people do it and wants to act like them. He copies people. He imitates them. And it's not enough for me. That's why I turn away. You know what he's like? He's like someone who tries to learn English by memorizing a page of writing. He can repeat that writing back and fool you into thinking he really knows English well. But he doesn't even know what it means. And he certainly doesn't know anything in English that wasn't written on the page. That's how he tries to learn how to love. He copies what he sees without knowing what it's all about. He doesn't really learn, he just imitates. And it's just no good any more. Not now."

What António was saying made sense. I said, "But maybe he's really learning how to love this time."

"It would be a big change. And I really doubt he's capable of it."

"People change if they have to."

"So after all that's happened you're still an optimist?" he asked.

"No, a realist. I've seen it happen. It takes a trauma sometimes. But it happens."

A cool wind was coming off the water. António hunched his shoulders and hugged himself. "Maybe," he said, but his tone indicated *I don't think so.*

"Come, let's go home," I said. "It's getting cold." We held hands again. I wanted to tell him I'd made love with his father, but was too nervous. Finally, just outside the hotel, I blurted it out like a confession.

"I know," he nodded.

"How?"

"He told me."

"He told you?"

"Yeah, yesterday."

"What'd he say?"

"He said, 'I let your professor suck me off.' He bragged about it. Like he was doing you a big favor. Letting the queer abase himself in frnt of the macho man." António shrugged. "It's typical."

"That's kind of hard to believe."

"Believe it! I told you, he's a wolf in sheep's clothing. He said you were begging for it. He also said he didn't like it that much because he felt so soiled afterward."

"It seems impossible. Why didn't you tell me sooner?"

"He only told me yesterday. It's one of the reasons we fought. Maybe I should have said something to you. But I warned you about him from the beginning. And then you told me today in the car not to meddle in your relationship with him. So I figured I'd done the right thing in keeping quiet."

Back in the hotel, I agreed to spend the night with the boy. I downed two of the three Spanish valiums I'd hidden in my wallet. António held my hand in bed. "I do love you," he said in a reassuring voice.

I turned over. "But you hate me just a little bit, too."

He slapped my belly. "Yes."

Ambivalent — just like his father, I was thinking. But I didn't know how to define Miguel anymore. I grew nervous. My legs began aching. I stretched them over my head while the boy slept. I got up and paced. I sat back down. I passed out.

In the early morning, I remembered having dreamt of spiders. Only it was a comforting dream. They were sucking blood from the bottom of my feet while I was resting in a web in order to purge me of poisons. Although it tickled a bit, it felt good and healing.

It was after that that I put two and two together from all the research I'd done about medieval Jewry and realized that the characterization of vampires as evil was wrong. They'd been feared as being different, *just like the Jews.*

I was so excited that I woke António. "What is it?" he said, sitting up. "You okay?"

"I'm fine. Listen... Who were the vampires? Were they a real people? What did they believe in?"

"What are you talking about?"

"Just listen... The only clues we have are that the same characterizations were applied to them as were applied to Jews. Don't you see? During the Middle Ages, for instance, Christian doctors said that Jews had horns and tails, and that their men menstruated. Clerics said that Jewish women had preternatural seductive powers. My God, Christians have been claiming for centuries that Jews are creatures of darkness, akin to rodents, that from the farthest corners of the globe they conspire together under cover of night to form an invisible nation of evil. In Poland, they still think that Jews are *bloodsucking* parasites."

He sighed and rubbed his face. "You woke me up to tell me that?"

I was too excited to stop. "Had the Jews been completely annihilated in the death camps or assimilated to the point of invisibility, we'd still be reading such lies about them. That's what I'm saying. We'd be told today that when the Jews still existed, it had been possible to tell them from human beings because they couldn't stand sunlight. And that they were only able to sleep in the soil of their homeland, Israel. We'd be warned that there might still be a few around and that they could even change us into Jews with their cunning magic if we weren't careful and always on our guard."

"I'm just going to sleep a little bit longer," he said. He puffed up his pillow and lay back down. He looked at me sympathetically. "Just a few more minutes. You can tell me what you want over breakfast."

Before he could close his eyes, I said, "António, if you substitute *vampire* for *Jew* then you realize that all the legends about nocturnal bloodsucking monsters are nothing more than Nazi-style propaganda. History is always told by the victors. And we all know that the vampire, unlike the Jew, is always a loser. In the end, the proud, Nordic-looking hero always manages to pound a spike into him. Into his heart, of course. In short, our legends about vampires are descriptions of a people whose history is lost to us, written by the ruthless and terrified men who've tried to destroy them."

"So what's the truth?"

"The truth? That vampire legends are the result of collective fear. About something so frightening to most men that the vampire's heart must be destroyed. Don't you see, they're afraid of us! We're their descendants and they're afraid of us."

António patted my hand and closed his eyes. In a few minutes, he was asleep.

It was Sunday and no banks were open. After breakfast, Miguel and I cashed some pesetas at the hotel. António took our loose change.

We hit the road. Content and calm, the boy sat in the passenger seat with maps spread on his lap, naming each French town we passed, pronouncing billboard advertisements in his best Gallic accent. I gave up on vampires, and we discussed music theory for a while. He bit his cuticles and watched passing cars. We listened to the radio. He drummed his hands against the glove compartment and sang along with Queen and Aerosmith. He smiled at me. I almost believed he was the old António. I kept looking in the rearview mirror at Miguel, however. He made faces at me as if to ask, *What's up with you?* I didn't answer; I didn't know.

We ate lunch at a rest stop off the freeway. I went to the bathroom to take another tranquilizer because Miguel's watchful eyes were making me jumpy. Now he was the one who was using up my air.

He followed me in. I was peeing by then because the first thing I'd done was down the pill. He stood next to me and unzipped himself. We were alone. "I want to suck your cock," he whispered in my ear. "Come to a stall."

I figured that maybe he was going to threaten me or even hit me. "Leave me alone," I said.

He brushed my cheek. I pushed his hand away. I zipped myself up and went to wash my hands.

"What's wrong?" he asked. He stood with his hands on his hips, casually irritated.

"Leave me alone," I said.

"I want an explanation. What did I do?"

I faced him. "Did you tell António we were having sex?"

"What?"

"You heard me."

"I heard you, but I didn't tell him anything."

"He says you did."

"Then he's lying."

"Or maybe *you* are, right?"

"Why would I lie?"

"Why would he?"

He stuck a cigarette in his mouth. "Because he's jealous."

"First you're jealous of him, now he's jealous of you. Give me a break!"

He lit his cigarette and in a cascade of smoke, whispered, "Not jealous of me, Professor. Of you!"

Miguel's words made me realize that our relationships were so knotted that I could never disentangle them. And I didn't want to hear anymore about them. So I patted his back and assured him with sincere nods that I believed him; it was simpler. On my insistence, he promised not to bring the subject up with António. He felt me through my jeans and told me he still wanted to give me a blowjob. "I'll be quick," he said.

"You might be, but I can't get an erection. You're dealing with a eunuch now."

He put his hands to my chest and said, "I didn't tell him," you know.

I held a finger to my lips and walked out.

My only goal now was to get to Paris so António could take his audition. I figured that afterward we could drive back to Porto in one twenty-four-hour flight to safety. None of these complications between father and son would matter in two days. I'd be home. Fiama could bake me codfish with potatoes and onions. I could even watch television next to her in her room if I was a good boy.

Maybe my mother would have sent another letter which I could burn.

And maybe the ghost of Nancy the Border Collie would be waiting for me and tell me what I needed to do to regain hope. I'd suddenly be able to interpret dog barking.

I bought a copy of *The International Herald Tribune* to make me drowsy and asked António to drive. Miguel agreed to sit up front so that I could have the back.

I read about:

fighting in Bosnia;

nursing strikes in Belgium;

the latest attempt to push a strong gun-control bill through the U.S. Congress.

I didn't wake up till we were twelve kilometers south of Paris. Miguel was shaking me. I switched seats with him and navigated us to the Place Saint-Sulpice. It took forever because cars seemed to have reproduced like rabbits since I was last here. I'd never seen such traffic outside of L.A. and New York.

"Oh my God," António kept saying. "Paris... I can't believe it."

He kept hitting his thigh and biting his cuticles.

The Hotel Greco did not look terribly promising; it was a thin four-story townhouse of flaking white paint guarded by two bushy plane trees. Between the second and third floor was clamped a vertical sign with gold lettering and two stars like you might see outside an American motel. We parked on the sidewalk in front. I went in. As Barabas had instructed me, I asked for Jean Floris. A man behind the desk with a round head, thinning hair and sleepy eyes told me that Jean was vacationing in Nice. The lobby was walled with fake wood paneling and the carpet was a deep copper brown. Wilted red tulips in a blue vase graced the desk. The place smelled of dust and ammonia. In my pidgin French, I mentioned Barabas and the possibility of a bargain rate. I was charming and humble in an American sort of way. The man pointed behind him to a rubber board with white letters stuck on it and said in a burdened voice, "Those are our prices."

I'd forgotten about Parisian hospitality. The board said:

Chambre double: 700 Francs

Chambre simple: 550 Francs

That was a hundred bucks for a single. *Merci,* I said. I got us three; I was taking no chances.

We carried our bags in ourselves, of course. The receptionist coughed as we passed through the lobby toward the elevator and said, "Breakfast from seven till ten."

There was no hint that he was going to volunteer information on where the breakfast room was. So I asked, *"C'est où?"*

"Où quoi? Where what?" he asked, as if offended.

"Où breakfast?!" I said.

He frowned and pointed down.

Hotel from hell, I thought.

The rooms themselves were hardly more than closets, and were painted the same flaking white as the hotel facade. There was just room enough for a spongy single bed with pink bedspread, writing desk and wardrobe. The bathroom was minuscule and was decorated with turquoise-blue tiles. No television. No bowl of fruit. It was clean, however, so I was happy. António had a view of the great columns of Saint-Sulpice just across the street. Miguel and I had a view of a dingy courtyard with a mangled baby carriage lying on its side at the bottom. I leaned out the window and looked for the baby's discarded skeleton, but I couldn't spot it.

When we were each settled in to our room, I called the desk for a line out. The same receptionist as before said, "One moment."

One moment turned to ten, then sixty. As I was wondering if he was torturing me on purpose, the line finally clicked in. I called Pedro back in Porto.

"How's it going?" he asked.

"I couldn't explain even if I wanted to."

"Good, bad...?"

"Both. And more... But I'm fine."

"You sound tired," he observed.

"Drugs."

"You're not back on tranquilizers, I hope."

"Limit your hopes and you shall not be disappointed."

"I suppose you know what you're doing."

"Not at all."

"You're stronger than you think," he commented.

"Pedro, you're a dear, but you think people are finer and more powerful than they are."

"I don't. It's just that..."

"You do," I interrupted. "You look at a mushroom and you think you see a tree fern."

He laughed.

"Anyway, have you spoken to Landero about António's audition?" I asked.

"All taken care of. Only one complication — he's not going to be at the Paris Conservatory this week. He's expecting you to call him at home."

Pedro read me the number. I repeated it back to him. "What should I say when I call?" I asked.

"You're the one who wanted to do this, don't you know?"

"Pedro, don't argue with me. My thoughts evaporate unless I make the greatest effort to freeze them. What do I tell him?"

"That António's the best student we've ever had and that he deserves him as a teacher."

"What should I tell the boy to play?" I asked.

"You know better than me."

"I don't."

"You do!"

"And what do I say about him being gay?"

"That's totally irrelevant," Pedro assured me.

"It is?"

He sighed. "Of course. God, why are you being so weird?"

"I'm nervous. I'm tired. I'm confused."

"I guess that's enough reason. Look, hang on for a few more days and come home as soon as you can. I'll have some maté tea ready for you."

"Oh Jesus, what a thought! valium with maté tea!"

After I hung up, I called Landero. I didn't want to take a chance on getting cold feet. He wasn't in. A taped voice speaking Spanish-accented French answered. António knocked at my door while I was waiting for the beep. I carried the phone across the room and let him in. I left a careful message in English with the name and phone number of our hotel.

I really must have had my brain in the clouds because I didn't even consider for a minute that António would find out my plan this way.

"What's this about an audition?" he demanded.

"Sit," I said.

He sat next to me, on my left side. I wanted him on my right. "Other side," I said.

He rolled his eyes.

"Indulge me," I said.

He got up and dropped down again.

"Now give me your hand."

"I don't want to."

"But I want to touch you."

He plopped his left hand on my thigh. I picked it up and starting kneading his fingers.

"What are you doing?" he asked.

"Look, it comes down to this," I said. "I'm trying to set up an audition for you with José Maria Landero. Do you know who he is?"

"I know."

I was silent. I couldn't think of anything else to say.

"But what's the audition about?" he asked.

"One of the reasons I wanted to come to Paris is that I was thinking while you were in the hospital that you deserved a better teacher. That you could go further. Just like you said. Turns out, we both must have been thinking the same thing. In a couple years, I want you to be playing concerts, you know."

He took back his hand and stood up. "You want me to study in Paris?"

"He hasn't accepted you yet. You've got to play very well at the audition. He gets the best students from all over the world. You'll be competing against blind, eight-year-old Israeli prodigies from Minsk who've mastered the guitar through braille Torah study and kabbalistic black magic."

He rolled his eyes. "This is crazy," he said. He began gnawing the cuticle on his right thumb.

"Leave your fingers alone!" I said.

He spit out what he'd gotten and turned around to gnaw some more.

"Why is it crazy?" I asked.

He faced me and threw his arms out. "I can't just leave Portugal."

"Why not?"

"For one thing, I can't afford it. My father isn't rich, or haven't you noticed? We don't have the money."

"You can get a part-time job here. Be a waiter or something. It'll be good for you. Or you can play at some romantic little café where lovers smooch in the corner."

"I don't want to play at a café."

"It can be a gay café," I said enticingly.

He rolled his eyes again.

"Look, I'm not telling you what to do," I said. "I'm just telling you that you're perfectly qualified to get a job like everyone else."

"It still won't pay my stay. Lessons, an apartment, food..."

"I'll help with the rest."

He sighed. "Why would you want to waste your money on my

lessons at this point?"

"After all this time, isn't it obvious?"

He frowned at me. "I don't want your money. I don't want to owe you any more money than I already do."

"You don't owe me anything."

"This money you've given me on this trip... I'll pay you back, you know."

"Forget it."

"No, I will."

"Fine. You can consider any money I give you a loan."

"No."

"António, what am I going to save my money for? There's nothing left for me to do. I'm not going to go trekking in the Himalayas or scuba diving in Brazil. And I'm not going to have children. So what's it for?"

"That's what this is about, isn't it?"

"What?"

"Me, your surrogate son. I'm not your son!"

He was taking the air from me again. I was dizzy. I sat up straight and tried my best to breathe deeply.

"What's wrong?" he asked.

"Nothing. Look, I admit I like it when people think we're father and son. But that doesn't mean..."

"I don't want your money," he interrupted.

"I thought we were past that?"

"We're not."

"Well, let's make believe we are. What other problems are there?"

"I can't just pick up and move."

"People do it all the time."

"I'm not people. Besides, now...now that I've got this in me."

"That makes no difference."

He was silent. He was standing now with his back against the window. His hands were crossed over his chest. He said, "I don't want to come to Paris just so you can say one day that you knew me when I was a nothing student. It's your dream that I play concerts, not mine. You're living through me."

"That's not fair. You've told me many times how you daydreamed about playing in Carnegie Hall and the Paris Opera."

"Daydreams... They're not real."

"Look, this argument is absurd. I'll set up the audition. You want to go, you go. You don't, don't."

"I won't go!" he declared. He glared at me.

I went to the bathroom to get my Turkish switchblade with the amber handle; I'd put it in my medicine bag for safekeeping. I came back and stood in front of him. I was very calm. I turned my hand over. I popped open the blade. I cut an inch-long canal of blood on the back of my wrist.

It only hurt a bit. I guess the valium made me a little numb.

"What are you doing?!" António shrieked.

"So you don't have to bloody your knuckles again. Or do something worse. I don't want you spoiling your chances."

"You're crazy!"

"Maybe so. But I bet you won't hurt yourself now."

I watched the blood dripping onto the gray carpet. It was pretty. I held my hand up to him. "Now go practice," I said.

António was frightened that a virus might leap from his mouth into my wound. He didn't say another word to me. He ran to fetch his father, then disappeared. In the bathroom, as Miguel attended to me, he kept saying, "What a stupid thing to do!"

It took forever for the bleeding to subside. I never felt faint, or even perturbed. I was convinced that it was the right thing to have done and that I would be none the worse for a little scar. Miguel demanded that I get stitches at a hospital. But I wasn't about to go to an emergency room and wait around with all those seriously ill and depressing people. He begged. I refused. By then, my pants and shirt were stained with blood. He began running the wound under hot water. Every minute for a half-hour, he told me in a furious, somewhat hysterical voice, "If this continues then you're going to bleed to death!"

A cup of me went down the sink. He worked on me for at least an hour. "What did you think this would accomplish?" he yelled when he finally let my arm go.

I had half a roll of toilet paper wrapped around my wrist at this point, and it was soaked red.

I knocked three times on the side of the bathtub with my other hand.

"I don't get it," he said.

"Words," I replied. "They don't fit sometimes. Bulls in a china shop."

"You're babbling. It's those tranquilizers. That's what it is! It's those fucking tranquilizers."

"I would have done the same thing without them. They just steadied my hand and made it hurt less. They're useful. Remember that Francis Bacon painting where the guy was coming apart in smudged space?"

He nodded.

"Think of how much better he'd have felt if he were drugged."

"You're crazy."

"That's an assessment that's getting a little old at this point. But if it's really what you believe..."

We sat together on the rim of the bathtub. "Can I smoke?" he asked.

I nodded.

He lit a cigarette. He sighed. He was sweaty and covered with blood. A smelly cloud of tobacco engulfed us, but I didn't mind. He said, "We're in Paris. And there's not a single thing I can think of that I want to do."

"Me neither."

He said, "It was meant for me."

"Paris?"

"No. This thing. This Aids thing."

"It wasn't meant for anybody."

"I'm the one who should pay, not the boy. It's because of me. He received my secret wishes. They made him what he is."

"First of all, it's just a virus. How many times do I have to tell you? It doesn't know who you are. Do you think that it can see you? That it says to itself like a lioness on the prowl, 'I think I'll go for that muscular old gymnast over there named Miguel?' Then it makes some sort of navigational error and hops into António by mistake? Is that what you think? It doesn't work like that."

He faced me. He was pale. "António's mother doesn't believe me. But if I could take this Aids thing from him, I would."

I nodded.

"I really would. I'd free him. I've lived enough." He shook his head. "The rest... It doesn't matter. I'd free him."

We sat without talking. Miguel finished his cigarette and dropped it into the toilet. He put his hand on my thigh.

"How do you get the virus? he asked.

"I'm sure you know."

"Can you get it from kissing?"

"No."

Miguel started conjuring up all those intricate hypothetical scenarios people do when they first get worried about becoming infected. Things like, *If I were to kiss a guy with the virus and then got a cut on my arm a half-hour later and sucked at the blood with my mouth could I get it?*

I listened patiently because he was scared. The thing is, you can never get enough information when you're panicked. There's always another scenario: *If I were to take a drink out of a glass that a person with the virus had drunk from, and if the glass suddenly broke and cut my lip...*

"You're safe," I assured him.

He looked at me skeptically and lit another cigarette.

The phone rang. I ran to get it. It was José Maria Landero. I introduced myself. His English was abominable. We spoke French. He would see António at his apartment the next day.

"Does it have to be so soon?" I asked, hoping the boy could get some more serious practice in.

"I have to go to Deauville the day after tomorrow," Landero explained.

We agreed on a time. I wrote down the address on an automatic teller receipt and then underlined it so hard that I broke through the paper.

27

I was glad that António had disappeared; I needed the peace. And seeing Paris alone would be a good experience for him. Miguel and I walked to the Deux Magots. We sat outside, in the section of the café guarded by the bell tower of the Saint-Germain church. I was cheered by the:

round marble tables with metal rims;

green umbrellas and awnings;

smell of Gauloise tobacco.

A fastidious waiter wearing a black jacket and bow tie took our order. Across the street, the green cross of The Drugstore was pulsating. The air was warm and comforting.

When my tea came, I found out that it cost twenty-four francs, more than four dollars. Which was fine, except that it was a bitter brew made from a Sir Tea tea bag and highly chlorinated French tap water. valium was making me thirsty and I didn't want to start hallucinating again, so I drank it anyway. Miguel sipped a double espresso.

We were having a fine time talking about basketball and watching our neighbors till a barechested man with a handlebar mustache started breathing fire right in front of us. He took in mouthfuls of gasoline, then spit it past his flaming torch to create an explosion of fire. Miguel and I paid our bill in a hurry and escaped to a Korean barbecue restaurant on the rue du Dragon. A tiny electric hibachi stood on each table. We grilled razor-thin slices of meat on it. I ate my beef, rice and kimchi with chopsticks. Miguel used a fork. I was deliriously happy for no reason. Miguel started remembering António when he was a child. His gripped my hand. "What a boy!" he said. "I used to love just to watch him run down the street. I couldn't hold him enough or kiss him enough." His dropped my hand and rubbed his cheek. "Maybe I kissed him too much."

"Eat your beef," I said.

"Do you think I kissed him too much?" he asked.

"No."

"We were too close," he said. "Then, when he began to frighten me, I moved too far away. It was the inconsistency which was wrong."

"Eat your beef."

"The *inconsistency*. I've got to tell that to António's mother. It was the *inconsistency*. She'll want to know."

When we got back to the hotel, it was near midnight. The light was on in António's room. I pushed a note under his door telling him that he needed to meet me in the lobby at one in the afternoon the next day so we could get to his audition by two. I didn't risk writing anything else. Standing in the hallway, I heard him pick the note up and crunch the paper. It hit against the door. "I know you're still out there," he said.

Apparently, António could see through wood. I poked my thumb between my index and middle fingers for protection against demons. I locked myself in my room.

At two in the morning, I awoke. There was an argument coming from António's room. I cupped my ear against the wall, but the French plaster was too dense for proper eavesdropping.

Muffled shouts went on for some time. When I heard what sounded like a body being tossed against the wall between our rooms, sweat beaded on my forehead. I was thinking: *António was right, Miguel wants to kill him! Maybe he's going to try to murder us both!*

I slipped on my pajamas and rushed into the hall. The boy's door was locked. I jiggled it and shouted, "Let me in!"

Silence.

"What are you doing in there?! Let me in!"

A crack in the doorway opened. I could see a sliver of António's face, but he hid his body from me. Miguel was standing behind him by the bed. He was naked. His hands were fanned over his sex. A condom sheathed his erection.

I stammered something in English. António reached out his hand and held mine tightly. "I'm okay," he smiled. "We'll talk in the morning."

I looked at Miguel. He nodded as if to say, *Everything is under control, Professor.* He bowed toward me in a ceremonial manner.

The door closed and the lock clicked.

I didn't sleep the rest of the night. I was thinking that I finally understood what Miguel meant by *I want to know my son.*

I remembered, too, all those questions he'd asked me about sex and what António liked in bed.

It didn't make me angry that he might have used me. If, after all that had happened, my heart and body could still serve as catalysts, then so much the better.

Yet I began to get worried that the chest hairs of a father and son rubbing together in a hotel room in Paris would have unforeseen consequences.

They were tempting the gods.

Then I considered that everything has unforeseen consequences. And that the gods could go fuck themselves.

So it shouldn't have mattered. Even so, I sat in my bathroom till four in the morning. I read the *Herald Tribune* front to back. I began having desperate, clinging thoughts because my chest was really hurting, so I turned on the shower to breathe the steam deep into my clogged lungs. I wanted to take another tranquilizer because I was very nervous. I simply couldn't get my leg muscles to relax, among other things. I sat on the floor and stretched them over my head. There were knots like tennis balls in my hamstring muscles. They defied my most earnest efforts.

I'd taken two tranquilizers before dinner. I measured the arguments for and against drugging myself further. I really didn't want to hallucinate. I opened my toothpaste tube. I got out a pill. I washed it off.

I took it quickly. I downed another one just to be sure I'd sleep without waking.

I regretted it afterwards, and I tried in vain to make myself vomit. Then I drank four glasses of water from the sink, figuring that it would dilute the active ingredients in my bloodstream.

I still couldn't sleep, however; now I was panicked that I'd taken an overdose. I ruled out calling the desk to see if there was a number for Poison Control. I thrashed around in bed.

I'd seen movies where people who've taken too many pills are made to walk around. I seemed to recall Susan Hayward in a nightgown. I started pacing.

A clinging depression began to weigh me down. Wherever I walked, I seemed to be lugging a dead child with my brother's face around my neck.

I imagined myself looking like a gorilla, with my knuckles swinging along the carpeting. My lips tasted rancid from the sweat sluicing down my cheeks.

I pictured myself on the deck of a ship that was swaying. It was a relief for a few minutes. Then it began to pitch too far to the side. I sat on my bed. But it was harder to breathe sitting down. I forced myself to stand. I saw myself in the mirror above the writing desk. I gripped the flab at my stomach in my hands. I ripped off the scab on my wrist. I painted my face with blood to look like an Apache. I sat down and stared at my reflection in the mirror. I told myself, *António will be all right. You must have faith. You just need another pill to see that clearly.*

So I took one more.

Then I thought: *You'll substitute him. God will take you instead. He won't realize the mistake till it's too late.*

So I took two more. That made five. On top of two I'd taken earlier that evening.

In a half-hour, I was so empty and thin that I figured I was made of black rice paper — a giant origami creature of darkness.

That amused me for a time. I think I actually laughed.

I closed the window though because the wind was fierce and I figured I'd blow around the room like a balsa-wood plane and break a wing.

I listened to traffic noises for a time.

Then I got real heavy. I pictured myself as a wafer made of lead.

In the mirror, my eyes floated on a sea of pink. I went to the bathroom and poured alcohol on my wound to stay awake. I sat at the desk and stared at myself again.

My heart seemed to stop beating for a time. I wasn't breathing.

I'm dead, I thought. *Yet there's something resembling me in the mirror.*

I suffered more illusions and half-dreams. It took all night, but finally, near dawn on Monday, I spotted António inside me. We had the same smile. He was my son. It was like the waiter in Salamanca had said: *Mi hijo.*

I wanted to tell Miguel what I'd discovered and that there was no reason to be sad.

So I trudged next door and knocked loudly.

Nothing.

My legs were hard and needle-like. They couldn't support me, so I sat in the hallway. I was thinking that it was good to sit on hotel carpeting. It was like being home in the world, like being a child again.

I knocked again.

Miguel came to the door. His hair was mussed. He looked down at me and furrowed his eyebrows. "Are you okay?" he asked. Then he noticed my wrist was bleeding and had a fit.

He grabbed my arm and tried to lift me.

"I'm fine," I said with bravado. "I just wanted to say that I found António in my face. He hasn't left us completely."

"What are you talking about?"

"I found him. It's true. He's not dead."

He lifted me up and took me inside. António was sitting up in bed. I was shocked that he was alive. I dropped through Miguel's hands to the floor.

I banged my elbow so hard against the metal frame of the bed that I thought I might have broken it. The next day, it puffed up and turned blue and yellow.

"He's done it again," the boy told his father.

"Done what?"

I said to Miguel, "António's alive. Then who was it? Who could it have been?"

The boy said, "valium."

"You don't understand," I told him. "You were dead and I was looking for your face in the mirror and it took all night..."

"Let's get him into the shower," Miguel said.

Two naked men pushing me. Antonio covered his hand with a towel so his *infected* skin wouldn't risk touching my wound.

Both of them held me securely. One was dark and had lots of body hair. He looked like a beaver. The other had such soft skin. He was just a baby. I began to stroke his shoulder. It was like marble. It was a dream come true to be held up by four hands.

"To be a piano sonata," I said. "To be a piano sonata played by two men."

"Sshhh," Miguel replied.

Just before passing out, I remember saying to them both, "I want you to just lay me on the bed and enter me one after the other. I don't need an erection for that. You won't mind, will you?"

"No," António said.

I caressed his cheek. "Promise me you'll both crawl inside me. You'll be safe inside there."

28

That was the last thing I remember. When I woke, António was sitting by the open window, looking out on the Place Saint-Sulpice. He was smoking.

I had a bad headache and I was very dry. "I always seem to be doing this," I said. I sipped some water from a glass on the night table.

He turned to me and smiled. He stubbed his cigarette out in an ashtray on the window sill which had a mound of other butts.

He sat next to me. His hands smelled of tobacco. I sat up and covered my face with them. "You smelled like this when we first met," I said.

"We called a doctor." the boy said.

"And what did he say?"

"To let you sleep. How many did you take?"

"I think seven."

He slapped the top of my head. "What do you think you were doing?"

"I was nervous," I said.

I looked out the window. I looked for a watch. I sat up. "Oh, shit," I said.

António read my look. "You missed it, all right. It's three-thirty in the afternoon. I've been back an hour."

"No, it can't be. What time is it really?"

He grinned. "It's three-thirty."

"But this can't have happened in real life. This happens in movies. The teacher can't sleep through his student's audition."

"It's okay. We could have awakened you if we thought it was necessary."

I began cursing. António stood up and started jabbering at me. I waved at him to shut up. He said, "No, you be quiet!" I was stunned. I thought he was going to be cruel to me. But all he said was, "Listen, my father just left to get something to eat. He's been sitting all day with you, you know. I never saw devotion in him like that before. It was incredible."

I sat all the way up. "Just tell me what happened at the audition."

"Don't get upset, but I don't think it went very well." He shrugged. "He only had me play for five minutes."

"You're not lying to me, are you? You went?"

"I went."

"Where'd you get the address?"

"You always keep things like that in your wallet," he noted.

"And?"

"And I already said. He had me play for five minutes."

"What did you play?"

"The Prelude from the Bach Cello Suite in C."

"That's it?"

He nodded.

Not *Recuerdos*?"

"No."

"But you play that better than anybody in the world."

"I played something I needed help on. There was no point in playing something I already have where I want it."

"That doesn't make sense," I said, but it did.

He shrugged. "It's not important. How do you feel?"

I waved away his question. "What was Landero like?"

He laughed at my insistence. "Handsome and young. Maybe thirty. He spoke Spanish really weirdly. He's from Mexico, not Spain, you know. Tijuana of all places. I didn't know real people were from Tijuana. Did you know that?"

"Gay?"

"I don't think so."

"Good," I said.

"Why?"

"We've enough complications."

António laughed again.

"What's so funny?"

"You."

"Now I'm funny?" I asked resentfully.

"Don't take it bad. Anyway, it doesn't matter that much."

"Of course it matters *that much!* Did he say whether he'd accept you?"

"No."

"What did he say?"

"He asked me how I liked Paris."

"That's it...?! How you liked Paris? Who is this Mexican idiot?"

"And how I'd pay for lessons if he were to accept me."

"What'd you say?"

"I said I didn't know."

"Schmuck!" I yelled in English. "Why didn't you tell him *cash.* That you had loads of money." I motioned toward the phone. "Bring me that!" I said.

"Why?"

"I'm going to call him."

"No, don't."

"Bring me the damn phone or I'm going to kill you!"

He brought it to me.

"And my wallet... Did you put the number back in there?"

I've got it. He took my automatic teller receipt from his back pocket. He read the number to me, then went back to his seat by the window and sat gnawing his cuticle. I dialed.

"Leave your fingers alone!" I told the boy.

He rolled his eyes.

A man answered. I said, "Is this José Maria Landero?"

"Yes. Oh, hi. It's you," he answered in French. "I just saw António. Sorry we didn't get to meet. You feeling any better? You should stay away from shellfish in Paris."

"I'm fine. Listen, how did it go?"

"He's good. He's very good. But I don't think I've got room right now. If you wait six months, I'm sure a space will open up."

"He's only been playing seriously for four years, you know."

"Your colleague Pedro told me. He's obviously extraordinarily talented."

"His *Recuerdos* is the best I've ever heard. He should have played that for you.'"

"Look, we know he's going to have a career if he wants one. But I don't have space right now. I'm recording next week in London. Then I've got a concert tour of Spain and France. I'm going to be back and forth like a madman for a while. I can't accept another student right now. But I can recommend another teacher. Or he can wait six months."

"He'll pay cash," I said.

"What?"

"Cash. You won't have to declare any of the money. And you could fit him in any time. When someone cancels a lesson, you call him."

He laughed at me.

Everyone obviously found me hysterical. Such is the empathy human beings exhibit during the last decade of the twentieth century.

I said angrily, "Don't laugh, this is serious."

"Sorry. It's just that the money doesn't matter at this point. Three years ago, yes, not now. So why is this so important to you?"

"I waited too long to find him another teacher better than myself. I was selfish."

António suddenly grabbed the phone from me and banged it down on the receiver.

"Why'd you do that?!" I yelled. "Now you've ruined everything!"

He sat with me and took my hands. "Can't you see what you're doing? You're begging. Stop it." He kissed my forehead. "Calm down. Nothing terrible has happened. I'm still here. You're still here. We're okay. Everything is okay."

Everything is okay.

He squeezed my hands and kept repeating that line till I almost believed him.

I didn't know what to say. It seemed like all had been lost and all had been found. My shoulders slumped. I drank more water. "I'm confused," I said.

"Everything's going to be okay," the boy replied. "That's what you told me when I auditioned for you at the Conservatory. Remember?"

I nodded.

"You know, I was thinking about our first day together while waiting to play for Landero, and I suddenly realized that my tempo was all wrong. And not just in the Bach. In everything."

"What are you talking about?"

He shrugged. "I know I'm not explaining well. It's like what your brother said about the Valley of the Shadow of Death. I've got to think of my life as music. As if it's something that needs to be played at the correct tempo." His eyes brightened. "That's what I realized when I was sitting there in front of Landero. From now on, my life has got to be music. You understand? It can't be what it was. I've got to be careful with it, be more conscious of it than I was before." He kissed my forehead. "Doesn't that make some sense?"

I nodded, then started to cry — not because of his words, exactly, but because of the effort he was making to explain himself to me.

He kissed my cheek and said, "I'm okay."

I hugged him and breathed in his scent for the longest time. When I finally let him go, he reached up and started combing my area of thinning hair. I wiped my eyes and said, "Forget it, there's nothing you can do. I'll be bald by this time next year." But his fingers felt so nice that I didn't twist away.

"No, if we arrange it right, then no one will notice," he replied.

"Thank you, but I don't want my hair *arranged just right.* You make me sound like a Barbie doll."

"You should eat more gelatin," he said.

I lifted my lip threateningly.

As he tilted my head down to look over his work, he said, "My father kissed me last night."

"And that's not all apparently."

"No, but kissing me was the most important thing. Afterward, he cried." António mussed up my hair playfully. "One last thing," he said, suddenly serious again. "I've always known I was gay. Always. You had nothing to do with that. I would have been miserable if I hadn't met you."

I shook my head. "No, you wouldn't. You'd have been fine."

"Why won't you let me tell you the truth? I would have been a basket case. I'd have never known there were gay people who were normal and happy and kind. I'd have been all alone. I'd have spent all this time in a closet, waiting, banging my head against the wall."

Life is one big repetition after a certain point; when Miguel got back from snacking and smoking, he flushed all my tranquilizers down the toilet bowl.

I confessed about my toothpaste tube. He held it up to me and squeezed it out like a gigantic white worm. He and António were laughing.

"Where else?" he smiled.

They were having such a good time that I handed him my wallet. "Next to my driver's license."

He tossed the last pill into the water.

"That's it?" he asked.

I nodded.

"Nothing up your ass?" António inquired.

"I beg your pardon!"

"I'll search if necessary!" he warned me.

"I assure you that there's nothing in there right at this moment," I replied. "And yes, I can always tell when something's inside me. It isn't that callused."

He jumped on the bed and lay next to me. He covered his face with my hands. He breathed in. "You smell like you for the first time in ages," he said.

"Is that good or bad?"

"Very good," he said.

"It's not my smell that's changed, you know. It's your nose."

"Where do you want to eat?" Miguel asked. He sat next to António and kissed his cheek.

The boy hugged his father's arms around him.

"Anywhere," I said. "Maybe the Korean barbecue again. It's nice doing your own cooking."

Miguel kissed the top of António's head. He said proudly, "Isn't my boy handsome, Professor?"

We took a cab to the Marais and ate Jewish food at Jo Goldenberg's on the rue de Rosiers. They'd never before eaten Jewish food.

I ordered for everyone. We got...

matzah ball soup;

stuffed cabbage;

hot pastrami;

and cheesecake.

I considered ordering gefilte fish but had learned that no one who isn't raised Jewish can stand the sight or taste of it. Henry The Beast once told me it looked like something Klingons ate on *Star Trek*.

Pastrami was the big hit of the evening.

I drank two espressos and three glasses of Evian water before the meal because I was drowsy and dehydrated again.

Miguel and António were playful. They needled each other. They tried each other's food.

They were holding hands under the table.

After dessert, António went to the bathroom. Miguel watched his son threading his way to the back of the restaurant. He lit a cigarette. "It's been a long trip," he said, sighing.

"Glad you came?"

He scratched the stubble on his cheeks. "Whatever happens, I'm going to get to know him." He shaped the ash at the tip of his cigarette by turning it against the glass of the ashtray.

I said, "And you'll always use a condom, right?"

He nodded.

"Always," I emphasized with a wagging finger. "And use only Harmony."

He smiled and nodded again. In his eyes, I saw that there was some worry he wasn't giving voice to, so I looked away to give him space. After a few puffs on his cigarette, he said, "Do you forgive me?"

"For what?" I asked.

"You know what."

"Miguel, there's nothing to forgive. I loved being with you. And I knew it wouldn't last."

He took my hand. "I know it's not a solution, but maybe it will help António. Not just now, I mean. But when he needs me. When he really needs strength."

"Knowing you're loved always helps," I said.

"I need to know what you think," he added. "I guess I need some strength, too."

I sat with my head down, considering my reply. But António appeared out of nowhere.

The boy didn't complain about his father smoking. They held hands again. Just before we left, they kissed each other on the lips.

Outside, as we were about to enter the Saint-Paul metro station, Miguel took my arm. He looked at me hopefully, asking for my approval again.

Dearest Carlos, what should I have told him?

My heart was pounding. I didn't think I could speak. "However you do it, love him," I said. "Listen to whatever he has to tell you and then just love him. What else is there in life?"

We hugged while António asked what was up.

He and his son slept together again in the boy's room.

On Tuesday morning, a telephone call woke me up. I could tell from the static it was long-distance. I thought: *Something's wrong with my mother!*

I jumped to my feet.

A woman said in heavily accented English, "My name is Victoria Atxaga. I received a phone call yesterday from José Maria Landero. He told me that a student of yours deserves the best teacher we can find."

She had a good firm voice.

I sat down. "We?" I asked.

"It's my English," she said. "You're American, aren't you?"

"Yes."

"From where?"

"New York."

"Ah, New York. My favorite place in New York is the courtyard at the Museum of Modern Art. You know it?"

"Of course."

"And Weiser's. I used to buy used books there. Lovely place. I spent two years in New York reading and playing guitar. My husband was with the diplomatic corps."

"How long ago was that?"

"During the Middle Ages. I don't remember the exact dates, but there were two popes, one in Rome, one in Avignon."

I laughed.

"Good, I've put you at ease," she said. "That's important. What I mean to say is just this… I am a guitar teacher. I was José Maria's teacher for six years. I used to be a professor in the Conservatory of Music in Madrid but I'm too old to maintain an interest in school meetings any longer. After a while you just want to slap the other teachers. And the noise! If I never hear another French horn again, it will be too soon! Anyway, José Maria told me that your student is very good. He says to me I would like him. That is good enough for me. José Maria is not as good a guitar player as he thinks, but he is an excellent judge of character. Excepting his own, of course. We can start whenever your student likes."

"I think I'm confused," I said. "Back up a bit. José Maria Landero told you about us?"

"Yes. He called yesterday. He'd fax me but I don't have a fax machine. Have you noticed that everyone is sending faxes these days? It's positively rude, don't you think?"

"It can be. What did José Maria tell you?"

"Just that your student is very talented and that he thought I could help. He's too busy for students now. It's a mistake, I think — to lose contact with younger people. But it's his life, as you Americans say."

I was silent, thinking of what to ask.

"Look, it's really quite simple," she said. "António, that's his name, yes?"

"Yes."

"António comes to my flat once a week for a two-hour lesson."

"Where?"

"Oh, I forgot to say. I live just outside Toledo. There's nothing to do but it's so very lovely. Have you ever been here?"

"No."

"You must come!"

"I will. But how much will lessons cost?"

"If he's really very very good, I will ask you pay my lunch at my favorite restaurant. That is the arrangement I had with José Maria after I quit the Conservatory. If he's only very good, it will cost ten thousand pesetas a lesson. I may warn you that being not so good may be less expensive, however. I only eat lunch and I eat a great deal." She paused for a moment and said, "That is a joke. But I'm afraid it is not very amusing in English."

"No," I replied. "But listen, why are you being so nice to us? I don't understand."

"Nice? I'm not being nice."

"Then why do you want him as your student?"

"Isn't it obvious?" she asked.

"No, not at all."

"Look, I'm a teacher. It's what I do. And if I have a chance to teach a very talented young man who I'm told is also very polite, I'm going to try to get that job, no?"

"Polite?"

"That's what José Maria said. Why, isn't he?"

"No, he is. Normally."

"How about abnormally?"

"Abnormally, he can be a real pain."

"That's good, too."

I was silent. I simply couldn't understand how I'd suddenly gotten a phone call from out of nowhere. When I told that to Victoria, she said, "Sometimes good things do happen, you know."

"I suppose."

"I don't mean to say it happens often or with any regularity, but it does happen. I myself have been very fortunate."

I was silent again. What was the catch?

"I understand your hesitation," she said. "You don't know me. I am an unknown entity, as you say. And I'm saying silly things because I don't understand telephones. I am nonplussed by technology."

"You're doing much better than me," I confessed.

"Yes, you have trouble with telephones, too, it seems."

"I have trouble with everything."

"Surely not."

"I'm just confused. I've been walking for so long without..." I was about to say *hope*, but I didn't want to use the word.

"Without what?" she asked.

"Without *expectation* of finding anything good. And then suddenly there's a phone call out of nowhere. You know what I mean?"

"It's simple. Logical, even. Look, my name is Victoria Atxaga, as I said. I studied with many people, most of whom are long dead and haunting my home. You'll see them if you ever stay over. I haven't played a concert in twenty-five years. I only made one recording. I was horrified by its quality and sent my husband out to buy up every copy he could find until it was no longer available anywhere outside Cuba. Apparently, I still have fans there. I had a family and started teaching. I enjoy teaching very much. But I've no patience for those without talent. It's a failing. Ask José Maria about me if you like. But don't you believe everything he says. He exaggerates."

She gave me her phone number and address.

As I wrote her last name, I remembered hearing about a woman named Atxaga once from a former teacher of mine at the Manhattan School of Music. "You studied with Alexandre Lagoya?" I said.

"That's right," she replied.

"And you knew Ida Presti?"

"Very well."

"And you once played the *Concierto de Aranjuez* under the direction of Leonard Bernstein in Jerusalem. I think it had something to do with an anniversary of the founding of the state of Israel."

"How do you know all that?"

"My teacher in New York was Juan Barrios. He used to call you Bibi."

"Oh, I remember Juanito! Always showing off. Juanito and I spent a summer in Buenos Aires together."

I said, "He told us you played the *Aranjuez* better than anyone."

"That's nice to hear after so long away. Oh good, it's wonderful to have Juanito in common."

"Bibi Atxaga," I said. I couldn't get over it. "You're famous!" She laughed.

"Listen, I'll call you back today," I said.

"No rush," she replied. "I'm not going anywhere."

"And you're not going to take back your offer, are you?"

"Goodness no."

I was silent because I didn't know how to end the phone call.

"Cheer up," she said. "I don't know what it's like in Paris, but it's a lovely day in Toledo."

Paris, Toledo, Porto... I didn't understand any of it. I looked out the window. I couldn't see the sky, only the cement walls of the courtyard. I said, "I think it will be a nice day here, too."

"Good. Go for a long walk. Go to the Eiffel Tower. I used to love going to the top. Go for me!"

It was eight a.m. I went down to breakfast. António and Miguel weren't up yet. I was very excited but I tried to eat slowly because I didn't want to make a thank-you call to José Maria Landero till nine. What was reputed to be the dining room, however, was a cave in the basement with pink walls and no windows. It was stiflingly hot and the coffee was undrinkable. I asked for tea. The waitress looked at me like I was a bad smell. I left and went next door to the Café Carillon and got two croissants and a cappuccino. A young man next to me with long black hair was reading *Une Vie avec une étoile*.

What are the chances of running into someone reading the same book as you in another language?

I realized then that only stories of misery, memory and death made any sense — not just to me — but to lots of other people as well. Would any of us ever read a simple mystery again?

I went back to my room and called José Maria. A woman answered. I explained who I was and why I'd phoned. She said she was his wife, Clara. José Maria had already left to give a private concert at a wedding in Deauville. He'd only be back the next day, and only on his way to another concert in Lyon. Her French was worse than mine. We spoke Spanish. She said, "Look, it's not for me to say, but Victoria is a wonderful woman. If António can study with her, he'd be very lucky. How can I explain. *Es luz.* She's light."

After I hung up, I kept repeating *es luz* to myself. I thought it would be good for the boy to study with a woman *who was light.*

I began daydreaming in bed about a Spanish fairy godmother. There was a knock on my door. "It's open," I shouted.

Miguel and António stood in the doorway. António was leaning against his father and raising his eyebrows like a mischief-maker.

A very perverse Norman Rockwell magazine cover, I thought.

"Ready, Professor?" Miguel said.

"For what?"

"Paris. We plan to see everything in the city before noon."

"Can we go to the top of the Eiffel Tower?" I asked.

I explained about the call from Victoria Atxaga as we stood staring at the facade of Notre Dame.

"Toledo will be easier to get to," Miguel noted.

"I haven't decided anything," António replied. "Just give me time to think."

"You only have to be there one day a week," I emphasized. "It won't be hard."

The boy shrugged.

"Listen," I said. "Life begins one minute, it ends the next. While you're waiting to figure out what to do, thirty seconds pass."

He nodded. "I'm just a little scared."

"We'll drive together to your lessons."

"But still..."

"Look, tell her to give you some duets," I said. "We'll practice together. I'm not too old to learn."

"Okay, okay, okay..."

We walked along the Seine to the Champ de Mars. The river was the color of pale green jade. All around us were apartment buildings of bleached blond stone. And above us were their sloping slate-gray rooftops, the chimney cones looking like thousands of terra-cotta beer mugs.

We stopped at an outdoor market just past the Museé d'Orsay to admire the fruit and vegetables. António spotted some plump cherry tomatoes and bought a box.

He ripped off the plastic cover and popped two in his mouth. He was suddenly staring at me nervously.

"I was right," he said, relieved. He wiped his mouth with the back of his hand and offered me the box. "It's just like I thought," he said, "I do like tomatoes. I finally remembered!"

The Eiffel Tower rose up before us like a giant erector set of mud-colored steel. It seemed powerful because it was a dream that any child might have.

On the elevator up to the top, Miguel hugged António. The boy looked at me over his father's shoulder and waved.

I realized that he'd been playful and kind to me that whole morning. I found myself hoping that the worst was over, that at least for now he'd found his correct tempo. It seemed possible.

I wanted to hope for a cure to Aids, too, but I just couldn't.

Paris looks like a pop-up postcard from a thousand feet in the air. The landmarks are all there, emerging from a circuit board of chimneys: Notre Dame, the Pompidou Center, the Arc de Triomphe, the Montparnasse Tower, the skyscrapers of La Défense, the Seine.

I spent most of my time staring at La Défense, thinking about New York and Los Angeles, wondering if I'd ever go home.

António couldn't get enough of it. He smiled and laughed. His hair blew in the stiff wind. He moon-walked in a circle around me.

When we were back on terra firma, Miguel said that they wanted to go see the Arc de Triomphe, then stroll down the Champs-Elysées. I told them I was feeling drowsy and would meet them back at the hotel. "No, you come, too," António begged.

"When you get home, come knock on my door," I replied. "We'll go for more Jewish food."

But I already knew I wouldn't be there.

Saying goodbye was difficult. The word formed a knot in my throat. I acted casual and said I'd see them later.

Then I turned and started off. My heart was beating wildly. I waved from a distance, but they were already lost in each other.

António's own courage prompted me to make an effort to walk calmly, and I strolled all the way back to the hotel like a gentleman out for a promenade. I forced myself to pack as if preparing for a picnic. I didn't think I could trust the bland-looking teenage girl at the desk to give Miguel my note, so I convinced her to give me his key. I sat at his tiny wooden desk and wrote. I looked in my face in the mirror from time to time. I sealed my note into an envelope and dropped it with the keys to the Batmobile on his pillow. I wrote:

My two handsome travel companions,
I understand now that I've done my part. You need time to be together. I'll see you back in Porto. When you get there, call me and we'll work out how we get to Toledo once a week. Don't forget to stop at Victoria Atxaga's house on the way back. I'll call her and tell her to expect you in about a week. Take good care of the Batmobile. I love you both.

I wrote Victoria's name and address below. Then I called her and told her she'd be getting a visit from António and his father.

"And you?" she asked.

"I'll come the week after that, for his first lesson."

"We'll go to lunch," she said. "I want to talk about New York. You must tell me about the changes there since my last visit. I bet there's been a lot!"

Too many, I was thinking. I packed my bag. António had left my guitar behind in my room after his audition. I balanced its body between my legs and started playing *Recuerdos del Alhambra.*

It seemed to me as if the guitar were speaking to me in its own language.

And do you know what it was telling me, Carlos? I was quite surprised by the message myself.

In its tremulous tenor, the guitar was saying, *You're not ever going to leave Portugal.*

You see, Carlos, it was telling me that my family, whether you believe it or not, is António and Miguel.

At the reception desk, I paid for three more days lodging for my travel companions. The only airport bus I knew left from the Gare de Montparnasse. I walked there. At three p.m., there was a TAP flight to Porto from Orly. I made it with two hours to spare and bought a ticket. On the plane, I sat next to an old woman in black who unwrapped a cheese sandwich over the Bay of Biscay. She offered me some. I thanked her but refused. "Whatever else we need, we all need food," she insisted.

I took a section of her sandwich. As I ate, I thought about my letter to you, Carlos, and what I was going to say about all this.

I'm not naïve, and I know that sex doesn't solve every problem. But maybe there are some men who can only express their love in bed. Maybe Miguel was one of them. So perhaps this was the best thing that could have happened. I'm not stupid though. I know it could end even worse; the hardest thing for lovers to do is to separate as friends.

I'm assuming that the same holds true even if they happen to be father and son.

I remember my brother telling me that the most important thing I ever did for him was cry over his coming death.

Miguel shed tears for his boy, and maybe that was what finally convinced António he'd learned how to love. Who knows for sure? Maybe António just got tired of fighting and gave up.

Will being able to love his father make a difference in his life? How long does he have before he hears the approaching footsteps of Death?

So many things we'll never know. We tend to make a fetish out of knowledge, but what good does it really do us? We still spend all our time plodding ahead into uncertainty.

But you know what, Carlos, that uncertainty no longer frightens me. Is it magic?

Or simply hope?

29

So here I am back in Porto, still suffering labor pains over this overgrown letter — a letter you might even refuse to read. But the contractions are growing ever closer together and there's no point in stopping now.

I've been back three days. Fiama is fine. She loved the earrings I got her. Pedro is well, too. He says that he hopes the book I bought him won't keep him up at night. Salgueiro was pleased that I'd picked out sweat pants for him in his favorite color. He says that I can live with him if I want to.

You know, if you reject my proposal, Carlos, I might even take the old bird up on his offer. In a way, it would be nice to have a boyfriend who's a grandfather and who's going to die of simple old age when his time comes.

Fiama insisted that I get the cut on the back of my hand looked at by a doctor. So I'm on antibiotics to make sure it doesn't get infected.

Only one piece of interesting mail arrived while I was gone: a letter from my ex-agent Libby saying that she was still interested in anything I came up with on Jews and traveling. Apparently, somebody was cleaning up files at Beacon Press and wrote her a letter out of nowhere saying that they were still *very* interested in the project.

I've already sent her a thanks-but-no-thanks letter. But what she wrote started me thinking... Maybe I'll change your name and mine and everyone else's and send her these confessions. I wonder what she'll make of it all. I'm the only Jew, of course, but it's got queers who...

play basketball and classical guitar;

fight and fuck in three different European countries;

and get hooked on tranquilizers and cruelty.

Why there's even a handsome love interest who can't decide which sexual gymnastics team he prefers playing on!

I would think that these characters might interest someone, somewhere. Other members of our sub-species, perhaps.

There was also a letter from my mother waiting for me. She's still having nightmares about my brother lying helpless on wrinkled *salmon-pink* sheets. She enclosed two flattened gardenia petals. She said she hoped they'd retain some of their smell for me on their trip across the Atlantic. They didn't, but I appreciated the thought.

I've mainly been sleeping and writing these words to you, dear Carlos. Nothing eventful at all happened until ten this morning. I was getting back from coffee at the Pérola Negra. The door to the apartment was open, but Fiama wasn't home.

I called for her. No reply.

Strange, I thought. But naturally enough, it didn't occur to me that Rui, my closeted Moor from the Algarve, had managed to break in to our apartment and was hiding in my bedroom. Things like that don't happen in real life, I thought; I'd forgotten that a Portuguese man bent on defending his machismo defies what passes for reality everywhere else.

After drinking a glass of litchi juice in the kitchen, I decided to finish up this letter to you. So I went to my room to work at the computer. I passed the door and was walking to my desk. Fists began crashing against my head and shoulders. Before I knew it, I was on my back with a crazy man on top of me. He had me by my ears and was hitting the back of my head into the wooden floor and shouting, "*Vou mata-lo, bicha de merda!* I'm going to kill you, you fucking faggot!"

Happily, my adrenaline kicks in pretty fiercely when I'm subject to sustained physical violence.

I threw him off me and managed to get to my feet. I realized then that it was Rui. "You! What are you crazy?!" I shouted. I felt the back of my head. Thankfully, it wasn't bleeding.

He was panting. "I'm going to kill you!" he said.

But he had no weapon that I could see. Did he expect me to lie down and say, *Yes, please, bang my head into the wood parquet until I'm dead?*

I took out my switchblade from my back pocket. I shouted, "Go away or I'll cut you!"

He crouched down with his arms out, like we were going to sumo wrestle.

I couldn't believe this guy's idiocy. Was I just fulfilling some self-destructive fantasy of his? Or were his ideas on the defensive abilities of American queers really this primitive?

When he grabbed for my arms, I stabbed him. In the upper thigh. He spurted blood and said, "Shit, you fucking cut me." He didn't shout. His voice was puzzled. It was like he was noting that he'd worn mismatched socks by mistake. He fell over on the floor and held his leg.

"Oh my God! I'll call an ambulance," I said.

"No," he replied calmly.

He grimaced in pain, got to his feet and hobbled to the door. Blood was sluicing down his pants leg.

"Are you nuts?" I shouted. "You're cut bad."

From the blood on my knife, I figured I'd gotten a good two inches into his flesh.

He didn't answer. He hobbled out the door and hopped down the stairs. He left a trail of blood.

I called 115 and told an emergency operator that there was a bleeding man leaving my apartment house. I gave her the address. I looked out the window for Rui, but he was already out of view. I didn't hear any sirens.

I started worrying that he'd die. I fantasized about the police coming after me.

As if I were a schoolboy dutifully doing his homework, I slipped my knife into a freezer bag to save it as evidence.

It was self-defense, I thought. *I'll get a lawyer.*

Then I realized that Rui was like you, Carlos, so he wouldn't want anyone knowing how it happened. He'd tell the folks at the emergency room that an accident had occurred at work: a window had fallen onto his hip and shattered.

Anyway, it was just a leg wound. He wasn't going to die.

That's what I began to think after a hot shower. I sat at the window drinking ouzo out of my Daffy Duck mug, waiting for Fiama to come home for lunch.

I'd done a first cleaning of my bedroom and the living room, but right away she noticed the missing throw rug at the door and the brown streaks on the wood floor. I explained. She said, "Men have been bothering me since I was ten. I'm surprised I never killed one myself."

She held up the freezer bag with the bloody knife and gave a long whistle. She made us tuna-fish salad for lunch. On my insistence, she called 115 and got a supervisor. She found out that Rui had been picked up in front of the old jailhouse and taken to Saint Anthony's Hospital.

Talking with her clarified some things. I realized that frustrated souls like Rui believe that people like me and António deserve to die not so much for being gay but for being *free.*

Free vampires are the scariest of all.

But poor Rui didn't really want to kill me or he would've brought at least a butter knife, don't you think?

So now that the excitement is over and the dishes are washed and I'm alone in the house, we come to my proposal:

Will you try to work things out with me?

I bet you never thought you'd hear me ask that.

It's just that we're all moving steadily toward the grave, even you and me. We've only got this one meager life. And I still love you.

After reading this letter, you have a much better idea who this man is who wants you. Will he be worth the risks you'll take? Only you can say.

I think you love me, too. I think that that's what scared you so much. Although maybe I'm reading too much into your actions. Maybe you just can't stand me. Simple as that.

I'll stay off drugs.

We'll make love gently. And only when we both really want to.

We won't talk about our past together anymore than we have to. Maybe there's still time for us to make some journeys together.

I've got no commitments that can't be broken — except of course to António. As I say, he and Miguel are my family now. I'll go with the boy once a week to Toledo, no matter what else happens.

If that makes you jealous, so be it; there are certain things I cannot give up, even for your love.

You're not stupid and you know there's got to be a catch, so here it is: we're not going to be able to withstand the pressure of you remaining in your dreary little closet. It'll poison everything we say and do and think, just like it did last time. So, you've got to open the door at least a crack and peer out.

The earth won't open up and swallow us.

You won't turn into a pillar of salt.

No Nordic-looking hero is going to pound a stake into your heart.

I promise.

Don't get frightened. Because I'm not saying that we've got to put an announcement in the newspaper saying you're gay or walk across Porto's main square in black leather with spurs on our motorcycle boots.

But if you don't admit what you like to do in bed — at least to yourself — then we'll always remain separate.

We'll never be able to talk about our lives.

We'll never have friends who love us.

We'll never learn how to give each other pleasure.

And we'll surely never be able to trust each other.

You know, in the nearly two years we were together, I can't remember what we ever discussed except your art. It wasn't enough. It *won't* be enough.

Wouldn't you like to live with a friend? Wouldn't you like for someone to know you? Wouldn't you like to walk down the street just once and not have to worry about what other people are thinking of you?

Because you'd be free.

I've journeyed through many years and countries and relationships to be able to write this letter to you. I'm filled with fears and regrets, as should be clear to you now. I'm haunted by the past. And there are certain to be more ghosts in my future. I'm fragile. You are too, of course.

So... Come to Porto one of these next weekends. Or I'll come down to Lisbon. We'll explore each other. We'll forgive each other. We'll see what happens. What do you say?

— *THE END* —

Gay Men's Press books can be ordered from any bookshop in the UK, North America and Australia, and from specialised bookshops elsewhere.

If you prefer to order by mail, please send cheque or postal order payable to *Book Works* for the full retail price plus £2.00 postage and packing to:

Book Works (Dept. B), PO Box 3821, London N5 1UY
phone/fax: (0171) 609 3427

For payment by Access/Eurocard/Mastercard/American Express/ Visa, please give number, expiry date and signature.

Name and address in block letters please:

Name
——————————————————————————————————

Address
——————————————————————————————————

——————————————————————————————————

——————————————————————————————————